Also by Antoine Vanner

Britannia's Wolf
The Dawlish Chronicles
September 1877 - February 1878

Britannia's Reach
The Dawlish Chronicles
November 1879 - April 1880

Being accounts of episodes in the life of
Nicholas Dawlish R.N.

Born Shrewsbury 16.12.1845

Died: Zeebrugge 23.04.1918

Britannia's Shark

Shark

The Dawlish Chronicles

April – September1881

By

Antoine Vanner

Published by Old Salt Press 2014

Old Salt Press LLC, is based in Jersey City, NL, USA
With an affiliate in New Zealand

www.oldsaltpress.com

Hard Copy: ISBN-13:978-0992263690
ISBN-10: 0992263697

ebook: ISBN 978-0-9922636-8-3

Prologue

One more day in a war without end

The ridge was all but bare and they waited until the sun had set before they crossed it lest they be outlined against the red of the evening sky.

Machado looked back eastwards from the crest, aware despite the darkness of the steep hills and broad valleys through which his column had carved a winding swathe of fury and destruction. He could all but see the burning fields, smell the sugar boiling in the blazing cane, hear the walls collapsing as the mills went up like torches, sense the terror of the cornered troopers ambushed on a forest track. There was a savage joy in knowing that the destruction wrought had hurt so badly, in profit as well as in lives, a satisfaction too in knowing that he was feared as well as hated enough to carry so high a price upon his head.

His men moved slowly down the track on the western slope, five only, with two laden mules and a heavier-laden prisoner. They had used this path a month before when they had marched to join the group which had assembled in a forest clearing thirty miles to the east. Others had come in threes and fours from the north and north-east so that at its largest the force had been sixty-one strong. Most had carried only machetes initially but small victories – dozing sentries at isolated block-houses, poorly-escorted transport wagons – had added firearms as the column snaked unpredictably from one valley to the next, growing more deadly by the day.

The temptation to keep the force together had been strong after the mounted patrol had been trapped at Yateritas. There had been twenty-four riders, six of them brought down in the first volley. The remainder had cowered among the rocks for two days, tortured by thirst and under constant fire. Ten had surrendered, most of them wounded, and if they had expected mercy then they had been mistaken. Their vanquishers had felt invincible, had been drunk with success, and they had clamoured to be led on to further triumphs. Machado knew that it was at this moment that he had most truly proved himself a leader. He had recognised that such coups could only invite massive response, larger sweeps and relentless pursuit by more powerful columns, and could only result in his force's annihilation. It was at this moment that it must melt away, that he must send its members back to their distant villages in twos and threes to bury their

5

weapons and wait for the call to assemble again at another place, another time. The men had disliked the order, but they had obeyed, their trust in El Jefe now absolute. The revolt had lasted years already, would last many more. Victory would go to those who endured longest.

All that was left with him now were these five, Ambrosio from Boquerón, his best man, the remainder from three other villages. The path was flanked by heavy growth, the going easier for being downhill. Even the prisoner was panting less than when he had strained up on to the ridge. He did not have a name – Machado had not allowed him to tell it, for that would make him a person, would make it harder when the time came. The man's feet were bloody, for his boots had been taken from him, and his shoulders were rubbed raw by the empty rifles he carried so that the more precious mules would be burdened less. He had given up pleading and seemed to be reconciled with mute misery to what he knew must come. He had seen it twice before, and knew by now that neither stoic reserve nor blubbering pleas would earn compassion.

The moon was bright enough to light the track and the urge to hurry was almost irresistible. Machado found himself aching for sight of the wife and children – a girl, two boys – whom he had forced himself not to think of in the past weeks. It had been enough to know that they were safe, that their presence in Porcuna, the village they had been brought to, could not be suspected. He had no family connection with it and it was too remote, and peons and escaped slaves who tilled its fields too few, to be worth official interest.

The sky was lightening in the east as the forest thinned on the lower slope. They were looking for a suitable place now, somewhere unremarkable but easy to find again. A lightning-scarred tree by the side of the track provided the ideal marker and they pushed through the foliage beyond it to a point hidden from any passer-by.

"This will do," Machado said.

The mules was tethered to a tree and offloaded. Machado picked up a spade.

"Lay your burden down, Amigo," he said to the prisoner. "Take this." He handed him the implement and saw that he was trembling, that against all reason he had still been hoping that this moment would not come.

They smoked as they watched him dig. He was weeping as he worked, slowly and steadily, and he raised terrified eyes to them at intervals as the hole deepened. Nobody wanted to look at him and nobody felt like talking. This had happened before. There had been some pleasure in it the first time but even those with most to avenge shrunk from the necessity now.

"That's deep enough," Machado said.

The weapons carried on the mules had been well-greased and wrapped in oiled canvas looted from a captured blockhouse. The covers were opened and the arms they and the prisoner had carried were added. There were five boxes of ammunition, worth more than gold, all unopened. Machado regretted most giving up the two Spencer repeaters – unequalled at close quarters – and he hesitated about leaving his own revolver, a Colt, just as the others must. Once they had descended to the valley, were heading for their own homes, it would be safer to be unarmed.

The bundles were laid in the bottom of the hole and the prisoner began to fill it in. He was young, but he seemed even more like a child now, sobbing, speaking brokenly about his mother, how she had already lost another son, how much she was to him, how she awaited his return. He had never killed anyone himself, had tried to restrain his companions, had wanted only to be back home across the ocean. If they spared him he would promise never speak of this, that he would forget all that he had seen. He fell silent as he threw on the last spadeful and patted the ground level. Ambrosio brought stones and piled them in a low cairn. A week's growth would cover the bare earth and shield the marker.

The second hole, twenty yards from the first, would need no marker but it should be deeper if animals were not to disturb it. The prisoner dug more slowly, his hands shaking so badly, his clothing so befouled after his bowels emptied, that even Machado pitied on him.

"Rest a little, Amigo," he said and reached his hand to him to pull him from the hole. He handed the spade to Ambrosio and told him to continue digging. "If you want to pray you should do so now."

The prisoner seemed not to hear him. It was easier, Machado thought, when they were defiant to the last, when they retained more dignity. It was hard to reconcile what must be done to this remnant of a man with the vision of liberty that inspired the campaign of resistance, justified its terror.

When it was deep enough Ambrosio pushed the prisoner to his knees at the edge. He did not resist but even now he must have retained some shed of hope for he turned and began "Por Dios, Señor, por Dios y su …."

His words were cut off as Machado took him by the hair with his left hand and dragged his head back. The throat was tight as the blade sliced across it

7

and blood was pumping from it as he pitched forward into the pit. They filled it in silence, beat the ground level, knew that it too would be covered by fresh growth within a week.

It was mid-morning, the sun high, when the forest died and the first cultivated fields came into sight. They reached a road, deeply rutted by ox-carts. They parted, four heading in one direction and taking the mules with them, Machado and Ambrosio in the other. There was a village ahead, a scattering of huts where a few pesos would buy food and drink for two peons returning from months of work on the sugar plantations. Their ragged clothes aroused no suspicion as they stood to one side, heads bowed, hats respectfully doffed, as a mounted patrol drummed past.

Nobody knew him at the village even though Porcuna, where his wife and children now sheltered, was scarcely two hours trudge beyond. The small cantina was only an open-sided shack but they could get beans there, and coffee, and benches on which to rest before embarking on the last stage. It would still be light when he got there, Machado told himself, the children still playing and looking up and recognising him, one running back to the hut with the news, the others rushing to him in delight, his wife emerging blinking into the sunlight, her face bursting into a smile.

While he had been lost in his reverie Ambrosio had been talking to the owner.

"Jefe." Ambrosio touched him on the arm. "Jefe..." He seemed to find it hard to continue.

Machado saw the horror in Ambrosio's eyes and knew the worst had happened even before he heard the name.

Almunia, the colonel, the devil, had been at Porcuna the night before.

Part 1

The Brotherhood

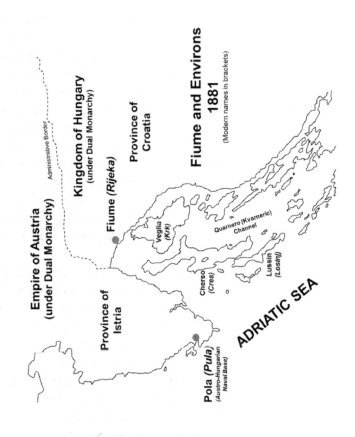

Empire of Austria
(under Dual Monarchy)

Kingdom of Hungary
(under Dual Monarchy)

Province of
Croatia

Administrative Border

Fiume (*Rijeka*)

Province of
Istria

Pola (*Pula*)
(Austro-Hungarian
Naval Base)

Vegilia
(*Krk*)

Cherso
(*Cres*)

Lussin
(*Losinj*)

Quarnero (Kvameric)
Channel

ADRIATIC SEA

Fiume and Environs
1881
(Modern names in brackets)

1

The sun was rising when the converted tug slipped from its secluded wharf, passed into Fiume's Porto Grande and chugged across the mirror-still basin.

April 17th 1881 promised to be another splendid spring morning. Commander Nicholas Dawlish regretted that he could not have spent this day, like the previous ones, exploring the old town, yet the act of leaving harbour excited him, as it done since boyhood, even if it was only, as now, for a single day. Merchant vessels thronged the port, but no warships – the main Austro-Hungarian naval base was at Pola, forty miles to the south-west. Steamers and sailing craft, sea-going as well as coasters, clustered along the quaysides, drawn by the wine and grain and timber the Hapsburg lands to the north and east produced in such abundance.

And people too, Dawlish thought, for an Austrian Lloyd cargo-liner was readying for departure, its decks thronged with bewildered and shabby Hungarian and Bohemian emigrants headed for an unknowable future across the Atlantic.

The tug rounded the Maria Theresia mole and encountered scarcely a ripple on the open waters beyond. Golden sunlight now bathed the islands of Cherso and Veglia to the south, and beyond them lay the broader expanse of the Adriatic. Dawlish stood on the bridge-wing, drawing on a cheroot, looking aft, content for once to be a passenger. Tarpaulins still shrouded the jumble of piping, air-accumulators and machinery on the afterdeck and they would not be removed until the craft was far enough from shore to make observation impossible. Most seamen here were Italian, despite the legality that their home port belonged to the Kingdom of Hungary, and two of them were now undoing the ropes securing the covers around the weapon. That was as far as they would go for now.

"Are you hopeful this time, Commander?" Scrivello's English was faultless even if his eyes were bleary from lack of sleep.

"My mind's open, Signor." Dawlish liked the engineer who had joined him, but knew also that he was feared by him. For his own judgement could either secure the future of the invention in which

Scrivello had invested so much of his life and passion or consign it to the catalogue of ingenious but futile technical dead-ends.

"It will be better today, Commander, I promise you. Much better."

And it will, Dawlish thought, *but will it be good enough?*

Scrivello and his team had not left the workshops for a week as they tinkered and modified to redress the problems encountered in the earlier trials. The company established so incongruously at this Hungarian port by Robert Whitehead, a Lancashire engineer, had not only invented the automotive torpedo but was now also supplying the world's navies with them. Whitehead had changed the face of war at sea – as Dawlish knew only too well – and now, with this new invention, hoped to do so again.

"A thousand yards minimum, Commander, not less than a thousand yards today."

"Let us hope so, Signor."

Dawlish did not remind him of an identical promise ten days before. He sensed the engineer's desperation. A single order from the Royal Navy, even a mere expression of interest, might secure this weapon's future. Yet he must remain scrupulously neutral in his evaluation, repressing the urge to roll up his own sleeves and join Scrivello at lathe and workbench to solve problems which intrigued him. Instead he had passed the delay pleasantly, spending his enforced leisure, like a tourist, with his wife Florence.

"Time now to tell the captain where we test," Scrivello said.

The tug had passed between Veglia and Cherso and the channel between was widening again. The choice between a half-dozen possible trial locations was always made this far from port. Whitehead's lead over its competitors was jealously guarded and an anonymous stranger's small payment to an impecunious seaman could well endanger it.

The site selected was in a small bay on southern coast of Veglia – Krk, to its Croatian inhabitants – a crescent of crystalline blue fringed with limestone cliffs. Pine and scrub dotted the slopes above. The tug slowed, circled, dropped a yellow target buoy and then headed seawards again. At what Dawlish was asked to confirm was a

12

thousand yards from the target an anchor splashed over the stern. The vessel nudged ahead, paying out cable aft, then dropped its bow anchor. The screw stilled and capstans rattled fore and aft, tautening both lines and mooring the tug in a fixed heading.

"Neatly done," Dawlish conceded. The target was almost dead astern.

Seamen stripped the tarpaulins away and Scrivello's mechanics busied themselves with preparations. The air-tanks, charged to capacity before departure, were confirmed to be holding pressure. Couplings and seals were checked and a nut tightened here, a stuffing box there. Polished brass gleamed in the sun, bright against black-painted cast-iron cylinders. Hand wheels were rotated this way or that, valves opened or closed in a predetermined sequence. The turntable supporting the twenty-foot long, heavily-flanged eight-inch projector tube was rotated to bear on the buoy.

"First a dummy, Commander." Scrivello's hands were trembling.

"So that's how you'll give me a thousand yards," Dawlish tried to inject lightness into his tone. "With a projectile as light as this you should promise me twice as much!"

"Just to test the mechanism, Commander." The engineer was too worried to joke.

A two-foot cylindrical wooden plug, with leather gaskets set into grooves in its sides, was loaded into the open rear of the smooth, unrifled, projector tube and pushed forward until it met resistance. A mechanic raised a threaded cast-iron cap and another rotated it shut. He used a hammer on its extended lugs to tighten it.

"A slow system, Signor," Dawlish said. A conventional gun would have fired and have been reloaded by now.

"A temporary expedient, Commander, for the tests only. In production we would have a better system, a faster one."

Earlier failures had cast a gloom over the entire crew – Whitehead had the ability to make every employee feel part of a larger family – and now even the stokers had come on deck to watch. Scrivello fussed over final settings, supervised the projector's elevation and jotted last observations in his notebook. A hush fell over the deck as he turned to Dawlish.

"Ready, Commander?"

"Your weapon, Signor Scrivello."

There was no explosion, no searing blast of flame and smoke, no rolling, thunderous roar as Scrivello drew back the firing lever, only a brief ear-splitting "pop", like the opening of a gigantic champagne bottle. The high-pressure puff of compressed air that sped the dummy up the tube shimmered for an instant at the muzzle as the projectile leapt from it, leaving the line of flight unobscured. The wooden plug, clearly visible and moving slower than any conventional shot, soared high over the buoy. It shattered on the cliff face three hundred yards beyond. The onlookers cheered and Scrivello flushed with pleasure and relief.

The breech was hammered open, ready for the projectile now being manhandled forward. It bore little resemblance to a conventional shell. A wooden-sheathed tinplate cylinder, eight inches diameter and thirty-six inches long, encircled at three points by leather sealing gaskets, its nose a half-dome, formed the elongated head of what might have been an enormous arrow. A three-inch tubular shaft extended three feet behind it, terminating in four sheet-metal fins. These were set at a slight angle to the axis to impart stabilising spin in flight.

"It carries no charge, Commander," Scrivello said, "but it weighs the same as if it did, and it's been balanced accordingly."

Dawlish did not object. Until the weapon was proved he had no desire to be close to dynamite. For all its awesome power, the new explosive's sensitivity made it unsuited to the shock of discharge from conventional guns. Such guns must still fire shells filled with traditional – and lower energy – black powder. Whitehead's pneumatic projector, with its gentler acceleration, was intended to bypass that embarrassing complication.

Scrivello took an age over the elevation – as well he might, for there were scant results so far to validate the trajectory calculations. Satisfied at last, he turned to Dawlish.

"Your weapon, Commander." He bowed, gesturing to the firing lever, a glint in his eye indicating confidence growing over earlier trepidation.

Dawlish fixed his eye on the target, then drew the handle back smartly. This close to the muzzle the loud "pop" made him jerk involuntarily but he recovered to follow the missile's majestic flight. It arced upwards, its spinning tail-vanes a blur, levelled briefly and then curved into its descent. Cheers broke from the crew as it became obvious that it would clear the target by a generous margin. Dawlish had to repress his own impulse to pound Scrivello on the back and shake his hand as it splashed down a full hundred yards beyond it.

It was only a start, but the projector was beginning to look as if it had a future – and if so, the Royal Navy would be the first to take delivery.

2

The Hotel Tersatica was a decade old, built when Fiume had passed under Hungarian control. The majority of its guests appeared to be senior officials on visits from Budapest. It lay directly on the coast, the view seawards from its terraced gardens superb. As always, the sight of Florence lifted Dawlish's heart when he returned there that evening. Her smile turned her plain bony face into something irresistible as she told him about her day while he changed for dinner. She was herself again, he told himself, full once more of life and fun and energy, and the joy of each other's company seemed greater each day. They had been close before, but the tragedy of the miscarriage four months previously – he tried to block the memory of pain and terror and blood-soaked sheets – had brought them closer still.

"You should have been with me, Nick! We thought the road from Ljubimec was bad!" The suffering of the bitter winter in Thrace that had united them was now long enough past to be laughed about. "But I guarantee you that road was nothing to my climb to the Pilgrimage Church today. Four hundred steps to reach it! It's a wonder I can still stand, much less walk!"

Guide-book in hand, Florence was an inveterate visitor of sights and monuments, compensation, Dawlish guessed, though she would never admit it, for her scant formal education. The present journey, with its opportunity to spend a week in Venice before continuing here by steamer, had been one of the happiest periods of her life.

And of mine, Dawlish thought, and its memory would make the separations that approaching promotion would make inevitable all the more poignant.

"Will there be time for us to visit Lussin?" she asked as they descended the main staircase to the dining room. Dawlish was pleasantly conscious of heads turning, drawn by her lithe figure, glorious blond hair and splendid carriage. "I heard today that the Emperor may be going there for his health next month," she said.

"If he comes here, Florence, he won't be Emperor, he'll be King of Hungary." He avoided her question, reluctant to reveal immediately that there would be little opportunities for further excursions together. The tests had gone too well today, seven successful firings. The real work, with live charges, could now begin. Long days lay ahead and afterwards his report would be needed at the Admiralty as soon as possible. As Senior Instructor at H.M.S. *Vernon*, the Royal Navy's Torpedo and Mine School at Portsmouth, Dawlish's opinion carried weight.

The dining room was full and a quartet played softly in the background. As Dawlish and Florence paused on the landing before the final flight of steps the violinist looked up, caught her eye and smiled. He nodded to his companions and the music flowed effortlessly from the *Blue Danube* into an air from *Pinafore*. Florence flushed with delight and Dawlish realised that she must have tipped the musician. She squeezed Dawlish's arm.

"And a very good captain too!" she sang softly, picking up the tune. "Soon, Nick! Not just very good. You'll be the very best."

The dinner was a pleasant one until half way – the moment, Dawlish realised afterwards, when the nightmare started, the nightmare of failure, of confusion, of realisation of weakness hitherto unsuspected.

Florence was at her brightest as she commented on the pomposity of their fellow guests and on what she had learned of Fiume.

"It's taken me two weeks here to work it out, Nick," she said. "The Hungarians think they run the city, the Italians say they run it, and the Croats ..."

She stopped dead, her wine-glass frozen inches from her lips, colour draining from her face. Her eyes reflected something between fear and disgust and were locked on some point behind and beyond Dawlish's right shoulder. He reached across, took her hand and brought it down gently on the table. It was trembling.

"Florence," he said, pained. He had seen her face Bashi-Bazooks with more composure. "You might have seen a ghost."

"I've seen something worse." Her hand still trembled but she tore her great brown eyes away from whatever held them and looked with something like an appeal into his. "Thank God I have you, Nicholas," she said in a low voice. "You're a good man."

Silence followed. She freed her hand, took her knife and fork again and made as if to eat, but Dawlish saw that it was for appearance only.

"Would you like to go to our room?"

She shook her head and Dawlish felt a surge of pride and love. Florence was not a woman to retreat.

Slowly, as if casually, he turned in his chair. The scene was as on any other night – more men than women due to the constant turnover of visiting officials, a few couples, obviously wealthy, here from Vienna or Budapest or Prague on a spring holiday, the odd uniform, even an elderly Mr. and Mrs. Bulstrode from Leicester who were here because it was cheaper than Menton. It was a gathering of the utmost respectability. He saw nothing untoward. He turned back slowly to the table.

Florence's eyes, cold and angry now, gave him his direction. "By the pillar, the one with the palm behind. Two men together. The one on the left."

He turned again and realised that he had glimpsed them both at the Whitehead works, visitors passing into the commercial office, part of the endless stream of overseas purchasers. The man who caused Florence such distress, and who seemed oblivious of her presence, was red-faced, balding and thickset, though the weight he carried seemed more like muscle than fat. He looked fifty, maybe older, and his closely cropped moustache was already white. His companion was long and lean and brown, with dark deep-set eyes and a closely cropped steel-grey beard. The immediate impression was of someone who had experienced much and could endure more. He might be any age between thirty and sixty. Such men seemed forty all their lives.

They finished the meal in silence and passed into the gardens. Pinpoints of light winked against the dark islands beyond and the night air was soft and warm, heavy with the scent of blossom. But Florence clutched her shawl closely around her, as if cold, and though they sat twice on palm-sheltered benches her restlessness brought her each time to her feet again. Dawlish knew better than to say anything. She would speak in her own time.

"Fentiman," she said at length. "Major Clement Fentiman."

"You knew him?" He could feel what the words had cost her. He reached into her shawl, took her hand and held it.

"At Kegworth's. He was a guest. He was there for the shooting. Eleven years ago. I was sixteen." When she had been a servant, days she seldom spoke of. The days before Lord Kegworth's daughter Agatha had made her a formal companion. The days which many, especially wives of other naval officers, still referred to with casual, mean-spirited, cruelty.

"He... he tried to bother me. In a corridor, late one night."

"Did he..." Dawlish was lost for words, overcome with love for her.

She shook her head. "I slapped his face, kicked him, warned him I had a father and two brothers." As she had, muscular coachmen who would have flayed anyone who abused her.

"Was that the end of it?"

Her voice was bitter with regret. "I should have spoken out – His Lordship never stood for that sort of thing – but I was young, and confused, and ashamed that he might even think that ..." Her voice trailed off.

"So it wasn't the end?"

"A year later, he was visiting again. Another girl – Beatrice Hollins – a lovely girl, two years younger than me. I hadn't spoken out, and it happened. She was cleaning his room and ..."

She was weeping very softly. He waited, pressing her hand, drawing her to him.

"I found out when she couldn't hide it any more – the baby that is. I told Agatha and she spoke to her father. He's a kind man, Lord Kegworth – you know that, Nick – and he had her looked after like she was his own daughter. And he must have taken it further, for we heard soon after that the major had to leave the army."

"And Beatrice?"

"She died. The baby with her. Women said afterwards she was too small down there."

"Then it's this blackguard who has it on his conscience," Dawlish felt anger and contempt, "though I'm damned if he has one. And, cashiered or not, he doesn't seem short of a shilling. He deserves worse."

Then, to his surprise, Florence began to laugh through her tears. She kissed his hand lightly and said "You look like you're going to horsewhip him yourself, Nick."

"If necessary." He meant it. "But he's no danger. He'd never recognise you now." Even as he spoke he regretted this reference to her previous menial status, was grateful that she ignored it.

They strolled on, each too-obviously shifting the conversation to the beauty of the area, the Roman remains, the *Don Giovanni* they had seen at the opera house the previous night. Out in the gulf lights still winked against the island masses. There, somewhere, in the coming days, the pneumatic projector would be tested live for the first time.

They paused on a balustraded terrace, palms rustling there in the slight night breeze. Dawlish put a cheroot in his mouth and produced his box of lucifers. Florence took it from him, slid the tray out – the habit that had grown between them that she would light his cigars when they were alone. She scraped the match and it flared briefly, then died.

"I'm sorry, Nick," she said, looking in the box. "It's the last one."

The sound of feet on the gravelled path caused them to turn. Fentiman's companion was approaching, now wearing a broad-brimmed hat and carrying a silver-topped cane.

"Forgive me intruding, Sir – and Ma'am – but I believe you're in need of a light."

The accent was American, with a hint of something else not immediately placeable. He bowed slightly, tipped his hat to Florence.

Dawlish sensed her freeze, then relax as the moonlight fell full on the newcomer's face. It had a dignity – even something of sadness – that was immediately winning. It had nothing of the coarseness of the major he had been dining with.

"I'm in need of a light indeed, Sir," Dawlish said. "I trust you can oblige me."

"With a cigar too, Sir – a prime Havana – if you'd care to save that cheroot of yours for another occasion."

Even as he drew in the flame from between the American's cupped hands Dawlish realised that the cigar he accepted was the best he had ever smoked

"You're a stranger here, Sir?" Florence's curiosity was almost palpable.

"Like yourself and your husband, Ma'am, if I guess right? I'd take you for Britishers."

Florence nodded, but the American was already stepping back.

"I'll wish you Good Night then Ma'am. And you too, Sir." He tipped his hat again. "I hope you'll enjoy the remainder of your stay in Fiume." Then he was gone into the soft darkness.

Florence, Dawlish knew, would not sleep tonight.

3

Both Fentiman and the American were gone from the hotel the next day. Dawlish spent most of it, and of the next, at the Whitehead workshops, observing the assembly of the live projectiles and fascinated by the complexities of their seawater-activated fuses. He chose his moment for enquiries carefully, a break when he shared coffee and a cheroot with Scrivello. He mentioned appearances, wondered, apparently idly, why they were here.

"You know our business is confidential here, Commander." The engineer's tone had a sudden wariness. "We don't discuss individual customers."

"But you are of course aware who your most important customer is," Dawlish said. He waited, savoured the tobacco, sensed the Italian's mounting unease. The Royal Navy purchased well over half of Whitehead's output.

"Major Fentiman is an independent agent." Scrivello looked around uncomfortably, as if fearing to be overheard. "He sometimes works with Belgian interests – small arms, light artillery. And he has bought torpedoes before on behalf of a number of countries."

"Which specifically?" Dawlish failed to sound casual.

Scrivello paused, looked around, saw no eavesdroppers. He shrugged and lowered his voice. "Spain, Venezuela, Uruguay, even Siam. Nowhere important, small sales only."

"And his friend? The long, thin one?"

"I don't know, Commander. That's the commercial department's business. He's new. I think from some South American republic, God knows where. And if he has left with the major it's because they couldn't afford our prices."

If Scrivello knew more – which was unlikely – he wasn't revealing it. Other than that the American called himself Miguel Gonzalez, a name comparable in Latin terms to John Smith in English, Dawlish discovered nothing more before the three-day sequence of live firings began.

The test site was a secluded bay on the eastern coast of Cherso. Two dummy firings went well. The range had been opened to twelve hundred yards. Every shot improved calibration of the elevation table and projectiles were soon being dropped within twenty yards of the target. It was encouraging, even if it was from a moored vessel in a dead calm and with no wind to deflect the slow-flying missile. At last it was time for the first dynamite-laden projectile. It carried a partial charge only – ten pounds, by comparison with five times what the casing was designed for. It was enough to start, enough also to test the fuses that Scrivello screwed into the rear of the main cylinder just before it was inserted into the projector. They had worked well in a tank ashore, sending an electrical current to blow their detonators ten seconds after they contacted seawater. It remained to be seen if they were rugged enough to withstand the stresses of firing and impact.

Silence on deck, many placing themselves apparently casually behind some stout obstacle in case of an explosion inside the projector tube. Dawlish stood to one side of the breech, glasses focussed on the target.

Then the champagne-cork report – he would never grow accustomed to it – and the projectile was soaring and spinning upwards, hanging for an instant, then plunging towards the buoy. It raised a splash ten yards to its right. The waters fell back and for two, three seconds the surface was broken only by the slightest ripples. Dawlish heard Scrivello's intake of breath and knew that he feared the fuses might fail, but then, suddenly, the sea itself heaved up like a mound and a white plume burst from it with a dull roar. Waves raced out as the fountain collapsed and moments later a reverberation shuddered through the tugboat's hull. The buoy had disappeared within the seething, expanding circle of froth. Slowly the white dispersed and the surface fell level again, dotted now with dead fish.

"You may have a winner, Signor." Dawlish could not withhold his admiration.

"You believe it now, Commander?"

"Get a large enough charge close enough to a hull, set it off twenty, thirty feet down, and you'll buckle the frames, rupture the plating and maybe even break a vessel's back."

He had seen it happen – to a Russian collier – though he was sworn never to speak of it. But moored mines that waited passively for their victim had been responsible then, not a portable weapon that could be brought to the enemy. The projector was still crude, but so too had been Whitehead's torpedo when Dawlish had first seen it tested in the *Oberon* trials a scant eleven years before.

Three further successful shots were completed. They headed for the harbour of Veglia, on the western coast of the island of the same name, to spend the night there. The tug had little accommodation, with only a tiny cabin available for Dawlish and Scrivello, and the remainder of the Whitehead team lodged ashore. A winter in Thrace had given Dawlish a loathing of lice and he was unwilling to risk any village inn if he could help it. The harbour was packed with fishing craft, mostly tunny catchers. He dined well with Scrivello at a quayside tavern before returning to the tug to write up his journal and read a few chapters of Trollope before sleeping.

The dawn found the weather changed, the sky overcast, a fresh breeze blowing in from the Adriatic, and strengthening, whitecaps forming in the waters beyond. Many of the fishing craft had departed already and others were hurrying to follow.

"They're heading for the eastern side of the island." Scrivello translated for Ruggieri, the skipper. "He says we should do the same. Conditions on the other side will be calm enough for the test."

"He's the captain," Dawlish said, "He knows these waters. We go where he advises." They had conducted tests in two bays on the east coast previously and either location would offer shelter against what promised to be a stiff blow.

"He says it will only cost us a few hours. He'll pass around the island's southern tip."

An hour was lost locating a mechanic who had drunk too much the night before, so that the tug was the last vessel to head out into an increasingly angry sea. Spray broke over the bows as she battered ahead and on the afterdeck tarpaulins were once more draped over the projector. The shrouds whistled plaintively and the short vessel plunged and rolled. Scrivello vomited over the side while Dawlish, oilskin-clad on the bridge wing, savoured the feel of salt spray on his face and felt content.

They sighted the fishing boat two hours later.

The island's southernmost promontory was two miles off the port bow and the tug was bearing eastwards to round it when the lookout called. The wallowing craft was perhaps five cables distant. It was low in the water and the waves were now high enough for it to be lost momentarily in their troughs. As it rose again Dawlish saw that it was half-decked and that the single mast had snapped. The gaff and mainsail and a mass of cordage lay half-overboard in a confused heap that dragged the hull beam-on to the waves. It rolled sluggishly, spray breaking across it. Four men supported themselves at the base of the mast, and a fifth was halfway up what remained of it, waving frantically.

The tug swung towards the stricken vessel, the skipper himself at the helm, the screw churning at maximum revolutions, the mate's yelled commands mustering crewmen on the port side with heaving lines and grapnels. Others were lugging rope fenders from the starboard flank and draping them to complement those opposite. An ashen-faced Scrivello joined Dawlish on the bridge.

"Is there hope for them, Commander? Their poor wives, their poor children…"

"They've nothing to fear," Dawlish said. "I've seen rescues in immeasurably worse conditions." And Ruggieri's handling skills had impressed him earlier.

The confidence was well placed. Slowing as he neared, the skipper edged his tug ahead to a point some fifty yards upwind of the half-waterlogged craft, killed his forward speed and lay beam on to the sea, screw stationary. The wind urged the tug, so much higher than the crippled boat, down towards it. The tug rolled violently as waves crashed over her starboard bulwark and surged ankle-deep across her deck. The distressed fishermen – sodden, bedraggled, but elated by the imminence of salvation – could now be seen to be atop a low deckhouse. One clung miserably to the mast ahead of it, head hanging, obviously injured, and one of the others was gesturing to him and indicating a broken arm.

The first heaving line snaked out, fell just short, was instantly retrieved. Another slapped down across the deckhouse roof, was grabbed by one of the fisherman. The separation was now twenty yards and another large wave might bring the tug crashing down on the smaller craft. Dawlish, a passenger without right of intervention, could sense the skipper gauging whether to signal for revolutions to carry him forward, away from the danger, or to trust his luck for

24

another ten seconds. But now two men on the fishing boat were rapidly drawing in the heaving line and a thicker rope was following it, and a third man was scrambling to catch another thumping down beside it. The injured man was thrust aside and the rope was secured about the mast. Cries and raised hands signalled success. Ruggieri rang for quarter revolutions and the tug nudged ahead. The tow tightened. A second cable was made fast about the mast-stump and then it too was tautening as the cripple lurched into the tugboat's wake.

It took another five minutes of cautious manoeuvring to draw the fishing boat alongside and by then it was obvious that it was past salvage. It had settled appreciably since first spotted and little more than the deckhouse remained above water.

Dawlish and Scrivello watched the fishermen helped on board. He could not understand the language but the rough kindness, the eagerness of every crewman to pull a fellow sailor to safety, had a warmth that transcended tongue or nationality. The injured man was first over – his left arm flapped limply and he screamed as the craft beneath him dropped away suddenly on a falling surge as he was hauled across. He slumped against the engine-room casing but refused to move until his companions were also heaved on deck. One by one they came up, weather-beaten, muscular men, stammering thanks, one even dropping to his knees, babbling prayers.

"God and his Mother have saved them and ..."

Scrivello's words ended in a choking gargle.

Dawlish turned to see Scrivello being dragged backwards, his face frozen in terror, his eyes bulging. The injured fisherman was on his feet, his recently useless left arm locked under the engineer's chin, drawing the throat tight against the thin blade his right hand held against it. He was shouting and the other crewmen were turning, momentarily shocked. Other knives were flashing out from within sodden shirts, and a deckhand was being grabbed by the hair and forced to his knees before one of the fishermen, a point pricking just below his ear lobe. Shouted warnings, emphasised by the extended knives of the other fishermen, drove the crewmen back in a bewildered half-circle.

The tug's mate, a heavy man, stumbled and fell. One of the fishermen stepped towards him, reaching, grabbing, menacing his throat. It was diversion enough for Dawlish. He had no weapon, and the tug carried no firearms that he knew of, but long experience had taught him that he must take the initiative. A wrench, a hammer – anything would do. He spun about, launching himself for the afterdeck. He heard feet pounding behind him and saw too late the coil of heaving line that tripped him and sent him sprawling. He felt hands on his shoulders, others reaching for his kicking legs. He managed to twist his upper body free and lash out with the binoculars he was still carrying, but he could only strike a glancing blow. Then he found himself totally overpowered.

Anger and a feeling of foolishness coursed through him, his whole being screaming that this could not have happened to him. He had faced Chinese cannon and Abyssinian swords and Cossack lances and a dozen other forms of death by land and sea and he had somehow survived, even prevailed. But now he lay face-down on a water-sluiced deck, surprised in peacetime aboard a civilian vessel on an errand of mercy, a Croat fisherman kneeling on his back and holding a knife to his throat, A small, cold internal voice told him that struggle was futile but acceptance of that fact was a humiliation in itself.

More shouts behind, protesting voices quietened by threats, feet moving past. The crew was being shepherded towards the stern, one prisoner's throat the guarantee of his shipmates' compliance. Dawlish thought he heard Scrivello sob, and then a metal door clanged shut and the sound was cut off. He recognised the voice of Ruggeri, the captain, yelling objections – he seemed to have descended from the bridge – and then his indignation seemed to stop in mid-sentence, replaced by stammered assurance of cooperation.

Then noises by the bulwark, sounds of exertion, of instructions when to jump, of first one body, then another being dragged over, of boots on the deck. It was obvious that two more men had crossed from the sinking boat. Dawlish could not see the newcomers but feet pounding on a ladder indicated they had gone straight to the bridge.

It was then that Dawlish knew for certain that this was no opportunistic piracy. There had been others hidden inside that water-logged deckhouse, awaiting their moment. The entire manoeuvre, desperate but perfectly timed, superbly executed, could have been planned with only one objective. And that was confirmed as the deck shuddered beneath him and as the engine shifted from slow to half-revolutions, and then to full, sending the tug battering forward again. She was heading not for the lee of the island now falling astern, but into the wide expanse of the Quarnero Channel, southwards towards the Adriatic. The tug herself was incidental. The half-proven weapon she carried aft was the real prize.

Dawlish was jerked to his feet, his arm doubled painfully behind his back by one of his captors, the second holding the blade to his throat. He had a brief glimpse of the deckhands and mechanics huddled in the lee of projector. Sheltered by a ventilator, one of the boarders sat on a bollard, covering them with a revolver – the first inkling Dawlish had that firearms had been brought across. He saw nothing more as he was hustled past the engine-room casing towards the small deckhouse beneath the bridge. He tried to look up to catch sight of the latecomers but a sharp push on his twisted arm forced his head down. The door to the captain's tiny cabin was pulled open, he was shoved inside and it was slammed shut behind him.

"Thank God they didn't kill you, Commander!" Scrivello's face was paper white as he rose from the single bunk on which he had slumped.

"They had chance enough but they hurt nobody I could see." Dawlish felt his knees weak, the reaction setting in.

"Who are they, Commander?"

"You know the languages here, Signor."

"They spoke Croat. I recognised the dialect, it's from farther south. From Hvar, I think, maybe from Mljet."

Local cut-throats then, but surely not the originators of the seizure. Scrivello had seen nothing of the others who had come on board, but it must be they who had set the tug's course southwards through a near gale, having cut the swamped fishing boat free to founder at its leisure. They had no doubt secured the co-operation of the tug's skipper and his mate and the engine room crew by the same means that held the remainder captive on the exposed afterdeck.

The cabin had a single scuttle, too small to offer escape. A glance through it confirmed that a now oilskin-clad boarder was stationed outside, a pistol in hand.

"They want the projector," Dawlish said.

"God and his Mother! You think it is a rival?"

"Another company? I can't imagine it." And Dawlish knew that no foreign power could risk the consequences of outright piracy so close to the Austro-Hungarian naval base at Pola. Yet no other explanation presented itself.

"If they want the projector, they'll want me as well." Scrivello's misery deepened with the thought. "Nobody understands it so well! My poor wife! Seven months we are married, Commander! So soon to be a mother, and already a widow!"

"Not yet, she's not." Dawlish felt compelled to show an optimism he knew was probably misplaced. But he was damned if he would be carried passively into captivity even if he had little idea yet how to prevent it.

Hours passed, the wind easing. Scrivello was sick again – as much from terror as from motion – but it gave a credible excuse to attract the guard's attention, to negotiate for an unwillingly granted bucket and to sneak a look outside. A mountainous shore lay as a rain-misted streak eight miles, maybe ten, to port. The tug must be close to the chain of tiny islands beyond which lay the full expanse of the Adriatic. A hunk of bread and a jug of water were passed in later and Dawlish demanded assurance through Scrivello that the crew aft were receiving as much. The fact that they were was reassuring. Outright murder did not seem part of the plan.

A dozen options churned in Dawlish's mind, each rejected in turn as more futile than the last. Only one idea buoyed him up, the knowledge that the captives outnumbered the boarders by some three to one. Even a fleeting moment of local superiority might be enough to unleash that potential. He could only wait for his time, only fight to ignore the fury and humiliation gnawing him.

It was late afternoon when shouting and sounds of shifting of heavy objects woke both prisoners from the doze they had fallen into. The tug seemed to have heaved to, her engine panting only enough to hold her stationary against the waves.

"The boat. They're swinging out the boat," Scrivello said. "They're forcing the crew to lower it." It was a stout craft, whaler-sized, carried as much for handling kedges and buoys and the other paraphernalia needed for the trials as for service as a lifeboat.

The view through the scuttle was limited. The boat's bows were briefly visible before dropping below the bulwark. Figures moved into sight, were lost again, one of the boarders, then another, both with pistols, urging the captive crew over the side.

"They're abandoning them here." Dawlish fought down the fear that he himself and the engineer might be detained on the tug. He wanted to be in that boat. Packed to capacity it might be, but he did not doubt he could get it ashore. Since his Anti-Slavery Patrol days off Zanzibar open boats in exposed waters held no fears for him.

Then Scrivello surprised him.

"You are a man of action, a man of decision, Commander." His face was deathly pallid, his front stained with vomit, but his eye glinted resolution. "If they bring us out, if you act, I will support you. I promise it."

"Why?"

Scrivello shrugged. "I will not be shamed. The projector, it's like … like my own child. They must not have it, not like this."

And Dawlish knew that he too could not meekly accept this humiliation, could not take a place in the lifeboat with the craven gratitude of a beaten cur spared another thrashing.

The last of the crew had been transferred to the lifeboat that must be plunging violently alongside. Two boarders were turning towards the small prison, revolvers raised.

Time for rapid instructions to Scrivello. Then the door was being thrown open, and they were being beckoned to emerge.

Scrivello went first, cowering, hands raised before his face as if to ward off any blow. He paused, blinking, as if the clean cold air and the brightness stunned him after the cabin's foetid gloom. Dawlish, following close behind, feared that the Italian's acting was almost too theatrical. The nearer captor was to Scrivello's right, half-amused, half-irritated by his cringing hesitation, and the second moved in behind Dawlish, urging him forward with a push between the shoulder blades.

"Don't shoot, don't shoot!"

Dawlish's English might be incomprehensible to the gunman, but his craven tone and his trembling hands rising slowly spoke unambiguously of submission. He moved slowly aft behind Scrivello. The lifeboat could be seen below the bulwark now, pitching wildly, held fore and aft by lines to the deck, filled to capacity by the chastened, spray-soaked crew. Even the skipper was there, and the engineer and the two stokers. Their presence told that the tug would not be travelling much further. Two men stood by the bulwark, one with a pistol in his waistband, both men who so apparently thankfully caught the heaving lines thrown to them as their fishing boat sank beneath them. They were now obviously ready to slip the whaler's mooring ropes. They seemed bored now, even casual, eager to be rid of their wearisome, compliant charges. Dawlish inched his head around, caught a glimpse of figures looking down from the bridge, could discern nothing of value before he had to turn away.

Then it was time.

He guessed that the gunman at his back was two paces behind. The weapon was not touching him and he had to assume it was aimed between his shoulder blades. Heart thumping, he knew he had one and a half seconds, no more, between any action of his own and any response by his captor. He breathed in deeply, felt the oxygen course though him, willed strength into his muscles, concentrated his whole being on absolute co-ordination of feet and brain and hands.

"Now!" He yelled as he spun about leftwards, his hands meeting in a double fist that swung over and down to smash on to the pistol that was indeed exactly where he had surmised. It fell from the gunman's grasp even as Dawlish's right foot kicked up violently

30

into his groin. The man collapsed, gasping, and Dawlish grabbed for the fallen revolver. He was conscious of Scrivello rolling on the deck, legs entwined with the other gunman's, both hands locked on his adversary's weapon and squirming to avoid the free hand that clawed at his face.

Dawlish had the pistol. Its owner was struggling to his feet but Dawlish brought him down again with a kick into his stomach. He swung around and drove his boot twice, with even greater force, into the side of the gunman who by now straddled Scrivello. It was enough to knock him sideways, enough for the engineer to twist from under him and wrest the second revolver free.

"Stand by me!" Dawlish shouted, backing towards the bulwark, raising the pistol, drawing back the hammer. Scrivello, panting, placed himself to his right. Their two vanquished captors were crawling hurriedly away.

There were shouts from further aft – two more of the boarders coming forward to investigate, one with a drawn knife, but hesitant as they sensed the fury of the two self-liberated captives.

"If they come closer, Scrivello, shoot!"

Dawlish raised his revolver towards the two figures silhouetted against the sky on the bridge above and to his left. They were leaning over the rail, apparently surprised by the sudden action, only now taking in the full import of the scuffle. Bracing himself against the tugboat's heave Dawlish lined fore and back-sight on the nearer figure – the more stocky of the two.

"Come down!" he bellowed. "Come down with your hands up!"

A cry from the right, a scuffling of rushing feet. The boarders who had come from aft had summoned their courage and were charging forward, one with outstretched knife, another with a length of pipe raised like a club. The recently disarmed gunmen followed more closely behind.

"Shoot them!" Dawlish sensed Scrivello's hesitation, the last-moment reticence of one who had never killed before to take the final step. "Shoot, Man!"

He swung his own revolver round, aimed for the chest of the nearest attacker – fifteen feet away along the heaving deck – and squeezed the trigger. He heard the hammer's click on an empty chamber an instant before Scrivello's weapon clicked just as uselessly. He thumbed the hammer back, pulled again, and to as little effect.

The nearest border was on them, slicing his blade horizontally towards Scrivello's face, missing by inches. Dawlish's reaction was automatic, born of thousands of hours of cutlass drill, to stamp forward and slash backhandedly with the pistol as if it had been an edged weapon. The barrel caught the attacker on the side of the head, ripping a scarlet streak along his temple. He fell as Dawlish thumbed back the hammer a third time, pushed the muzzle towards the next boarder, whose piping length was raised to beat down a shock-numbed Scrivello.

And for a third time the hammer clicked on an empty chamber.

The pipe flailed down. It might have brained Scrivello had the vessel's roll not unbalanced his attacker, but was it was enough to shatter the engineer's collarbone with an audible crack. He dropped, howling in agony.

Dawlish lunged forward but the boarder with the pipe was faster. Tall and massive, he stepped back, his seven-foot length of tubing extended before him like a pike. Getting inside it to flail with the empty pistol would be impossible. And the two disarmed gunmen were edging out from behind them, the memory of their kicking all too clear upon their faces, one holding a length of timber, the other a knife. Dawlish paused, mind racing, seeking some alternative to vengeance that could only be merciless. He stepped back slowly, his hand moving back to grasp the bulwark. If he could vault across, swim to the boat alongside, and if it could cast loose…

A single shot rang out and something screamed between Dawlish and the three men inching towards him with murder on their faces. All froze. He turned to see a thickset man at the base of the ladder from the bridge, a revolver in his hand. His single barked command sent the boarders back, leaving Dawlish standing alone.

The pistol edged round, its muzzle a black dot aimed straight at his face.

There was a terrible inevitability in the watery-blue eye that squinted down the sights being that of Major Clement Fentiman. A python might view its prey with more pity.

Dawlish raised his hands slowly but knew already that it was hopeless. For Fentiman meant to kill him, he realised. His knees were shaking and he fought down the urge to be sick. Images of Florence flashed through his mind – on that chilly morning off Troy when he had first spoken to her, swearing at a recalcitrant mule in a Balkan caravanserai, laughing on a balloon ascent at a British fete, horrified only nights since by the reappearance of this monster who boded even greater ill for her happiness than she could have feared.

"You! You're the Admiralty buyer, aren't you?" The major's voice trembled with suppressed fury. "Answer me, damn your soul!"

Dawlish nodded. He wanted desperately to live, to hold Florence in his arms again, to bury his face in her hair and the urge to beg for mercy, however fruitlessly, was strong. And to save himself from that shame at his end he shouted out "You blackguard, Fentiman! I know you!"

"You couldn't leave well enough alone, could you?" Fentiman advanced closer, his pistol all too clearly cocked, rock-steady despite the tugboat's heaving and his own anger, and aimed straight between Dawlish's eyes. "You couldn't leave quietly with the others when you were given the chance! And now you know me, so the whole damn lot of you are going to have to die!"

For a heavy man Fentiman was fast. He flailed the pistol suddenly, catching Dawlish on the cheek – his left cheek, laying it open just above the livid florin-sized scar he already carried there – and all but knocking him off balance. Dawlish clapped his hand to his face, felt the blood wet on his fingers and looked up to see the revolver held rock-steady towards him again.

"On your knees." Fentiman said through gritted teeth and at this last extremity Dawlish saw that his death, his humiliation, would give this man infinite pleasure.

He shook his head slowly.

Fentiman spoke again. "On your knees, I said."

Dawlish shook his head again.

Time stood still. He felt the wind cold on his face and the water in the scuppers sloshing across his feet and heard the wind singing in the mast-stays and tasted his own blood salty on his lips. His heart was pounding and his knees weak but life had never seemed dearer. He had faced death in action a dozen times and now he realised how much easier it had been than awaiting execution. He closed his eyes, summoning Florence's image, focussing all his being on her as he waited for the final darkness.

"Drop it." An American accent. American, with a hint of something else.

Dawlish opened his eyes. Miguel Gonzalez – if that was his name – was standing to the right and slightly behind the major and holding a cocked pistol against his temple.

"He knows us, damn your soul!" Fentiman snarled. "We can't let him go, not him, not any of them." His face was redder now than ever but the pistol he held on Dawlish never wavered. "He had his chance," he said. "He could have gone in the boat."

"You knew that wanton slaughter was never part of the deal, Major." The American's tone had a menace all the more deadly for its weary patience. "You knew that when we agreed that only you and I would carry loaded weapons."

"What's he to you? Since when did you start valuing Englishmen?"

His words were ignored. Again that quiet voice, its resolution unmistakable. "We have what we came for, Fentiman. So now be a reasonable man now and drop that revolver. Because if you don't I'll blow your brains out."

Rage and humiliation and resignation passed in rapid succession across the major's countenance. He lowered his weapon and stamped towards the bridge ladder, brushing the American's pistol away with a contemptuous sweep of his arm. "You'll regret this," he muttered, "you'll regret this bitterly."

"You'd better be on your way now, you and your friend." The American had turned his weapon towards on Dawlish but there was no malice in his voice. "I'm sorry about your face." He reached in his pocket with his left hand and extended a clean folded handkerchief. "It was a cowardly blow, but I daresay you and I have both survived worse."

"You'll hang for this," Dawlish said. Pride stopped him thanking this man for his life. But he took the handkerchief, pressed it to the gash.

The answer was a shrug. "It'll be wet and cold in that boat, but I've no doubt you'll make it to shore. I'll have food and water put in before you're cast off. Then we'll be on our way ourselves."

Dawlish and Scrivello found themselves ushered into the crowded boat that plunged and rolled alongside. The lines were cast off and with only a single pair of oars, and neither mast nor sail, they found themselves abandoned thirty miles from the mountain-fringed coastline to eastward. They watched as the tug drew away, battering into the oncoming waves, its screw once more thrashing the waters astern to a white froth.

On the western horizon was a smudge of black smoke, another vessel, larger. Towards it the tugboat forged, the tarpaulin-shrouded projector clearly visible on the after-deck, until the rising waves blotted it from view.

But the two dozen men cramped in the open boat had no eyes for this. Survival was now their only concern.

4

The child, a boy, now almost three, had fallen asleep in Dawlish's lap, tiny fingers entwined in his beard.

"I'll call for Mrs. Gore." His father reached for the bell pull. "It's time Edgar was put to bed and his mother should see him first."

"Time enough," Dawlish said. "I don't see him often."

The late May evening was dying at last but the lamps in the study in the old house outside Shrewsbury were still unlit. Dawlish had a sudden memory of himself ensconced here with a book as the shadows fell and hoping that his own nurse, that same Mrs. Gore, younger but no less kindly, would not direct him too soon to bed.

Almost a quarter century had passed since he had been a permanent resident of this house.

"It's like James was given back to me."

Dawlish's father's voice trembled with emotion. He drew back his hand, left the bell untolled. Only recently, for the first time in a decade, could he bear to mention again the name of the older son taken in his prime, his neck broken in the hunting field. James. The brother Dawlish still missed no less keenly and to whom he had been so long unfavourably compared.

"He has a look of James too," Dawlish felt almost weak with affection for his tiny half-brother. "And he'll follow you into the firm too. No doubt of it."

His father would be eighty before the child could join him in his solicitor's office. Dawlish realised with a pang that he himself might well become his guardian long before then. The thought was not unpleasing. There was every reason now to believe that Florence and he would never have a child. She would love this boy, that he knew, should she ever see him. But she would never enter this house while his father lived, nor his strapping young step-mother either. Any reference to Florence by Dawlish was pointedly ignored. The stigma of life as a servant, however brief, counted for even more here than among navy wives. Dawlish's father had been content for years to comfort himself with servants – there were rumours of half-brothers other than Edgar – but he would never regard one as family.

"That ship you saw today, Nicholas, will it be yours to command?" This too was new, a curiosity about the Navy, as if Edgar's birth had at last freed Dawlish from the endless entreaties to leave it, take articles, bury himself in a market-town solicitor's office. "Will you be captain?"

"I don't know, Father."

He could not keep the longing from his voice as he glanced at the file on the desk beside him. It had absorbed him since leaving Pembroke that morning. The thick bundle of technical specifications, builder's reports and performance estimates all confirmed the impressions gained in his two-day visit to the dockyard. "There are many besides myself eager for her," he said. "Older officers, better qualified, better connected,"

"But not men who've commanded an ironclad in battle, Nicholas. Only my son did that." The hint of pride was touching.

"Ottoman service doesn't count for much at the Admiralty," Dawlish said, but a small silent voice told him *"Except with Topcliffe"*. He hoped it was true.

HMS *Leonidas* might still lie in the fitting-out basin at the Pembroke Dockyard, her completion still months distant, but she promised to exceed every expectation placed in the new class of cruisers of which she would be the first completed. Her sleek lines, her ten six-inch breech-loaders, the five and a half thousand horsepower that would urge her 4300 tons in excess of sixteen knots and, above all, her steel construction marked her as a vessel apart. On the day she commissioned she would render obsolete dozens of ponderous iron-hulled cruisers, British as well as foreign. Sisters would follow – *Amphion* had succeeded her on the slip at Pembroke and *Arethusa*, *Leander* and *Phaeton* were in varying stages of completion at Napier's yard in Glasgow – but command of *Leonidas*, first of her type, would be an honour that a score of ambitious officers aspired to.

Yet that honour might just be his, Dawlish reflected as his train pulled out of Shrewsbury the next morning at the end of his flying visit. Topcliffe had implied as much in his brief note. It had contained the briefest acknowledgement of the exhaustive report Dawlish had prepared on the Fiume affair and the advice *If you have business in South Wales you might with profit view progress on Leonidas.*

The hint had been broad enough for Dawlish to find urgent need to investigate the potential of fixed torpedo tubes to augment Milford Haven's seaward defences. He was planned to leave *HMS Vernon* within months, and his contribution there – and certain services that appeared on no official record – had made promotion a near certainty. It would mean Captain at thirty-six – an achievement confined to the merest handful of coming men. Fisher had managed it, the midshipman with whom he had shared his first terrifying taste of action on the mud-flats before the Taku forts two decades before.

Fisher now commanded *Inflexible*, the navy's most powerful ironclad. And now such distinction might be within his own grasp also.

Dawlish stared out across the rich landscape, seeing none of.

Leonidas.

The Spartan king's name was somehow appropriate for something slim and deadly, a rival for his love, a bait, tentative, tantalising, from that old tempter Topcliffe. His patronage had brought Dawlish opportunities and advancement, though always at a price. And this time, Dawlish suspected, would be no different, though the price was still unspecified.

There had been two reports to write when he returned from Fiume.

The first, for the Admiralty, contained little more than he had stated to the Austro-Hungarian naval authorities. They had been eager to hush up the embarrassment of brazen piracy committed so close to their main base and Dawlish had been more than ready to co-operate. He had said the minimum about his own role. He disliked being a victim, and his failure to navigate the packed boat to shore – there was little to be achieved with two oars, he told himself, but it still rankled – and its ignominious rescue by a local fishing vessel after two miserable days were hardly achievements to be proud of.

The second report was longer and intended for the single reader. Heavily wrapped and sealed, it was delivered personally into the hands of Admiral Sir Richard Topcliffe by the man Dawlish most trusted.

"He ain't an easy man to track down, Sir." Egdean was just back from London. The excursion had been a novelty for the seaman, a break from his duties as helmsman on the *Lightning*, the torpedo-trials vessel attached to HMS *Vernon*, which Dawlish kept in almost constant employment. But their bond was closer than that, for all the differences in rank, and based on debts each owed the other for his life.

"Sir Richard wasn't at the Admiralty?" Topcliffe had dominated Dawlish's life for four years now but hitherto it was always he who had initiated the contacts. Though Dawlish had once heard Topcliffe's role defined with elegant inexactitude by the previous Prime Minister he was as unclear as ever as to what precisely the admiral did. He was not even sure how to find him.

"The porter at the Admiralty said he hadn't had an office there for years," Egdean said. "Thought he was on the retired list, he did." And that was the general view of Topcliffe, a half-forgotten name, a dauntless commander once tipped for the office of First Lord who had somehow slipped into obscurity without ever attaining it.

"But you found him in the end?" As Dawlish had known he would. Egdean was not a man to be defeated.

"At his club, Sir. The porter – an old seaman, Sir, served on *Argus*, invalided after Kagoshima – he told me where I might find him. And when I did, Sir, why, Sir Richard remembered me! Tipped me a guinea he too, he did."

Dawlish had waited for the Admiral's summons – the theft of a weapon in which the Royal Navy had taken so keen an interest must surely be his concern – but none came. Nothing but the advice to view *Leonidas*. Nothing but the bait.

And then at last, a fortnight after the Pembroke visit, the two separate invitations came to the rented villa in Albert Grove, Southsea. It was close enough to the dockyard and to the moored hulk that was *HMS Vernon* for Dawlish to spend most nights at home.

"You'll see Agatha then," Florence said across the breakfast table. Dawlish had passed to her the gilt-edged card that invited him to dine at Lord Kegworth's London address.

"I don't know," he said. "It says nothing about who else will be present."

"Tell Agatha that she must come here again. That she'll always be welcome. Miss Weston was so grateful for her support."

Ignoring the fact that Florence had once been her maid, Lord Kegworth's daughter had not only stayed in Albert Grove before but had flung herself into helping Florence, and her friend, Miss Agnes Weston, in converting an old public-house into a Sailor's Rest. It provided cheap meals and beds for enlisted Navy personnel ashore and support for their families when they were at sea. Lady Agatha hesitated as little now to roll up her sleeves as when she had cared for refugees in Thrace.

But Dawlish knew that Kegworth was not inviting him to meet his daughter. It was surely no coincidence that the same post had brought an invitation to meet Topcliffe at his club on the afternoon of the day of the dinner.

On the last – the only – occasion when Dawlish had entered Kegworth's Piccadilly mansion it had been Topcliffe who had introduced him.

*

They met in the library of the same London club in which Egdean had run Topcliffe to earth. A single volume lay on the table beside him. He, like Dawlish, was in civilian garb and no casual observer might have guessed their calling.

"A thorough report, Dawlish." In all the initial pleasantries there had been no mention of *Leonidas*, and yet the name hung like something palpable between them.

"One I'd have preferred not to have had to make, Sir."

"I'm surprised to see Fentiman involved. Too clever by far for him alone." Topcliffe sounded reflective. "Embezzlement of mess funds and general beastliness were apparently more in his line – we've checked with the Horse Guards and his old regiment. I won't embarrass fine officers by naming it. Some bad business, women involved, I'm afraid. He'd peddle himself to Satan himself if the price was high enough. He did well from it when he served the Madrid Government against the Carlists a few years back. I've an unconfirmed report that he's been seen recently in Cuba – he'll have friends no doubt in the Spanish administration and there's always some revolt there for him to help them repress. And your wife is certain that it was Fentiman?"

"Absolutely certain, Sir."

"A desperate business, but superbly managed." Topcliffe could not keep the admiration from his voice. "A handful of local brigands who doubtless knew nothing and cared less about who paid them

40

when they were dropped at some Dalmatian island, a small steamer lurking offshore to meet the tug, an expenditure of perhaps two thousand pounds – and Whitehead's latest invention has vanished into thin air."

"They almost certainly scuttled the tug. The Austro-Hungarians had checks made at every Adriatic port," – Dawlish had learned as much from August von Trapp, the tight-lipped fregatten-kapitän who had led the enquiry – "but nothing comparable had been located."

"That's correct," Topcliffe said. "I had separate enquiries initiated myself."

"Only the American could have planned it." Dawlish could see him still, could almost feel his absence of personal malice and the sad look in his deep-set eyes. "He called himself Gonzalez but I'm damned if he's a Latino."

Topcliffe smiled and flipped the book beside him open at a place identified by a marker. He turned it towards Dawlish. The right page was a sepia photographic reproduction, the left text, the heading indicating the volume's title, *Operations of the Army of the Potomac 1864-65*.

"Look closely at the photograph, Commander. Tell me if you recognise anybody."

Dawlish did. Ulysses S. Grant was unmistakable, sitting stiffly in a ceremonial uniform he was clearly uncomfortable in and flanked by similarly gorgeously attired officers to either side. Another row stood behind, all immaculately turned out. The caption was superfluous – the photograph could only have been taken at the end of hostilities. Indomitable men who had overcome brutal obstacles, recorded in their moment of glory.

"Grant, of course", Dawlish said, "and the short man must be Sheridan…" He scanned the front row, recognised no others, shifted to the back row. And there, looking out at him from deep-set eyes was the man who had spared his life on that spray-lashed tugboat deck. Sixteen years had passed since the photograph had been taken but the face had hardly changed.

"That's him!" Dawlish said. "That's him to the life."

41

"You see the senior officer sitting directly before him, Commander?" A handsome, high-cheekboned man with a dark imperial, a face vaguely familiar. "That's General Hancock, Commander of the Army's Second Corps and…"

"Democratic candidate in last year's presidential election." Dawlish finished the sentence. The candidate defeated by another wartime general, James Garfield.

"The gentleman behind Hancock was his Chief of Intelligence, one Stephen Driscoll," Topcliffe said. "They've remained close friends since. Hancock credits Driscoll with delivering him the votes of the Irish community last year."

"Driscoll's Irish?"

"An immigrant. From Limerick I believe, only a youth when his parents fled the Potato Famine. His father died at sea, the mother arrived penniless with four children. He got himself an education of sorts, God knows how, and was a clerk in a New York shipping firm when he enlisted as a private in the Sixty-Ninth Regiment at the outbreak of war. He was a captain by the time of Fredericksburg – which was when his courage drew Hancock's attention – and a Brigadier-General by the war's end. He was wounded three times and his reputation on the battlefield was exceeded only by his skill in intelligence operations."

"So how does he end as a common pirate, Sir?"

"Through the Irish Republican Brotherhood, Dawlish, the Fenians. Founded in America and dominated by Union veterans. Driscoll never forgot his native country, never forgave either. He's one of the Fenian leaders, probably their most clever. He participated in two of their incursions into Canada after the war and those failures convinced him of the futility of that approach. So in between his other interests – and they're extensive – he's been searching ever since for a way to strike back at what he regards as the old enemy. He never married and enmity to Britain dominates his life."

"So he's been responsible for the dynamite campaign?"

A series of outrages by Fenian nationalists had brought sporadic terror to the streets of Britain's cities even as Irish members in the Westminster Parliament disrupted debate after debate in their campaign for land reform. Rural Ireland was convulsed in rent-strikes, intimidation and massive obstruction of government.

Topcliffe shook his head. "He's too clever for dynamite atrocities, Dawlish. Too humane also, I suspect. The slaughter he saw in Virginia inclines him to indirect approaches, ones that inflict damage without head-on attack. The Brotherhood is split on the use of force and Driscoll is seeking a way that will injure us far more effectively – economically and commercially – than random blasts that kill only cabbies and paper-boys."

"So why he does he want the pneumatic projector? Those other interests you mentioned, Sir, could they offer an opportunity?"

"He spent time in recent years in Central America. Very profitably, I understand," Topcliffe said. "It's always been an area of United States interest – Brother Jonathan nearly annexed Nicaragua in the '50s. Driscoll represented some New York commercial interests, groups with affiliations to the same Democratic Party that regards him as such an asset."

"But how could that support help him exploit the projector?" Dawlish was genuinely bemused.

"Finances, my dear Commander! Finances far in excess of what the petty contributions of a million Irish immigrant road-menders and scullery-maids could furnish him! What Driscoll has in mind demands money, a very great deal of money. And the commercial interests in which he is a major shareholder, and which he has assisted to secure certain advantageous contracts in a vast and ambitious project, can provide cash in such quantities. I'm speaking of the Panama scheme. You know of it, Commander? The canal."

Dawlish nodded. The project was ambitious, perhaps insanely so, but success would unlock riches untold.

Topcliffe's voice dropped. "We can only be thankful that Garfield now sits in the White House! Had Hancock occupied that position Driscoll would be yet more dangerous!"

"What has he in mind, Sir?"

"A submarine boat," Topcliffe said. "Not one. A fleet of them. But one to start."

Dawlish smiled. "Surely fanciful, Sir? There have been experiments enough, God knows, but none that could be taken seriously."

He knew that there had been several attempts at building and employing such craft, most recently in America. A contraption operated by Confederate forces had managed to sink a Union warship, but it had sunk itself also, and her crew, with it.

"I wouldn't want to be making the experiments," Dawlish said. "I can't think of any weapon more dangerous to the user than to the intended victim!"

Topcliffe's tone was suddenly icy. "Not this time, Dawlish," he said. "Driscoll has found a natural genius to help him. He's been working in secret with Fenian funding. We've reason to believe that this man has found practical solutions to the problems that dogged every previous experiment. It carries two men, it can sink and manoeuvre underwater and it can rise again."

"And there's no doubt that it's practical?"

"None. It's been under test for months. And only a weapon was needed to make such a boat deadly. Now Driscoll's theft of the pneumatic projector satisfies that requirement."

"And you want this boat for the Royal Navy, Sir?" Dawlish still felt that the idea was absurd, an imaginative fiction created by some squalid informer to justify his pay.

"I don't want it, Dawlish. I want it forgotten, every trace of it wiped clean from the slate of history," Topcliffe said. "The submarine boat's day may come in time – rather will come – but when it does it will be the poor man's weapon for challenging the power of every major navy, ours most of all. I want to delay that day beyond my lifetime – beyond yours also, Commander, if possible."

Then Dawlish knew what was coming, the proposal he could not refuse. Such moments had come before. They had almost killed him but they had also bought advancement.

"You'd like me to destroy it, Sir." He looked the Admiral straight in the eye.

"I'd like you to steal it, Dawlish, and to learn all you can about it, then destroy it. I want you to spirit it away from a friendly country which will look askance on any such action. And tonight you'll meet the gentleman who'll assist you to do just that."

"And afterwards?"

"And afterwards, Commander Dawlish, there could be promotion, command of a certain vessel now undergoing completion and continued active interest in your career by certain highly placed persons."

No real choice then, not with the Navy his life, advancement his goal.

"Then I look forward to meeting the gentleman you speak of, Sir."

And with that Dawlish moved one step closer to the nightmare.

5

There were no carriages in front of the Piccadilly mansion. This was no great occasion, or else Dawlish was early. As he pulled the bell he remembered that it was through this door he had for the last time seen the frail figure of Benjamin Disraeli, Lord Beaconsfield, pass into the night. The wizened old genius who had sent him on a mission that must never be breathed of had passed into history while Dawlish himself had been tossing on the Adriatic in an open boat. A more cautious, sanctimonious hand now held sway in Downing Street. The imperial power, grand designs and bold strokes that Beaconsfield had delighted in had little appeal for Gladstone's worthy Liberals. How Topcliffe had accommodated to his new masters could only be guessed at. Kegworth, Tory grandee that he was, would not have welcomed the change.

The servant took Dawlish's hat, cloak and cane and ushered him, not up the sweeping marble staircase he knew led to the reception rooms above, but to a small room on the ground floor, a study rather than a parlour. Chaos reigned there. The desk, most of the floor and even the swivel chair and the chaise-longe were strewn with papers and journals. Bookshelves lined three walls – the fourth was a window looking out on a tiny walled garden, exquisite in the late evening light – and the titles on the volumes filling them, mathematical treatises and historical studies, left no doubt as to whose domain this was.

"Lady Agatha will be with you directly," the footman said, then left him.

Dawlish recognised the photograph in a silver frame on the desk, was suddenly back in the Istanbul studio where it has been taken three years before. He himself, gaunt and haggard, his Ottoman uniform hanging loosely on him, stood flanked by Florence's slim form and Lady Agatha's solid bulk. Behind them was an ill-executed painted backdrop of Aghia Sofia. The photograph had been Agatha's idea – "To cheer you up, Commander!" – on the first day he had been strong enough to venture out. The women's faces registered pride for nursing him as he had lain delirious in the back of a jolting wagon on that nightmare retreat across Thrace, gratitude also for his own earlier rescue of them. And in Florence's face something more.

Agatha burst into the room, heavier than ever, her great sheep's face beaming, her pince-nez flashing as it caught the gaslight.

"Papa told me you would be coming, Commander," she said, taking his hand "I asked him to have you come before the other gentlemen. I so wanted to see you again."

She glanced around, seemed to see the disorder for the first time. "But we must find somewhere to sit," she said and began hastily to sweep books and papers to the floor. Dawlish joined in, smiling, as exhilarated again by her enthusiasm as when he had once encountered her, unkempt but indomitable, stirring a cauldron of soup in a filthy caravanserai. He cleared a place for himself on the chaise-longe and Lady Agatha settled herself on the swivel chair. Its creak told that it would not sustain her weight for much longer. She beamed at him.

"You have been doing great things, Lady Agatha," he said. "The newspapers seem full of you – and not just your charity work in the East End! The first lady to present a paper to the Royal Society! Recognition from Cambridge of your mathematical work and your astronomic calculations! And your monograph on Piri Reis has finally been published!"

She flushed with pleasure. "You once implied mathematics a strange occupation for a lady," she said in that sweet voice that was always so at variance with her appearance. "Do you think so still, Commander?"

He did not, though many did, and the *Spy* cartoon, entitled "*Minerva*", which had marked her Royal Society success had more than a hint of malice about it. To many it seemed cruelly appropriate that a woman with a mighty intellect should have it enclosed by so unprepossessing a body. Yet she seemed to accept that fact with a cheerfulness Dawlish found touching, just as she accepted that as a daughter she would inherit little and that her appearance doomed her to spinsterhood.

"You've been in South America, Commander. Florence wouldn't speak of it but Papa told me something. Confidential Hyperion business apparently. He said you achieved much, though he would not say what."

"Little enough, Lady Agatha." The look of admiration, almost adoration, and with a hint of longing, in her eyes, made him suddenly uncomfortable. He forced a smile. "But I did see a railway engine called after you." It was better not to mention the horror of the circumstances.

She laughed. "That was Father's idea. And the other engine sent to the Hyperion estates was called after my sister Sophia."

A discreet tap on the door. The footman entered. "The other guests have arrived for dinner, Milady," he said, then left.

"I'm losing you too soon, Commander," she said, rising. "The dinner is for gentlemen only."

He left her in the study and fancied that he heard a sob as he closed the door.

*

There were four others around the dinner table. Kegworth had clapped Dawlish warmly on the shoulder when he entered. He could be relied upon not to allude to the embarrassing fact that he employed Dawlish's wife's father and two brothers as coachmen.

"Hyperion's trading at two and thruppence halfpenny, Commander, and still climbing steadily." His Lordship's pedigree was ancient enough that he did not need to feign the contempt for trade and commerce professed by many whose ennoblement was more recent. "It's thanks to you more than to anybody, Dawlish. It's a damn shame you refused those shares!"

The price stood at almost six times what it had been eighteen months before. Dawlish had little doubt that Kegworth and the other directors had bought up every available share before the San Joaquin expedition had been launched. On his return Dawlish had refused not just the shares but the valuable honorarium offered. Kegworth, as Hyperion Chairman, had over-ridden the objections of another director to make the award and had been amazed when Dawlish would not accept. He could have done with the money too. His farms in Shropshire yielded little and he had been on naval half-pay while in Paraguay. The Rio San Joaquin had cost him more than nightmares and bitter memories.

"There's no reason the shares shouldn't keep rising!" Topcliffe too was present. "None whatsoever!"

Bur seeing Kegworth's eldest son Oswald was a surprise. He seemed as querulous as ever, yet in his own way glad to see Dawlish. He had not forgotten the rescue of his sister, for which he had been thankful enough at the time – his love for her was about the only redeeming feature that Dawlish had ever found in him. He was on leave from his latest post, First Secretary at the Washington embassy – "a damn unpleasant city, like a steam bath in summer" – and less than enthusiastic about returning there.

Only the fourth guest, who had entered with Topcliffe, could be the gentleman whom the Admiral had promised would assist Dawlish in his new mission. He was a short, powerful-looking man, perhaps in his late thirties, with a square, pleasant face. He carried his elegantly-cut evening clothes to perfection. His thick dark hair was cut short and, otherwise clean-shaven, his moustache curved to meet his side-whiskers. But it was the dark, almost black, eyes beneath

48

thick eyebrows that arrested Dawlish, clever eyes that somehow also conveyed warmth and humour even before he spoke. He did so with a cultured American accent.

"Henry Judson Raymond, Commander." He did not wait to be introduced and took Dawlish's hand in a firm grip. "A pleasure to meet you, Sir. The Admiral has been loud in your praises."

"I understand we should congratulate you on a certain acquisition, Raymond," Kegworth said.

"The matched pair? Beauties, My Lord, though until the final bid I thought Rothschild's man would have them for him."

The meal passed uneventfully, the conversation superficial and yet Dawlish knew this was no mere social event.

"You are resident here, Sir?" Dawlish asked. Raymond was seated to his right.

"For some years now, Commander, though I travel extensively." He looked across the table towards Topcliffe and a brief smile flashed between them. "British society agrees with me. I've encountered a welcome from every class, from the highest to the lowest."

And the highest included a stratum Dawlish could never aspire to familiarity with. Raymond did not boast – was pleasantly self-deprecating indeed – but casual references to his mansion near Clapham Common, to his house in Brighton, to his chambers off Piccadilly and to his shooting box in the New Forest, where Kegworth was apparently a frequent guest, and the Prince of Wales not unknown, left little doubt as to his wealth and acceptance. By the time they adjourned to the smoking-room for brandy and cigars Dawlish had him placed, a rich American expatriate who like so many of his kind had tired of the vulgarity of his native land and who had chosen to live as an English gentleman. Dawlish could not imagine how such a person, however influential, could aid him in a venture which might border on the criminal.

Topcliffe opened the evening's real business when the last servant withdrew. "The other gentlemen are familiar with the topic we discussed this afternoon, Commander," he said, pausing to draw on his cigar. "We can talk freely."

"A damn trickish affair nonetheless." Oswald looked far from comfortable. "Gladstone prefers to know nothing of it officially, and he'll want to know even less if it turns out badly."

"He won't be with us forever," his father said, and there was a hint of something very hard, very determined, beneath the familiar bland smile. "But the People's William is a sly old hypocrite and he's had the sense to seek aid from the quarter best able to provide it, party lines or no party lines. He knows that Britain has interests that will outlive him and if this isn't one of them then I'm damned if I know what is. You agree, Topcliffe?"

The Admiral nodded. He turned to Dawlish. "I trust you've no qualms about legalities, Commander?"

"None," Dawlish lied. "But I imagine I'll once more be signing three letters of resignation."

"Bravo!" Topcliffe laughed, "You're ahead of me this time, Commander. Two will be enough, one for myself and one for Lord Oswald in Washington. It's better you don't carry one yourself and you'll be using another name anyway. Both letters to be destroyed on your safe – and no doubt successful – return."

Dawlish could almost feel again the oilskin envelope that had nestled within his clothing through his months of Ottoman service. The evidence, whether he was dead or alive, that he had no further connection with Her Majesty's Navy. The act of burning it – on the same day that photograph in Lady Agatha's study was taken – had been one of the most satisfying of his life.

"Leave of absence won't be a problem, Admiral?" Kegworth asked.

"A word in a certain ear will be sufficient, My Lord. The Commander's assignment at *Vernon* is near its natural end. And for a short absence young Jackson will no doubt cover satisfactorily – you agree Commander?"

He did. Lieutenant Henry Jackson had arrived only months since from *Agincourt*, but already his combination of scientific insight and obvious command ability was making its mark.

"Admiral Topcliffe mentioned an inventor, Mr. Raymond," Dawlish could contain his curiosity no longer. "A natural genius, he called him. You've met him, Sir?"

"Holland - John Phillip Holland, Commander. I guess it'll be a name to be remembered if you don't put a spoke in his wheel. I can't say I've met him, but some of my... my associates have had contacts."

"You're sure he has constructed a submarine boat?"

"Not just constructed it, Commander – at the Delamater Iron Works, at the expense of the Skirmishing Fund of the Irish Republican Brotherhood of North America – but tested it repeatedly in New York Harbour." Raymond said. "There's no doubt he can control it, sink and rise at will. He has navigated it under barges, may have been as deep as forty feet and he's been down for up to two hours at a stretch – stationary, in a dock basin – though I hear he and his helper were half-suffocated when they emerged."

"It's propelled by an oil engine, a Brayton, fifteen horsepower," Topcliffe said.

"That must need air," Dawlish said. "How does he supply it underwater?"

"Storage tanks."

Dawlish was intrigued now, more by the mention of duration submerged than by any other fact. The makeshift craft crewed by desperate Confederate volunteers had operated little more than awash and mainly with hatches open. Propellers cranked by hand, there had been no engines.

"How large is it?"

"Thirty feet, about twenty tons displacement, a crew of two," Raymond said. Then, noticing Dawlish's incipient disbelief, he added "I assure you my sources are reliable, Commander, and independently corroborated. Workers at the yard, harbour-craft crew, even two members of the Brotherhood."

"Informers," Topcliffe said. "Always the Irish weakness."

"The damn thing's an open secret in New York." Oswald sounded unimpressed. "One of the newspapers even had a story about it, called it the Fenian Ram – they guessed that it was intended to sink ships by ramming and the name stuck. Another paper nicknamed it the Boilerplate Shark. But it was a nine day's wonder – there's always some fellow or other in the United States tinkering in a shed with the latest invention that's going to change the world. And that's the last you hear of it."

"*Ex America semper aliquid novum,*" Topcliffe murmured.

"You have drawings of this ram, Mr. Raymond?" Dawlish was already prepared to trust the stranger's judgement over Oswald's.

"Sketches, reconstructions from memories, Commander, but close enough. I can show you tomorrow. My chambers are close by, 198 Piccadilly."

"This Holland, just what is he?"

"A schoolteacher, Commander, and – what was the phrase you mentioned? – a natural genius. A not-inappropriate description. He seems to have been some kind of teaching monk in Ireland until a few years ago. His health failed, he threw it up and came to the United States, taught school in New Jersey. It appears he had been thinking about submarine boats for years, making small experiments until…"

"Until Brigadier Stephen Driscoll recognised that he might be more than an eccentric." Dawlish saw the pieces falling into place now.

"You're acute, Commander," Raymond said.

"And you're well informed, Sir. But what might your interest be in this?"

"You might say that it's my business to know such things." Raymond seemed to catch Topcliffe's eye and he smiled. "And to act on that knowledge of course, when it's in the interest of certain friends of mine."

"As it is on this occasion?"

"As it most assuredly is on this occasion, Commander."

"Mr. Raymond's associates have been keeping us informed for over a year," Topcliffe said. "And to be frank we were not unduly worried. But the theft of Whitehead's pneumatic projector changed everything."

"I received news a fortnight back that the underwater boat had been drawn up on the Delamater slip again. That's the same yard, at 13th Street, where she'd been built," Raymond said. "Work proceeded night and day but there were enough of Mr. Holland's countrymen guarding the place to ensure we couldn't see exactly what was happening."

"That information, together with your report, Commander, clinched the matter." Topcliffe's eyes gleamed with triumph at his deduction. "Driscoll and his associates are on the brink of possessing a weapon that can be transported to any harbour in the world in the hold of an innocent-seeming merchant ship. Driscoll has a whole fleet in mind eventually but one alone can do damage enough!"

"Hang it all, Admiral!" The brandy Oswald was drinking heavily had not mellowed his temper. "Aren't you laying it on a bit thick? I don't mind playing along, even acting as messenger between yourself and Dawlish when Father tells me that it's needed, but do you really believe a gang of Fenian ruffians can manage the like?"

"Just as effectively as they sent the whaler *Catalpa* from New Bedford to Western Australia and back five years ago to snatch half-a-dozen of their members from hard-labour. It was an exploit I'd have been proud of myself." Topcliffe was quietly angry. "We've been deceiving ourselves too long with Punch cartoons showing Irishmen as chimpanzees. There's nothing stupid about these people, gentlemen. They're clever and they're dangerous, with long memories to boot, and since we haven't had the sense to treat them fairly and make friends of them in the past we've now no option but to strike hard now before they injure us seriously."

"But we have the most powerful navy afloat, Admiral." Kegworth sounded eager to deflect attention from his son's boorishness.

"It's not our navy that worries me, My Lord," Topcliffe said. "It's our merchant fleet! What do you think a few random sinkings at apparently safe berths around the world would do to insurance rates? To balance sheets? To dividends? To British prestige?"

"I understand you can assist me to prevent all this, Mr. Raymond?" Dawlish was less interested in potential disasters than in the task confronting him.

The American smiled. "With men, contacts, purchases, identities, Commander, and with all else you'll need to be a successful thief. With everything except luck. You'll have to supply that yourself."

"You seriously think we can cut out this craft from a yard in the heart of New York and get away with it?"

A look of quiet pride spread over Raymond's face. "I'd be reasonably confident, Commander. I have some experience in such things. But it won't be necessary. I've telegraph confirmation that Holland took the ram across the Hudson under her own power three days ago. She's at Jersey City now – a much quieter location. And yesterday he dived at least twice and brought her back safely to the basin where they're keeping her."

"The projector seems to have been installed successfully and there's now little time to lose. You'll be sailing for New York within the week, Commander." Topcliffe's tone left no room for argument. "Mr. Raymond will precede you. He has access to the necessary funds to support your efforts. As you too will have."

"I'll be in Washington but you'll only contact me *in extremis*, Dawlish." Oswald's words were slurred. "And then only by telegram, mind you. Topcliffe will give you the code."

"It's late, Gentlemen," the Admiral said, "too late for business, and we presume too much on His Lordship's hospitality. Mr. Raymond – might Commander Dawlish and I call on you in the morning? Ten o'clock, shall we say? We can plan in more detail then."

Kegworth saw his visitors personally to the door. He shook Dawlish's hand warmly as they parted. "It will be a signal service, Commander," he said. "A signal service. And it won't be forgotten, that I assure you."

"It's a fine evening," Topcliffe said. "I believe you're lodging at the Charing Cross Hotel, Commander? Good! I'll stroll that far with you. And Mr. Raymond – you'll join us for the first few yards? I imagine you're staying at your chambers tonight?" He signalled his waiting coachman to follow.

Topcliffe and Dawlish left the American at the entrance of an imposing block, a liveried porter fulsomely ushering him inside. They lit cheroots and walked on past the Royal Academy.

"You'd never guess, would you, Commander," Topcliffe said, "that our friend is the lover of the Duchess of Devonshire?"

Dawlish stopped, looked at him appalled. "Sir..." he began, and then words failed him. However true, a lady's name could never be mentioned in such a context.

Topcliffe was smiling and Dawlish realised that he was enjoying the outrage he had provoked. "The Gainsborough, Commander," he said. "The portrait that disappeared five years ago from a gallery not four hundred yards from this spot."

It had been a nine-days' wonder at the time and ever since unsubstantiated accounts of its sighting, or of demands for its ransom, had surfaced in the press. The voluptuous duchess was sequestered in a Belgian chateau, in a London vault, in the schlöss of a German princeling. She had crossed the Atlantic to the United States, to Brazil, to Mexico. She was gracing the boudoir of a French demimondaine, the saloon of a private yacht, the smoking room of a San Francisco sporting-house. Rewards had been offered for her return, guarantees of anonymity, solemn undertakings not to prosecute. All to no avail.

"What are you saying, Sir?" Dawlish knew most of the story. Florence, like half the nation, had followed the intermittent saga with breathless delight.

"That our charming Mr. Raymond is a thief," Topcliffe said. "A most accomplished and successful one. That's why he's so useful to us."

"But he seemed..."

"Exactly what he is. A clever, cultured, agreeable American gentleman, whose profession just happens to be larceny."

"Is he aware you know this, Sir?"

"He wouldn't be helping us if I didn't. The Duchess is the least of his misdemeanours. He watches his step here in Britain – and he's welcome to her for all I care. But others may be less forgiving. The Pinkertons want him for a string of bank burglaries in his native land, his robbery of the Calais to Paris Express earned him a twenty-year sentence in absentia, the Cape-Colony authorities didn't take kindly to diamonds disappearing in transit last year and your erstwhile Ottoman employers took similar exception to an avalanche of forged letters of credit."

"Does Kegworth suspect? Or the Prince of Wales?"

Topcliffe shrugged. "Does it matter? He's a delightful companion. His name isn't Raymond, by the way, it's Worth, Adam Worth. He's generous and he's entertaining." Suddenly his voice was cold. "And he likes the company of the prince and his friends even more than they like his, and he craves acceptance and respectability more than you crave advancement, my dear Dawlish. That's why he's useful to me, he and his whole web of informants and confederates and accomplices across four continents."

"But what was the Duchess to him?"

"God knows. An ideal of beauty and grace for the son of a penniless German immigrant who grew up knowing neither? The embodiment of wealth and elegance for a youth from a Boston slum whose first gains were accumulated by bounty-jumping from one Union regiment to the next, just one step ahead of the firing-squad? Does it matter, Commander? By now he'll have taken her out from her hiding place in those tastefully-appointed chambers where we'll visit him tomorrow and he'll be gazing enraptured on her beauty."

"But can we trust him?"

"The Duchess's loss would mean more to him than his liberty, even his respectability. And a man who once escaped from hard-labour at Sing Sing prison will take every measure to avoid returning there. He'll support you to the hilt, Commander, depend upon it. I've little doubt that together you'll take the wind from Brigadier Stephen Driscoll's sails."

They reached the Crimea Memorial at the bottom of Regent Street. "I'll leave you here." The Admiral shook his hand. "My way is to the right. Good Night, Commander."

Dawlish strolled on, knowing now that only grand larceny on foreign soil could earn him *Leonidas*.

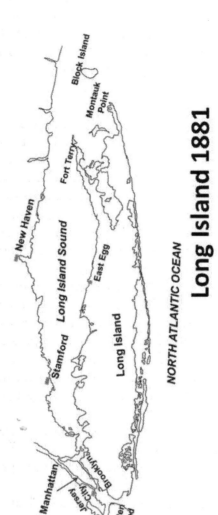

Long Island 1881

New Haven

Stamford   Long Island Sound

Fort Terry

Block Island

Montauk Point

East Egg

Long Island

NORTH ATLANTIC OCEAN

Manhattan

Jersey City

Brooklyn

Staten Island

6

The Narrows widened and the liner *SS Germanic*, sleek and black-hulled, nosed slowly into the Upper Bay. Her engine was at half revolutions for the first time since she had departed Queenstown, the only brief break since Liverpool, eight days since. The weather had been favourable, the crossing comfortable and now she was arriving at her destination in afternoon sunshine.

"It's wonderful, Nicholas!"

Florence gripped the rail before her with white-knuckled delight as the bows swung over. The full expanse of the harbour opened before them – Manhattan's clutter on the far skyline, its buildings half-obscured by a forest of masts and rigging, the factories and piers along on the opposite Jersey waterfront dim beneath a haze of smoke, shipping and grain elevators lining the Brooklyn wharves to the east. The waters ahead were alive with vessels of every tonnage, through which the *Germanic*, siren blasting intermittently, forged her majestic path.

Florence reached for Dawlish's hand, brought it to her lips, kissed it. "Thank you, Nick," she said. "Thank you for bringing me."

He was excited enough himself to forget momentarily why he was here. He had seen this harbour once before, as a young lieutenant marvelling at a nation's explosive growth in the aftermath of war, but that memory had not prepared him for the changes now apparent. Even the rural Staten Island shore slipping past to port was showing signs of industrial development.

"Take these, Florence." He passed her his binoculars. "There, follow my finger, above those masts."

The tops of two great stone towers were just visible, huge cables draped from them in graceful catenary.

"That's the great new bridge that they said could never be completed," he said. The epic of ingenuity and perseverance that was now almost ready to span the East River had received wide coverage in technical journals and he had followed its progress avidly.

"We'll see it together, Nicholas," she said. "That and all the other wonders we've read about."

He realised he had never seen her happier and reminded himself that it was not meant to be like this. Florence – Mrs. Page, just as he was Mr. Page for the duration of this assignment – was with him for purposes of deception. That was how he had rationalised it when he had finally surrendered to her demand to accompany him.

"It's private, not Navy business," he had told her.

"Like when you disappeared to South America? God knows what you did there, Nick, but ever since you got back you've raved in your sleep at least once a month."

"This will be easier this time, Florence. I'll be back before you know it."

"It won't be easier. I can see it in your eyes, Nicholas."

"There will be no danger," he lied, "nothing to worry about."

"I'll lose you, Nicholas." She was suddenly quiet, embarrassed by the tears welling in her eyes. She reached up, touched the scar on his cheek. "I'll lose you, Nicholas, sooner or later, on one of these tasks you never want to talk about. I know it, and I accept it. I just want a little longer with you before it happens."

He had not yielded then, nor the next time, but in the end he had, and when he mentioned his decision to Topcliffe with deliberate casualness at their last meeting before departure the Admiral had pronounced it a capital idea. "Your wife, Dawlish? A splendid woman – I met her once, remember? An ideal cover. Together you'll play the part to perfection."

So it had proved in practice. Neither at the *Germanic's* captain's table nor in the saloon, not even during the Sunday service at which Dawlish had read the lesson and at which Florence had impressed all by her piety, had anyone doubted the credentials of the squire of Silverbridge Court, Shropshire, and his lady, wealthy tourists venturing to the New World for the first time. Raymond had pressed a hundred guineas on Dawlish for her wardrobe – "Essential expenses, I'll be settling otherwise for them," he had said. Explained by Dawlish as a stock-market windfall, Florence had protested only briefly before ensuing that the best dressmakers and milliners in

Portsmouth hurriedly provided her with discrete elegance, wealthy provincial taste rather than ostentatious fashion.

They stayed on deck, picking out sights, as the vessel nudged into the Hudson. The First-Class tender edged alongside, past the hovering tugs that would lodge the liner in her berth further upriver. It was time to go ashore and Egdean, uncomfortable but correct in a serge suit and starched collar, was already below by the entry-port with their trunks and cases. He would never make a valet but Dawlish needed somebody by him whom he could trust implicitly. The seaman who had stood so resolutely by him in Africa and Paraguay, and who had served him so competently helmsman in so many torpedo trials, could be relied on to the death. His leave of absence from the Navy had been easy to arrange.

Nobody met them – Raymond had specified it must be so – and their impersonation of bewildered visitors fighting their way through the chaos at the Castle Garden arrival station was convincing because it was genuine. Egdean pushed through the press to secure two cabs, in one of which he would follow with the baggage.

"It's different, Nick," Florence said as they clattered and swayed towards Union Square. "They speak English but it's somehow different. And it's so loud, so... so rough, and so busy."

Her elation was tempered now and Dawlish fancied he could read her mind, her uncertainty. It was little different to his own. The unreality of shipboard life was over and the game was suddenly serious, the more so since he still could only guess at much that lay ahead. And Florence knew less, far less, than he did – she clearly distrusted his story of a technical investigation – and dreaded more.

The Kennebec Hotel was small and well appointed, a block away from Union Square. "It's as comfortable as the Clarendon or the St. Denis," Raymond had said, "but it's quieter – fewer coming and goings, and that, I imagine, is to our mutual taste." Its furnishings, patent safety-elevator and private bathrooms made Fiume's Tersatica seem by comparison like a village inn.

A single stampless envelope awaited Mr. Page's arrival at the reception.

"Hand-delivered?" Dawlish asked.

The clerk shook his head. "Dropped in the mail-box, Sir."

Dawlish waited to open it until they had reached their room. He found a single sheet of paper and two unsigned lines in a flowing script. *"Pier 21, East River, 10 o'clock tomorrow. A yachting excursion. Your wife will enjoy it."* Nothing else, not even an initial, and yet the implied instruction was as clear as any hint of Topcliffe's. It indicated too that the necessary charter had been effected, the first steps taken, since Raymond had arrived via Canada. The long border provided opportunities for avoiding any official on the lookout for Adam Worth at an American port.

*

The streets were hot, airless and humid as their cab carried them south and east the following morning. Dawlish's light suit was damp with perspiration and Florence's hair was sagging, much to her annoyance, long before a shower of sparks from the overhead railway at Third Avenue drifted through the open window and dotted her cream linen dress with tiny black spots.

"What will Mr. Raymond think of me?" she said. "Or his wife either?"

"I don't think she's here," Dawlish said. "I believe she lives in London."

There might not even be a Mrs. Raymond. Not for the first time Dawlish reflected that knew so little of him, that he was placing infinite trust in Topcliffe's assessment of the man.

Florence sensed his unease and lapsed into silence. They were passing through an increasingly squalid area, high tenements with open windows and gaping doors, washing hanging from sills, slatternly women gossiping on doorsteps, filthy children playing in the gutters, urchins running up to hang on the back of the cab until dislodged by a quick backwards crack of the driver's whip. A tough-looking group of loafers at a street corner eyed the cab hungrily and one, catching sight of Florence, raised a laugh from the others with some inaudible obscenity.

Dawlish found himself fondling his cane's lead-loaded head and was grateful for Egdean's solid bulk on the seat opposite, knowing that he carried a life-preserver in his inside pocket. His disquiet was ridiculous, Dawlish told himself – he had braved hazards a thousand times worse than robbery in a New York slum – but he recognised beneath it an awareness that he was acting, for the first time ever, without any shred of support from an official organisation. Topcliffe had entrusted him with complete discretion – with a budget to match, though he suspected Raymond had been induced to contribute most of it – but he knew that failure would result in his total abandonment. No single-worded telegram to Oswald in the embassy at Washington would save him from the quarries of Sing Sing.

Pier 21 was a commercial one, its sides flanked by small coasters, its planking piled with crates and sacks and barrels, salt and flour and potash and sugar and rice, horses and drays moving between them, netted loads swaying overhead, longshoremen shouting instructions and warnings. Egdean paid off the cab and they stood, slightly bewildered, amid the bustle. Then, out on the grey, filth-streaked river, incongruous against the stark utility of trade, screw churning gently to hold it stationary against the current, Dawlish saw the small steam yacht. Her white hull, varnished teak upperworks, brass-framed scuttles and buff funnel gleamed as if she were a toy upon Kensington Round Pond. Two rakish masts and the bowsprit jutting over the clipper bow served no purpose but elegance, but strings of coloured bunting had been stretched between them. A huge and unfamiliar ensign, probably that of some yacht club, flapped weakly at the stern.

"Is that Mr. Raymond's ......" Florence began, no less impressed than Dawlish himself, for it was a thing of beauty, a millionaire's whim, splendid for its unattainability.

"It is indeed, Ma'am."

They turned and there was Raymond, no less immaculate than the small palace out on the polluted stream.

"And you can only be Mrs. Page. A pleasure, Ma'am." He took her hand.

He was charm personified, handing Florence down gallantly into the pulling cutter that had manoeuvred to steps between two moored schooners. The oarsmen were uniformed in white duck and tattoos on bare arms indicated that several had served in the American Navy. As they neared the yacht Dawlish saw the name "*Tecumseh*" on the bow.

"A magnificent craft, Mr. Raymond," he said. "I had envisaged something rather more modest."

The foreboding that had plagued him all morning had a focus and a justification now. They had agreed in London that a nondescript tug, prosaic but powerful, would best answer their needs. He could not envisage committing what amounted to piracy with this floating mansion.

"Perfect for Long Island Sound," Raymond said, "Perfect, and not out of place, I assure you, Mr. Page, and indeed modest by the standards of many you might see off Newport. You've heard of Newport, Mrs. Page? The resort of our best families in the summer months."

Dawlish wanted to remind him that their business lay in a small, congested industrial basin somewhere behind Jersey City's waterfront and not among fashionable dilettante sailors but they were drawing alongside the yacht now. Raymond was on his feet and preparing to pass Florence up with the same elaborate courtesy as before.

It was no surprise to find the decks holystoned to a standard that would have done credit to a Mediterranean Fleet ironclad, nor a brass-buttoned steward in snowy white waiting with ice-cold champagne on a silver tray, nor the captain – Elias J. Swanson, as he introduced himself – to be a sharp-featured, taciturn Yankee whose manner conveyed competence. Florence, for once not sensing Dawlish's mood, was glancing about with barely concealed delight and, no, she did not wish to go below briefly. She would be delighted to accompany the gentlemen directly to the bridge.

"A pleasure and an honour for us all then," Raymond said. He swept her with him, leaving Dawlish to follow, angry at his failure to fathom what was happening, fearful lest his frustration show.

The *Tecumseh* was under way now, the helm over and the long bowsprit sweeping around to point downriver.

"On your first day in New York, Mrs. Page, I thought a circumnavigation of Manhattan might assist your orientation," Raymond was saying. "You'll excuse American pride when I say it's always impressive – but today, quite coincidentally, there's an extra element of interest."

"The Great Bridge?" Florence said. She looked at Dawlish. "The one you spoke of Nicholas?" The huge granite towers were visible upstream, a half-completed roadway suspended from the massive twin cables draped between their pinnacles.

"There's something to show you that's no less impressive than the bridge to Brooklyn, Ma'am, and related to an undertaking even more audacious. And quite a gala occasion to celebrate it – which is why the *Tecumseh* is dressed so gaily today." He gestured to the bunting overhead.

"You disappoint me, Mr. Raymond! I thought it was in my honour!" Champagne in mid-morning was clearly too much for Florence, Dawlish thought, seething quietly.

"Patience, Mrs. Page," Raymond was laughing. "You'll find the spectacle worth the wait – and I suspect your husband will find it of no less interest." Then he was pointing out the Navy Yard on the eastern shore – he might have owned it for the pride he seemed to take in it – and a belching line of factory chimneys rising beyond. He was reeling off some meaningless statistics that seemed to impress not only Florence, but Egdean also, who was standing respectfully behind.

The yacht glided smoothly past other river traffic, barges in the wake of straining tugs, small traders pushing slowly upstream and high-decked ferries crossing with screaming whistles, vessels soon be rendered obsolete by the bridge's completion. Dawlish lifted his field glasses and marvelled at the soaring towers and the human swarm labouring high above. The air was heavy here with the mixed smells of spices and grain and roasting coffee wafting out from the shoreline. Downriver shipping-congested jetties and piers jutted from the waterfronts on either side.

"There's the entrance to the Atlantic Basin. You'll have heard of it, Mr. Page? The largest enclosed dock in the world."

More shipping, more grain elevators, more warehouses, more superlatives.

The steward hovered close with more champagne. Dawlish motioned him away with a scowl, silently angry that Florence accepted another glass. The southern tip of Manhattan was slipping past to starboard and he waited impatiently for the moment when the bows would swing across into the Hudson. The Jersey City wharf where Holland's submarine boat nestled was little over a mile away and Dawlish's urge to sight the location, if not the craft itself, was almost unbearable. But instead the yacht forged southwards, between the Brooklyn shore and Governor's Island, heading towards a cluster of boats and shipping a half-mile head.

"Take my glasses, Mrs. Page. You can focus them? Yes! An accomplished lady indeed!" Raymond pointed. "There! There's the spectacle I promised!"

Whistles and sirens blasted and a flotilla of smaller craft circled a huge, slow vessel. Four steam yachts, each larger than the *Tecumseh*, and a flag and banner-festooned ferry kept pace with it as it moved towards the Narrows. Two feathery streams of water rose vertically to either side of a red-painted fireboat off to starboard and a uniformed band was crashing out on the ferry's upper deck.

"What's that enormous ladder sticking up?" Florence asked.

A jagged pyramid extended above the craft that was the centre of attention. Dawlish adjusted his own glasses to reveal a sloping iron lattice. Topped by a national flag, it rose high, like a tilted coal-pit winding tower, over a superstructure that seemed to consist of a jumble of metal boxes pierced by several spindly funnels. Banners stretched between them, bellying slightly in the gentle breeze. Red, white and blue bunting had been strung from every possible point.

"It's a dredger," Dawlish said, "A bucket dredger."

The name was all it had in common with any machine Dawlish had ever seen keeping open the approaches to a port or dock-yard. This was gigantic, a low-freeboard rectangular raft at least three hundred feet long and surmounted with boiler and engine-rooms, winches, spud-legs and the great inclined ramp that carried the endless chain of huge toothed buckets. Piled crates and tarpaulin-draped machinery filled the spaces between the deckhouses. The nearer end – bow and stern were almost meaningless terms – was occupied by a three-decked structure, obviously crew accommodation, and on the galleries that surrounded it another band thumped and blared, oblivious of the competition on the ferry. No mud or silt streaked the dredger's pristine paintwork and absence of smoke from its stacks indicated that its furnaces were cold. At the other end huge hawsers linked it to two smoke-belching tugs – large, ocean-going vessels with high bows – that drew it forward at little more than walking pace.

"A great day for the Isthmian Dredging Corporation," Raymond said. "Splendid, is it not? The largest of its kind ever built."

"But where's it going?" Florence asked. "Why such a carnival?"

"To Panama, Ma'am, to realise the dream of centuries. To link Atlantic and Pacific by a ship-canal, to make the navigation of Cape Horn a memory and to change the entire pattern of maritime trade. It's got a long, slow tow ahead of it but they're giving it a fitting send-off."

"Is it for that Frenchman, Nicholas? The one who dug the canal at Suez?" Florence was an avid reader of illustrated papers and recent proposals for an inter-oceanic canal had received extensive coverage.

"de Lesseps," Dawlish said. "But he might have bitten off more than he can chew this time." Every article he had read had been sceptical of the plan's feasibility.

"The Vicomte de Lesseps' Compagnie Universelle du Canal Interocéanique," Raymond savoured the title, "granted a New York syndicate the main contract for excavating the eastern section of the canal."

"And this dredger, the *Jeremiah Jessup*" – Dawlish could just read the name painted in large black letters against the accommodation's white – "will do the job alone?" Large as it was, the machine seemed puny for a task so Herculean.

"The first of two," Raymond said. "The Isthmian Corporation has high ambitions – but justified ones, given the strength of their backing." He turned, nodded to the captain and the *Tecumseh*, whistle blowing, slowed and took station off the ferry's port bow. Its decks were thronged and several of the passengers, ladies as well as gentlemen, waved towards the newcomer. Raymond lifted his cap in acknowledgement and Florence swept her handkerchief slowly above her head.

"So this is what you came to see, Nick!" she whispered, coming close, her face showing a relief that touched him all the more for the fact that it must ultimately be disabused. "Not such a great mystery after all!"

"Do you recognise anybody, Mr. Page?" Raymond turned to him with a smile. "There, on the middle deck – there, in that group with the ladies in white."

Dawlish raised his glasses and recognised a scene reminiscent of what he had once witnessed at Epsom Downs on Derby Day – a knot of wealth and ostentation, silk, linen, feathers and gold, a diamond flashing as it caught the gleam off a wave, a parasol slowly twirled, elegance mixed with raw vulgarity, new money and old families mutually parasitic. Fleshy, sweating men with cigars clamped between their teeth slapped the backs of embarrassed acquaintances who seemed to recoil from their touch. Women with the features of fishwives, their bulk straining through bulging gowns, laughed with open mouths and drained champagne side-by-side with ladies who seemed shamed by their presence.

"I see nobody I know." Dawlish felt proud of it, could not keep the distaste from his voice.

"Not among the aristocracy of our young republic, Mr. Page? But no – your friend has turned away for now but in a moment you'll recognise him."

The group was shifting, new faces coming to the fore, a stout, red-faced, white-haired gentleman pointing towards the dredger, obviously explaining something, heads nodding around him in half-comprehension.

"That's Mr. Jessup himself, the president of the Isthmian Corporation," Raymond told Florence, "the man who promoted the entire venture and convinced the backers. And that's Kelly to his right – Boss Kelly of Tammany, a relation of Cardinal McCloskey –

and behind him that's Metcalfe the stockbroker, the fifth most powerful man on Wall Street, and Gage of Elliot and Gage, the banking house. And you see the man with that lady in blue? That's O'Dowd who delivered Brooklyn for Hancock last fall and on her other side that's Broderick of the Nashua and Montpelier Railroad and that's…"

"Brigadier Stephen Driscoll," Dawlish said.

His gaze had been fixed on the back of the long, lean figure that had seemed vaguely familiar. As it turned his lenses caught the dark deep-set eyes he had last seen when they granted him mercy on the deck of a heaving tug. The face creased into a smile in response to some remark and then was suddenly solemn again, the face of a man in company but not of it, sharing perhaps something of the distaste that Dawlish himself felt even at this distance.

"Driscoll indeed, Mr. Page," Raymond said, "the darling of the Democrats as long as he assures the Irish vote, the toast of the Isthmian Corporation for securing the Panama dredging contract and the Brotherhood's preferred candidate for first president of an Irish Republic while he still keeps the funds flowing to them."

"It's that man from Fiume." Florence was trembling, had lowered her own glasses. "The friend of…" She stopped, unwilling to pronounce the name. "The man, Nicholas, whom you said stole that tugboat, who abandoned you…" The colour was draining from her face, her lower lip quivering and now he knew she was creating her own vision of menace and threat, all the worse for her partial knowledge. He took her hand and she said very quietly "Take me away from this, Nicholas. I don't want to see any more."

Raymond had sensed her distress and was signalling to the captain. A clipped command, the telegraph ringing for full ahead and the *Tecumseh* surged forward, well clear of the ferry. Her bowsprit was almost level with the poop of the large steam yacht ahead before the helm was thrown over and she headed out into the clearer waters towards the centre of the bay. Dawlish fancied he saw Driscoll's face turned to them as they forged ahead but he must surely not have recognised them, not so unexpectedly. The wheelhouse blocked them quickly from view and Dawlish's attention was now fully focussed on Florence.

"It would be tedious to follow the *Jeremiah Jessup* to Panama." Raymond flashed Dawlish a look that told he was ready to change the subject. "I suggest we cruise the western shore for now and then head northwards up the Hudson, but slowly, to give us time for lunch. May I lead you to the saloon, Mrs. Page? Some modest refreshments await us there."

The buffet was sumptuous, laid out in silver trays on a snowy cloth, amid furnishings that would have done credit to Kegworth's mansion. Yet none of them did more than taste a token quantity and the conversation was stilted and formal, with long silences. Dawlish sensed Florence's fear and he himself felt doubt and apprehension knotting his stomach. The game was more complex, vastly more so, than he had supposed. Driscoll at the heart of Democratic wealth and power was somehow more formidable than Driscoll the cool pirate of the Adriatic.

The yacht had reached the Staten Island shore and now it turned north, steaming calmly at quarter revolutions. Through the open ports they heard the faint, discordant strains of the bands still playing across the bay as the floating pageant crawled seawards.

"Perhaps Mrs. Page would like to rest?" Raymond said. "I had a stateroom prepared for that purpose."

Dawlish's slight nod told her to accept. A uniformed maid, unseen before, materialised to conduct her aft.

"A cigar, Mr. Page?" Raymond opened a large box. "A Havana? A Sumatra perhaps? Or a mild cheroot?"

7

They went on deck, moved aft, lit up. The nearest deckhand was ten yards away.

"What the devil are you playing at, Raymond?" Dawlish could contain himself no longer. "Do you seriously propose to spirit away the submarine boat from under the noses of a gang of Fenian desperadoes with this, this….. this floating gin-palace?"

Raymond looked at him with tolerant, even affectionate, amusement. "I do, as a matter of fact, Mr. Page." He seemed to take a delight in using the nom-de-guerre even when they were alone.

"You're telling me that we're supposed to go up there," Dawlish gestured ahead towards the acres of factories and mills and foundries vomiting their contributions to the smoke-heavy pall hanging over Jersey City and Hoboken. "We're to lie unobtrusively off a squalid canal basin in the hope Driscoll's friends will think some eccentric millionaire finds it a scenic location for mooring for the night? And row ashore, secure this underwater boat, this ram, and make off with it before they notice?" He resented his mounting anger, felt it made him slightly foolish, yet could not help himself. Raymond's calm smile infuriated him even more.

"That's not what we're going to do at all, Mr. Page," Raymond said. "As I told you earlier, the *Tecumseh* will be anything but inappropriate for where we're headed."

"So we're headed to Long Island Sound, I think you said? I didn't come here to take part in some regatta!"

"The game has changed, Mr. Page. Holland has lost his Fenian Ram."

"What? You mean it's sunk?"

"I mean it's been appropriated by the Brotherhood. It's no longer in Jersey City."

"You know where it is?"

"I wouldn't have chartered this yacht if I didn't"

"What happened?"

"A falling out, I believe. Holland and Driscoll, Holland and the Brotherhood – it's apparently been simmering for months. Funding is at the root of it and Holland wants to experiment, to perfect his invention, and that eats money, but the Fenians want action, British shipping sinking mysteriously in neutral ports. And once the projector had been tested successfully – twice, according to my sources – they decided to move."

"How?" Dawlish sensed another humiliation piled on that of Fiume, his own plan pre-empted by the man to whom he so resentfully owed his life.

"Simple. While Driscoll was being very publicly feted at a dinner arranged in his honour at the St. Nicholas Hotel by the Isthmian directors a tugboat with a half-dozen of his confederates appeared at the Morris and Cummings pier where the ram was tied up. They had a note signed by Holland – forged of course – to authorise the craft's removal. The night-watchmen – Irishmen themselves – saw nothing strange about it being moved under cover of darkness. Driscoll's men took it in tow and the whole business was concluded most efficiently in a quarter-hour."

"Where did they take it?"

"Across the Hudson, up the East River. They reached the Sound by dawn, moved slowly through the daylight hours, entered New Haven two nights later."

"It's there now?"

"Lying at a brass foundry on the Mill River. The owner, Reynolds by name, is of the Brotherhood, one of Driscoll's inner circle. He helped finance the Fremantle rescue."

"How long have you known?"

"Five days, since just after the event." Raymond looked pleased with himself. "But time enough to charter this vessel, to draw on certain contacts to crew her, to rent a certain property on Long Island and to put one or two other measures in hand."

"And to flaunt her before New York society in general and Driscoll in particular. You've got a damn strange way about managing clandestine affairs, Mr. Raymond."

"When you've been as long as I have been in my particular line of business, Mr. Page," Raymond's tone had a hint of ice, "and when you've indeed thrived in it, as I have, then you'll understand that a bold front and a respectable image are your greatest assets. You know who own those yachts escorting the *Jeremiah Jessup*? Walton the meat packer, and Verbrugge of Pompeii Insurance and Demaine the oil man and Tylee who damn nearly owns the Comstock Lode, that's who. And after our appearance back there they'll be enquiring who chartered the *Tecumseh* and by morning their womenfolk will be scanning the society columns and learning that a certain wealthy

Englishman and his elegant wife will be spending the summer exploring the eastern seaboard in style and comfort."

"And you'll have planted the story!"

Raymond shrugged modestly. "I told you my contacts were extensive. I guarantee that afterwards nobody will see anything strange about this yacht cruising the Sound or lying off any town on it."

"We agreed none of this. Why should I consent to it?"

"Because it's the only way, Mr. Page."

Dawlish fell silent. The foreboding that had oppressed him all day had now evolved to something close to despair. He had already lost control of this expedition – had never had it in the first place, he now realised bitterly – and its success was in the hands of a criminal and a fantasist in whom his trust was falling by the minute. But the alternative was retreat, return like a whipped cur, Topcliffe's frigid judgement on his failure, a lifetime at his present rank commanding some shore-establishment in a backwater.

"You said the ram was up some river?" He forced calmness into his voice, the first step towards regaining the initiative.

"A mile up it, on the edge of New Haven, too narrow for the *Tecumseh*. And Driscoll's men will be alert to any tricks like they played themselves. They'll be armed and alert and guarding Reynold's wharf like it was the National Mint."

"You can't secure the services of a company of marines?" Dawlish felt a childish pleasure in the sarcasm.

"No, Mr. Page. Not serving ones, that is. But I may be able to arrange the co-operation of someone even more helpful."

"And who might that be? General Grant? General Sherman perhaps?"

"John Phillip Holland," Raymond's slight smile confirmed that he enjoyed Dawlish's look of amazement. "I'm not certain yet, but if all goes well we should be meeting him tomorrow evening."

"You mean…"

But further discussion was impossible for now, for Florence was emerging on deck, composed once more, and Raymond was moving towards her with a smile.

"Well timed, Mrs. Page," he called. "You're just in time to view Manhattan from the most flattering vantage."

Dawlish stayed at the stern, drawing on the cheroot he had smoked to the butt without noticing, his pulses racing, his emotions churning. The Battery was slipping past to starboard and off the port bow lay the basin of the Morris Canal from which the Fenian Ram had been spirited a week since.

It would have been easy, so very easy.

*

The circumnavigation of Manhattan ended where it had started and Raymond remained on the yacht, which would moor higher upriver for the night. He had however arranged for a cab to meet them and as it bore them back to the hotel Egdean's presence was enough to ensure a strained and icy politeness between Florence and Dawlish. It ended when they reached their room.

"Now tell me the truth, Nicholas," she said.

He recognised the same steely determination that he had seen, and loved, when he had found her facing death, and worse, in the wake of a defeated army. He tried prevarication, and it failed.

"You're using me, Nicholas," she said. "You're using me as a mask, as a disguise. I guessed that, ever since you agreed to bring me, and I accepted it. I still accept it – God knows I love you enough for anything – but only on the condition that you tell me the truth. That man from Fiume – Gonzalez you said his name was, but it isn't – he's involved in this, isn't he?"

"His name's Driscoll." Her courage and love moved him as it always did and he could not lie. "He's a Fenian."

"One of those wicked Irishmen who commit dynamite outrages?"

"He seems better than that," he said. "Better, but more dangerous."

"And Mr. Raymond? Just who is he and what's he to us?"

74

"He's a… I'm not sure what he is, Florence. But certain gentlemen in London whom I trust have infinite confidence in him. And so therefore too must I."

"You're a fool, Nicholas. You always were, but a brave one, and that's why I love you." She reached out, drew herself to him. He kissed her moist eyes.

"I'll need you still for my disguise," he said, "but for more than that, Florence. Always for much more than that. You know it."

He told her all he knew.

What had seemed comprehensive in London sounded pitifully scant to her, and the gaps in his knowledge now seemed enormous. The very size of the city around and of the vast continent beyond it, and the vibrancy of its wealth and growth and energy were like oppressions in themselves. More than ever in his life he felt puny, inadequate, even lost. To nobody other than Florence would he have admitted it.

"There's only one thing to be done." Florence broke from him, stepped towards the long mirror on the wardrobe, smoothed her hair and contemplated her slender figure. She looked superb.

"What's that, Florence?"

"To play the part to the limit," she said. "Mr. and Mrs. Page of Silverbridge Court. And we start tonight. You've let Egdean go?"

He had. The pious seaman had hinted at a desire to attend a Moody revival and had even shown Dawlish a handbill advertising it. He had remarked pointedly that 26th and Madison must be in walking distance. "We were at Zanzibar when Mr. Moody visited Portsmouth with Mr. Sankey," he said, "but many that was there told me 'twas an uplifting occasion." With a five-dollar bill thrust in his hand Dawlish had freed him to enjoy an energetic evening of hymn-singing, drink-denunciation and collective prayer.

"Then you'll go down to see the porter yourself, Nicholas." Florence picked up the morning's discarded *New York Times* and turned to a page of advertisements. "There's an opera called *Der Freischütz* at the Academy of Music tonight and…" she scanned further "and at Walleck's Theatre there's a play called *The Noble Jilt* and at the Steinway Hall a Madame Nilsson is giving a recital and…

75

and there's lots more. Here, Nick," she thrust the paper at him, "find something. Have a boy sent to get us seats. I don't care where we go, as long as it costs a lot and as long as we're seen."

He began to laugh, for the first time that day, and he reached for her but she thrust him from the room.

"On your way, Nick," she said. "I must start making myself beautiful for tonight. We may not be worth a million pounds, but we're going to behave as if we do."

*

They never knew if the impression made by Florence's queenly entrance at the Academy was responsible, or some intervention of Raymond's, but the morning saw an invitation addressed to Mrs. Page carried in with the breakfast trays.

"From Mrs. Mabel Bushwick! I've never heard of her, but I'm impressed." Florence frowned with mock seriousness. "She invites me to take coffee with her at the Astor House Hotel at eleven this morning." She scrutinised the card. "It looks expensive, Nick. The Lord knows who she is but I'll meet her anyway. You can amuse yourself without me?"

She left him to fret for word from Raymond that never came. The porter had proved useful for more than tickets – he had located a map of Long Island for Dawlish that showed enough of the Connecticut and Rhode Island shores to give basic orientation. Egdean, edified by his previous evening's entertainment, had returned from a bookshop with a guide to New Haven and environs and a map of the city. There was a bonus. Reynold's foundry was among the businesses that advertised on the borders of the map and a numbered reference showed its location.

The river was winding and narrow, partly canalised in its lower reaches, seemingly lined there by industrial sites and warehouses and crossed by several bridges. Bringing the ram up there must have been difficult and the tug used must have been a small one. Getting it back down, possibly in the teeth of opposition, would mean running a very narrow gauntlet. Dawlish covered page after page of a scribbling

76

pad with ideas for one futile plan after another, his frustration rising. His gibe to Raymond about needing a company of marines now had an ironic ring of truth about it.

Florence arrived back just after one o'clock.

"You'll never guess what Mrs. Bushwick is, Nicholas!" she laughed. "She's a lady journalist! Did you ever hear of such a thing? She writes for the *Columbia Home Gazette*, told me her job was" – she frowned, dropped her voice to make a fair imitation of an American accent – "*A sacred charge for the betterment of womankind*, no less!"

"So she wanted to write about you?"

"For her journal, yes. She wanted to know what a British lady thought of American fashions and whether women – *'our sisters'* she called them – should be permitted to vote." She laughed again. "And had I met the Prince of Wales and Princess Alexandra and if I was acquainted with many of the aristocracy – and whether Silverbridge Court was large and how much you were worth – yes, Nick, even that! They've no hesitation here in talking about money."

"And you told her what she wanted, Florence?"

She threw herself back on the bed, shaking with merriment. Then, partly recovering, she numbered her fabrications on her fingers. "I told her I was stunned by the grace and elegance I had seen so far, that of course ladies should have the vote, but only married ones over sixty, and spinsters over eighty, that I had taken tea twice with Her Highness at Marlborough House, that Lady Agatha Kegworth wasn't just the cleverest woman in England, but the kindest too – that wasn't a lie, Nick – and that Mr. Page wasn't just the most handsome squire in Shropshire – and that wasn't a lie either – but worth thirty-five thousand a year to boot, which was a big one! And the best of it was that that woman wrote it all down – every word of it, and she didn't smile once – and would have swallowed as much again if I wasn't afraid I would collapse in fits. You'll have to buy the *Gazette* to find out the rest!"

Dawlish was laughing himself now. A knock on the door stopped him.

Another silver tray, another envelope, the handwriting of the address now familiar. He tore it open.

A cab would collect him from the corner of Union Square at nine o'clock.

"H" had consented to the meeting.

8

The cab's blinds were drawn, despite the warmth, and Raymond greeted Dawlish from the stuffy gloom. "Only a short drive, Mr. Page."

"Where to?" Dawlish could not shake of his feeling of being half-lost in this unfamiliar warren.

"33rd. Just off Third Avenue. A respectable address."

Respectability seemed more important to Raymond than to any man Dawlish knew. He was dressed formally and a silk hat rested on the seat beside him. He seemed to study Dawlish, take in his light tweed suit, broad-brimmed soft hat and the short dark double-breasted woollen coat he had worn on deck on the voyage across and which now hung open.

"You look like a gentleman on a surreptitious visit to a house of ill fame," Raymond said. "Are you carrying a weapon?"

"Only a loaded stick."

"More than enough, Mr. Page. I carry nothing myself. In my line of business I've found that violence too often evokes an excessive reaction from the other parties involved."

Dawlish has a dozen questions but sensed he would get an answer to none. They lapsed into silence. The cab was passing up Third Avenue now, a rush and rattle overhead periodically signalling the passage of a train on the elevated railroad.

They dismounted outside a row of solidly bourgeois four-storied brownstones. It was almost dark now, the lamp-standards casting soft pools of light along the street. The driver must have been pre-paid, for the cab moved away immediately and Raymond was swiftly mounting the steps of the nearest house. He produced a latchkey and they passed inside. The marble-floored hall echoed to their footsteps and Dawlish had an immediate sense that it was unoccupied. Raymond led the way through the gloom with a sure step and they passed into what must be a parlour towards the rear. Guided by the blue glow of the pilot, he reached up and adjusted the gaslight. It revealed a heavily-curtained room, overfurnished, immaculately clean and freshly aired, though with a strong scent of beeswax. A tray with decanters and three crystal glasses stood on the otherwise empty table.

"The owner is away," Raymond said, "but he extends his hospitality. A brandy perhaps before our friend arrives?"

The doorbell rang before he had finished pouring. "Stay here," he said, and disappeared. Then the sound of the hall-door opening and closing, a murmur of voices, cautious introductions, reassurances.

The man Raymond ushered into the room a minute later was slight and pallid, with a receding hairline, high cheekbones and a heavy moustache. From his cheap dark suit Dawlish might have judged him a clerk – or a schoolteacher – had not the intense eyes behind thick, rimless lenses caught his attention.

"Mr. Holland – Mr. Page." Raymond was at his most gracious.

"An honour, Mr. Holland." Dawlish extended his hand.

The newcomer stepped back, obviously alerted by Dawlish's accent. He turned to Raymond. "He's an Englishman," he said. His voice was more reproachful than angry. "Nobody said anything about an Englishman being present."

"I don't deny it." Dawlish forestalled Raymond's explanation. "And you can like the fact or not, Mr. Holland, but we're meeting on neutral ground and I'm giving you my word that nothing we say in this room will go beyond it without your knowledge."

"You're a spy then," Holland said. "That's worse in my book." His accent was still strong, the enunciation slow, the Munster cadence unmistakable.

"I was an officer of the Royal Navy, though I've left the service."

"At least you're an honest man," Holland said, "but it's little business we'll be doing together. I'll wish you a good evening and a safe journey home." He made for the door.

"Give me five minutes, Mr. Holland," Dawlish's heart was thumping, his stomach hollow. Failure was imminent. "I'm somewhat of an inventor myself and I was observing the tests of the pneumatic projector when Driscoll took it and..."

"You want my invention, Mr. Page." Holland had turned back. "You're another of the damn fools who thinks it can be perfected in a week. Like the Brotherhood's Skirmishing Fund, that wants its ten cents of revolution every week and is impatient when it can't be delivered."

"It'll be twenty years before Britain's or any other Navy come knocking on your door to buy your invention," Dawlish said. "That, and longer perhaps, before you've got a viable weapon. You've made a beginning, come further than any man in history, if Mr. Raymond's intelligence is even half-correct, but I'll wager that beginning's just enough to alert you to what the real problems are. Solving them will take you years – and a fortune. And that you don't have."

"With the help of God I'll find a way."

Only once before had Dawlish heard a man speak with such total conviction, – a Paraguayan visionary whose dream had ended in the deaths of thousands. And the unlikely figure now before him was perhaps driven by something stronger, something even more irrational. Against all odds, without technical training or government funding, supported only by a group of embittered exiles, toiling in petty workshops and testing his creation at the risk of his life, he had somehow proved his dream to be more than a chimera.

"When the Brotherhood took your boat you lost the only backers desperate or crazy enough to support you," Dawlish said.

Holland flushed. It might have been with the embarrassment of poverty. "The United States Navy..."

"...is a fourth rate institution today that's hard pressed to keep a handful of ageing gunboats at sea." Dawlish finished the sentence. "It's got neither the money nor the inclination to support experiments."

"The proposal you submitted was dismissed by the Secretary of the Navy as *'The fantastic scheme of a civilian landsman'*." Raymond was quiet, matter of fact. "I've sighted the actual note, Mr. Holland. I can provide you a copy if you so wish. You'd never have been dealing with the Brotherhood if you'd won support from that quarter."

"You want my invention for the British Navy." Holland was trembling. "That's what you want, isn't it? To buy me off with your Judas silver."

"I want your invention out of the hands of the men who robbed you of it," Dawlish said, "and you wouldn't be here tonight if you didn't also. What happens to it after we get it back we can haggle about."

"You do want it back, Mr. Holland?" Raymond's voice, soft, understanding.

"I don't want those bloody fools to use it stupidly." Holland spoke with sudden vehemence. "I don't want to see it used before its time and made a laughing stock and maybe written off as just another crazy notion. I want those twenty years you mentioned, Mr. Page. I want to spend them quietly, building on what I've found already about how a submarine boat should be shaped and trimmed and powered and steered and dived and fought, which no other living man knows, and with God's grace and aid I'll make at last a weapon like the world has never seen!"

"Why?" Dawlish felt slightly repulsed. War was his own trade, necessary but ugly. Weapons, though they sometimes delighted him, were a means only to an end.

"Why?" Holland seemed surprised by the question, as if he had never considered it himself. "It's because... because it's my idea." He seemed to grasp in the air before him as if he could somehow catch some vision that eluded him. "Because... because I must." His hands dropped and he seemed at once lost, vulnerable.

"Sit down, Mr. Holland," Raymond said gently. "You'd like brandy? Or whiskey perhaps?"

Holland shook his head. "I don't touch the stuff."

But he sat at the table. Raymond settled next to him, Dawlish opposite.

81

"You've nothing to worry about, Mr. Page, not yet," Holland said. "It's a death-trap for anybody but myself and it was only God himself and His Holy Mother who saved my own skin once or twice. Those fellows will kill themselves the first time they try to dive it."

"It's that difficult to control?" Dawlish knew that he had to keep him talking.

"There's both the buoyancy and the horizontal rudders to manage. I've got the hang of it now, but 'twas murder to start with. And then there's air to be bled in from the tank to feed the engine, and the fumes from the engine are a holy fright even when it's running well."

"Does she steer easily?"

"She does, but it's the navigation that's the problem. You can hardly see a damn thing and the compass is no bloody good in the middle of all that iron. I've got to rise more often that I'd like just to take a look around and see where I am."

"It didn't stop you testing it."

"You can get handy enough if you're calm about it and if you think about what you're doing." Holland might have been discussing fly-fishing rather than near-suicidal dives in an all but home-made contraption in some of the busiest waters in the world.

"Did you have much experience with boats before this?" Dawlish was intrigued.

"My father, God rest him, was a coast guard. And I was on a ship on the way across." He stated it without irony, as if a ten-day Atlantic crossing was explanation enough for his achievement.

"I understand you've built in the pneumatic projector now. Does it make a difference?"

"The ballast tank's at the middle. The centre of gravity didn't move much."

A writing desk stood in the corner. Dawlish moved to it, took a sheet of notepaper and a pencil, laid them before Holland. "I can't visualise it," he said. It was untrue – the sketches Raymond had shown him in London had given a reasonable impression – but he knew his only hope was to keep this besotted and unlikely near-genius speaking about his creation.

A few deft pencil strokes – Holland could draw well – delineated a cylinder that tapered gracefully with convex curves to points fore and aft, the stern terminating in a single propeller, a rudder mounted beneath it. The middle section was surmounted by a low boxlike structure, along the side of which Holland sketched three separate ports.

"I'm doing you no favours by showing you this, Mr. Page." He smiled. "I think half New York and all the newspaper men in it must have seen it at some time or another, not that any of them think it's more than a joke."

"Where's the horizontal rudder you mentioned?"

"Here." A thick slash on the paper close to the stern.

"I suppose the Brayton engine is amidships?"

"It is – and it exhausts through check valves here." Two circles abaft the superstructure. Then Holland looked at him sharply. "I think you know a lot more than you let on, Mr. Page. How do you know it's a Brayton?"

"Sources closer than you'd like to think."

"Then they probably told you too that Brayton got more for his engine than it's worth – but it's the best we have for now, God help us."

The man had to be mad to sit in a closed compartment beside a slow-running oil engine, bleeding compressed air to it from a tank, trusting that vibration would not fracture the exhaust pipes and leak deadly fumes. But personal safety, Dawlish now guessed, was a concern that did not trouble Holland much. His imagination was for one topic only.

"How much did all this cost so far?"

Holland paused, thinking, then said "Eight, maybe nine thousand dollars."

"I'll offer you twenty." Dawlish had no authorisation for so much. But success would cancel all sins of presumption.

"I told you. I don't want your money."

"But you want your boat out of Driscoll's hands. And I want it destroyed – but you'd have two weeks testing of it first. I promise you that, and Mr. Raymond has located property where you can conduct your trials in peace. You'll have the observations that will let you design the next version, which may not be a death-trap, and you'll have the funds to continue your work for another few years. You would have something the United States Secretary of the Navy would take more seriously when you approached him again."

"I told you I didn't want your money. No man can buy me."

"If I was trying to buy you I'd offer thirty, thirty-five thousand, even forty," Dawlish lied. "I'd need extra authorisation for more but I'd wager that one telegram would get twice that."

"I want the boat, I told you. I don't want money."

"You'll never recover it on your own," Raymond said, "but I can provide the men, the boats, the money that could get it back for you."

"I'd guarantee you the fortnight's testing," Dawlish added. "All the observations, all the readings you'd care for."

"And then you'd want it destroyed." Holland rounded bitter.

"Or disposed of in some other manner that would put it equally outside the reach of the Fenian Brotherhood and of the Royal Navy. A manner you'd have the right to approve of." Raymond had drawn close to Holland's ear, his voice an insinuating whisper. "A manner that would compromise neither your principles nor your patriotism."

Dawlish looked at Raymond in amazement. This was a new proposal, as audacious, as improvised, as his own cash offer. Raymond flashed him a look of caution – *Leave it to me now, I can handle it.*

And Holland was biting.

"I wouldn't want it destroyed. It would kill me." A simple, sad statement of fact.

"It doesn't need to be destroyed, Mr. Holland." Raymond's voice was soothing. "Not immediately. Not before you had learned all from it that you could use for a better design."

"No?"

"Disposed of in a manner you would have to approve of, I said. And I mean it. But we'd have to act soon, very soon. Before Driscoll's men drown themselves in it."

"How do you expect me to trust any Englishman? No offence to you personally, Mr. Page, but I've little reason to trust you or the people who sent you."

"But you can trust me, Mr. Holland, you can trust me." Raymond reached out and patted his hand, like he would a child's. "If you can't trust me, then you can trust nobody."

And then, incredulously, Dawlish perceived Holland beginning to yield. Adam Worth, alias Henry Judson Raymond, lover of the Duchess of Devonshire, had inspired confidence where a commissioned officer of Her Majesty could not.

Now final capitulation could only now be a matter of time.

9

They left the house two hours later by a back entrance and gained what must have been 34th Street through an alley. A single cab clattered by, a few staid couples passed. Holland had been adamant that he must return to Jersey City this night, despite Raymond's offer of a hotel.

"The last ferry runs at one o'clock," he explained. "The El will get me to the jetty in time aplenty."

Talked-out now, the outlines of a deal agreed, they headed towards Third Avenue, the lattices of its overhead railway visible in the lamplight at the end of the block. Out on the street Holland was suddenly insignificant, the man who dreamed of epoch-changing weapons once more a nonentity to be passed unnoticed.

"Five houses ahead, to the right, in the doorway." Raymond did not raise his voice, nor slacken his pace.

Beyond a lamp-post's lighted circle Dawlish caught a glimpse of a figure shrinking rapidly into the shadows at the top of the steps leading to the door. It might just have been a householder returning late and fumbling for his key but the movement seemed too deliberately furtive for that.

Senses immediately alert, Dawlish was immediately conscious of footsteps behind. He looked back. Two men on the sidewalk directly behind, a half-block distant. Another roughly level with them on the opposite side. Imagination perhaps, but their pace seemed to slacken as he turned towards them.

"Keep walking," Raymond said. Holland was to his left, guilelessly bewildered. Dawlish shifted to the inside, his hand slipping down to catch his stick close to the lower end, his head down, watching the doorway ahead from under his hat-brim, sick with apprehension. It might still be an innocent householder.

They were almost level with the entrance.

A rushing, rattling sound at the end of the street and then the spark-showering passage of a tiny locomotive overhead and the clattering sway of five brightly illuminated coaches. It was little enough distraction, but Dawlish could only hope it had drawn the attention of the lurker in the doorway for a split second. He could afford no hesitation and he launched himself up the steps. Behind him Raymond was urging Holland into a run and ahead of him a figure was emerging from the darkness of the porch – a tall, rangy figure in workman's clothes, with a cap pulled down over his face. He had a pistol in his hand, and he was raising it.

The man was unused to firearms – or perhaps he had been counting on intimidation, not murder – for he would have had ample time to have fired twice into Dawlish's chest as he dashed upwards. But instead he hesitated, started to speak, and in that instant Dawlish's loaded stick slashed down like a cutlass and smashed his wrist. He cried out, dropped the revolver – it fell off into the shadows by the side, and Dawlish knew there would be no time to find it – and the half-pound of lead moulded into the stick's ornate head was already swinging back to catch him on the temple. He crumpled down silently but Dawlish was already turning away and rushing back down the steps.

Raymond and Holland were already fifty yards ahead. Dawlish pounded after them. A glance up the street had told him that the men behind him had started to run and one was pulling something from an inside pocket as he did. Odd windows were bright on the houses to either side but the brief fracas had attracted no attention. The corner ahead was brightly lit and traffic moved there beneath the railroad's girders. The two fugitives reached it, turned right and disappeared from sight. Dawlish was seconds behind them.

An elderly couple, soberly dressed, white-haired, loomed in his path as he careered around the corner. He tried to side-step them, failed, and the old man tumbled to the ground. His wife cried out indignantly and Dawlish called an apology as he rushed on, conscious of other heads turning towards him. The sidewalk was broad, sparsely sprinkled with pedestrians, and he searched frantically for some sign of his companions among them. He felt panic rising insidiously – the sensation of being alone, virtually unarmed, in a human ant-heap he did not know, was overwhelming – and he forced himself to scan the pavement ahead for Raymond's silk hat. He slowed to a fast walk – it looked less suspicious, drew less attention – and glanced back for signs of pursuit. It gave no reassurance that he saw none, for there was nothing to distinguish his hunters from anybody else on the street at this hour. He grasped his stick more tightly and longed for the reassuring grip of a cutlass hilt or pistol butt.

Vehicles moved in both directions, cabs, carts, drays, and through them he strained to see some sign of Raymond on the far side. Still none. Trembling of the girders overhead foretold the advent of another train and drew his attention to the heavily shadowed roadway stretching beneath the elongated bridge that carried the railroad up the centre of the avenue. A hundred yards ahead it seemed to swell out slightly to occupy a greater breath and there, beneath it, was a brick structure with two lighted windows and gas-lamps flaring on either side of a cast-iron stairway. It must be a station. Then, suddenly, he saw two figures flitting between the horse-drawn traffic towards it, one bareheaded, carrying his silk hat, but made unmistakable by the moustache curving to meet his side-whiskers.

Dawlish glanced back. No other pedestrians separated him from two men striding not twenty yards behind, gazes fixed on him. One was clad in workman's clothes and carried a stick, the other in shabby respectability, his right hand pushed beneath his coat and obviously holding something. To their left a third man, heavy, massive, dressed in check, was slipping into the roadway, dodging between the traffic and into the space beneath the railroad. He was moving fast, despite his bulk. Dawlish realised he was being outflanked.

Raymond had paused at the lighted windows ahead – buying tickets, perhaps – and then hurried towards the stairs, hustling Holland ahead of him. Dawlish broke into a run. He threw himself between two passing cabs, close enough for a placidly trotting horse to shy and whinny. A crack by his left told of the driver, swearing, lashing a whip towards him. He almost blundered into one of the railroad's cast-iron pillars ahead. Just to its left he saw the check-suited bruiser racing forwards, momentarily oblivious of his change of direction.

It was an opportunity to lower the odds that was not to be missed, even if the other two must be close on his heels. Dawlish flattened himself for an instant against the column, heard panting and footsteps nearing from the other side, grasped the stick by its brass-encased lower end. As the stout man lurched into sight Dawlish emerged, swinging the stick at shin level. The man half-turned to him, surprised, and the leaden head smashed into his leg. He went down, shouting, more in anger than in pain, but Dawlish was already sprinting towards the gas-lit stairs now fifty yards ahead. Raymond and Holland had disappeared. There was an eight-foot high barrier ahead, bars, what looked to be turnstiles, a uniformed attendant in a booth to the side.

Shouting behind him now and more running feet, and then a sound that chilled him, a long blast on a whistle. A memory stabbed from his brain of reading somewhere that half the policemen in this city were Irish. He pelted onwards, heard a cry of "Stop Thief!" He forced himself not to look around but realised that others, passers-by perhaps, had joined in the chase.

The girders above began to shake again, and accumulated soot drifted from them like dark snow, and then a louder rattling announced the arrival overhead of a train from the south. Brakes squealed as it drew to a halt. It was his life line, and his companions'.

The barrier was a wall of spike-topped iron bars but the space beyond was free for the moment, though soon disembarking passengers would be streaming down into it. That would be to his advantage if he were already on the other side. Then he saw the attendant stepping hurriedly from his booth, thrusting aside the newspaper he had been reading, his attention drawn by the whistle that blasted again.

The turnstiles, intermeshing bars enclosed in part-cylinders, offered no pathway. Three horizontal bars linked the barrier's vertical spikes, the highest just below the ornate spearheads, the middle bar at chest height. Agility learned as a boy on white-knuckled ascents of masts in Atlantic gales and honed in the years since was now Dawlish's best asset. He threw his stick across like a javelin as he neared the iron hedge, then launched himself upwards, hands reaching for the spikes. He grasped, heaved up with his arms and his feet sought toeholds on the middle bar. One held, one slipped.

A voice – an Irish voice – shouted "Grab the bastard!" and he felt a hand on his ankle. He kicked back and the grip loosened. Then he was somehow dragging himself up towards the spear points, his stomach level with them. His coat was thick enough to protect him against immediate impalement, but he still took as most of his weight on his arms as he propelled himself up from the bar beneath, one leg hooking on the spikes to his right, the other flailing wildly.

For an instant Dawlish was balanced on the line of skewers, conscious of a shouting cluster below him and a policeman pushing through them with a long club upraised, then he was toppling over and somehow breaking his fall by shifting his grip. His arms were almost wrenched from their sockets and pain lanced up his legs as he hit the ground, but he was still on his feet and his stick was only feet away. The attendant was shrinking back, his face ashen. "No trouble, Mister," he said but he was edging towards the turnstile and Dawlish realised that he was about to release it, to allow the pursuers through.

Figures crowded the top of the steps, passengers descending. Dawlish grabbed his stick as the police whistle blasted again and a voice roared "Stop that man!" He heard the turnstile rattle behind him as he threw himself up the steps. The figures above him were mainly couples, respectably dressed, returning from theatre or concert, and the women shrank back. One began to scream. The entire structure began to vibrate again – another train coming in, this one from the north. There would be more passengers in a moment, more confusion on the platform above. Dawlish rushed on upwards.

One man, middle-aged, respectably dressed, was moving to block him, raising his cane, and his wife was trying to restrain him. "Don't be a fool, John!" she cried, pulling his arm down, and Dawlish dodged past.

Three steps to go and the open platform, flanked by two stationary rows of carriages, lay before him. It was momentarily almost empty – passengers from the newly arrived downtown train were still opening doors and across from it the uptown train was ready to depart. A single figure stood by an open door – Raymond – and then another whistle blast, shorter, sharper than the policeman's, announced departure. There was nobody ahead, but as Dawlish threw himself forward his toe slipped on the edge of the last step and he sprawled to his knees. A cry behind made him twist and he saw that his tall workman-like hunter was three steps below, a knuckle-duster gleaming on his right hand. The shabby-genteel pursuer was close behind, his hand still clasped inside his coat and the bruiser tripped earlier was following an equally heavy policeman through the now freely-spinning turnstile.

Dawlish struggled to his feet, taking the stick's end in both hands and drawing it back over his right shoulder. The workman below – his cap had fallen away to show reddish hair and a freckled face and buck teeth – paused and began to move to the left but Dawlish had started his swing. The man twisted to avoid the blow, so that it caught him on the shoulder rather than the head, but it was still powerful enough to send him reeling backwards into the throng below. A man beneath him stumbled and fell, dragging his screaming wife with him and tumbling back into another couple. The policeman was bellowing for a path to be cleared and the check-suited thug was flinging a woman aside as he stormed up.

The uptown train was drawing out as Dawlish staggered on to the platform – he had a glimpse of Raymond swinging himself inside

90

as it pulled away – and several passengers were emerging from the stationary downtown train, still oblivious of the fracas on the stairs. A guard, with a club like the policeman's, was hurrying down to investigate. Dawlish realised that only bluff could save him now.

"There's a fight down there!" He hoped to sound somehow both respectable and shocked. "A lady's been attacked. There's more than one of them! Be careful! They're armed"

The guard took him for what he seemed, a gentleman outraged by violence, but too timid to intervene, and he rushed past, club raised. Dawlish raced up the platform, darting between the disembarking passengers, mingling with those boarding and seeking an empty place.

The carriages were low, smaller than a normal train, and poorly lit by oil lamps. He thrust himself through an open door in the middle, found himself in a long, open compartment and sought a free seat. The departure whistle was shrilling as he settled himself, his back to the platform, between a sleeping labourer in dusty clothes and two middle-aged women who smiled when he nodded to them. He reached up to tip his brim over his face and realised that he was now bareheaded. His hat contained nothing more incriminating than the name of a Portsmouth hatter but the loss still worried him. A door slammed shut behind the last passenger to board – Dawlish did not recognise him – and the train lurched into motion as the full mass of the indignant throng erupted from the stairs on to the platform, shouting and beating on the carriage windows.

"What's happening, Sir?" One of the ladies looked frightened.

"A pickpocket, I think, Ma'am." Dawlish was uncomfortably conscious of his accent.

"Mercy help us!" said the other woman. "Are we safe anywhere?" But neither she nor any other passenger showed any suspicion of him.

Dawlish slumped back, feigning exhaustion, disguising his heaving breath, aware that the train was swaying and lurching southwards with gathering speed. He evaluated his options rapidly. Holland and Raymond were now longer a concern – the plausible thief was probably already alighting calmly with Holland at some uptown stop and hailing a cab. But Dawlish could not yet feel secure himself. Even the trivial matter of leaving a station was a concern – the protocol for doing so without a ticket, while not raising an alarm, was a mystery to him. As gas-lit second and third-floor windows of flanking houses slipped past he consoled himself that the train was at least carrying him in the general direction of his hotel. Its security could not be more than a half-hour away.

The train screeched to a halt at the next station. Passengers left and boarded, none paying him any heed. It lurched into motion again. A painted board above the seats on the opposite side indicated the stations on the line. It was hard to read in the dim light but Dawlish deduced he had boarded at 35th Street. He knew the track ran directly south along Third Avenue – they had crossed it yesterday en route to Raymond's yacht. Another three stations then should bring him close to the hotel – the 16th Street stop would be the nearest. He was weak now with the reaction from the danger he had passed through, his knees and hands trembling, his heart racing. He forced himself to breathe deeply, to seem like another weary citizen returning home.

Two more stations passed. He had decided now how he must approach the guardian of the turnstiles when he alighted. He would claim loss of his ticket, offer payment and profuse apology. Should he offer something more, or would a gratuity be interpreted as a bribe? Once again he was painfully conscious of how alien he felt, for all the similarity of language, and of how little his status of gentleman might count for here. The carriage was crowded – only a few seats were vacant and several occupants seemed to prefer to stand, holding vertical stanchions.

The two ladies got up and left at the next station. He helped one to the door with her laden valise, thinking that the action made him seem more unexceptional and then, as he returned to his seat, he froze. The door at the end of the carriage, which gave passage to that behind, was swinging open and a burly figure in a check suit was pushing through. Dawlish ducked for his seat and the train jerked into movement again, but as he did he glimpsed the last passenger to enter at the other end. His right hand was still buried inside his shabby coat and Dawlish recognised him as another of his pursuers. He shrunk back into his seat, raising his collar surreptitiously, knowing that he was trapped. Both men had managed to board immediately after him, though in different cars, and they had been searching systematically ever since, moving from car to car at each station.

There was something dreadful in their studiedly casual onset, moving slowly towards him from either end. The bruiser had seen him almost at once and a nod to his confederate had confirmed it. Both men were nearing, neither hurrying, apologising to others for toes stepped upon as they lurched with the sway. They raised no hue and cry and Dawlish realised that their intention was to take him with them without fuss. He glanced towards the heavy man, and met a steady gaze that told him that the blow on his shin would be paid back in full. He had dropped on to a seat diagonally across, eight, ten, feet distant, produced a handkerchief, pushed back his billycock hat and mopped his brow. His eyes did not leave Dawlish.

16th Street Station now and Dawlish should have been stepping out. Florence was ten minutes' walk away and Egdean would be in his attic room, thumbing his Bible. The seaman would be well capable of flooring these cutthroats, or a half-dozen like them, but he might have been a million miles distant, for Dawlish did not dare to move. He could not risk these men tracing him to the hotel and learning his identity, for he guessed that he was a mystery to them, that it was Holland whom they had trailed to the rendezvous. His mind was churning alternatives for escape and the train was rattling southwards again when his second pursuer approached and leaned down.

"This seat is free, Sir?" His voice was loud enough for others about to hear, courteous enough not to raise alarm. "Then I'll take it. Thank you, Sir." The accent was American, but with just enough underlying lilt to betray its true origin. He settled next to Dawlish.

They sat in silence, close enough for Dawlish to smell stale tobacco-smoke on the other's clothing and see the shine on the knees of the threadbare trousers. He felt something hard nudge into his left side and was almost sick with fear, most of all because nobody knew where he was. He could disappear without a hand lifted in his defence, could disappear without a trace. His only hope lay in somehow keeping control of the situation. To test it he made to rise at the next stop.

"I wouldn't do that if I were you." The voice was soft, the tone low, and all the more chilling for that. "We'll be getting out soon enough."

"Where?"

"You don't need to worry about that." Then silence again.

Another station and the composition of the passengers was different now, more working clothes, less finery, more sweat, lower affluence, greater fatigue. Dawlish had an impression of working people going unwillingly to their shifts or leaving them exhausted, the sour smell of poverty growing stronger, the lights in the windows sweeping past dimmer, the houses more squalid.

The train was juddering to a halt again, brakes screaming.

"We'll be coming down here, so you'd better be quiet." The man had something of Holland's inflection and he pushed harder into Dawlish's side. "I'll have this thing pointed at the small of your back," he said, "and I'd be pleased if you went down the steps in front of me. My friend will be ahead of you."

"I won't give you any trouble." Dawlish meant it, for now at least, for he could still think of no alternative and he was fighting down despair.

"My friend will take your stick now." The large man passed before them, stretched out his hand as he made for the door and Dawlish passed over his cane.

The platform was almost deserted – a half dozen weary passengers waiting for an uptown train, only two others alighting besides Dawlish and his captors. The tall, ill-lit houses flanking the railroad structure were no less redolent of poverty than the dark roadway below. Acres of slums extended in every direction, as capable of swallowing the stranger as irrevocably as the most dismal swamp.

"Just walk a little ahead of me, slowly, if you please." The voice was as soft as before but Dawlish knew that the pistol was still lined

94

up with his spine. The check-suited man had moved ahead and was already disappearing down the steps towards the entrance.

"If it's money you want…" It was futile, but Dawlish could think of nothing else.

"Shut up and keep walking."

From the top of the iron steps down to the entrance Dawlish saw the last of the other passengers exiting through the turnstile. Check-suit had gone ahead and was passing money to the attendant, obviously settling for three missed fares. He glanced back and raised Dawlish's own stick in mocking salute.

Dawlish was half-way down the stairs when figures came into view beyond the turnstile, half-obscured by the iron railings to either side. Two women, one old, one middle-aged, poorly clad, were pushing what might have been an invalid chair with a withered, blanket-swathed figure crouched in it. The attendant had not seen them yet – he was moving back to the comfort of his booth – and the check-suited bruiser's back was turned to them. But they would not have manoeuvred their pathetic burden to this point without a reason and hope flared within Dawlish that they might somehow provide a diversion. He did not slacken his pace nor move his head and only his eyes followed the women's progress to one side of the barrier.

"Can you let us through, Mister?" The older woman's voice, tired, almost a whine.

The attendant came reluctantly from his booth. "You're too late, Ma'am," he said. "There's nobody to help you up to the platform."

"Please, Mister."

"I can't leave here. Regulations, Ma'am."

"We'll carry him ourselves." Her whisper told of expectations disappointed, of hope long abandoned, and was so low that any outside her direct vicinity might not have heard her. But Dawlish did, every sense at a peak of awareness, and he realised that he had perhaps five seconds advantage before his two warders realised what was about to happen. And in those seconds his brain was racing, planning, reluctantly accepting that the only course open to him was probably suicidal.

Check-suit was by the turnstile, Dawlish was two steps above ground level and behind him his shabby captor was two steps higher. The attendant had yielded, was moving towards one end of the railing and producing a bunch of keys. The barrier must be hinged there, a gate that would allow the wheel-chair to bypass the turnstile.

"God bless you, Mister." The women had lined up the invalid with the gate and Dawlish's mind was made up.

The bruiser had entered the turnstile. He filled it, and for one giddy instant of optimism it looked as if he might jam there, but then he was though, waiting on the other side for Dawlish and the second thug to follow.

The attendant's key clicked the deadlock free as Dawlish stepped on to the level. The gate was starting to swing inwards, and the women were pushing the rickety, home-made wheelchair into the gap. Dawlish knew that an unseen pistol was pointed towards him – to his head, to his back perhaps – and also that a little over a second would be needed for the instruction to fire to flash from the gunman's brain to his trigger finger. One second's advantage... and the man was still moving, still had two steps to descend, was perhaps now glancing over towards the women's clumsy manoeuvring by the gate, was maybe distracted by the moaning issuing from the pitiful bundle slumped there...

Dawlish whirled around.

The gunman was still descending, and on the point of colliding with him. For an instant Dawlish saw confusion, surprise, and his captor's right hand jerking from inside his jacket, a small pistol grasped in it. Dawlish's own hands swung to make a single fist and pounded into the other's stomach. Shocked, the man cried out, flailed blindly with the pistol and staggered forward down the last step. Dawlish knew that he had momentary supremacy – his reactions were sharpened by two decades of cutlass drill and his adversary was no more than a back-street ruffian – and the knowledge lent power to his next blow. His still-joined hands swung upwards under the gunman's chin, jerking his head back and sprawling him on the steps behind. Dawlish kicked him in the side as he went down. The man was groaning, dazed, but he still held the revolver and was raising it again. It wavered as his eyes sought for a target but Dawlish was already stepping across him, his left foot stamping down on the outstretched arm. The pistol blasted – the noise was deafening in the half-enclosed space – but the aim was wild and Dawlish's boot was already driving the arm down. It crunched against the step's metallic edge and the man cried in agony as it snapped.

The older woman screamed and then the second joined her.

Dawlish had the taken the pistol now – a cheap nickel-plated small-calibre revolver, puny, but a weapon nonetheless – and he sprinted towards the open gate. The women were trying to drag the wheel-chair away from it but one wheel had caught in the frame but in their alarm they did not notice and they still jerked frantically. The chair's occupant, a child with a hideously large head, whimpered in terror. The attendant was backing away, hands raised. And the man in the check suit was lumbering up behind the women, ready to block Dawlish's exit.

There was no option but to go through. Check-suit was dragging the older woman aside. She staggered, fell, and then he was grabbing her distraught companion, hurling her clear. Dawlish was almost at the gate and raising the pistol. The bruiser had grasped the handle on the back of the invalid-chair with one hand and was wrenching it towards him. He was raising Dawlish's own loaded stick in his other hand – and that was enough to tell that he carried no firearm. Fear on his face now, he dragged the chair violently towards him like a shield. The force was too much for the ramshackle object and check-suit fell backwards, the chair's handle ripped from it and still grasped in his hand.

Dawlish was conscious of the women scrambling from his path but his glance and his pistol were riveted on the man on the ground. He was struggling to rise but he froze as the saw the revolver.

"Don't shoot me, Sir." The gleam in the pig-like eyes lost between folds of fat belied the cringing tone. "For God's sake don't shoot me, Sir! I've got a wife and…"

"Throw the stick over to your right. A yard more than three and you'll get this in the stomach." Dawlish drew back the hammer, pointed. The stick was scarcely worth four pounds, had no associations, and yet Dawlish wanted it back, was damned if he was going to leave it like some token of defeat.

The stick clattered down. Dawlish edged towards it, still holding his aim.

"Kill the bastard, Matt." A gasping, painful howl from beyond the barrier. The shabby man had lurched to his feet, his arm flapping.

"Don't try it, Matt." Dawlish scooped up the stick in his left hand, raised the pistol until fore and rear sights aligned on the bruiser's meaty face. He saw cunning mixed with terror there, and then surprise, as he lashed with the cane. The lead-loaded head smashed into a check-encased shin. The man cried out as Dawlish swung again and then he dropped.

And now flight.

Dawlish was aware that the women were shrieking still and that the whole structure overhead was starting to tremble – another train was approaching and more passengers would be disembarking. Twenty, thirty yards ahead on the street half-a-dozen figures were moving uncertainly towards him and a dray had stopped and its driver was gesturing. Brawls must be sufficiently common in this neighbourhood, and perhaps deadly enough, that nobody was going to rush precipitously to investigate. He ran to his right, turned the corner of the ground-level entrance structure and pounded onwards, keeping to the shadows cast by the lattice structure above. It shook and rattled as a locomotive and cars rumbled over, brakes complaining, darkening the shade further. He uncocked the pistol as he ran, stuffed it into his inside pocket and forced himself not to look back. The sooner he could slow, dodge down a side street, look like some respectable citizen, the better – though he looked possibly too respectable for this neighbourhood. He knew he was headed uptown, little more, and one thought dominated him, to reach the security of the hotel.

A cart was approaching on the narrow roadway to the left of the railroad structure, a weary nag, head down, plodding towards rest, the driver slumped in a half-stupor of fatigue. It was still just beyond a street intersection. Dawlish dashed forward until he was just short of the crossing, then froze in the shadow of a pillar. He glanced back. Two, three figures were advancing some hundred yards behind, their cautious hesitance indicating that they might be following. He waited until the cart jolted past, then flitted across behind it and into the street beyond. There was a chance, the merest chance, that the vehicle had masked his movement.

The street was narrow, poorly lit and smelling of poverty. There was more life here, scattered groups congregated on steps leading to yawning doors, men playing cards, somewhere a woman laughing shrilly and another echoing her, even a few barefoot children still at play. Dawlish forced himself to a walk and knew that it could be only seconds before his pursuers gained the intersection. A drunkard staggered towards him, vomit staining his ragged front, and he was suddenly aware of just how incongruous his own clothing was and how his lack of headgear marked him.

It took another fifty yards before he found what he sought, an open door above deserted steps with nothing to distinguish it from a dozen similarly unattended ones on the street. Dim lights burned in the rooms above and to either side of it. He entered and found himself in a dark hallway smelling of urine. In the half-light he saw a bare stairway ahead, broken banisters, sagging treads. He passed peeling doors, heard sounds of activity inside, mounted, found himself on a landing. More doors and another flight beyond. He stumbled over something soft, and it moaned, and there was an odour of alcohol and human waste, but he passed on and upwards again. A dozen families, perhaps three or four score people, might live in this putrid warren and movements on the stairs would attract no attention. He mounted another two levels and it grew yet warmer, more foetid and airless. At last found himself on a small landing below a sagging ceiling so low that he had to crouch. If there were

99

occupants in the garrets to either side they were asleep for no light glimmered beneath their doors.

Dawlish settled himself to wait, still revolted by the stench, his flesh crawling as he brushed against the greasy walls. Something rustled closely and continued irregularly – rats, almost certainly – and below a baby was crying, endlessly and inconsolably. The combination of isolation, strangeness and fear that had oppressed him almost since he had arrived in this city was at its strongest now.

He knew his hunters were probably still out there somewhere. They were not working alone, had probably hundreds of sympathisers within a few blocks and, worst of all, they could describe him. His accent would have betrayed him in the railroad car and there had been ample time to study his appearance. Holland had been followed to the rendezvous and now the Brotherhood would be in little doubt that something was afoot, and that an Englishman was involved. The guard on that yard in New Haven would be reinforced and here in this city, where there must be Irish chambermaids in every hotel, the hunt would intensify. But first he must survive tonight. Violent death could not be unusual in this area and another stripped and battered corpse would be just another statistic, with nothing to link it to the lady who even now must be fretting in a luxurious hotel not two miles distant. The thought of death was bad enough but that Florence might never know what became of him was intolerable.

Sounds came from below – three times residents returning, one of them singing in an unknown tongue, then somebody leaving with a woman screaming abuse in his wake – and though Dawlish froze each time nobody climbed as high as his level. It was too dark to read his watch but he guessed an hour had passed, and he forced himself to wait as long again in the foul darkness before he left. The steps creaked beneath his stealthy descent but nobody came to investigate.

The street was deserted when he emerged. He hastened down it – his grasp of the local geography was hazy but Broadway must be somewhere ahead. He moved towards it by a series of rights and lefts, approaching it diagonally through streets that were sometimes

100

sunk in squalid torpor and others where music and raucous laughter spilled from gaudy taverns and rouged harridans with rotting teeth plucked at his sleeve. He dropped the pistol into a kerbside drain, glad to be rid of it lest some policeman question his movements.

At last he found a cab. Obviously not unused to gentlemen guests returning dishevelled, the Kennebec's night-porter smirked when Dawlish pushed a dollar into his palm.

Florence disguised her relief with anger.

"You're a fool, Nick." She was beating her fists on his chest even as she kissed him. "They'll kill you yet. And Raymond… he's using you like you're using me." She turned her face away, embarrassed by her own tears.

And Dawlish knew that she was right.

Raymond had been lucky tonight – but he suspected that Raymond was always lucky, made his own luck, and that his disdain for violence was possible only because others were stupid enough to commit it for him. But he was stuck with Raymond as a partner – and somehow also with that half-madman, half-genius Holland also – and if he was to command *Leonidas* a long, uncertain game remained to be played.

"You smell like a pigsty, Nicholas." She pushed him from her. "Where have you been? Don't come near me until you've bathed and cast off those clothes."

Her back was to him as he slipped into bed and he felt her still stiff with fear and indignation. But as he extinguished the lamp she reached for him and held him fiercely and silently.

And that was some comfort.

10

"Chinese or Indian, Mr. Holland?" Florence's hand hovered over the silver pots.

"Just tea, Ma'am." This was the second time they had performed the ritual on this terrace overlooking Long Island Sound, but the Irishman was still uncomfortable in her presence.

She dropped sugar from a silver tongs into his cup — she had remembered his preference — and passed it to him.

"I don't know what to make of him, Nick," she had said earlier, "I can't imagine what he's praying about when he goes to that church in the village. When he's not dreaming up ways to slaughter his fellow man he's on his knees there counting his rosaries or doing whatever else that Romans do."

Dawlish settled back in his wicker chair, accepted his own cup and looked out over a tranquil Sound towards New Haven, almost directly across but hidden by haze. Raymond should have left there by now, his joint reconnaissance with his associate in the city complete. Dawlish had wanted desperately to accompany him — his own life would depend on the findings — but his encounter with the Brotherhood six nights before had almost certainly ensured that the watch at Reynolds' yard would be on the lookout for a dark-bearded man with a scarred left cheek. He looked beyond the *Tecumseh*, which lay alongside the long wooden jetty extending from the lawns running down towards the water's edge, and searched for the first sign of the *Putnam*, the rented steam launch which had carried Raymond across.

The *Tecumseh* had carried them first to Newport. They had disembarked two days in succession and had taken ostentatious carriage rides to view the mansions along the shore. Mrs. Page had carried off the part of elegant but discreet visitor splendidly, wielding her parasol and turning heads with a grace that even Mr. Page, himself modestly reticent about his wealth, found impressive. Only Holland had stayed on board, unseen, working assiduously from memory on a diagram of the ram's interior to replace one he had not dared return home to collect after that night in New York. It was essential if Dawlish was to be familiar with the vessel in the venture now being plotted.

Raymond had arranged an introduction — a Denver dry-goods merchant who boasted that he was worth twenty-three million, ate food off his knife and spat when he forgot himself, and whose silk-encased wife had the hands and manners of a washerwoman. Others at their dinner table were scarcely more refined. They might summer in near-palaces with marble floors and tapestried walls but they were flattered by the presence of English landed gentry at their dinner-table and fascinated by Florence's account of her dear Papa's coach and its matched greys. She omitted to mention that he was paid to drive it. Dawlish suspected that there might be more exalted company in Newport than the assortment of miners and cannery owners and their over-bejewelled women from whom Raymond had secured invitations. That was of no concern — it mattered only that they listened to his tales of the hunting field with such pained attention and to Florence's accounts of tea with the Princess of Wales. By the time the *Tecumseh* weighed anchor the ostensible reason for her presence in the Sound was well established.

Eight men were quartered in the outbuildings attached to the large holiday mansion that Raymond had rented at East Egg on the Long Island shore. Half were there when the *Tecumseh* docked, and the remainder drifted in individually later, rough, hard-looking men in nondescript working clothes. Their presence filled Florence with foreboding, even if they kept far from the terrace where she read novels, smoked an occasional cigarette and dispensed afternoon tea beneath a fringed shade.

"You can't trust those men, Nick," she said. "Most of them look like criminals."

"Most of them are."

Dawlish had met them all by now, had heard their particulars from Raymond, knew that they included an ex-soldier and three ex-seamen. Carter, a muscular, sandy-headed ex-marine, had rolled up his trouser to show the crater torn in his calf by a Korean musket ball at Kwangsungbo a decade before. "An inch to the right and I'd have lost the leg," he said.

"You were discharged afterwards?" Dawlish asked.

"I had some other opportunities."

Despite their service ashore or afloat none of these men showed the cheerful deference Dawlish would have expected from their British counterparts and they showed a wariness of Egdean, and he of them. Others described themselves as warehousemen, which probably meant something worse. There were Germans and Swedes among them, but no Irish. The food and ample drink they were provided with seemed enough to quell any disquiet about their confinement to the small estate.

"They've all worked with me at one time or another, Mr. Page." Raymond had said. "They're reliable. They'll do the job they're paid for, and no questions asked before or after." None knew yet why they had been gathered and now Raymond was due back with the intelligence that would allow finalising plans for their employment.

Holland heaved himself to his feet, muttered thanks for his tea and went inside. He seemed obsessed with the idea that his vessel would soon he in his hands again, if only for the brief period of trials agreed. He had had interminable discussions with Raymond on its eventual disposal, none conclusive – which was what Raymond intended.

It was time for Dawlish to join the Irishman, to go over the drawings yet again until he could visualise the position of every lever and hand wheel within the diving boat's dark maw. He laid his Trollope aside reluctantly – he would willingly have spent a lifetime with Florence on this sunlit terrace – and raised his field glasses to scan the misty horizon before he went inside.

There was a smudge of smoke there, and beneath it a small foreshortened hull heading directly towards this spot. Raymond's scouting mission was complete. Action would be initiated twenty-four hours from now.

*

Dawlish had known this moment a dozen times before – the moorings slipped, the vessel gathering speed, the land dropping away astern, the knowledge that he was sailing deliberately towards danger, perhaps death, the twinges of doubt about his own courage and resolution.

Yet this was different.

Whether manning open cutters or swift torpedo-boats of the Royal Navy, or Ottoman ironclads, or ramshackle paddle-steamers on a Paraguayan river, his crews had known what lay ahead and had accepted it, willingly or unwillingly. But now the *Tecumseh's* crew – even Swanson, her master, whose past had proved less innocent than it had appeared initially – believed they were heading towards New Haven to drop off their charterers for a summer ball at Yale University. Only the presence of the dingy ex-marine, Carter, now drinking coffee by the galley, might raise suspicions that anything else might be afoot. He was down on his luck, Raymond told Swanson, and he was arranging employment for him in a friend's mill in Hartford. He had worked for him before, a reliable man. Offering him passage was an act of charity.

And it was different for another reason. Florence was on board. Not just to lend credence to the story of the ball, nor because she had been immovable when Dawlish had suggested otherwise, but because she, and Egdean, were the only ones on this entire continent he could trust to the death. Both now knew what was in the offing, one resolute but filled with foreboding, the other silently promising the dogged loyalty that was his hallmark.

Dawlish reached for Florence's hand and drew it to his lips. Neither spoke as they watched the sun setting spectacularly to port. The Connecticut coastline was clear ahead and the *Putnam* steam launch, on which tonight's success for failure would depend, was far ahead off the starboard bow. Three more of Raymond's recruits crewed her – also reliable men, according to him, respected on the New York waterfronts – and she carried out of sight in her tiny saloon the remainder of the ruffians he had assembled at East Egg.

"Soon you must feel unwell," Dawlish said. That would be the pretence. Florence would stay on board while he went ashore with Raymond and the others.

"I don't need to pretend," she said. "It makes me ill to think of what's ahead."

He went below. A last conference with Raymond and Holland, poring over a city map, memorising street names and layouts, fixing again in his mind the twists of the Mill River and the four ominous bridges that spanned it between Reynolds' foundry and the harbour. The ram had still been secured against the wharf there twenty-four hours previously Raymond had seen her himself – and there was no reason why she should have moved since.

"Were her bows pointed upstream or down?" Dawlish asked.

"I can't say." Raymond studied the drawing intently. The small humped superstructure was symmetrical and gave no hint of orientation. He and his New Haven contact had been more intent on ascertaining the strength of the watch on the yard. "Is it important?"

"Of course it's bloody-well important!" Holland showed animation only when his beloved submarine was mentioned. "The rudders and screw are delicate. They'll catch easily on any snag."

Nor was there any way of knowing if the hatch was secured, or if the engine had been run recently. Neither point was insuperable but they were complications. Dawlish glanced towards the bespectacled Irishman. He looked more than ever like some puny clerk or fussy schoolteacher and not the companion he would have chosen for robbery in the teeth of armed opposition. But Carter, the marine veteran was, he comforted himself. Together they were going to have to shepherd and cosset Holland like an invalid.

The sky was still bright and the tide flowing as the *Tecumseh* nosed slowly into the inlet that jutted northwards into the Connecticut shore, low coastline to port and starboard.

"West Haven off the port, New Haven dead ahead." Swanson knew these waters well. Dawlish was by him on the bridge, scanning the shore through his glasses, imprinting every detail on his mind, giving substance to the features he had memorised from the chart.

The city lay at the head of the bay, the spires and towers of Yale University to the west contrasting with the jumble of mills and factories eastwards, where several ships lay alongside docks, warehouses beyond. Dawlish located the Quinnipiac River by the high bridge it exited under at the harbour's apex and by the *Putnam* loitering two hundred yards short of it. The Mill, the small river the launch would ascend, joined the Quinnipiac a little upstream of the bridge.

"Where will you anchor?"

"There, off the Long Wharf." A slim wooden finger extended from the low shore a mile west of the river and main docks. Shunting locomotives and rising steam identified marshalling yards and Union Station beyond.

"It looks like a fine city, Captain," Dawlish said. "My wife had so wished to see it, but it's for the best that she rests tonight." He looked embarrassed. "Women's complaints, I fear." He was enveloped in a long opera cloak that covered the workman's clothing he wore beneath and he carried a silk hat. Raymond had provided similar garb for himself and Holland.

The *Tecumseh* anchored. A boat had been swung out and it pulled for the jetty as the shoreline shadows lengthened. Dawlish, Holland and Raymond sat in the sternsheets, Carter among the rowers, the very picture of a down-at heel labourer. A scuffed leather tool bag at his feet contained a jemmy, a bolt-cutter, a hammer, a hacksaw and an assortment of spanners specified by Holland. And no knives or firearms. Raymond had been adamant about that, and before they set off he had checked the *Putnam's* complement to ensure that nobody carried anything but knuckle-dusters.

Dawlish looked back at the receding yacht. Florence would be watching from her cabin and a burly figure waved from the poop – Egdean, who had begged to come but could never have fitted in with the gang of thugs on which success depended. And then, suddenly, Dawlish's attention was drawn to the shore by the sound of music wafting across the tranquil waters from the direction of the station. A brass band was thumping into *Hail Columbia* and cheers were echoing as a rising plume of smoke identified a train drawing slowly into the station from the south.

"You didn't say you'd arranged a reception." Dawlish glanced uneasily towards Raymond.

"Some guest at the ball, somebody up from New York." For there was to be a ball at Yale that night. Raymond's deceptions always seemed to be built on a strong foundation of truth.

They landed. Carter was audibly grateful to Raymond for the passage across, then hurried ahead alone. Raymond was in no hurry. He dispensed cigars – Holland refused – and lit up before sauntering up the deserted walkway, the picture of ease. The cheering was louder now, almost drowning the band's enthusiastic blare. Dawlish recognised *The Wearing of the Green* and sensed that Holland did also, though he said nothing. It was an unwelcome omen but the sight of the *Putnam* disappearing slowly under the bridge and up the river gave some reassurance.

A cab waited beyond the jetty, the driver on the box and a small man in a dark suit by the open door. Dawlish already knew his name, Heimbach. He greeted Raymond with a mixture of obsequiousness and unease. He saw them inside, then followed. Carter was already within and the blinds were drawn. The vehicle lurched into motion. *The Battle Hymn of the Republic* contended with more cheering across the tracks to the left.

"It's Driscoll." Heimbach said. His tone told that he knew that he had let Raymond down.

"Driscoll? How the hell…" Raymond was angry.

"He wasn't to have been here. Nobody expected him. It was just to have been a small dinner, an Irish veterans' reunion."

"You knew about it? And you didn't tell me?"

Heimbach squirmed. "I didn't think it was important. These damn Hibes are always commemorating something. If it isn't Patrick's Day then its Fredricksburg or Gettysburg or the Fighting 69th."

"When did you find out?" Dawlish said.

"At midday. It seems Driscoll had refused the invitation before, then changed his mind yesterday. And because he's here half the Fenians and Ancient Order of Hibernians and Sons of Erin between here and Hartford have turned out to welcome him. The host is Reynolds, the foundry owner."

"Where's the dinner?"

"Academy Street, the side of Wooster Square." Heimbach said.

"Half a mile from the river." Raymond was clearly shocked.

"Can it be a coincidence?" Dawlish looked hard at him.

Raymond shrugged. "It must be. But it'll keep them busy. Give them two hours and half of them will have drunk themselves under the table." He looked uncomfortable nonetheless.

"We can't wait two hours." Dawlish felt the nausea of dread. "The *Putnam* is already half-way the Mill River. It's too late to turn back." He saw that something was slipping between Holland's fingers. Rosary beads. His lips were moving silently.

The cab turned a corner and was rattling over cobbles now. The noise of cheering and marching feet was close. Dawlish plucked back the blind slightly to see flaring torches and waving banners filing past an intersection a block away. The band was beating out *A Nation Once Again!* and a thousand voices were joining in.

"Maybe we can dispense with the diversion? It might draw this crowd." Raymond sounded uncertain.

"No," Dawlish said. "We need the diversion. We'll never get past eight guards without it."

For that number patrolled Reynolds' foundry by night, as Raymond well knew since he had bribed the information from workers there and had confirmed it by personal observation. Those not armed with pistols carried buckshot-loaded shotguns. The Brotherhood was taking no chances.

They lapsed into silence as the cab trundled north and the noise of celebration grew more faint. It was fully dark now, the streets still residential and gas-lit but soon a bumpier surface and a sharp odour of coal-smoke and factory waste told that they were entering the industrial quarter.

Holland's Fenian Ram 1881

Overall length: 30 ft
Displacement: 19 tons

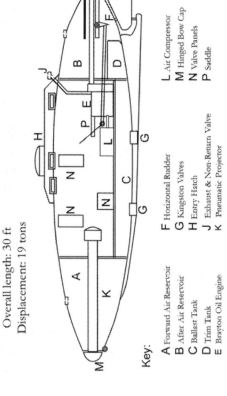

Key:

A Forward Air Reservoir
B After Air Reservoir
C Ballast Tank
D Trim Tank
E Brayton Oil Engine

F Horizontal Rudder
G Kingston Valves
H Entry Hatch
J Exhaust & Non-Return Valve
K Pneumatic Projector

L Air Compressor
M Hinged Bow Cap
N Valve Panels
P Saddle

Not Shown: Internal piping, projectile storage and fuel tank

11

Two thumps on the roof from the cabby.

"We're getting close," Heimbach looked out. "We'll turn right at the end of the block and then drop off at the bottom of the street."

Raymond removed his cloak. Dawlish and Holland did likewise. All three were clad in rough, tattered and patched clothes, short jackets and shapeless trousers.

"Here, Mister." Carter dug into his bag and drew out two caps and a battered felt hat. Dawlish took the hat and dragged the sagging brim close over his face.

The cab slowed, then manoeuvred sharply and stopped. They alighted to find themselves in a small courtyard piled with timber, a double gate behind. The driver was already moving to close it. He would wait here with his vehicle, Raymond's getaway.

"You've got the necessary?" Raymond asked Heimbach.

"Here." He lifted a sack and there was a chink of glass. To Carter he passed across a thick roll perhaps a yard long. It was bound with rope and a loose length running from end to end allowed him to sling it over his shoulder.

A doorway took them into a narrow alley, Heimbach and Raymond leading. Somewhere close-by an unseen stationary engine panted rhythmically and leather belts slapped on drive-wheels and shafting. They passed into a wider street, walking boldly, like men heading to a shift-change. Raymond confidently called greetings to labourers loading a dray. Another turn, another alley and then a narrow street flanking a mill with rows of lighted windows and beyond it a factory where furnaces cast a scarlet glow into the night sky. The strains of the brass band were distant now, interrupted at intervals by cheers.

"They'll be playing in the street outside Reynolds' house." Raymond flashed a smile. "They'll be cheering Driscoll and his cronies every time they show themselves at a window. The good Protestant Yankees of New Haven will be apoplectic. We might even see a riot – and that would be all to our good."

Then the last alley.

"Reynolds' foundry is down there." Heimbach's face was white and he was already turning to leave.

"You'll stay with me," Raymond hissed. "Leave now, Mr. Heimbach, and the Pinkertons will have enough by Monday morning to see you breaking rocks for ten years."

Heimbach led them on, paused at the corner ahead. A long, unlit cobbled street stretched on either hand, deserted between flanking walls and brick buildings. The night was clear and the half-moon cast long shadows. Heimbach pointed diagonally to the left. "That's Reynolds'."

It was exactly as Raymond had sketched it – the fifty-yard frontage, broken glass topping a ten-foot wall, a dray-wide wooden door piercing it to the side of a two-storey building, the office, its unlit ground-level windows barred. Over the wall, to the right, there would be a row of lean-to storage sheds against the dividing wall with the next property, and in the centre a large, high-roofed, barn-like structure that housed the moulding shop, furnace and casting area. The Mill River served as the far boundary, and along it was the small wharf from where many of the bells and other foundry products were shipped by barge. And where the Fenian Ram now lay.

They waited silently, three minutes, four. No sound of movement or voices beyond the wall, though eight armed men might be patrolling there if some had not yielded to the temptation of joining Driscoll's welcome.

"No reason to delay," Dawlish said. "Let's get started." His hands were trembling. Years of hard labour in an American gaol were a worse prospect than swift death.

"May God and his Holy Mother protect the lot of us." Holland crossed himself gravely. He had secured his spectacles with string across the back of his head.

Heimbach extracted two bottles from his sack, opened one and dribbled lamp-oil from it on to the rags swathing the necks of both. Carter undid the knots securing the roll he carried. He flattened it, a hair mattress cut in half and sealed with twine stitching. He thrust it at Holland. "You take this," he said, "and this, and this", and handed him the tool bag and a length of rope. Carter seemed wholly calm. He had done something like this before, Raymond had said, had done it satisfactorily. He had been no more specific..

Raymond and Heimbach left the alley, walked towards the office, one slowing the other to a calmer pace and glancing casually up and down the length of the street. Half-way, Raymond raised his arm. *All Clear.*

"Now us. And slowly, Gentlemen, calmly," Dawlish said.

Carter and Holland followed him to the point to the right where Reynolds' wall met that of the neighbouring business. A transition from broken glass to iron spikes marked the boundary and the shadows there were reassuringly deep.

The others had reached the office. Raymond looked towards Dawlish, who raised his hand – *Go Ahead.* A tinkling of glass announced a pane broken – the windows there were divided in small panels and the sound was low. Another tinkle, then a match's flare, and a second, and then two bottles of lamp oil thrown in to shatter in the rooms beyond.

Even as the two arsonists hurried away towards the alley they would escape through Dawlish was cupping his hands and Carter was stepping on them. He steadied himself against the wall, mounted Dawlish's shoulders. Dawlish straightened up – the ex-marine was heavier than he would have wished – and hissed "Now, the mattress!" to Holland.

An orange glow flickered from one of the office windows, grew, then exploded to greater intensity as something large inside caught light. A blaze was growing at the second window also and smoke was jetting from it and billowing skywards.

"Look there, Tom! There's a fire!" A shout from beyond the wall. Another answered and there was the sound of running feet.

Carter took the mattress from Holland's up-reached hands. He almost fell as he swung it towards the wall's crest and the effort was unsuccessful. He tried again, Dawlish shifting beneath him to keep balance as Carter's boots ground into his shoulders. This time the mattress flopped down over the glass and Carter reached for the last of the neighbour's spikes and used it to drag himself upwards. He gained the top and straddled it, protected from the glass shards by the cushioning beneath. "It's clear," he hissed, "the fire's drawing them."

Flames now roared through every window on the ground floor. Unseen men shouted and a dog barked furiously – a bad omen, for Raymond had said nothing about dogs.

"The rope! Then yourself!"

Holland tossed it up to Carter, then mounted Dawlish's cupped hands and shoulders and was heaved upwards. He half-scrambled, was half-dragged, to the top, then disappeared over to slide down the sloped roof of the lean-to shed beyond, the first inside the yard. Carter slipped the bowline on the rope's end over the nearest spike and Dawlish began to haul himself up. He froze for an instant as he did – the gateway close to the burning office was swinging open and men were pouring into the street. The floor above was now alight also and the buckets some carried could have no impact on the inferno. One glance down the street might have revealed him suspended half-way up the wall but their attention was wholly focussed on the flames. He dragged himself up, reached for Carter's outstretched hand and was then somehow resting on the mattress. Together they dropped down three feet to the sloping corrugated roof beneath, slid down it and lowered themselves to the ground.

Heaped coal to the left provided a dark nook in which Holland crouched. "I counted six of them," he said. "One of them's Tom Rooney. I know him – he's a fierce hard man."

Dawlish glanced around the coal. The building was burning on its inner side also and the first glowing edges were showing through the roof tiles. Three men were scuttling to and fro with buckets – there appeared to be a water-tank or stand-pipe at the further end of the large workshop that occupied the centre of the yard. Their efforts were as futile as their companions' on the street side. Dawlish knew that if they had any sense then one at least of their number must already be speeding to alert the local fire-company.

"It's clear. You first," Dawlish motioned to Carter.

Fifteen yards took Carter into the cover of the workshop and he disappeared down its flank towards the river, turned its corner, and was lost to sight. Holland crossed himself yet again, then followed. Dawlish waited thirty seconds, then hurried behind, painfully aware of the crunching of the cinder-strewn surface underfoot. He paused at the workshop's furthest corner. The river was twenty yards ahead, the waters dark and sluggish, foul with scum washing down from factories upstream, a lifeless mill and warehouses on the opposite bank. On the near side, thirty yards to the left, he saw Reynolds' wooden wharf with its open-sided loading shed and a small stiff-leg loading derrick. Shadows moving between crates stacked there told him that Holland and Carter had reached it.

Shouting still came from the direction of the now-unseen fire, the night sky above it crimson, sparks rushing skywards with the rolling smoke. The dog was barking again and snatches of the brass band's remorseless thumping echoed incongruously in the distance. Thus far the guards did not seem to have recognised the fire as a diversion but Dawlish knew he could not count on that luck holding. He edged along shadows of the workshop wall, eyes searching downriver – and there, lurking in the dark bend a hundred yards downstream, only the merest glow from her funnel betraying her presence, was the *Putnam* with her desperadoes.

He flitted across to the shed, joined Holland between the crates.

"The hatch's padlocked," Holland said. "Mr. Carter's down there now."

Dawlish moved to the jetty's edge and felt a thrill as he beheld for the first time, four feet below him, the short, hump-backed cylinder, nine-tenths awash, that had drawn him so far. Carter was crouched on the low boxlike structure that surmounted it, straining on the bolt-cutters. He looked up in mute appeal. The padlock's hardened steel was too much for him alone. Dawlish lowered himself, stepped across and felt the ram lurch slightly like a living being. He stooped to face Carter and grasped the cutter's dual handles just short of the other's hands. It was like a shears, but with a toggle action designed to multiply force eighty times, and its tempered blades were already biting deep into the shackle of the lock securing the domed twenty-inch hatch in the centre of the box. Both men gasped with effort and then, with a snap, the metal parted and they sprawled forward, their energy dissipated. Dawlish heaved on the hatch and it swung open. A warm, oily stench wafted up as he lowered the hinged cover to rest on the surface behind.

"Come down, Mr. Holland," he called softly. He helped him across and seemed to sense a new strength, elation even, in the slight Irishman as his feet touched the rounded iron surface.

"She's pointing downstream, Mr. Page. Thank God for that," Holland said. "Now help me in. It's a tight squeeze." He dropped a leg inside, reached for a ladder rung, found it and then slipped through as Dawlish assisted. "I'll trouble you for the tool bag too," he said and then disappeared into darkness.

Carter had felt his way towards the bow on his hands and knees, half-submerged. "I've found the towing shackle," he whispered to Dawlish. "We can signal for the *Putnam* now."

The launch was invisible from this low – Dawlish would have to mount the jetty again. As he did he heard the insistent clanging of a bell, still distant, but drawing nearer, the unmistakable sound of a fire-engine racing towards the conflagration. He thought he heard cheers too but the roar of the flames was louder still and they were rising in great licking tongues beyond the roof of the intervening workshop.

A low growl froze him as he gained the wharf. A large mongrel, teeth bared and hair bristling around its neck, tail rigid and twitching, crouched between the crates not ten feet distant. Retreat was impossible – climbing back down would only expose his face and shoulders – and Dawlish began to edge slowly to his left, avoiding meeting the beast's direct gaze. Heart pounding, fearing it must be smelling his terror, he slowly opened his jacket and slipped his right arm from the sleeve. The dog's nose and jowls were scarred, one ear missing – no stranger to fighting – and it growled again as it paced forward another foot.

Dawlish hoped to wrap the jacket round his left arm to parry the animal but it moved first, springing forward as he freed his right hand. He side-stepped and it smashed into his right leg, head flailing as the fangs sought purchase. For one dreadful instant he felt the jaws open around his thigh and he beat down with his fists and twisted himself as they closed. The heavy dungaree material of the stained workman's trousers he had flinched to don saved him. The teeth skidded, gripped on the slack of the cloth and the animal held and dragged, thrashing its head side to side. The fabric must rend at any moment and then those teeth would be seeking new purchase. Dawlish fought to keep his feet and somehow pulled his jacket free. He held it stretched between both hands, then jerked down, striking the ravening beast hard on the nose. It yelped, relaxed its grip for an instant and somehow the jacket was passing under the jaw and chin. Dawlish pulled hard, drawing the garment tight around the head like a hood, jerking the writhing body upright. Sharp-nailed paws tore at him but he had his hands around the throat now and was pressing deeply with this thumbs. He kicked hard, twice, three times, but the frenzied creature hardly seemed to notice and he doubted he could hold the strong, flailing body much longer.

"Carter!" he gasped, "For God's Sake! Carter!"

He threw himself down, aiming to smash the mongrel's spine with his knees, but it lashed to one side and he came down heavily and almost lost his grip. Man and dog rolled together and Dawlish felt his shirt ripping and furrows torn on his chest by the flailing paws. Then Carter was over him, swinging down the bolt-cutters, thudding them into the heaving carcass, increasing its frenzy. Dawlish shoved the jacket-encased head from him — for one instant he saw the flash of white teeth working through — and Carter hammered down again. Blood burst through the fabric and he struck again, and again. A spasm ran through the animal, and then it stilled.

Dawlish staggered to his feet, shaking, his chest bloodied from the hound's raking. He stammered thanks to Carter and then was arrested by the clanging of the fire-bell.

"They're near," Carter said. "And they'll bring the engine here for water."

Flames soared unabated beyond the workshop and still the tolling bell drew nearer. A black shape, the *Putnam*, was separating

117

itself from the shadows at the river bend and pushing resolutely towards the jetty.

"Go on board," Dawlish said. "Get ready to fix the tow."

Carter scrambled down, sloshed his way along the curved hull towards the bows. Dawlish followed and crouched over the open hatch. There was a small glow of light inside, enough to show Holland kneeling between a jumble of piping, flywheels, gauges and levers. He glanced up.

"I've got the pilot flame going," he said. "And there's air in the tanks, nearly two hundred pounds pressure. They've been running the engine all right, and there's another three hundred in the projector accumulator." He sounded as calm as if vengeance was not fifty yards distant.

"Stay there," Dawlish said. "We'll be under tow in a moment."

The *Putnam* passed, figures crowding her deck. She slowed, reversed her screw and began surging back and forth to point herself downstream – the river was too narrow here to permit a single sweeping turn.

Suddenly there was cheering from the direction of the blazing office. The clamouring bell was announcing the fire-engine's arrival with a score or more of volunteers. The launch's slow manoeuvrings were a torture as the seconds slipped past, but at last the bows were heading for the ram and she glided alongside, momentum dying as the engine was reversed again. Boots thudded on iron as four men jumped across, one carrying the tow cable. Guided by Carter, Dawlish edged along the flooded foredeck and both men plunged their hands under to make it fast on the shackle. The others leaped towards the jetty, heading for the mooring ropes fore and aft.

The shotgun blast caught the third man as he hauled himself on to the wharf. Shocked by the sound, Dawlish looked up to see him stagger back and drop with a splash between the ram and the piles. He was conscious of another of the landing party – a self-styled warehouseman – rushing towards the figure emerging, shouting, between the crates with a smoking weapon. A fist encased in a knuckle-duster caught the gunman across the jaw. He went down, his shotgun's second barrel blasting uselessly as it hit the planks. Another guard ducked into view and too late saw the warehouseman leaping towards him from the shadows. A blow in the stomach doubled him over and a backhanded swing took him on the temple and brought him sprawling. The second man ashore was lifting the bow mooring-rope from its bollard and casting it into the water.

Shouting now, running feet, the drumming of hooves and the insistent tolling of the bell. The fire-engine was being driven to the wharf to pump water so hoses would be run from it to the blaze. It was bringing dozens of helpers with it.

"The tow's secure," Carter yelled. The man with him was already scrambling across to the *Putnam*.

Moaning and weak thrashing from the water alongside. The wounded man was grasping a slimy ladder-rung, his face and arms running scarlet. Dawlish lowered himself, half-squatting, across the curved deck towards him and caught him by the collar. "I have you," he called and then, louder, for concealment was already forfeited, "Carter! Here! Help me!"

Together they dragged the casualty on to the ram. Boots thudded down next to them – the warehouseman. "Get him over!" Dawlish shouted, and they lugged the wounded man across, groaning, to be lifted on board the *Putnam*.

The after-mooring was cast off and the last man ashore was sprinting towards them as a knot of men burst on to the jetty, the fire-engine clanging behind. Blocked, he turned and leaped for the waters astern of the ram, landing with a splash. He struck out for midstream, beyond the *Putnam's* sheltering bulk, but no shots followed for his pursuers were suddenly arrested by the scene before them.

The launch was pulling out slowly, the tow-rope jerking taut as she took up the slack, and the ram was nudging from the jetty in her wake. Only Dawlish was now left exposed on her curved, water-lapped deck. He looked back aghast to see a score of surprised faces, and then hear a roar of wrath and fury as the full significance dawned on them.

A shot rang out – a pistol – and another, wild but terrifying. Dawlish scurried to drop through the manhole into the vessel's dark belly. The launch gathered speed, the submarine oscillating wildly astern as it surged towards the centre of the river, and men leant over to drag their swimming comrade from the water. Another pistol shot – the bullet screaming close – and Dawlish had his legs down the hatch and felt Holland guiding them on to rungs inside. The hatch cover was hinged towards the stern and he caught it and raised it like a vertical shield just as a jolt and a "ping!" told him it had saved him. He shrunk down, only his eyes raised above the opening's rim, and looked aft.

Figures were running along the shore, parallel to the river, yelling angrily, but their pursuit was cut off by the boundary wall with the next yard. Two figures on horseback were forcing their way through the throng, both incongruously in evening clothes. One, florid, heavy, his face rabid with indignation and loss, could only be Reynolds, the foundry owner, but the second's deep-set eyes and closely cropped steel-grey beard marked him as Brigadier Stephen Driscoll. He reined in and yelled "To the bridge, boys!" with all the authority that had inspired men to follow him suicidally up the corpse-strewn slopes above Fredricksburg.

Dawlish dropped inside, frightened now, knowing that four bridges and a mile of winding river lay between here and the open harbour. He fought down a rising feeling of claustrophobia. Study of Holland's drawings had not prepared him for the actuality of confinement in this tiny iron compartment.

"They've looked after her well." Holland seemed oblivious of the tumult outside. "The steering's free, and the horizontal rudder too." He screwed down the cover over the pinpoint of the pilot light in the combustion chamber between the Brayton oil-engine's two cylinders, plunging the interior into almost total darkness. The only light now, dim at that, came through the three small thick-glassed windows on each side of the tiny box-like superstructure.

Dawlish's eyes were becoming accustomed to the gloom and he recognised the layout he had memorised so intently. The convex disc that sealed the after tank closed off the rear of the six-foot diameter compartment and was pierced in its centre by the tube and seals and bearings that carried the propeller shaft. Ahead of it, the

Brayton occupied a full third of the compartment, its compression and power cylinders in the centre, and above them a saddle-like seat on which Holland now perched. From here he could peer through the thick windows and manipulate the levers on either side to operate the vertical and horizontal rudders. A rocking beam and cranks behind him linked the cylinders and the two enormous flywheels to port and starboard, one driving the screw by a train of gears, the other the air-compressor. Air piping, valving, gauges and the fuel-oil and ballast tanks congested the remainder of the compartment. The forward air tank's convex wall closed off the bow and a flanged cylinder protruding from the centre showed where the pneumatic projector had been mounted.

"The crank's behind you," Holland said. "Turn her over five or six times and then I'll close the compression. With God's help she'll fire up."

God's help was badly needed, Dawlish thought, as he bent over, knocking his forehead painfully on some projection, and feeling for the crank handle. If Driscoll and his crew reached the bridge first – it was two hundred yards downstream – then the *Putnam* would have no option but to slip the tow and make her escape. Only with her engine running would the ram have a chance, a small one, of running her iron-plated bulk through the gauntlet.

Dawlish grasped the crank, threw his weight on it, felt the flywheel rotate slowly, gather speed. He swung round into the second revolution, and it was accelerating, and hope was rising in him when Holland called "Stop!"

Dawlish looked up.

"The mooring rope, Mr. Page," Holland said. "Could it snag the screw?"

It could, and Dawlish should have remembered.

He reached into the tool-bag and felt for the hacksaw he knew was there, then levered himself up the ladder, through the open hatch. Yards, warehouses and jetties were slipping past. The *Putnam* and her tow had already rounded the bend, losing Reynolds' foundry astern and the girders of the first bridge, a railroad trestle, were a hundred yards ahead. Water foamed and creamed around the ram's small superstructure – the pointed bow had dropped under the force of the tow. Dawlish groped under the swirling water aft and located the trailing cable. He sawed rapidly, felt it part, then threw it clear. Ahead, the launch was passing under the girders and as Dawlish clambered back, and heaved himself into the access shaft again, he saw dark figures moving on to the bridge from the right.

A single shot rang out – wild – and then two, three more as he dropped back into the stuffy interior. A shadow passed over the open hatch for a moment – the bridge – and more shots followed, but he knew the first obstacle had been passed. It was little comfort. The street-map he had so carefully memorised flashed in his head and told him that the pursuers would be rushing down East Street, parallel to the river, heading for the more accessible Grand Avenue Bridge. At the *Putnam's* current speed it could be only three, four minutes away.

"Try her again, Mr. Page," Holland said. "She's free enough. She'll fire."

Dawlish took the crank again, swung the flywheel over, felt it grow lighter with each turn.

"Now!" Holland called, and closed the compression. The engine shuddered and the flywheel slowed and stopped. "Again," he said. "She'll fire this time."

She did not, and not on the third or fourth attempts either, though she choked and spluttered, but on the fifth she came to life in a series of slow coughs. The flywheel's rotation stabilised and the rocking beam behind Holland began its monotonous rise and fall. Dawlish found himself immediately intimidated by the close proximity of so many moving parts. One lurch, one slip, could mean a mangled limb.

"She'll need to heat up before we load her." Holland already seemed one with his craft. "She's temperamental."

Dawlish raised himself to peep over the lip of the access hatch. He felt a small flow of air across it, drawn in by the now reverberating engine. Aft, the exhaust burbled up from the check valves on the submerged exhaust pipe. Ahead, the *Putnam* had reached the point where the river divided around a small island. She was ploughing into the narrower, and shorter, westerly channel and the single-arch Grand Avenue Bridge was just coming into sight. Workshop yards and warehouses still formed a barrier to starboard but fifty yards ahead of the launch, between her and the bridge, they seemed to peter out into an expanse of open waste ground. And suddenly there were men there, a handful on horseback – Driscoll must be among them – and others plunging on foot through the tangle of reeds and overgrown grass at the water's edge. A ragged mix of a cheer and a howl of fury told that they had spotted the oncoming launch.

"They're ahead of us," Dawlish called down. "The *Putnam* won't make it."

Admitting it chilled him. He had planned for this eventuality, had discussed it with Raymond's cut-throats, had gone through it step by step with Holland. But now that the reality was on him of placing his only hope of survival in a temperamental, fifteen horse-power oil-engine that seemed barely capable of keeping itself idling the gamble seemed hopeless.

"I'll open the throttle, then, speed her up a bit," Holland yelled over the racket. "She's heating up nicely. She won't stall."

Shots rang out ahead. Water boiled at the *Putnam's* stern – her screw was being reversed, killing her forward speed. The ram lurched and slowed as the tow slackened. The *Putnam* was trying to turn back to run upstream again. On her deck men were hauling in the dripping tow-cable, dragging it along the side and clear of the thrashing propeller as she now surged ahead and astern in short rushes as she tried to turn in the narrow river.

More shots, more voices rising in anger and triumph as fresh arrivals clustered at the bank downstream.

Dawlish dropped down and felt again for the hacksaw. "Engage the screw when I tell you!" he shouted. "I'll cut the tow and then I'll con you downstream." The *Putnam's* crew might be able to escape but there could be no hope of turning the wallowing, clumsy ram in this cramped channel. The gauntlet must be run. A shaft of moonlight reflected on Holland's spectacles as he nodded agreement, his face intent, a man unafraid, Dawlish realised, because it had not occurred to him to be afraid.

The *Putnam* had turned by the time Dawlish regained the hatch and she was surging upstream, a wave creaming around her bows, heading for the junction with the other channel. There she could be abandoned at some secluded yard and her crew and passengers could disperse rapidly into the maze of workshops and factories beyond. Immediate pursuit would be unlikely since all attention would be focussed on the ram.

"Now!" Dawlish yelled. "Engage the screw"

"Cut the tow! Cut the tow!" A figure in the launch's bows was shouting and gesticulating as she drew level with the ram.

Dawlish struggled from the hatch and crawled on hands and knees along the curved deck, spluttering as the *Putnam's* bow-wave washed over him. Gears grated and the hull shuddered under him, then lurched forward as the ram's screw bit. His hands found the rope and he sawed frantically. He was not through it as it tightened – both craft were urging in opposite directions now – but it was weakened enough to part with a splashing whip. He looked up to see the narrow channel ahead empty, the bridge perhaps a hundred yards away and a ragged fusillade barking from the open ground a third of that distance before the bows.

He gained the hatch, swung his legs inside, driven now more by the fear of running aground than by the ill-aimed gunfire. The ram was still in mid-stream, but judging direction was difficult with no bow visible ahead and a wave breaking over the low superstructure and slopping at intervals through the hatch opening. The speed was little over walking pace.

"A half point to port!" Dawlish shouted but Holland knew neither port nor starboard and he lurched for the wrong bank. Yelled corrections, left and right, brought the ram in a sinusoidal course down past the open ground. Dawlish had all but closed the hatch-cover over his head and peered out from the gap remaining. The target presented was a tiny one, and black against the shadowy, scum-laden grey waters and the few shots that screamed overhead were wide. Ten, twenty men lined the bank, one causing Dawlish to slam the cover closed momentarily as he raised a shotgun and blasted. Most were merely shouting abuse. But the majority had rushed on towards the bridge, and the parapet was already black with figures.

"Hold her steady now," Dawlish called.

Shots rippled from the span ahead, wild, undisciplined, but close enough to raise spurts in the water to either side. Closer now, close enough to hear the shouts of anger and hatred, to pick out individual faces illuminated by the single gas-lantern on the bridge and to see men wearing scraps of uniform, worn caps and tattered jackets that were proud mementoes of war-service, donned to welcome Driscoll. Several rounds impacted harmlessly against the superstructure – like the hull it was constructed of three-quarter inch charcoal-iron, tough and thick enough to stop any small-arms fire. Again Dawlish slammed the hatch closed and trusted that the ram would not wander as it ploughed the last yards towards the arch.

Something large clanged against the hull forward, making it lurch, a heavy object dropped from above, harmless in itself but deflecting the vessel's course. Dawlish pushed up the hatch. The ram was now under the bridge and veering to port. He shouted a correction to Holland and they were back in midstream as they emerged on the far side and another hail assaulted them.

"We're past!" Dawlish could not contain his delight.

"Thanks be to God and His Holy Mother," Holland shouted. "We're making it, Mr. Page! We'll do it!"

The firing died away and the ram moved steadily through the now-widening waterway close to the end of the island. It curved here to rejoin the second channel and soon there would be another bridge, at Chapel Street, but the prospect no longer seemed so daunting. And the Brayton was behaving manfully, beating regularly, even if the temperature in the compartment was rising steadily. If it was like this with the hatch open, Dawlish thought, it would be unbearable running closed, on air released slowly from one of the tanks. Yet that was how Holland had run this contraption underwater, fifteen minutes at a time, feeling his way blindly around the channels on the New Jersey shore and out into New York Harbour and even the Narrows, coming up briefly to clear the

125

compartment of fumes, then diving again. He might almost be a genius, but there was much of the madman about him as well.

Past the extremity of the island now, and the river was a now twenty-yard wide channel. The ram yawed around the next bend and Chapel Street Bridge came into view. A few figures had reached it but the river and the banks above it were dark and the ram was almost below them before they spotted the vee of ripples thrown off by the superstructure, the only part visible. Dawlish slammed down the cover at the last moment as rocks and abuse were hurled down. A few harmless pistol shots echoed but then the obstacle was slipping astern and the Mill River was funnelling out in the last two hundred yards before it flowed into the wider Quinnipiac. One bridge remained.

Dawlish conned the wallowing craft into the confluence. The Mill's flow has been negligible, but the larger river's stronger current added impetus and the shores slipped faster by. Ahead was the last road-bridge, a high trestle structure, two piers and three spans. A dark shape moving on the far side resolved itself into a small tug towing three laden barges upstream through the central gap. Dawlish headed the ram towards the nearer span. The barge-string's wash sent a cascade of water over the hatch rim. He ducked, slammed the cover closed, and waited until the heaving subsided before throwing it open again.

The broad, open harbour spread before them, calm, rippled by only the slightest breeze, reflecting the moon and the lights of the town and of wharf-moored shipping to either side. And best of all, less than a mile to starboard, was the *Tecumseh's* white hull, ghostly against the darker waters, lights winking along her deckhouse. There Florence would be watching with infinite patience, and Egdean by her, encouraging her hopes with clumsy kindliness.

"We've done it, Mr. Holland!" Dawlish felt elation rise within him, "and now for …"

A single shot echoed from port.

He turned and saw a vessel pulling out fast from between the shipping moored along the wharves there. It was another steam launch – larger, heavier, than the *Putnam*, smart and official-looking, a pilot craft perhaps – with men crowded in its bows and a white wave creaming at its stem. It was suddenly clear why passage of the last bridges has been so easy. Driscoll and a handful of supporters had banked on the ram heading for the harbour, not up the Quinnipiac, and had raced here to call on the loyalty of some Irishman in the harbour service.

Dawlish ducked down, shouted at Holland. "Driscoll's got a boat and he's coming for us!"

"How far?"

"Three hundred yards."

And the launch must be making eight or ten knots to the ram's three. It could overhaul her, land men on deck, force ignominious surrender at gunpoint – or those sharp bows could come crashing into the submerged hull, rolling her over, and once the open hatch was under she would fill and sink like a stone.

"You're sure they've seen us?" Holland said.

"Only too well."

Dawlish felt anger and despair. To have got this far...

He pushed his head out again, ducked involuntarily as another shot rang out.

And then Holland's words stilled him, assured and confident even if he did have to shout above the Brayton's clatter.

"Shut the hatch, Mr. Page. Secure it tight. I'm taking her down."

12

The hatch clanged shut and when Dawlish pushed the locking dogs tight the darkness was total. Terror of entombment surged through him and for an instant he feared he could not master it. Then Holland's shout roused him.

"Come down, Mr. Page – that's it, face ahead. You'll find the forward reservoir valve by your right foot."

He had throttled the Brayton back to a tick-over but each beat was still sucking in precious air from the small compartment. Within a minute human breathing would be difficult, within two the engine would falter and die. Dawlish groped for the valve – he had memorised the position of every tap and lever beforehand, but the reality was somehow different in the darkness. He located the knurled hand wheel.

"I've found it!" A tiny victory, a flush of hope.

"A half-turn, Mr. Page."

He cracked it open, felt the air-stream jetting from it. "A half-turn! It's flowing!"

"Now, a foot and a half to your left, there's a lever. You've got it? Good! Open it fully."

Air roared through the vertical two-inch pipe rising from the ballast tank that formed much of the deck underfoot. It belched from the hull through a vent just ahead of the superstructure and water rushed in to replace it through ports in the bottom. The hull lurched slightly, then seemed to settle.

"Enough! Close it!"

As he acted Dawlish felt Holland's fist nudge into his back, pushing forward the long lever controlling the horizontal rudder. Not only was the ram sinking below the surface but her slowly beating screw was now also driving her down further.

"We're submerged?" The motion seemed to be smoother now, the inclination towards the bows eight, ten degrees.

"God knows how deep, twelve or fifteen feet, I think." Holland was levelling the craft now. "It's too bloody dark to see any light from the surface."

Then a noise louder than the engine's idling, a rhythmic, swishing rumble beating closer and reverberating through the side plating, the beat of another propeller.

Somewhere above – perhaps close enough for her bows and keel to strip the ram's boxlike superstructure from the hull – the launch was quartering the area where it had last sighted her quarry. And Driscoll would know exactly what to watch for, the tell-tale bubbles rising from the exhaust's check-valves, and could calculate how long the ram could stay below before suffocation of crew and engine would drive her to the surface. He would know from the reports that Holland had submitted weekly on his dives and hair's-breath survivals off Jersey City, reports Brotherhood had paid for.

The thrashing screw grew closer. Dawlish dug his nails into his palms, realised he had a weakness he had never suspected, a horror of enclosed darkness, of premature burial. He fought down the urge to cry out in despair.

"They're wide, they're twenty yards at least to the right." Holland seemed to sense his alarm and his voice was calm. "I'm turning away from her."

Dawlish sensed the hull nudge to starboard, the bows dipping slightly. The Brayton's revolutions were slow enough to count. Heat radiated from it – Holland must be broiling on his saddle – and though the compartment's sides were cool to the touch the atmosphere was uncomfortably warm. The beat of the launch's propeller drew more distant.

"Crack that valve open another quarter-turn," Holland ordered.

The airflow increased. Holland centred the rudder but there was no way of knowing in what direction they were heading. The tide must be ebbing now and there was also the added impetus of the Quinnipiac's outflow to carry the ram further into the harbour. With luck they would be moving towards more open waters but there was also a chance that they were heading straight for the shore.

The searching launch's beat was growing louder again. The rhythm seemed to find some response in the ram's plating and it boomed and echoed as the slicing propeller drew ever closer. Dawlish was biting his wrist rather than cry out. *Don't let me die like this*, he wanted to howl at the God he sometimes doubted but to whom he turned involuntarily when death was close – *not in this foul, warm, oily darkness!* Death on a Cossack lance or on a gunboat's exposed bridge on a sluggish Gran Chaco river would have been better than this!

The sound was deafening but Holland's shout was louder. "They're over us, Mr. Page," he called, "and they haven't seen us, or they'd have slowed. And they'll never pick-up the exhaust with the wake they'll be throwing up."

The beating above reached a climax, then passed, the tone changing, the intensity falling.

Three, four minutes passed, the ram's own motion imperceptible. Dawlish found himself sweating heavily and short of breath – the engine was taking most of the air bleeding in from the storage tank forward and his head was starting to pound. It took an effort now to hear the launch's distant screw.

"We'll give her another few minutes, and then we'll blow the ballast," Holland said.

Unseen in the darkness, Dawlish nodded dumbly, grateful that the insignificant Irishman had so easily taken control. His study of the drawings and long conversations with Holland had been insufficient to prepare him for this nightmare.

"If they've lost us perhaps we can run on the surface to the *Tecumseh*." Dawlish wished desperately that it could be so. The prospect of pushing his head out into the night air was irresistible. Salvation could not be more than a mile away across the harbour.

For a few seconds a brief scraping sound, and then a lurch that sent Dawlish sprawling forward and brought his barely controlled fear to a new level of shame and misery.

"We're touching bottom, and we're dragging." Holland must have heard his intake of breath. "It's nothing to worry about. It's happened me often enough before. The keel's strong enough, God knows."

Then it was suddenly calm again – the current had pulled the ram free. The next minutes were like hours, and Dawlish fancied his own breathing was louder than the slow panting and clicking of the Brayton and the low rumble of the bevel gears driving the propeller shaft. The sound of the launch's screws had died completely.

At last Holland spoke. "The long lever to your right, Mr. Page. You're sure? Not the one you pulled before? Good. Count to three, open it to the count of ten, then close it again."

Dawlish felt for it, found it, pulled. Air surged into the ballast tank, expelling its contents slowly through the bottom ports. He began to count and felt the deck heave gently beneath him. Simultaneously Holland pulled back the horizontal-rudder lever and the bows rose slightly. Dawlish pushed the lever to the closed position.

An eternity passed and then there was once more the slight, unmistakable sway of a vessel rocking on the surface.

"I think I can see lights." Holland's face must be pressed against one of the glasses. "Open the hatch, Mr. Page. Careful as you do."

Dawlish was not careful enough, had not reckoned on the rise in internal pressure due to the airflow. As he slipped the last securing dog the hinged cover was blown upwards, swung on its hinges and clanged on the iron deck behind like the clapper of some huge bell. Anybody within a mile must have heard it, he realised, as hot air rushed past him, must wonder what caused the report. But for the instant he had eyes only for the moon and a starry sky above that had never seemed more beautiful. He thrust his head and shoulders free, gulped in fresh air, sought his bearings. Tide and current had carried the ram further south than he had expected and it was now moving slowly southwards not five hundred yards off the eastern shore, almost level with the last of the wharves and moored shipping. He recognised what must be the lights of East Haven off the port bow and way astern was New Haven itself, and the finger of the Long Wharf and off it, a mile distant from here, impossibly far, the lights of *Tecumseh*.

But more ominous still was what lay between, the trim hull of the launch that had hunted and lost the ram so recently. She was creaming around into a turn, and heading this way, alerted by the hatch's clang.

He felt Holland's hand jerking his shirt, demanding information.

"They're coming again," Dawlish called, "They're still about a mile away."

"Come down then, fast. Close that air valve."

The forward tank was still bleeding precious air. Dawlish closed it.

"We'll have to dive again, Mr. Page, but we'll need more air first if we're to keep the Brayton going. I'll increase the revolutions now and when I give you the word, shove that bar over and engage the compressor."

They ran south, paralleling the shore, the engine now at full throttle, urging the ram into what might have been four knots, the compressor's hammering adding to the noise. Head exposed, Dawlish conned and watched the launch's steady, inexorable progress. It had already halved the intervening distance. There were men in the bows, surely directing the helmsman towards the ridge of white foam thrown up by the ram's superstructure.

Dawlish forced himself to ignore his fear, to think of this vessel as one like any other, but with a cloak of invisibility that could be adopted at will. The night's light breeze raised only ripples but they were enough to disperse the exhaust – looking aft he could not detect it himself. The launch had missed them once, had passed directly over, and there was no reason why she should not do so again. But the shallows to port were the greater enemy and the ram must head into more open water where she might blunder blindly without fear of grounding.

He had to take control. He must conquer the terror that had unmanned him in the first dive. Holland was the engineer, but he was the captain.

"Prepare to dive in two minutes, Mr. Holland," he shouted down in that long-learned quarterdeck tone that brooked no hesitance. "I trust your air-chamber is primed?"

"We need longer."

"Diving in two minutes, regardless." By then the launch would be two hundred yards away, already too close for complacency. "Maintain course." The last Driscoll and his confederates should last see the ram steering due south.

Dawlish lowered himself, grasped the hatch, slammed it shut, pounded the dogs closed.

"Now!"

Holland was pushing the horizontal rudder down to dip the bows while Dawlish scrambled for the air valve – a full turn, for the Brayton was still beating at full revolutions – and for the ballast lever, flinging it over to let water surge into the tank. He felt terror rise again – the dark, the heat, the reverberations in that iron tomb – but concentration on tasks now half-familiar seemed to slow it. The compressor was still engaged and he dragged its clutch lever into neutral.

"We're down," Holland shouted, "I'm throttling back." The noise and revolutions fell. "Now close that air valve, Mr. Page. A quarter open, no more."

The churning of the launch's screw was close, and coming closer.

"Turn her to the right, Mr. Holland." Even at this extremity the landsman's phrasing was offensive, but Dawlish felt the hull lurching over. There was no way of judging the rate of turn. He wanted to carry her over by a full eight points, straight towards the centre of the harbour. He counted to thirty. "Now centre her, Mr. Holland. Steer straight ahead."

The propeller beat above rose to a crescendo. Dawlish fancied that it came from somewhere astern, but that might have been wishful thinking. Then it began to diminish, the tone changing. He kept counting, pacing himself to account for seconds, and two minutes passed, then three. Then the launch was closer again – still distant, but closer. He put his ear against the plating to either side. It was splendidly cool compared with the hot, oily air that was already shortening his breathing. To starboard, above the slow swish of the ram's own screw vibrating through the hull, he heard the launch's growing thrash. She was somewhere between them and the city, blocking return towards the *Tecumseh*.

Three more minutes passed, the engine throbbing slowly, the temperature rising. The launch came close again, then retreated, yet remained somewhere near. Dawlish could imagine her cruising parallel tracks, the men on deck straining for some sight of the exhaust, turning her towards some imagined sighting with excitement growing, then hope dashed, frustration rising, the methodical search resumed.

And all the time the tide was ebbing and the submerged vessel might be drifting steadily towards the Sound. Even had Driscoll's launch not blocked the course towards the *Tecumseh*, it was uncertain if the straining engine could carry her back that far against the current.

Dawlish's mind raced – he needed a change of plan. He made the harbour-chart concrete in his mind and the effort quelled that terror that was growing again. He visualised the eastern shore below East Haven – Fort Hale Point, and Morris Cove beyond, and South End at the extremity. If the ram could grope her way there, crawl on the surface to lurk in some shadowed refuge, he might swim ashore and find his way back to the town and get out to the *Tecumseh* by sunrise.

But first they would have to come to the surface, find their bearings. He told Holland. They had been well over a quarter-hour under now, longer than the engine had ever been run underwater before and the discomfort was extreme, each breath an agony, heads aching, stomachs on the edge of nausea. At last the launch seemed distant enough to justify the risk of coming up.

The sequence was now familiar, the ballast blown, the upward lurch, the rocking that confirmed that they were on the surface. Dawlish hung his weight on the hatch as he released the securing dog but even so it almost lifted him as the air gushed out.

The lights on the eastern shore were well over a mile distant in isolated clusters. The city was well astern and the bows were headed for the open Sound. For all Dawlish knew the ram might have described one or more complete turns while submerged. He strained to locate the launch – and there she was, well over a mile to the north, foreshortened, cruising slowly, methodically, parallel to the shore. There was no indication that the ram had been spotted – she was virtually awash, it would have been unlikely – but there was every chance that Driscoll had reasoned as Dawlish had done and was now systematically patrolling along the shoreline, hoping for an interception.

"Let me come up for a moment." Holland levered himself past Dawlish, leaving the engine idling, and pushed his head out. The moon cast deep shadows over his gaunt face. His face glistened with sweat and he looked drained, close to collapse. But his voice betrayed no lack of resolution.

"We'll have to run-in submerged," he said. "We might surface once or twice to get out bearings, but they'll see us if we stay up."

And that meant running the compressor again – with all the racket that it would bring.

It seemed louder than before, the rattling and clanking issuing through the open hatch even as fresh air was sucked into the interior and pushed into the reservoirs fore and aft. By a mixture of ingenuity and trial and error, Dawlish reflected, Holland had solved the problems of sinking and rising under control, and even of steering underwater, but navigation and propulsion shortcomings still restricted his invention to the status of a curiosity. Feeding an air-hungry oil-engine from a reservoir of limited capacity was a solution that only a madman – and Holland was little short of that – could cope with.

"They've heard us." The Irishman scrambled down, heaved himself on to his saddle again. Dawlish took his place at the hatch.

The launch was swinging towards them, still almost a mile distant. The sooner the ram could be brought under, the more difficult her pursuers' task would be.

"Have we air enough?"

"We've never enough. But 'twill do, with the help of God and His Holy Mother."

They remained on the surface as long as possible, crawling towards what looked like an attractively dark shore that must be Morris Cove. Dawlish was unsure if ram had indeed been spotted. It was the noise that still seemed to betray her, judging by the sinuous course the launch seemed to take in her general direction, the helmsman obviously now swayed one way by the indications of the observers on her bow, then another.

"Prepare to dive, Mr. Holland." The searchers still six hundred yards away.

Dawlish swung himself down into the noise-filled darkness, secured the hatch. The growing familiarity of the sequence was comforting. He told himself that though the fear of confinement would not leave him – it gnawed like some foul parasite whose very presence was shaming – he could at least control it.

"The lowest revolutions, Mr. Holland, the very lowest."

With the compressor disengaged, and the engine barely turning over, it was hardly necessary for Dawlish to raise his voice. The launch's screw was audible now, somewhere to port. It grew steadily louder.

Minutes passed, dreadful as before as the searcher's beat rose in intensity, made worse still by blindness and ignorance. Nothing in Dawlish's career – over twenty years of routine punctuated by sudden violence – had compared with this passive, sightless waiting in smothering darkness. He found himself gripping something before him with an intensity that almost burst the blood through his wrists and realised it was the breech of Whitehead's pneumatic projector, the weapon that had brought him to this dark misery. It was useless now – there were no projectiles on board – and without it the ram was impotent. As the propeller-beat rose louder still he wanted desperately to be on the surface again, to be able to manoeuvre the ram stealthily, half-submerged, towards her tormentor and to hurl a dynamite-laden arrow to blast it to matchwood.

"They're past, Thank God."

And they were, and receding, obviously chasing some new chimera. The ram crept onwards, five, six, seven minutes, and still the dreadful swishing, churning beat did not return. Both men were short of breath again and the heat and oily vapours were bearable only because salvation, an open hatch, the night air gulped in the seclusion of a shadowed inlet, was minutes away.

"Prepare to rise, Mr. Holland." A feeling of liberation. "We must be…"

Suddenly Dawlish found himself flung against the bulkhead and Holland, thrown from his perch, impacting into him. All sensation of forward motion ended instantly.

"We're aground," Holland gasped. But though the engine was still panting evenly there was none of the grinding beneath the keel that had attended the previous brush against the bottom. "We're stuck," he added. "It must be muddy here."

"Can you free her?" Dawlish's terror was raging back.

"I did before. Twice before, off Communipaw." Holland did not sound unduly alarmed. "And 'twas after the second time I thought of the marker buoy." He struggled to his feet. "We'll shift the screw into reverse, Mr. Page and then I'll give her full power and you'll blow the ballast tank clear. With the help of God we'll be on the surface again before we know it."

Holland clambered back on his saddle and Dawlish groped for the horizontal reversing lever, almost flush with the deck. Gear teeth juddered as he dragged it across.

"Now Mr. Page, open the air valve two full turns." Air screamed from the reservoir to feed the Brayton while Holland opened the throttle slowly. As the revolutions increased the hull trembled. Even with the compressor engaged the engine had never been loaded like this. "Now blow the ballast."

The ram lurched, the stern rose and then stilled again, leaving the deck canted at perhaps fifteen degrees. The noise was deafening, the heat and fumes overpowering in the blackness, and bearings screeched and gears protested and vibrations racked the hull. And still no further movement.

Then, suddenly, a report like a pistol shot, followed by the clang of something lashing into the side plating. The Bratyon died and the silence was broken only by the scream of air jetting from the reservoir.

"What's that?" Dawlish felt despair rising.

"I think it's one of the valve rods," Holland sounded shocked for the first time. "The bloody things are weak, I know that. One went before, at the quayside."

"Can you repair it?"

"Not without a forge and a machine shop."

"What can we do now?"

"Close off that air valve, Mr. Page. We'll have to husband what we have."

Entombed.

The word rose unbidden in Dawlish's mind as he shut off the flow. His hands were shaking and he choked back vomit.

"Can't we shift her?"

"We can release the buoy," Holland said. "Somebody might see it. And if God wills it then the tide or the current might free us. We must be stuck in mud."

Dawlish groped above and to the left for the hand wheel that would release the buoy. Lodged in a vertical six-inch pipe closed off by a gate valve, the red and yellow-striped cylindrical marker sat above some ten fathoms of line. Holland had been proud of the innovation when he had explained it at East Egg – his assistants had located him twice when he had tested it. Dawlish had refrained from pointing out that they had known roughly where to look. Now he held his ear to the pipe as he cranked the wheel open and fancied that he heard air escape and water cascading in. A slight scraping sound followed but there was no way of knowing whether the buoy had floated free.

"What now, Mr. Holland?"

"Now we make our peace with our Maker, Mr. Page. We might be answering to him soon."

13

This was hell.

The air was already foul but it grew worse quickly. Holland squirmed beneath the engine to locate valving that allowed bleeding from the compartment into the exhaust, and that provided some immediate relief, but the knowledge that their span of life depended on the contents of the reservoirs fore and aft lay heavy and unspoken on both men.

Dawlish spoke at last. "What was the longest you've remained down?" He already knew the answer, yet wanted desperately, irrationally, for it to be different.

"Four and a half hours. Beside the quay, in the Morris Canal Little Basin. 'Twas a test. The engine wasn't running. And I believe medical men say we need less air if we keep still."

It grew cold surprisingly soon and Dawlish found himself shivering in his saturated clothing. His head ached and he tried not to think of the odds of anybody, a fisherman, a passing pilot boat perhaps, spotting the buoy, if indeed it had reached the surface. But there was little to invite curiosity. It might be a small boat mooring that had dragged and anyway daylight must still be three or four hours distant. By then they might be dead.

A potentially feasible method of escape had already failed. If the compartment could be flooded slowly to raise the pressure to that of the water outside then the hatch might be opened and they might get out. That Holland could not swim and that Dawlish would have to support him seemed a minor complication. They debated using air-pressure for the purpose but rejected it – any miscalculation and it would blast them out too violently. Only through the exhaust was such flooding possible. Holland wriggled beneath the engine to break a piping coupling but no hoped-for jet of water came spurting in. The exhaust's check valve was serving its purpose all too well, blocking all flow back into the ram from outside.

The only sound now was the click of Holland's rosary. He seemed composed, resigned even, yet he was assiduous in his instructions to bleed fresh air into the compartment while he vented the over-pressure through the exhaust.

"Don't let yourself drift off, Mr. Page." His throat and tongue must be as parched and swelled as Dawlish's, for his voice was a croak. "If we fall asleep we're finished and where there's life then maybe the Man above still has something in store for us."

They struck matches twice to view the pressure gauges. The flames guttered and died quickly but lasted long enough to tell of just over a hundred pounds pressure in the forward tank and almost twice that aft. They lapsed into silence again, each sunk in his own thoughts. Dawlish caught himself on the edge of an hallucination once – he was on horseback, and a pack was in full cry – and he struggled to his feet, ran his hands over the levers and gauges and engine, seeking some diversion from the thoughts of Florence that now tormented him. A will lodged with a Southsea solicitor would leave her comfortable. But if his fate was undetermined, if his body was never found, would it be valid? He could not imagine his new step-mother allowing anybody but his infant half-brother to have ultimate possession of the Shropshire farms he had inherited from his uncle. His father, an attorney himself, would contest the will with a relish that would give zest to his declining years. And Florence would know service again if she were not to starve.

"Mr. Page?" A hoarse whisper from Holland. "Do you hear something?"

Dawlish roused himself, pressed his head to the plating. The remote thumping was as welcome now as it had been feared previously, but it was distant, far distant, and the rhythm was different to the launch's swishing bite. Then he recognised the cadence. And hope died.

"It's a paddle steamer," he said. "One of the boats on the New York to Providence run."

He had seen them beating their way up the Sound, huge floating palaces, and he knew that they put in briefly at New Haven. It would have departed New York last evening. Dawn must be close. He peered through the thick glass ports in the superstructure. The dark above seemed lighter now, the slightest hint of grey, the promise of daylight. *Not that it matters,* a small voice told him, *down here it is night eternal.*

Dawlish lapsed into a cold, breathless half-stupor, aware that death was close now and regretting rather than fearing it. He tried to hold Florence's image, felt it slipping from him. He had no idea of how much time had passed before Holland prodded him gently.

"If I've offended you in any way, Mr. Page," he said, "I want to ask your forgiveness now."

Dawlish, touched, felt for his hand and shook it. "It's I who need yours, Mr. Holland," he said. "I fear that it was I who brought you to this pass."

"It's God's will and not yours, Mr. Page. And I wouldn't wish for better company at this moment."

"Even though I'm an Englishman?" Dawlish tried to laugh but produced only a rattle.

"It'll be all one soon enough. But I've read what medical men say about cases like ours. 'Twas always a possibility and I wanted to be prepared. It seems that at the end there can be a sort of madness, a frenzy for air, and that men can rage and tear each other like wild beasts. If it should come to that, I'll be glad if you'll know that it wouldn't be conscious will nor hatred, but just the poor weak flesh at the last extremity. Perhaps you could forgive it."

"As you'd understand and forgive me in your turn, Mr. Holland."

A little later, after they bled more air. The flow was weak now from the forward reservoir. Holland said "I believe you're a Protestant, Mr. Page."

"I am."

"But 'tis the same God we worship. It would be a great comfort if you were to recite the Lord's Prayer with me. I don't believe the textual differences will count for much at this time."

They whispered hoarsely through parched lips. Holland's missed out Dawlish's reference to *"the kingdom, the power and the glory"*, then lapsed again into a silence that lasted scarcely a minute. For reverberating weakly though the plating, distant still, but growing, was the slow beat of a screw. They listened, transfixed.

"It's not the launch," Dawlish said at last. "It's slower, larger, I think." He hesitated to pronounce the word *Tecumseh*, but he was almost certain of it.

It was close now, very close. Holland grasped a spanner and hammered on the side. Dawlish followed suit, great smashing clangs.

"Hold!" Holland panted. "Listen now."

Then pitch was changing, and the intensity falling again. The long, swishing beat decreased and soon was but a whisper again.

"Some coastal tramp." Dawlish found he was almost sobbing.

But the whisper never died completely. It hovered somewhere near, sometimes louder, sometimes weaker, slower now than when they had first heard it. At intervals they beat again on the plating, unsure whether the noise might carry, or whether any on that unseen vessel could hear it, but it was impossible, intolerable, to wait passively with human presence so near.

And then the screw came close, changed speed and pitch suddenly, then died. A low, dull boom followed and a series of short crackles.

"They've moored," Dawlish cried. "That was an anchor! I'll stake my life on it. They've seen the marker buoy!"

"God and His Blessed Mother be praised!"

Ears flattened against the plating, their discomfort was forgotten as each external sound was pounced upon and interpreted. And sounds there were, muffled, confusing, yet pregnant with hope for all that. They hammered regularly, the hull a great echoing chamber, then listened with rising frustration for some acknowledgement. A milky brightness had appeared outside the glass ports now – it was dawn up there in that precious freshness – but the water outside was turbid and opaque.

A single reverberating clang echoed through the compartment and both men jumped.

Hope blazed, yet Dawlish fought it down. Disappointment now, he feared, could snap his last tendons of self-control. "Did you do that Mr. Holland?" he shouted, but even as the Irishman denied it he was struggling up to push his face against the ports.

"There's something, somebody, out there!"

Something large loomed indistinctly through the murk, and for an instant there was a glimpse of a hand grasping a rope – the marker buoy's mooring surely – before swirling particles obscured it again. Then another clang, and the softer, scrabbling sounds that might have been a man groping along the curved deck.

Holland beat out four raps on the plating, and was answered by another resounding clank.

"He's going back up!"

A surging eddy of silt washed around the port and Dawlish fancied he saw bare feet and white-trousered legs kicking amidst it before all fell silent again.

"God be praised," Holland said. "They've found us,"

Who it might be they did not debate. Speech was an effort and with the excitement their breaths were shorter now, more painful.

"He's back!"

Dawlish felt a surge of relief and gratitude. It could only be Egdean. Nothing could keep him on the *Tecumseh's* deck if he suspected that the officer he had endured so much with was trapped beneath.

No clang on the hull this time, nothing visible through the drifting murk, and yet the confused mix of clawing, scraping, slithering sounds somewhere aft were undeniable. Holland clambered up to his seat over the engine and pressed his ear against the plating above.

"He's over the stern tank."

A clumping and thudding confirmed the words. It continued fifteen, eighteen seconds longer, and then there was a single dull blow, followed by silence.

"He's gone back up," Dawlish said. "He couldn't hold his breath any longer." But Egdean would not be giving up.

Two minutes later the swimmer was back, a shadow in the pale mist, enough to send particles surging past the glass. Again there was noise aft, low, impossible to interpret, but indicative of activity of some sort, more than mere observation. Dawlish silently counted out the seconds and reached thirty seven before a last dull thud confirmed the swimmer kicking himself again towards the surface. He returned three minutes later – the intervals were increasing, and he must be tiring – and they greeted him with sharp knocks on the plating, were answered by a single sharp rap.

He left them and this time did not return.

"What do you think, Mr. Pa...?" Holland's words were lost in a surging, swishing sound outside and the slow, by-now unmistakable beat of a screw biting water.

In one glorious instant of revelation Dawlish realised what was happening and he shouted "Hold tight!"

For two, three, seconds, shudders ran through the hull and the plating seemed to pant, then suddenly the entire vessel seemed to be leaping upwards, stern first. Dawlish grabbed for a handhold, missed it, and was hurled to the deck. An instant later he felt Holland pounding down on top of him, shouting in surprise, and then breaking into a fit of choking, panting laughter.

"We're up, Mr. Page!" he gasped. "Up into God's own light of day!"

A dull light had pervaded the compartment, little more than a twilight but enough to throw outlines and shadows. The glasses above were bright and beneath them the vessel lurched and rolled. Propeller noise still reverberated through the plating from outside, then it reduced and died, and the small craft's motion with it.

Holland struggled to his feet, reached upward for the hatch. "Hold me!" he cried. "The pressure's high enough to blow me out!"

Dawlish grasped him around the knees as he pounded at the securing dogs. Outside, something grated against the hull, followed by the unmistakable sound of feet thumping down on metal. And Dawlish knew already who was out there and his heart leapt in exultation and in love. Florence would never have abandoned the search, nor would Egdean have hesitated to dive down, again and again until his lungs burst, to secure a line on the vessel that entombed his beloved Commander. He had only one idea now, to enfold Florence in his arms, to pump the honest seaman's hand and disregard his inevitable protestations that his feat had been little more strenuous than a morning dip.

One last clang as the hatch, released, slammed over on to the deck. A gale of foul air blasted upwards and Dawlish found himself jerked off his feet as it clawed Holland unsuccessfully with it. Then it was past, and they were slumping down again. There was a disk of light above them, white, diffuse and milky, and they knew the air there would be cool and fresh and desirable above rubies.

"You first, Mr. Holland."

Dawlish pushed him up, but now there were voices there, and bare arms reaching in, dripping and brawny. The small Irishman disappeared through the access and then Dawlish groped after him, dazzled by the light, his head throbbing with pain, his breath deep and rasping, but his heart singing. Then he too felt hands on his shoulders and he too was hauled on to the sloping deck. He crouched on hands and knees, half-blinded, gulping in great, searing, delicious lungfuls, conscious of two sodden, trouser legs before him.

Dawlish looked up into a face he did not recognise, round and meaty, flushed with exertion, sandy hair plastered across it.

And despair filled him.

He looked around. Three figures, equally unknown, were ankle-deep on the curved deck, one of them hauling Holland to his

144

feet. A dinghy bobbed behind them, and beyond, half-lost in the mist that drifted across the still waters, lay the rust-streaked hull of a harbour tug he had never seen before. A thick manila hawser drooped from her stern and was lost from view but a glance at its direction told that it been used to drag the ram free from the mud. The panting, dripping man before him had somehow managed to thread the cable around the ram's propeller or rudder post.

A larger boat was moving across from the tug, oars rising and dipping. It bumped alongside and a tall figure jumped over.

"Commander Dawlish, is it not?" The hint of something else in the accent that had been unplaceable in Fiume was now all too recognisable as Irish.

Dawlish raised his eyes to meet those of Stephen Driscoll and recognised both anger and respect. A hand reached out. Dawlish took it and was pulled to his feet.

"Thank you." The words were involuntary.

"You're a very persistent man, Commander," Driscoll said. "I thought I recognised you the day we saw off the *Jeremiah Jessup*. Maybe Fentiman had the right idea after all for dealing with you."

"Your quarrel is with me, not with Mr. Holland." Dawlish found his voice was a croak, was ashamed lest it be interpreted as from fear. "He shouldn't suffer for this."

"My quarrel is with your whole damn country, Commander." Driscoll looked past Dawlish, spoke to the others. "Get them across. Quickly now, they're half dead. Then get a secure tow rigged."

Growls of hostility met them as they were half-lifted, half-pushed on to the tug. Figures in dishevelled evening dress or street clothes were mixed with jerseyed crewmembers.

"You're a Goddamn Judas, Holland!" A stout, balding man spat in his face and cuffed him about the head. Somebody pushed him from behind and he stumbled.

"And you're a bloody English bastard!"

Dawlish felt spittle on his own face, ducked to avoid a clumsily aimed fist.

"Stand back there, Lads!" Driscoll shouted. "Leave them be now! They're brave men if nothing else and we've need of Mr. Holland still. Leave them be, I said!"

They were pushed into the wheelhouse and Driscoll called for blankets and coffee. Moored on the tug's other side Dawlish recognised the steam-launch that had hunted them earlier. The mist was thinning and the cable that had dragged the ram to safety was already being attached to the towing shackle on her bows. Dawlish sipped the coffee gratefully, silently searching for options and finding none.

"You did well to find us," he said.

Driscoll shrugged. "Captain Keogh has worked this harbour for years and he had a good idea where the tide might carry a drifting object. It was lucky he was at the dinner last night and luckier still that we spotted your buoy – the mist was a lot thicker earlier – and 'twas lucky too that Mick Slattery has such a good pair of lungs and that he's such a determined man. But you've been bleeding, Commander. Do you need it seen to?" He pointed to the torn shirt.

"A dog did it. It's only a scratch," Dawlish said. The incident already seemed a lifetime away. "I'll survive it." He was loath to accept help beyond the blanket he clutched around him.

Driscoll turned to his pale, still-shivering compatriot. "I hope she's not damaged beyond repair, Mr. Holland? We'd take that very unkindly."

"A valve rod," Holland said. "Any decent blacksmith could fashion another one."

"A decent blacksmith will, and you'll be helping him, Mr. Holland. And then you'll be giving some teaching to a few of the boys – you always were a great man for the teaching – and then maybe we'll yet part as friends."

"And Mr. Page? You wouldn't be thinking of…" Behind his thick lenses Holland's eyes registered concern and alarm.

"So it's Mr. Page now, is it Commander?" Driscoll turned to him. "But you're a damned nuisance, whatever you're called, and you know a lot more than is good for you. So you're a problem for me now, Commander, that's what you are."

"If you're going to kill me, do it now and get it over with."

Driscoll sounded more thoughtful than vengeful. "We'll have to hold you for a bit," he said. "It will be uncomfortable for you until we have you settled but if you're sensible you'll make the best of it. So drink up your coffee now and we'll be on our way."

He gestured towards the steam-launch. Holland made to move also but he raised a hand to stop him. "Not you, Mr. Holland. You'll be staying on board here."

Before he left the wheelhouse Dawlish reached for the hand of the small bespectacled figure.

"Goodbye, Mr. Holland."

"God bless you, Mr. Page."

The launch pulled away, Dawlish settled in the cockpit with Driscoll and was covered by a pistol. The tug's screw was already churning and the towing bridle tautening to draw the ram in her wake. Her course was opposite to the launch's, away from New Haven. Within minutes she was lost in the drifting mist.

The sun broke through as they approached the city and began burning away the last of the haze. There was no sign now of the tug or of her charge, but far out on the wide, still waters Dawlish caught sight of a trim white hull surmounted by a buff funnel. It appeared to be crossing and re-crossing the harbour in methodical sweeps and he fancied that even at this distance he could make out a figure on the bridge who would demand that the search continued even after all hope was gone.

It was her love and her loyalty that made his failure so hard to bear.

14

The launch moored at a remote jetty on the eastern side of the harbour. The workers unloading two barges and a coastal schooner spared no glances for the small party that moved quickly towards a shed, part-office, part-store, at one end of the adjoining warehouse. There was no hope of escape. Beneath the blanket draped over his shoulders Dawlish's hands were tied behind his back and he was painfully conscious that the guard from Reynolds' foundry who walked beside him was itching to use the pistol he ground into his ribs.

"You killed my dog, you whore," he had hissed as they disembarked. "You murdered my poor Bran."

Dawlish was left alone with Driscoll – who held a pistol of his own on him – while the others were despatched to secure transportation.

"You're formidable as well as persistent, Commander," Driscoll said. "You made a few enemies that night in Manhattan and that was a respectable little force you unleashed last night. You damn nearly succeeded too. But I doubt if those fellows of yours have much loyalty to the Widow of Windsor. Would I be right there, Commander?'

"You know this idea of yours is insane." Dawlish ignored the question.

"It's war." Driscoll showed no animosity. "That's what your people never seem to understand and we'll fight it with whatever weapons are necessary. I probably dislike it even more than you do, Commander, but we're stuck with it, you and me, professionals both, and there's no sense in making something personal out of it." He glanced out the window. "That's Jamesey Ennis coming back with a cab now. He'll be taking you where you're going."

Ennis proved to be the dog-owner and Dawlish sensed that he and his companion, another raw-looking bruiser in workman's clothes, were gentle while they trussed him yet further only because Driscoll was present. They knotted a rag around his mouth as a gag, laid him on the floor, bound his feet and then bent his knees back to secure the rope-end to his wrists. He had never felt more helpless, more humiliated. Then Ennis produced a sack, a large hempen one, dusty with chaff.

"I'm sorry about this," Driscoll said, "but down in Virginia we found it the most effective way of getting certain gentlemen back to our lines. It's uncomfortable, and I hope you've got a strong bladder, but you'll be none the worse for it if you don't struggle. I'll say goodbye to you now, Commander, for I've got to be on my way myself."

They manhandled Dawlish into the sack and he did not resist, knowing it to be futile. He felt terror of darkness and suffocation rise within him as they drew the neck over his head and bound it closed. Dust prickled his nostrils and he sneezed helplessly and violently, then somehow composed himself to endure.

"Carry him carefully, boys," he heard Driscoll say as he was lifted. "I won't have him hurt."

Only now did he realise that the ram's choking interior had been but the anteroom to Hell.

*

When he finally came-to Dawlish reasoned that wherever Driscoll might be going his return to New Haven was not expected soon. Otherwise Ennis and his crony might have refrained from kicking him into oblivion.

They had lugged him not ungently into what he had assumed to be a cab. They left him undisturbed on its floor for what might have been anything between thirty minutes and an hour – it was impossible to judge time while he half-suffocated. The vehicle lumbered and swayed across cobbles, ruts and potholes. He tried to distance himself from his discomfort, to pick up some inkling of his whereabouts, but the snatches he did discern of street noise, hawkers' cries and, later, sounds of lowing cattle told him nothing.

Once arrived at some unknown destination they heaved him to the ground. The shock of landing on his back and the pain in his bound limbs all but made him black out. Then they began to kick, taking care nonetheless to avoid his head as he thrashed and wriggled. "And that's for Bran," he heard as a boot smashed into his side, "and that, and that, you bastard!" as another, and another, landed. Fighting for breath through air passages already clogged and prickly with dust, blind inside the thick sacking, incapable even of gasping in his agony, knowing he might not survive this pummelling, he wanted nothing but that it might cease. When at last it did, the kicking, though not the pain, he drifted into unconsciousness while they were dragging him, still trussed, across some smooth surface.

He struggled into wakefulness on a flagged floor, surrounded by warm, musty darkness. His face was uncovered, his mouth free and his limbs unbound and, by some miracle, unbroken. But there his blessings ended, for every breath told him that two, maybe more, ribs were fractured and every joint screamed as he explored his body, finding bruises at every point. His throat burned and he longed for water.

With infinite caution he raised himself on hands and knees, moaning involuntarily as the effort lanced pain through him. He crawled forward until he encountered a wall. His fingers detected dry brickwork. He edged to the right – three feet, then a corner, another three feet of wall, and there an empty, open-topped barrel that smelled of whale-oil, and a corner beyond, and then a blank wall eight long, its corner giving on to a wall containing a locked wooden door. It was a windowless cell some eight feet by seven, and making its circuit had brought him near collapse. He eased himself into a sitting position, rested his back against the wall – there was little comfort in that, but he feared the agony involved in lying down again – and tried to collect himself.

Driscoll must have left New Haven, the ram most likely also. The last sight of her as she disappeared into the mist in the tugboat's wake indicated that Reynolds' yard must now be judged too insecure a shelter for her. Dawlish dismissed as too obvious the possibility that he was now in that same yard himself. It was some reassurance that Driscoll had rejected cold-blooded murder for the second time but he wanted him out of the way nonetheless. There was no good reason why he should not rot here unless he stirred himself. He discovered new aches as he heaved himself to his feet and groped towards the door.

"Let me out of here! Let me out!" He beat on the rough planks, not in any expectation of release, but in hope that someone would appear and provide a clue to his circumstances. Nobody did, and the hollow reverberations seemed to confirm the emptiness of the building.

He lowered himself again, denying his growing despair, and concentrated his mind on an image of Florence happy and smiling at the *Germanic's* rail, and so drifted off again into comfortless but necessary sleep.

*

"He's alive, Jamesey."

One of his tormentors was bent over him, breath whiskey-laden, candle in hand. It gave illumination enough to show the other in the doorway, holding a pistol, and darkness beyond. It was night and he must have been at least twelve hours here.

"I want a blanket, and I want water." Dawlish heard his voice as a croak.

"The gentleman wants a blanket and water," Ennis's attempt at mimicking Dawlish's accent was a failure. "Is there anything else he'd like? A porterhouse steak and a glass of beer maybe?"

"Water will be sufficient." Dawlish levered himself to his feet and the nearer man stepped back from him. The candle flame threw deep shadows on his features but he looked marginally less venomous than Ennis.

"We can't let the man die of thirst, Jamesey, nor of hunger neither."

"Damn little his sort thought of hunger when it was our turn, Dan," Ennis said. "But go on, get him something."

Dan left.

"How long are you going to keep me here?"

"We'll worry about that, Mister. But long enough to knock that bloody British arrogance out of you. And there's two of the fellows who were hurt at Reynolds' last night who might be thinking of dropping by for a visit when they're out of bed again."

"I'll be tracked down, dead or alive. I'll be found. You must know that." It was a long shot, but Dawlish knew he had to sow some seed of doubt. "You'll do yourself no good by keeping me here."

151

Ennis laughed. "You think anybody gives a damn about you or that the commotion in town last night? It's forgotten already because there's bigger news. The president was shot today and that's all that interests any citizen of the nation tonight!"

"The president?"

"Mr. Garfield to you, Mister. Shot and wounded this morning in Washington."

"Was it some enemy…" Despite his own misery Dawlish found himself shocked – but then politics here were different to the polite verbal jousting of the Commons and anything seemed possible in this thrusting, profit-crazed society.

"Some madman, they say." For a brief instant Ennis was no longer the gaoler, but a casual acquaintance drawn into conversation.

And that familiarity might be of value.

Dan returned with a chipped delftware mug and a stale quarter-loaf. Dawlish forced himself not to slurp the water down before them, nor to gnaw the bread.

"Will Mr. Garfield live?" He was desperate to prolong the conversation.

"If prayers and beseechings are of any use then he'll live," Dan said. "Half New Haven and all the denominations are out tonight marching and thundering condemnation of the foul deed and drawing up addresses of sympathy and praying for the fallen hero's recovery. And if they voted for Hancock last fall then they're praying all the louder lest any man think them disloyal Americans."

The idea seemed to amuse Ennis. "I'm afraid you'll be missing it, My Dear Sir, though I think I'll be off now to see some of the fun."

"Enjoy yourself then, Mr. Ennis" Dawlish tried to sound as if he bore no grudge. "I won't be escaping tonight. But I'll need a bucket for slops. And something to close it off with."

"You see that barrel? Isn't it big enough for you?"

"A bucket would be easier for all of us. You'll be coming in here from time to time."

"I'll get him a bucket," Dan said.

When he returned Dan brought not only a rusty pail and a scrap of canvas to cover it, but three threadbare sacks as well. "Something to sleep on," he said Then they closed the door and consigned Dawlish once more to the warm darkness.

Short spells of sleep ended when agony brought on by involuntary movement shocked Dawlish into wakefulness. Memories from the last thirty-six hours tormented him before he lapsed again into comfortless drowsiness – the Mill River gauntlet, the claustrophobic horror within the ram and the slow approach of smothering death. But most of all the memory of failure and of the image of the distant *Tecumseh* so patiently searching the harbour, and of Florence on her bridge, patient and faithful as Penelope.

The night passed somehow, until a stripe of dull brightness beneath the door told that daylight had penetrated the recesses of this building, whatever, wherever it might be. He suddenly longed for that sunlight and resented the long day, perhaps days, maybe weeks, he must endure without it. He forced himself to his feet, began to pace and to stretch his aching limbs. He steeled himself against the pain that every breath brought and was sure that two ribs were broken. He hammered on the door, but brought no response, and once more he suspected that the building was deserted. He recognised the first stirrings of panic – the spectre of abandonment and starvation in this dark confinement were no less terrible than suffocation in the ram's maw – and for now he quelled it, though the fear did not go away.

The hours dragged by and the silence was oppression in itself.

He did not know how long or how often he slept and afterwards thirst tormented him again, for even here he could feel that the day must be a warm one. Sucking a button wrenched from his jacket gave little relief. His fingers now knew every inch of the door – its planks were solid and it was rigidly anchored – and, though he had felt every brick individually by now, none was loose. His gaolers could abandon him here with total confidence that he would still be here when, if, they returned. Always his own thoughts drifted back to Florence. The thought of the agony she must be going through was as terrible as his own discomfort, and he could not imagine how it might ever be relieved. And so, reluctantly, he would turn from her image and seek solace in recalling snatches of poetry, visualising Shropshire mornings, remembering boyhood days in Pau, reconstructing plots and scenes from Trollope and pacing the cell for the hundredth time, ignoring his bruises and aches.

It was dark when they returned and by then his thirst was intense. They must have known it, even felt uneasy about it, for Dan had brought an earthenware pitcher of water in addition to several thick slices of bread and a piece of sausage. They watched from the doorway as he drank and ate.

"How's the President?" Dawlish was glad of the neutral topic.

"Bad, they say. The newspapers is full of it."

"It would do you no harm to let me see a paper."

"D'ye hear him, Dan?" Ennis sneered. "The bloody Englishman thinks he's a cat!"

"You could let me have a candle. Just a stub."

The door's slam and the grating of two bolts were their answer.

Dawlish settled himself for another uncomfortable night. He slept better this time though his ribs were painful enough to wake him when he twisted on his sacking bed. In what he judged was early morning he roused himself and hammered on the door and shouted loudly. He continued for ten, fifteen minutes. There was a perverse pleasure in it, even if his sides were tender, for it was an assertion that he was unbeaten still. He got no response. It was as he suspected. He was alone in this building and his captors visited in the evening only. The thought gave him new hope. He had twenty three hours in the day to work on the door, to find and exploit some weakness.

He got to work, seeking any space, and chink, between door and frame. There was none. He sought a tool. Were he to break the pitcher his action would be detected and anyway the shards would be unlikely to make any impression on the hard, close-grained wood. He needed metal. His slop bucket had no handle. His pockets had been emptied when he was brought here but a single coin – a five-cent piece, he guessed from the size – had worked its way through a hole and was lodged between the jacket's fabric and lining. Given its size, it would take a century to abrade the slightest depression in the door.

Only the barrel offered promise and he examined it minutely. The lowest hoop's surface was rusted, and the wood beneath it shrivelled slightly, though it still seemed firmly locked in place. His fingers probed the two rivets that bound its ends together. They were firm and rigid – no hope there. But there was space enough round much of the circumference to insert the coin between hoop and stave to lever downwards. There was no detectable movement at first but he persisted. He pulled the barrel away from the wall and began working around it systematically, one push after another, edging around a quarter of an inch each time, until his thumbs were aching and several nails broken from the coin slipping. But at last he sensed a downwards shift of the hoop, an infinitesimally small shift, and it gave him vigour to continue.

He did not know how long he worked – time had no meaning in this darkness – but when at last he felt exhausted the hoop seemed to be shifting ever so slightly, a sixteenth of an inch, maybe even less, with each now-painful levering of the coin. Contented, he pushed the barrel back against the wall, slumped down on his sacking and slept sounder than before.

And so this day passed, the streak of daylight under the door giving the faintest illumination to his efforts. His fear of abandonment and, worst of all, of panic was less now that he had something to occupy him that gave hope, however tenuous, of escape. He worked as long as he dared. Now that he had water, and had come to know and accommodate his aches, the ignorance of time was not the least of his torments. At last, worn out, he stretched out to sleep while light still seeped under the door. He was convinced that by now he had shifted the entire hoop downwards by perhaps an eighth of an inch.

They found him sleeping.

"You're getting too damn comfortable here!" Dan smelled again of whiskey when he shook him. Ennis was once more in the doorway, pistol levelled. Another pitcher, bread, no sausage.

"I'll eat it later," Dawlish said, but he drank some water.

"The President's no better," Ennis volunteered. "There's a battalion of doctors attending him. And Mr. Arthur's in control now."

"The Vice-President?"

"A New Yorker. Some say he'll be glad if Garfield dies. He'll be President himself then."

They had noticed nothing. They left him and when he had eaten, and was sure the building was again deserted, he started work, reasonably confident that interruption was unlikely through the night. He kept going, with short breaks, until dawn showed beneath the door and by then the hoop was moved down a quarter of an inch. It seemed to have stuck fast however, for though the barrel tapered below, the hoop had now risen from the slight channel it made when it had shrunk itself into the staves. There would be nothing for it but to scrape down the wood below its lower rim. That job could wait until he was rested.

The next day passed, warmer and more uncomfortable than before. There must be a heat wave outside. Another man came with Ennis in the evening. Dawlish did not learn his name, but he spat into the pitcher when he handed it to him. This time there was a piece of bacon fat with the bread and the slop pail was removed, and brought back. "I never thought I'd live to carry an Englishman's dung," the newcomer said as he threw the empty bucket back to clatter on the floor. Darkness again, and the labour recommenced.

A night and a day passed shaving sliver after sliver from the barrel. Dawlish's fingers were raw and splinter-tortured now and when he rested it was largely to allow feeling to return to them. He worked in a crouch, so that his ribs and chest ached and breathing was often painful. But still he persisted. The name *Leonidas* flickered in his consciousness and he nurtured it. For he was not beaten yet, though the hoop was still stuck firmly.

Dan was back with Ennis that evening.

"You're a smoking man?" he asked suddenly, after they had discussed Garfield's condition – stable but no better.

Dawlish sensed they were as glad as he was of some topic unconnected with his incarceration. "I'm missing it, yes," he said.

Dan produced a single poor-quality cheroot and lit it for him. The pleasure was exquisite.

"You're too bloody soft, Dan," Ennis said. Not on this, not on any earlier visit, did his pistol's muzzle deviate from Dawlish's chest, yet his voice conveyed marginally less venom and contempt that before.

Dawlish savoured each draw. "I'm sorry about your dog," he said to Ennis. "I've got a dog myself, a tough brute, but I'd resent his loss also. But it was me or him."

"Bran was afraid of nothing," Ennis sounded wistful. "Even as a pup he'd take on twice his size."

"There's always one in the litter like that," Dawlish said. "Not always the biggest either."

"My father had one like that. In Kerry, it was," Dan chimed in. "A great dog for sheep."

Dawlish kept the conversation going so he could sneak unobtrusive glances towards the barrel. There was no sign of his efforts — he had gathered the microscopic wood shavings and dumped them inside it. The hoop looked more corroded than he had guessed and that gave hope that he might be able to expose a sharp edge by breaking it. When the cigar was finished they left him again and he resumed work.

That night saw his greatest progress so far. He had pared the wood down sufficiently for him to lever the hoop downwards by a full quarter of an inch over much of the circumference, a little more in places, before it jammed again. Another ridge held it, but below that point the barrel tapered sharply. Were he to surmount this obstacle the entire hoop would drop freely to the floor.

As he worked, he tried to imagine himself in Florence's — and perhaps more importantly, Raymond's — mind when the ram had disappeared. Florence would have pressed continuation of the search and the sheer force of her character was such that he did not doubt that Raymond and Swanson would have yielded to her. But a day's search, even if it had been supplemented by some hastily-rented vessel that could venture closer inshore than the *Tecumseh*, would have been enough to prove beyond reasonable doubt that the ram had disappeared. Florence would be distraught, but not hysterically, irrationally so. She would seek confirmation, from whatever source.

And the only source could be the Brotherhood.

Dawlish would not put it past her to seek out Driscoll personally, though Raymond would urge some more cautious and plausible course. That systematic, lucid criminal mind would be seeking other avenues. He too had a stake in this, protection of that position in British society he set such store by. Topcliffe's continuing favour could only be bought with definite information as to the ultimate fate of the Fenian Ram. The thought that Raymond and his network of criminals and informers might still be busy cheered Dawlish when he lay down to sleep soon before dawn.

It took all of his self-control to conserve his water through the hot day that followed. By what he estimated was late afternoon he guessed the hoop was ready to fall. There was no sense risking detection so close to success and he drowsed off on his heap of sacking until Ennis and Dan arrived. There was fatty bacon again, and a single shrivelled apple. The talk of dogs must have softened some hearts.

"You can have this," Ennis did not move from the doorway, but he threw something with his left hand. Dawlish bent and found a folded newspaper. "Give him that bit o' candle, Dan," Ennis said.

Dan fished in his pocket and produced a three-inch stub. He lit it.

"Don't put the place on fire now," Ennis said as they left.

Fearful of some trick, Dawlish waited ten minutes after their footsteps faded before he examined the barrel. He hungrily scanned the newspaper, the *New Haven Post*. It was two days old and creased and folded as if it had been lodged in a pocket. The news from Washington filled a quarter of it. The doctors still had not located the bullet lodged somewhere in Garfield's body and Mr. Arthur had the reins of government firmly in his grasp. Verbatim listings of loyal messages of sympathy and outrage occupied a quarter more. General Hancock's statement was gallant and generous and Brigadier Stephen Driscoll had spoken on behalf of the entire Irish community when he denounced the cowardly deed at a mass meeting in Boston. Of the tumult in New Haven almost a week before there was no mention and much of the remainder of the paper was occupied with trivial local news, advertisements, trade notices and shipping movements. A small item noted that the second dredger to be commissioned by the Isthmian Dredging Corporation was due to depart for Panama from the Stamford shipyard where it has been built. And the older citizens of New Haven were feeling the present heat intensely and ice was selling at a premium.

Dawlish turned from the news reluctantly, still hankering for assurance that a world still existed outside this foetid cell. But his candle was burning down rapidly and its light would allow faster work than by touch alone. He attacked the barrel again, the guttering flame permitting him to concentrate on the half-dozen spots where he could now see that slight swelling of the wood still restrained the hoop. He gouged the coin's edge like a chisel, pushing away a tiny fuzz with each stroke, abrading one obstacle after another. The pain in his hands, above all the aching of his thumbs and forefingers, now eclipsed all other discomforts, for a quick examination of his body by the candlelight had told him that most of his bruises were fading to purplish-brown. He had by now become adept at holding himself and breathing carefully so as to minimise the pain from his ribs.

A half-inch of candle remained when the hoop fell to the floor.

He lifted the barrel, drew the metal ring from beneath. One section seemed rustier than the rest and when he laid it vertically against the wall he located this portion uppermost. Thankful that they had left him his boots – stout, scuffed workmen's boots that had been part of the disguise Raymond provided – he stamped down. The hoop sprang away and clattered across the cell. He tried again. This time it bowed under the blow. He kept stamping, a dozen, fifteen times more, before it broke with a snap. He was left with a long, floppy strip of iron, rusty but sharp at either end. He shouted in delight and triumph. He had a tool at last.

The flame died as he examined the door. Its planking was old and granite-hard and no one point seemed to be weaker than another. He fixed on the bottom left-hand corner as his objective. He scraped the outlines of a rectangle, twelve inches off the floor horizontally, eighteen inches from the brickwork vertically. Then, in the warm, velvety darkness he began to sharpen one of the hoop ends against the flags below where the barrel normally stood. It took perhaps an hour, and he used his urine to cool the metal as he ground, but at the end of it he had a fair approximation to a chisel.

The real work could now commence.

15

Dawlish guessed now that his two captors must be employed somewhere – at Reynolds' foundry perhaps – and that they came to check his presence on their way home. The knowledge made him more confident about undertaking long working sessions through the night and early daylight hours. When he guessed the sun must be at its peak he carefully smeared the ever-deepening channel he was gouging with dirt from the floor, looped the hoop once more around the barrel, jamming it with wedges of newspaper, and settled himself to sleep.

Another five days passed and he was making progress, slow, but progress. From furtive glances stolen when talking to his captors – the topics extended now beyond the President's continuing agony and the merits of dogs each had owned to the rigours of the summer heat – he knew the door to be some two inches thick. Nowhere was the ragged trench he scooped even half so deep. He seemed to spend as much time re-sharpening his improvised chisel as he did using it. Yet the sight of the shreds of wood drifting down like snowflakes into the crack of light beneath the door heartened him. It might take another week, but if his efforts were not detected there was no reason why he should not find his way to freedom.

There was little enmity in their dealings now, even if Ennis never relaxed his guard. Dawlish complained of the heat – the foulness of his own body repelled him – and they brought more water, and a small enamel bowl and some soap, so that he could make an attempt at cleanliness. One evening Ennis did not come and, while Dan covered Dawlish with the pistol equally effectively, the man who had spat before handed him his food. This time he was

160

more restrained. Twice more there was a cigar, and once again an apple, but the greatest pleasure were the candle stubs that appeared infrequently, and dog-eared newspapers, and once *The Police Gazette*, lurid with mayhem and bloodshed, which Dawlish read as avidly as if it had been a Trollope.

"How long are you going to keep me here?" he asked one evening. Dan had given him a cigar, was smoking one of his own also. The mood was without rancour.

"A while yet." The answer he had expected.

"The Brigadier's a tough man, but not a hard one," Ennis volunteered from the doorway. "He said he didn't want you hurt. You'll be going somewhere better when it's ready."

"Better for you or better for me?" Dawlish tried to sound casual.

"More secure, but a bloody sight more comfortable for yourself."

And the attempt by Mr. Alexander Graham Bell, the inventor, to locate the bullet inside the President by a specially designed electromagnetic detector had failed.

"How could he hope to do such a thing?" Dan was bemused.

Dawlish explained in simple terms – the newspaper had outlined enough for him to deduce the principle involved – and both men seemed to understand.

"It's no surprise then that you got on so well with Mr. Holland." Ennis spoke with grudging respect. "You seem to be a bit of an engineer yourself. It's a pity you couldn't stick to that. You could be a decent man then, even if you're an Englishman."

It was the closest they might get to cordiality, Dawlish reflected, as he resumed his scraping after they had left. And it might earn him another cigar, and with luck a piece of bacon, or even an apple, twenty-four hours from now. For he would still be here then because it would still be days before the wooden rectangle would be weakened enough for him to kick open. But another fear began to haunt him, that he would be shifted to the new prison, more secure even if more comfortable, before he could break out. The thought that his labour thus far could be in vain was intolerable and he set to work with renewed energy.

He hardly slept in the next two days. The right-angled channel was now sufficiently deep to give hope that he might smash through. He lay on the ground and pounded both feet at it, like a horizontal pile driver. The effort drew gasps of pain – his ribs were still capable of inflicting agony – but he persisted, longing desperately for the sound of splintering wood. None came. He could only resume his slow, methodical shaving.

Detection all but came when he least expected it.

The strip of light was bright below the door and the temperature, already close to intolerable, was still rising. It could hardly yet be midday. He was bathed in sweat and was promising himself a break, and a mouthful of water, in another five minutes. Then, as he finished a long, dragging gouge and lifted the tool to make the next, he heard a door creak open at some distance, and the sound of voices, still remote, and the echo of footsteps. He scrabbled frantically to scoop dust from the floor and rub it into the freshly scored groove, then swept his hand across the accumulated shavings to scatter them evenly. There was no time to jam the hoop around the barrel – the voices and footsteps were ever closer – so he dropped it inside. Then he was down on the floor, stretched on his blanket, hoping that his heart might not be pounding loud enough to betray him.

The third man had come with Dan. Their visit was short, perfunctory, and neither gave attention to either the door or the floor, though the light streaming through showed Dawlish that his hasty attempts at disguising his labour had been ineffective in the extreme. He was already unkempt, for all his efforts to wash, and his clothing was engrained with the floor's dirt, and so the visitors saw nothing amiss in his sweat-soaked, grimy appearance.

"This will have to do you for a bit, so go easy on it," Dan said when the water was passed over.

"Will you not be coming tonight?"

"Just go easy on it."

And as he surmised, they did not come.

The groove was now well over an inch deep and he thought he might just break through that night. But the close-grained, age-hardened timber defeated him once more and when daylight came exhaustion claimed him. The heat was intense. The whole building must be like a brick oven and he was at its parched, baking core. Thirst woke him several times and he forced himself to be content with single mouthfuls of tepid water. His frustration was growing. Progress seemed slower by the day and as his loathing of the heat and dark grew, so too did new stirrings of the panic that had threatened to overwhelm him on his first day here. He found himself longing for the nightly visit by Ennis and Dan, for the brief snatches of inconsequential conversation, for the glimpse of a newspaper, for a candle's soft glow. When the longing grew unbearable he began to scrape again, tearing away yet one more sliver that would bring him closer to liberation.

The light had died when they came, not two, but three of them, and this time there was no water, no bacon or apple or bread, no *Police Gazette*.

"Lie on your face!" As always, Ennis was armed and blocking the door.

"What's wrong?" Dawlish fought to keep the fear from his voice, but the two others were advancing on him and one carried a bundle.

"Shut up and lie down. You won't be hurt if you don't struggle." Dan spoke with more regret than menace, but a knuckleduster armoured his right fist.

Dawlish was on his knees already but a shove from the third man sent him sprawling. He groaned as his ribs ground against the flags and his lung exploded in pain. He felt knees impacting on his back and coarse, scaly hands reaching for his and dragging them behind him.

"I've got him, Dan," he heard, "Bind them good and tight there. That's it, tight now!"

Tears started to his eyes and he repressed a sob, not from pain, though that was intense, but from disappointment. For he knew now that what he had feared was upon him, that he was being shifted to yet stricter confinement at the very moment when a splintering, crashing kick through the weakened door was imminent. His patience, his ingenuity, his relentless dedication had been for nothing.

"Lie easy now and don't be a hero," Dan told him. "If you're calm you'll be in your new quarters before you know it."

They were trussing his ankles now, then doubling his legs back and lashing feet and hands together. He fought to slow his breath, to brace him for the smothering horror to come.

"Open your mouth."

He forced himself not to retch as the filthy rag was drawn tight to lock his jaws open. Then they lifted him, pulling a sack around him, and the same dusty, prickling darkness as before enveloped him as they drew the neck closed above him and bound it tight. They turned him on his back and dragged him across the floor – it seemed a thousand times rougher now than before. They manoeuvred him through the doorway and along what he surmised what must be a passage, and then he was half-lifted, half-pulled, up five steps, a bump on each shooting agony though his chest and sides. They passed two doors – he heard keys chinking, locks turning and knocks triggering the drawing of bolts on the far side – but he could make nothing of the words exchanged, for sound was muffled for him. But there were more men than three now and even through the sacking he sensed that they had reached open air.

A rumble of wheels and the plod of hooves told of a vehicle coming closer. More indistinct instructions and then he was being hoisted from the ground.

"He's heavy, be Jasus!" a voice said close to his ear, "You're sure he's not a real dead weight, Jamesey?" and others laughed.

Then he was resting on a smooth surface that twice tilted slightly as other weights were added to his. A slamming door confirmed where he was – once more on the floor of a cab. An instant later it lurched into motion.

The only sounds were of the vehicle's movement. There was no rattle of steel tyres on cobbles, no noise of passers-by, no hint of other traffic. The road surface was uneven. Wherever they were, it was outside the city. Dawlish felt something nudged gently against his side, the toe of a boot, he surmised, enough to tell him that he was under guard. Ten minutes passed before the vehicle slowed to a halt.

"What's that, Dan?" Ennis's voice. "We're not there yet."

A body moving, the swish of a roller blind being raised.

"It's a cart," Dan said. It looks like it's lost a wheel. The whole bloody lane is blocked."

"I don't like it. Let me have a look." Ennis again. A pause. Then he said: "It's a woman. It's safe enough I think."

The driver seemed to be shouting something down to them and the vehicle lurched – another man coming down off the box, Dawlish guessed. Muffled conversation followed and then Ennis, closer by, said: "You go and help, Dan. I'll stay here to cover our friend."

Dawlish felt the floor tilt again. The door was opening – Dan was getting down – and then closing again. A minute passed, then another. He sensed Ennis moving to the window, craning out to follow the activity on the road ahead.

Suddenly there was a crash, and wood splintering, and Ennis was swearing and a pistol barked. Noise then from the opposite side, as if the door was being ripped from its hinges and a body was flinging itself into the interior. The vehicle was swaying wildly and a horse whinnied in shrill terror. Shouts and another gunshot, close, deafening, and all the more terrifying for the blindness in which Dawlish lay.

He felt feet stumbling across him, and then a body – no, two – sprawling across him, and himself writhing beneath them, and blows impacting against something soft, and then a single cry, suddenly cut off. Part of the weight was levering itself up but the other remained slumped across him. There were other sounds further away – one more gunshot, and a confusion of shouting and thuds, and then sudden silence.

A voice, homely, instantly recognisable. "Are you all right, Sir?"

He could answer only by beating his forehead against the unseen floor, but joy coursed through him. Now the load upon him was being drawn away and through the thick hemp he felt hands

165

close around his face, seeking the cords that held the sack's neck closed.

The cloth was drawn away, and in the dim interior Egdean's honest face was close to his, eyes shining in triumph, and beyond him, at the door, were the faces of Raymond and of Carter.

But Dawlish had eyes for none of them, only for the figure they were lifting into the vehicle, laughing and weeping simultaneously.

Florence, faithful and patient as Penelope, had just proved herself wiser than Minerva and braver than Bellona.

16

Florence cradled him to her as the carriage rattled over the cobbles towards the port.

"You're half-dead, my poor darling," she kept repeating. "What have they done to you?"

"You came for me, Florence." His voice broke. "You never gave up." He wanted to hold her tighter but was ashamed of his filth, his matted hair, his foul clothing. Yet he knew it did not matter to her.

"We've known for two days where you were." Raymond spoke from the seat opposite. The interior was dark, the blinds drawn, the vehicle a different one, larger, that had been kept in hiding in a cluster of trees a half-mile from the ambush site. Egdean was riding on the box with the driver.

"Money conquers everything. Especially patriotism," Raymond said. "Once Heimbach had identified which of Reynolds' workers had the sick baby, the invalid mother, the bastard-child his wife knew nothing of, it was easy enough to direct our funds where they'd do the most good."

"I'll never forget when Mr. Raymond told me he'd learned that that diving boat had not been sunk. That Mr. Holland and you were still..." Florence was fighting back tears.

"One of the gentlemen lying back there in the field helped us immensely," Raymond said. "He needed the cash badly. Carter gave him a sufficiently convincing black eye that none of his friends will suspect he was the traitor among them."

Four of them lay in that field – Ennis with his head bleeding, unconscious from the blows Egdean had dealt him, Dan, and the driver and one other, all dazed, bruised and tightly bound. The cab that had conveyed Dawlish, one side smashed in by the sledge-hammer that the ex-marine had wielded, had been pushed into a ditch and its horse turned loose. The wagon that had caused the obstruction, its wheel restored, was being driven away by Carter and Heimbach in the opposite direction.

"You were superb, Florence," Dawlish said. "You always were, always are."

She had played her part to perfection, the helpless farmer's wife distraught at the accident that had spilled her produce into the roadway. She had pleaded for help so convincingly that Dawlish's captors had been taken wholly by surprise and overwhelmed in under a minute. The shots they had loosed had been wild and wide, and the rescuers had sustained no injury.

"Where was I?" Dawlish asked.

"Five miles north of the city. An old mill, deserted," Raymond said. "We couldn't be sure how many of them there were. Once we learned you were to be moved it was safer to wait and to take you like we did."

Dawlish laughed despite his aching ribs. "There was nobody there. You could have walked in anytime."

A steam launch, another, not the *Putnam*, lay at a small pier on the docks' western fringe. Dawlish fell asleep in the cockpit even before it chugged out into the calm, moonlit waters.

*

The Long Island shore was a narrow streak and the sun a scarlet ball inching above it. Dawlish had not wanted to stay below after he had first woken and he was ashamed to admit it even to Florence. He dozed now under a rug in the open cockpit, his head slumped against her shoulder. He started into full consciousness at intervals, savoured the daylight and the freshness and dropped off again. It was not only the memory of his terror of darkness and confinement and near-suffocation that troubled him, but the awareness of a weakness he had never suspected, of a fear that had come close to unmanning him.

"How far now?"

"I can just see the house at East Egg." She stroked his temple. "Sleep now, Nick, there's time enough."

The *Tecumseh* lay at the jetty, pristine white. Raymond left them after they docked.

"There's more you need to know, Mr. Page," he said had said. "A lot more. But it'll wait until you've slept." He had changed on board the launch and in his immaculate linen suit and straw hat he was once again a discretely wealthy man of leisure enjoying a country retreat.

Before Dawlish and Florence had reached the house a matched pair was hastening Raymond towards the nearest telegraph office. Dawlish had dictated the single word, "*Tancred*", that would confirm that he was alive. Topcliffe had chosen it, the title of a novel by the wizened old genius, now months dead, who had so brilliantly steered Britain's course. It would flash to a modest private address somewhere in Washington and some unknown and unknowing messenger would carry it to the Embassy there. Within the hour Oswald, Lord Kegworth's son, the first secretary, would be relaying the news to London.

News of survival. And of failure.

"We're free now, aren't we Nick?" Florence said.

Dawlish was soaking in his bath, his euphoria at his liberation ebbing. The awareness of just how deep his failure had been oppressed him. Florence ignored his mood.

"We could perhaps see the Niagara Falls," she was saying. "They can't be that far, Nick, can they? And the St. Lawrence River and Quebec, where Wolfe fell – a hero, like yourself, Nicholas – no, don't shake your head." She frowned in a way that made him laugh, as it always did. "You're a hero even if you're not safe to let out alone, even if you do consort with ruffians and garrotters and I don't know what, and even if you did need me and Mr. Raymond and Jeremiah Egdean to save you in the end! And you're going to give Jerry something generous for it, aren't you, even if he is going to spend it on tracts and prayer meetings and soda water?"

He let her run on, unwilling to spoil her happiness. "We'll see, Florence," he told her as she towelled him dry. His ribs still gave him agony but he was now clean enough now not to rouse the suspicions of the doctor summoned from the village – no stranger to ministering to the ills, real or imaginary, of wealthy summer tenants – who waited below to see him.

"We can't plan anything yet," he said. "And once I'm strapped up I'll need to rest for a day or so."

Even as he drew her closer, and buried his face in her hair, and never wanted to leave her again, he thought of *Leonidas*, and her sleek lines and her ten six-inch breech-loaders and the five and a half thousand horsepower that would urge her four thousand three hundred tons in excess of sixteen knots.

She had slipped through his fingers with the ram.

*

He rose at midday, body refreshed, mind despondent. He immediately sought Raymond and found him sitting alone on the terrace.

"Where's the ram?"

"Somewhere on the high seas to the east of the Chesapeake, I'd guess." Raymond looked dejected.

"What the devil is it doing there?" The very unlikelihood of the answer gave it a horrible air of truth. Dawlish felt sick at the implications.

"Deck cargo on the *Hiram Metcalfe.*"

"The *Hiram Metcalfe?*"

"The IDC's second dredger. There are so many boilers and tanks and pipes and smokestacks on the damn thing that nobody is going to take any notice of one more black cylinder."

And suddenly it was obvious. Dawlish realised that he should have seen it back in his cell, that he should have recognised the news of this second, less spectacular, sailing as the perfect cover for spiriting the ram from American waters.

Raymond's weary tone told that he shared Dawlish's sense of failure. "The ram was loaded on board at Stamford a week ago. Driscoll had it towed there directly after he recovered it. The *Metcalfe* left two days later, up the Sound – past here, if we'd only known it – en route for Panama. And Holland is on board, willingly or otherwise."

"When did you find out?"

"Too late."

"She can't make Panama without intermediate coaling."

"We don't yet know where she'll coal. But some friends of mine are finding out."

Dawlish churned the news. The ram might be on the high seas, but on an unhandy carrier. It was inconceivable that a towed, wallowing dredger could provide permanent or even convenient cover. And Panama was too remote from main trade routes to serve as a long-term base. Driscoll's plan must be yet more complex.

"Does Topcliffe know?"

Raymond nodded. "By coded message, sent through our friend in Washington."

"And any word from Oswald himself?"

"He wired that he'll be here tomorrow. He also said that a separate message would be on the way for you." Raymond thrust a telegram into his hand, three pasted strips of jumbled letters. "Here it is. I waited at the post office for it."

Oswald had relayed a reply that the admiral had most likely encrypted himself.

Dawlish locked himself away. The code, a Playfair, was simple, but virtually unbreakable in a short message, and this looked less than twenty words. The key he had agreed with Topcliffe – *"Gelendzhik"* with the second "e" omitted – not only evoked memories of victory at an obscure Russian port but also had improbability and an unlikely letter sequence.

He took a pencil and pad, then rearranged the alphabet in a table of five rows and columns, starting with the key – the "i" did duty for both itself and "j" – before dividing the message itself into pairs of letters. The Playfair's beauty was that each letter was encoded differently each time it appeared, depending on its neighbour in the pair, so that in a short message there would be no obvious patterns. The decryption took less than two minutes. Even before he broke the continuous string of letters into individual words he had the gist.

"STAY PUT AWAIT LORD OSWALDS ARRIVAL AND INSTRUCTIONS YOU HAVE FULL DISCRETION REGARDING EXECUTION TOPCLIFFE"

He stared long at it, foreboding growing within him. The game was not played out, perhaps had not truly begun, and an ocean away the admiral was plotting his next move with cold, merciless cunning. And for himself *Leonidas* was perhaps not lost, but if he wanted her then he too must play his part in that remorseless contest. He burned the decoded message in an ashtray.

Florence deduced his discomfort from his uneasy silence over lunch. She took him aside afterwards and asked him directly. He told her that there would be a delay, perhaps a long one, before they could leave. It might have been easier had she reacted angrily. But instead she was sad, even hopeless.

"I won't stop you, Nick," she said. "But it's madness, whatever it is, and you know it. I've always known that you could be taken from me and when I thought you had been it was even worse than I had dreaded. And now it's starting again."

"But Topcliffe..." He stopped. His ambition seemed unworthy, selfish, in the face of her misery.

"I can bear it when the Navy calls you," she said. "But not this, not these criminal antics they'll disown you for when it suits them."

"Oswald will be here tomorrow." He thought it might divert her attention and he showed her the other, uncoded, telegram that Raymond had brought.

"So he's in it too! But he'll be far from any blame!" Her eyes flashed. "Master Ozzie's been shifting it to someone else ever since he was a boy. I saw it often enough. Servants see these things! The sly little toad! You'll be a fool, Nick, if you let him use you!"

But that was unavoidable, Dawlish knew, and he remembered her words the next day when a maid found him in the library and told him that a gentleman had arrived.

Uncomfortable, icy politeness pervaded the terrace where Florence dispensed tea to Raymond and the newcomer. Scarlet-faced, puffy and sweating heavily, Lord Kegworth's eldest son had the look of an obese turkey-cock encased in a linen suit two sizes too small.

"Mrs. Page has been looking after me handsomely." His words carried no conviction as he extended a flabby hand. Not even shared experiences when Russian armies had pressed on Istanbul had mellowed Oswald's resentment of his sister's elevation of her maid to the status of companion.

"My wife can be relied upon in any circumstances." Dawlish touched her hand. "She saved my life two days ago, Lord Oswald." He looked at her and saw pride and gratitude. "But then you may remember that I would not be here if she and another splendid lady had not saved mine once before."

"I imagine you'll want both tea and Lord Oswald's news, Nicholas," Florence said. "He's been appalling us with details of the tragedy in Washington. One does so grieve for Mrs. Garfield, does one not?"

They left her ten minutes later and gathered in the study.

"It's damnedly inconvenient having to rush here at this time," Oswald said. "Sir Edward, the Minister, that is, needs me badly. Condolences, letters of sympathy, enquiries about the President's state – amazing how that man just hangs on at death's door – and all that sort of thing, Dawlish. Or Page, I must call you, I suppose. You enjoy such childish subterfuge, don't you? I can assure you I was damn hard put to think up a reason for getting away."

"If we'd had advance notice of Mr. Garfield's misfortune we might have arranged things differently." Raymond's broad smile offered no offence.

"You've made a mess of this business, both of you." Oswald sounded personally aggrieved. "It seemed like a damn simple task to me and I can't for the life of me understand how you could let a gang of ignorant ruffians get the better of you."

"You'd have managed it better, I take it?" Dawlish knew it was stupid to let himself be provoked but he could not help it.

"Fellows like you, Dawlish, are trained to do this sort of thing. Not well enough, it appears, in your case. Because of you this damned underwater boat is now somewhere at sea."

"So a fellow like me will just have to find it and sink it? There are naval ships enough on the West Indies Station and a limited number of ports where the dredger and her tugs can put in to coal. It can't be too difficult to find her."

"It's not quite that simple, Dawlish. There are rather larger issues involved." Oswald's tone conveyed a weary acceptance that minds less subtle than his own might not comprehend such matters easily. "Issues of neutrality, Dawlish. This wretched dredger is sailing under American colours and the Isthmian Dredging Corporation has support from the most exalted levels of American society."

"Like Driscoll?"

"Like Hancock and certain Democratic interests. And if Garfield dies and Arthur – a weak man by the way – succeeds him, then the Democrats could supplant him at the next election and be the power in Washington three years from now. Her Majesty's Government can't afford to antagonise them."

"Then it sounds like we can all go home quietly." Raymond smiled innocently.

Oswald ignored him. "We just can't embarrass the Washington administration by confronting it with the facts and demanding the ram's removal, not at such a damned sensitive time. They might well brazen it out – freedom of navigation, sovereignty of the American flag, and the confounded Monroe Doctrine to boot. They'd have the press behind them. Driscoll and his cronies have substantial backing there."

"Admiral Topcliffe's telegram mentioned instructions."

"Oh they're quite straightforward, Dawlish," Oswald said, then stopped. "You're sure we can't be overheard?" He looked towards the open window.

Raymond stood up, walked to it, put his head out briefly and then said solemnly, "Not a single Fenian on the terrace, Lord Oswald. I reckon were safe enough to talk if we keep our voices down."

Oswald detected no irony. "No notes either, gentlemen!" He turned back to Dawlish. "You're to destroy this blasted Fenian Ram. Preferably without damaging the dredger, and more importantly, without embarrassment to any of the principal parties."

"Just like that?"

"Well, yes, Dawlish. Yes, that's the idea. You'll have Raymond's support of course, and the necessary funds. Just see it as a chance to redress your previous failure."

"Would you have any advice as to how to go about it?" Dawlish could not disguise his anger. He might have taken this from Topcliffe, but not from this glorified go-between.

"Don't presume on our acquaintance, Dawlish," Oswald's sneer told why Florence and a houseful of servants had despised him. "There's no need for sarcasm."

But Oswald was near-enough an irrelevance, Dawlish knew, unimportant except in so far as he might furnish information. Topcliffe had stressed that he himself had full discretion. He was under no illusion as to what that meant – he could take his own decisions but be confident to be disowned in the event of failure. Nor would success ever be referred to, however guardedly. Any promotion would be portrayed as appreciation of his efforts at HMS *Vernon*.

"You're game for this, Raymond?" Dawlish ignored Oswald.

The American shrugged. "Nothing's impossible, Mr. Page, when there's money to pay for it. There's a steam-yacht lying out there that crossed the Atlantic twice in the last three years and I reckon she's a lot faster than the *Metcalfe* and her tugs, so I don't see why we shouldn't be there ahead of them, wherever they're going. And if we are there, why, Mr. Page, I guess we should be able to think of something to satisfy the admiral."

"We'd better start planning then," Dawlish said.

But he did not know where to start.

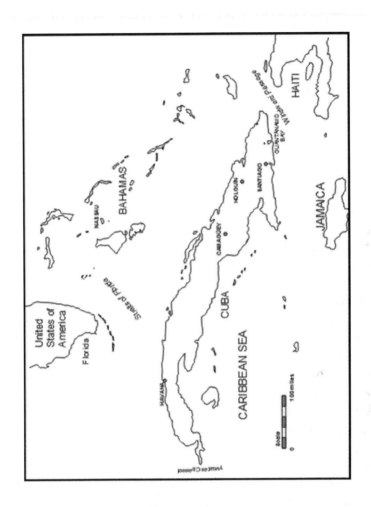

Cuba and the Carribean

17

They talked about it late into the night and got little further. Oswald had brought maps – the man was good for something, even if they were not maritime charts – and it was not difficult to identify the general route the dredger must follow initially, down the east coast, towards the Florida Straits, probably giving the Bahamas, a British possession, as wide a berth as possible.

But thereafter there were two possibilities routes into the Caribbean, and on the one chosen by the IDC would depend the coaling opportunities. The dredger must be boarded – that was unavoidable – but whether doing so at sea or while replenishing represented the better option would depend on the *Metcalfe's* route. And Raymond did not expect to know that for forty-eight hours. He had exchanged telegrams with a certain lady of his acquaintance who needed time to work on a certain gentleman.

But in the early morning hours, as sleep still eluded him, the solution burst on Dawlish like a revelation.

Fentiman!

Dawlish remembered Florence's horror when she had recognised the florid major across a crowded dining room, remembered the watery-blue eye that squinted down the sights of a revolver held to his own head, remembered the demand that he should kneel before him on a heaving deck.

Fentiman!

Topcliffe had dismissed him as a subordinate and transient player and had concentrated, rightly at the time, on the more subtle Driscoll. And the renegade major's whereabouts – Cuba – had not been significant while the Fenian Ram still nestled in a New Jersey basin and when there had been a reasonable expectation of cutting her out from there. But now the primitive, stealthy but potentially deadly weapon was on her way south, with Holland, under duress, perhaps training a crew for her. And Cuba was in the dredger's path and...

Dawlish struggled from bed. He gasped as he wrapped a dressing gown about him – the stabs of pain his ribs could inflict still surprised him. He hushed Florence back into sleep as she enquired drowsily where he was going and he set off down the corridor to hammer on Oswald's and Raymond's doors.

They gathered again in the study, bleary-eyed and yawning in a circle of soft lamplight, Oswald reluctant and sullen, Raymond already excited by the insight.

"Cuba?" he echoed. "It makes sense, Mr. Page. A long shot, maybe, but it makes sense."

"Topcliffe indicated he had an informant there." Dawlish said. "We need more details on Fentiman. Where is he exactly, what's he doing?" He turned to Oswald. "Can you manage the contacts with London? You can handle the coding?"

"I've normally got a clerk for that." Oswald sighed, then seemed to sense Dawlish's urgency. "But, very well, yes, I can do it, if you insist."

"Would you have any contacts in Cuba, Mr. Raymond?"

"Not directly. But I think I might know a gentleman who might have supplied certain items there during the insurgency."

"I need to know more. I know nothing about the place," Dawlish said.

Nothing except that it the last significant toehold of Spanish power in the Americas and that Madrid's grip was tenuous. Vicious civil war in Spain itself had ensured that there were never enough troops to suppress the Cuban revolts that seemed to drag on almost perpetually.

"It's quiet enough there now," Oswald said. "Spain signed a treaty with the rebels two years ago. But I doubt if much has changed in practice. The Spanish won't honour promises about reform if they can help it. I imagine the old enmities are far from burned out."

"There must be somebody in the embassy who can prepare an appreciation for you." Dawlish felt the joy of taking the initiative again. "Yes? Good! And then dry docks. Dry docks and floating docks."

"Dry docks?" Oswald looked bemused.

"Not just in Cuba. Anywhere within five hundred miles, United States, Haiti, Santo Domingo, Mexico, anywhere except a

177

British possession. I want to know the location of every dock capable of accepting steamers of a thousand tons and upwards and I want details of every job they've undertaken in the last three months."

"That's consular work, not diplomatic," Oswald protested.

"Then mobilise the consuls, Sir! They're all close to telegraphs, aren't they? And Mr. Raymond, I imagine you can assist in the matter? Yes? Then go ahead."

The sky was lightening and a long day lay before them. Dawlish went back to dress. He did not light the lamp, moved as silently as possible lest he disturb Florence.

"It's not finished then." Her voice sounded from the half-darkness.

He sensed that she had been awake while he was absent, hurt that he had not shared his worries with her.

"It's not finished, Florence."

"It's that thing, that awful underwater boat, that ram, you call it, isn't it? You'll promise me, Nick, that you'll never enter it again?"

"I won't need to. I'll just have to find it and destroy it."

"You're sure it won't destroy you? Destroy us?"

He had no answer, was silent, felt her tremble with anger. But at last he told her, not everything, not Cuba or Fentiman, but enough.

"It's ambition, Nick, isn't it? Is it worth so much?"

"Yes, Florence, it's ambition."

The admission seemed somehow shaming, yet he knew he wanted command and advancement almost as badly has he needed her, that he could not live without them.

She spoke at last. "I'll go with you, Nicholas – no, Nick, don't protest!" She pushed him from her so she could see his face in the growing light and so he could sense her resolution. "If the Navy sent you, even if it were to Hell itself, I'd willingly see you go alone. But this, this piracy, this insanity they'll disown you for, when you've nobody but Jerry Egdean and me myself whom you can trust, or who cares a jot for you, I hate it and I will not lose you to it!" She brushed her welling tears away impatiently. "If you're chasing that hideous machine again then I'll be there with you. I'm all you have Nick, and you're all that I have too, but I'll leave you now, this very day, if you say otherwise."

"You could be killed. Or worse." His spirit shrivelled at the recollection that he had once come close to putting a bullet in her brain to save her from the worse. "I can't allow it, Florence."

They argued, but she was adamant, her fists clenched, her eyes blazing. "I'll leave you, Nick! I could make a life here in America, I've seen that." Her ferocity left no doubt of her determination. "Nobody will care here that I've once been a lady's maid, and I can start again as one if it comes to it. I love you more than you can ever know but I'll sooner earn my bread in servitude here than see you throw your life away in a stupid escapade and deny me the right to stand by you."

She did not so much demolish his objections as ignore them.

Dawlish never agreed outright but by the time they descended for breakfast they both knew that it was settled and that she would come. On her fierce love and courage and intelligence he could rely to the death.

He only wished he could be as sure of himself.

*

The *Tecumseh* must head south immediately. Every hour she lay alongside the East Egg jetty was bringing the *Metcalfe* and her cargo closer to some unknown rendezvous. Information was essential but Dawlish knew it would be useless unless he could get there ahead of the *Metcalfe*, wherever "there" might be.

"Swanson will be game," Raymond had already spoken to the *Tecumseh's* captain.

"You're sure?" Dawlish asked. He was poring over a map of the eastern seaboard. "We're asking him to turn pirate."

The price could be high. Oswald had reminded him that afternoon how the Spanish authorities had detained an American vessel, the *Virginius*, in international waters off Jamaica eight years since. They had brought her to Cuba on a charge of gun-running to the rebels there. The captain's nationality had not saved him, and

179

despite all Washington's fulminations, he had been shot with fifty-two others.

"Swanson's a devoted husband and father," Raymond said. "He has an idiot daughter and a wife who has collapsed under the strain of looking after her. He's got no female relatives to care for them, a house that's too small and he's already borrowed money to pay for one nurse by day and another by night. Swanson's price won't be particularly high."

No higher than his scruples then. Raymond, no patriot himself, had hinted at Swanson's blockade running to the Confederacy. Dawlish felt an instinctive distrust of a man who had sought more lucrative and traitorous employment when the Union Navy had cried out in its hour of crisis for experienced seamen.

"And the crew, Mr. Raymond?" They had a list before them.

"Reliable enough until you get to Norfolk, Mr Page."

They had already agreed the Virginian port as the first objective. It was close to Washington, had good rail and telegraph connections and the brief visit of a rich English tourist's yacht would raise no suspicions. And it was four hundred miles closer to Cuba.

"I'll have some other men for you by then, reliable men, and we can pay most of these others off." Raymond gestured towards several of the names through which he had drawn a line. "I'd recommend you keep a few of the men we had that night at Reynolds'. Like Sam Eames for example, and Aaron Powell – they'd go to Hell and back if there was money in it for them. And Carter – he's good to have around. And not just like rough stuff, like that night. But delicate work too, if you need it, very accurate, very effective."

Dawlish looked bemused.

"If you'd mislaid the key of a safe, Mr. Page." Raymond smiled. "Or if you'd lost your bankbook. Carter's good with explosives."

While Raymond and Oswald busied themselves with drafting telegrams – the wires of the local post-office might well be burned out by evening, given the volume – Dawlish saw Swanson and confirmed that he was indeed game. An inspection confirmed that there was coal enough to make Norfolk and that the boiler and engine rooms would have done credit to one of Her Majesty's vessels. Swanson was competent – he would not have lasted ten years in the China trade otherwise. He had already taken the *Tecumseh* twice to the Cowes Regatta, where Raymond had first encountered him, and to cruise the Norwegian fjords for the banker who owned her and had afterwards tired enough of her to put her out to charter. But competence was not loyalty, and it was that quality above all that characterised the navy Dawlish had grown up in. In every extremity he had faced for that service he had relied on others' loyalty, and in his turn had been relied upon for his. But now he would be dependent on mercenaries pure and simple, criminal mercenaries most of them, and the prospect did not reassure. He returned, troubled, to his maps.

Cuba lay like a narrow, seven-hundred mile rampart across the dredger's southerly course. She might pass westwards, past the great harbour of Havana, then southwards into the Caribbean through the Yucatan Channel. Or she might head towards the Windward Passage that separated the great island from Haiti. In this direction lay major ports, Santiago de Cuba, Port-au-Prince, and a host of minor ones where the simultaneous presence of the dredger and of some innocuous merchantman would rouse no curiosity, where the ram's stealthy transfer to a vessel converted to receive and carry her unobserved might proceed with confidence. And southwards lay Jamaica, and beyond lay dozens of other islands and harbours to and from which British shipping carried valuable trade. A few ports might boast a half-rotten guardship, a converted pilot boat armed with a ten or twelve-pounder, the token navy of an unstable Central or South American republic, but the majority were unprotected. Once the ram and her carrier were united Driscoll would have scope aplenty for his furtive assault on British commerce.

Frustrated, Dawlish turned from the map. Until Fentiman's location was known further speculation was useless.

They gathered in the library before dinner, the last they would eat in this house. Raymond would return to New York in the morning. Telegrams had confirmed that contacts had been established with a Cuban revolutionary group and he might have to travel further south if they were to be followed up. For hard cash, or for arms, the group's co-operation might be forthcoming. Oswald's wires had alerted a dozen consuls but their replies as to shipyard activities would be directed to Washington, where he himself was headed by train on the morrow.

Dawlish had had a coded exchange of messages with London. His own had been brief, an assurance, more confident than he felt, that he was doing his damnedest. Topcliffe's had been briefer. Florence herself had taken it from the messenger who had ridden across with it from the post-office. He had seen that her hand and lip were trembling as he took the envelope from her.

"I knew it would be important to you, Nick," she said. "So I brought it myself."

He tore it open. The pasted strip carried a single word – NLDMALTK.

Even without reference to a Playfair table he could deduce its meaning.

LEONIDAS

His career still had a glimmer of hope.

*

"I guess it's time to go, Mr. Page." Raymond nodded towards the seamen busying themselves with the mooring lines. He reached out his hand. "If not in Norfolk, then we'll meet further south. With definite news, I trust."

Dawlish turned towards the gangplank, boarded and went to the bridge. Florence was there already, at Swanson's invitation, and the pressure of her hand as Dawlish joined them told that she was thrilled by the drama of the night sailing. Doubt about her presence stabbed him once more but he pushed it aside. Too late for second thoughts.

"A good night for departure," Swanson said.

Ragged clouds were drifting across the moon and the Sound's waters were dark. *Tecumseh's* leaving would draw no attention and she would have cleared Montauk Point and be over the horizon long before dawn.

The last line was cast loose. The yacht nudged away from the pier, leaving Raymond standing alone by the green light at its end. Oswald had not bothered to leave the house.

"Is it always like this, Nicholas?" Florence asked as the bows swung north-eastwards towards the beams of the rotating beams of the Montauk Point lighthouse at the island's extreme tip. "Is it always so exciting?"

It was, though he found it hard to explain the mixture of trepidation and challenge that coursed through him on every occasion since boyhood when he had set off towards some unknowable destiny. Nor could he tell why the feel of a deck beneath his feet and of a breeze against his face exhilarated him. Now they did so all the more keenly because he had by him the woman he loved and feared for.

There was a slight swell now and *Tecumseh* was swinging due east, with the lighthouse on the starboard beam and Block Island a dark mass on the horizon. Far short of it the yacht would bear south by west, paralleling the coast on the long haul to Norfolk.

And somewhere far ahead, wallowing astern of two massive tugs, the *Hiram Metcalfe* was also straining southwards, blithely unconscious of the stalker hurrying in her wake for an unexpected rendezvous at some unknown anchorage.

Part 2

Five Stripes
and
a Single Star

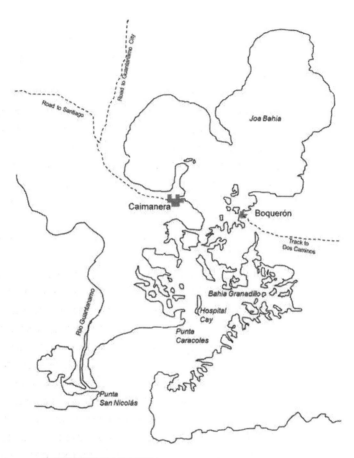

Road to Santiago

Road to Guantánamo City

Joa Bahia

Caimanera

Boquerón

Track to
Dos Caminos

Bahia Granadillo

Hospital
Cay

Punta
Caracoles

Rio Guantanamo

Punta
San Nicolás

CARRIBBEAN SEA

Guantanamo Bay 1881

18

"That's Cuba."

The man standing by Dawlish on the bridge spoke in Spanish and with what might have been halfway between a sigh and a growl of menace. His great black eyes were glistening.

"That's Cuba," he said again, "that's my country."

His use of the word *"patria"* told that he meant more than the geographical feature that lay as a thin green trace along the starboard horizon. Piled-up clouds obscured the mountains beyond.

"That's Punta Guarico. You know this area, Señor Machado?" Dawlish had found that his own Spanish had revived since Raymond had brought this heavy, muscular exile on board at St. Augustine in Florida.

"La Provincia Oriente," Machado said. "It was – it is – my home." His voice faltered.

Dawlish could feel this man's grief and anger even if he could not penetrate his reserve. Resentment and thirst for revenge seemed to consume him. This die-hard had never accepted the terms which had ended a decade of savage warfare between rebels and Spanish overlords two years before. Even during those endless and merciless campaigns the dark skin and crinkly hair that attested Machado's part-African ancestry had set him apart from Cuba's other revolutionary leaders – polished lawyers and academics of unblemished Hispanic ancestry – and he had never earned their full acceptance. Now he alone was the revolution, its living embodiment, the last leader untempted by promises of limited constitutional freedom under Spain. He was the untiring force that might urge the smouldering embers of resentment among the poor and dispossessed into another blaze of outright revolt.

"Another day, Señor, and you'll be home."

Dawlish regretted the hollowness of his words even as he uttered them. The next day and night would bring the *Tecumseh* sweeping southwards through the Windward Passage that divided Cuba and Haiti, and westwards towards her landfall, but Machado's home could only ever be a metaphorical one. A night of insane cruelty by a Spanish column five years before had seen to that and now it must seem real to him again as he stood, gripping the rail, his pock-marked face wet with tears.

It was on the resolution and guile of this angry, wounded man that Dawlish knew his own success would rest, on Machado's local knowledge, his contacts, his ability to evoke loyalty from a population cowed by reprisal and oppression. Dawlish had known him – or rather had hardly known him – for just a week and from tomorrow his dependence on him would be complete. But the die was cast and he had no alternative to relying on him. For a decision taken in Washington while he had pared at that iron-hard door in foetid darkness at New Haven had ruled out any possibility of boarding the dredger either at sea or in port.

Oswald had dropped the bombshell when he had arrived incognito at Norfolk shortly after the *Tecumseh* docked there. He had travelled from Washington wrapped in a white duster coat, face shaded by a broad-brimmed straw hat and eyes lost behind green spectacles. He demanded brandy, thrust a wadge of hand-written papers entitled *"State of Cuba"* at Dawlish and flung himself into the nearest armchair in the yacht's saloon.

"Arthur gave them a naval escort." His tone conveyed disgust.

Vice President Chester Arthur, now President in all but name, had proved more amenable to representations from the Isthmian directors than the still lingering but despaired-of Mr. Garfield might have been. Democrats the directors might be but with the presidency now only a feeble pulse away the Republican Arthur was in no mood to make enemies.

And yesterday, just before dusk, when Andros, the largest of the Bahamas, had lain unseen to port, and Cuba still far to the south, the evidence of the escort had been plain to see one point off the starboard bow.

Three long trails of smoke drifted above the horizon. The vessels beneath them were hull down across a calm sea – only the thinning plumes betrayed them – but their close, ordered spacing told that these were no tramps toiling independently towards the Windward Passage. Two heavy black columns marked the progress of the *Hiram Metcalfe's* tugs but a lighter wisp identified the USS *Kanawaha*, her furnaces and engines all but unloaded as she crawled in two-knot company. Her officers and men must already be all but berserk with boredom.

It was a measure of the United States Navy's third-class status that an obsolete double-ended side-wheeler gunboat was the best available for this service but her presence was enough to make the dredger inviolate. When he left East Egg Dawlish had vaguely envisaged a boarding operation, a bloodless one, a close reprise of Driscoll's exploit off Fiume, and there would be a satisfactory appropriateness were it to culminate in the ram's scuttling. The *Kanawaha's* presence had killed all hope of that.

Raymond had not been at Norfolk – "PROCEED TO SAINT AUGUSTINE FLORIDA STOP WILL JOIN YOU THERE," his telegram had read – but he did send a dozen capable-looking men to replace the seamen paid off there. *Tecumseh* re-coaled and continued south, leaving Oswald to scuttle back to embassy duties which he implied were both onerous and momentous. Dawlish could see no way to secure the ram's destruction. He could only plough doggedly, hopelessly, in her wake. Something had to turn up.

And that something was Julio Machado.

Raymond had located him among the penniless Cuban exiles in Tampa, brooding and plotting and dreaming among the cigar-makers and day-labourers whose contributions of single cents might someday raise enough to spark one more futile insurrection. Even after his associates had negotiated a peace of sorts Machado had fought on, the desperate leader of an ever-diminishing band, hunted without respite by mounted forces that all too often included ex-comrades eager to prove their rediscovered loyalty to Madrid. His fugitive group of peons and escaped slaves – for slavery was still legal in this outpost of Spanish civilisation – had somehow reached Cuba's northern coast. There they had commandeered a schooner to carry them to Florida to join the destitute refugees already congregated there. A year before, on the Rio San Joaquin, Dawlish had learned how men and women with nothing to lose – and Machado had less than nothing – could fight with a brutal intensity that was all the

189

more remorseless for its lack of an alternative. And, unlike in Paraguay, these people would be on his side. The shipment of five hundred Springfield rifles that Raymond had promised would guarantee that.

But the *Tecumseh* carried no firearms, no weapons other than the crew's knives. A search by Swanson and Dawlish personally before they had left St. Augustine had ensured that. There was every chance of examination by a Spanish patrol vessel and with the *Virginius* precedent in mind – and Florence on board – Dawlish was taking no chances.

Florence was happy when she briefly forgot her apprehension of what lay ahead. At such moments it was not her life as a privileged guest on this rich-man's plaything that enchanted her, nor the panelled stateroom, nor the lavish meals, nor her delight in learning elementary Spanish, but rather the very fact of being at sea.

"I've always known I had a rival, Nick," she had confided one evening as the sun set in an explosion of reds and pinks, "but I never knew she was so beautiful. I know now why you want so badly to return to her." Veiled against the sun, she spent hours on end on the bridge, entranced by crystal waters, dolphins, sharks and rays.

"You can't judge the sea by this," he told her, reluctant to shatter her illusions too soon. "Even now it could change within hours. This ship could be fighting for survival."

For the hurricane season was on them, and each day when the horizon did not darken, when the first flurries did not presage fury inconceivable, was a boon gratefully accepted. The Isthmian directors must have been desperate to secure shareholder confidence by starting work, Dawlish reflected, if they were prepared to gamble the *Metcalfe's* passage at this time. But caution would have cost five months, maybe longer, enough perhaps to scare the more nervous investors, trigger a collapse in share-price. Isthmian was gambling everything on the tracks of the year's hurricanes snaking clear of their slow leviathan.

"Captain Swanson says the *Tecumseh's* well capable of weathering any storm." Unlike Dawlish, Florence had managed to penetrate the quiet Yankee's reserve, even hear details of his daughter. "Is he correct, Nick?"

"He's right, Florence, and if he's not you'll still have me to take command," he said, smiling, "and I'll commission her on the spot as a Queen's ship and sail her safely through hell and high water!"

His confidence did not match his words, for uncertainty dominated the task ahead. Only the briefest of encrypted messages despatched by Topcliffe, and relayed by Oswald to St. Augustine, had identified Fentiman's whereabouts. From somewhere – in Spain, in the United States, or in a half-dozen locations in Central and South America – information from venal local officials and shipping agents and British consuls would have reached Topcliffe in London. The information would have been sifted, cross-checked and validated and if Topcliffe had endorsed the conclusion then it was almost certainly correct.

Examination of the charts had confirmed that Fentiman's location would be ideal for Driscoll's purpose. The secluded anchorage had been large and sheltered enough for a British fleet to have attempted to hold it during a war with Spain more than a century before. It offered every opportunity for coaling the dredger, her tugs and her escort – and for stealthy offloading of the ram and for its seclusion at a small sugar-export port. Afterwards the *Metcalfe* would crawl away towards Panama, and a week later the ram's carrier would arrive to collect her, like some marsupial mother seeking to tuck her child within her. Then the Brotherhood's furtive assault on British commerce could commence.

"If Machado has the support he claims," Raymond had said, "then he can deliver us the port without the rifles. What he does with them after he's received our shipment is his own affair. We'll be long gone by then."

"You're sure the carrier is ready to sail by now?" Dawlish had asked when Raymond had reappeared at St. Augustine, exhausted but triumphant after his criss-crossing by rail of the south-eastern states.

"Five hundred dollars sure, paid by myself to the yard foreman."

Raymond had seen the vessel briefly himself – she even had a name, the *Old Hickory* – when he had been smuggled in workman's clothing past the Brotherhood guards at the graving dock at Mobile, Alabama. Oswald had sufficiently overcome his aversion to consular work to produce a list of dry-docks and repair yards and Raymond's contacts and his own tireless persistence – and money – had done the rest. He had seen the rectangular gap cut in the twelve-hundred ton steamer's flank plating below the waterline to give access to the hold beyond. The pumps and piping for flooding and emptying the space were already installed and the watertight door that would seal it off lay on the dock's floor, ready for mounting. There could be little doubt that Isthmian funds rather than pittances of Irish road-menders and scullery-maids had made the conversion possible.

The *Old Hickory's* crew was already gathering in Mobile. Raymond had even drunk with some of them, tough Irish seamen and barge hands, war veterans among them, whose bitter memories extended back beyond the Union's endless blockade and thundering ironclads on the Mississippi to the despair of the Potato Famine and the horror of the coffin ships that had carried them westwards.

"Driscoll?" Dawlish asked. "Any news of Driscoll?"

"Only that he's not on the *Metcalfe*. Otherwise not a word, not that it means anything."

"But we can depend on it that he's not sitting still."

But now, as night fell and as Cuba's eastern extremity drew ever closer, that ruthless intelligence was not Dawlish's most immediate concern.

For when the sun next plunged he would be going ashore. Alone except for Machado.

*

Morning saw *Tecumseh* through the Windward Passage and heading westwards along Cuba's southern coast at reduced revolutions. There was time in hand before nightfall and, with encounters with Spanish patrols a real possibility, there was every necessity to play to the limit the role of millionaire's yacht on a summer cruise. Holystoned decks, soap-washed paintwork and gleaming brasses proclaimed a tycoon's darling. The crew was uniformly turned out in duck trousers and striped cotton shirts. Buttons glittered on Swanson's jacket and Raymond paced the deck in immaculate white, once more the assured man of wealth and breeding, the friend of the Prince of Wales, his part not so much assumed as lived. Florence, a vision in cream linen, never lovelier, her face and golden hair shielded from the sun by a lace parasol, counterfeited by her poise her claim on the owner no less than on the vessel. Raymond had slipped back into a familiar personality but her pretence – and it must be a long one – was just beginning.

Dawlish knew that she was frightened. He felt it when they sat beneath an awning in the afternoon, an incongruous pair, she exquisite, he already in the soiled and tattered cottons that would be his own disguise, rehearsing the plan for the last time. The stratagems that has seemed so subtle, so certain of success, when first discussed at St. Augustine and refined endlessly since, suddenly seemed insanely optimistic now that commitment was imminent. Florence was right to be frightened but he knew she would have died rather than admit it.

"I won't fail you, Nicholas."

In her voice he heard a trace, the slightest of hints, of that regional flatness of accent she so resented and which she had striven so assiduously to repress. Anxiety alone could have wrung it from her. He found it moving.

"You could never fail me," he said, "not as long as you draw breath." He would have held him to her were a seaman not swabbing the deck close by. Instead he lifted her hand to his lips.

At last he said: "You'll be guided by Mr. Raymond as if he were me. You promise it, Florence?" She nodded mutely, sadly. "It may mean leaving Cuba without me. He won't do so unless it's necessary – but if it is, you'll do it."

She was silent, looked away. He pressed her again, and at last she agreed, though he doubted her. But there was no time to discuss it further, for the light was fading fast and *Tecumseh* had edged closer inshore. On the bridge Machado was pointing out landmarks to

Swanson and presently the bows were swinging towards the landfall on the steep, green-shrouded coastline.

Night had fallen when the *Tecumseh* hove to, the coast a mile distant, the jagged Sierra del Convento beyond, a dark mass against the cloud-heavy sky. Two isolated pinpricks of light flickered to the east, towards Bahia Sabanalamar, humble shanties on the shoreline. There was no other sign of habitation. The boat was bobbing alongside, four seamen at the oars, Machado in the stern sheets and Egdean at the tiller – he had respectfully but firmly made it plain that he would trust nobody else to land his Commander safely. Dawlish shook hands with Swanson and Raymond. They stepped back to allow him a moment with Florence.

"I love you, Nicholas," she said as they broke their embrace.

"I love you too, Florence," he whispered. A sudden memory overwhelmed him of a time before, on an Ottoman ironclad in the Golden Horn, when they had also parted to face their separate dangers. Their love had been unspoken then, unacknowledged even to each other, and he did not know whether the pang was more dreadful now than had been then, for in the years since they had known joy and contentment together.

And then, as he heaved himself over the rail towards the ladder, and gasping at the stab of his still-unhealed ribs, she was disguising her concern by a mock frown to make him smile, as it always did, and calling: "Don't let me hear from Mr. Machado about you charming any Señoritas!"

He dropped into the boat and it pulled shoreward. The *Tecumseh's* pale bulk faded astern and he forced Florence from his mind, focussed on the nearing beach and the uncertainty beyond. Machado was at his side, as raggedly clad as himself, and Dawlish could sense his tenseness, his excitement as the land he had fled as a fugitive drew closer.

The keel grounded. Two seamen leaped out to drag the craft further up the beach.

"God bless you, Sir." Egdean helped Dawlish across the gunwale – his ribs were assuredly not mended – and handed him his rope-trussed bundle. "And don't you be worried about Mrs. Dawlish, Sir, not while I'm there to protect her!"

"Por aqui, Nicolás!" Machado was already disappearing into the darkness and his tone was peremptory, its harshness and informality announcing that here, on home soil, he was no longer the penniless dependent he had been through the voyage but rather Dawlish's equal and confederate.

"Vengo, Julio, vengo!" Dawlish called softly, lapsing into the tongue he must now think in even in his sleep. He hoped that the dialect he had picked up along that blood-fouled Paraguayan river was not so different from the local Spanish as to brand him an outsider. "Vengo!" he called again and hurried on down the beach after the dark figure striding ahead. Somewhere behind, the unseen boat was already stroking back towards the yacht, where Florence and Raymond would be turning their minds to the deception they must now carry off.

But Dawlish faced a masquerade of his own, his own identity abandoned. Poor, tattered and sandal-shod, his worldly possessions slung in a roll across his shoulder, Nicolás Quinones, labourer, whose mental capacities bordered on the feeble, plodded down the beach behind his more astute compañero Julio Paz.

A long trudge lay ahead if they were to find the track that would lead them by morning through the thickly forested coastal hills and towards the sugar country beyond. Already he could feel insects nipping at his bare ankles and sweat soaking his shirt. It was going to be a weary and comfortless night.

19

A few coins purchased a meagre meal and a few more bought shelter in a corner of a single-roomed thatched shack occupied by a man, his wife, his mother and his five children, all darker, more African, than Machado. It was one of a dozen huts that fringed a forest clearing that contained several untidy vegetable plots. The bedraggled travellers prompted no curiosity when they arrived, exhausted, shortly before midday. By then it had been raining for four hours.

The hut's floor was liquid mud and the grandmother and younger children occupied the single hammock slung diagonally across it. The others crouched on makeshift benches and watched the downpour with listless eyes. What possessions there were had been slung from the roof for protection from the ooze underfoot. A wood fire on a raised ledge near the open doorway did more to fill the interior with eye-smarting smoke than to boil the pot above it.

While Machado negotiated hospitality Dawlish hovered behind and tried to look blank. Machado dropped his voice, nodded towards him and tapped the side of his head discreetly. Dawlish caught the whispered assurance that he would be no danger to the children. He ate an unidentifiable paste from the bowl presented to him – his stomach recoiled from it, hungry as he was, but he was ashamed when he saw the children's huge eyes follow every mouthful longingly. Then, urged by a display of Machado's rough solicitude, he found the driest spot he could against one wall and slumped down to uncomfortable sleep. He drifted off to the sound of a baby's endless coughing.

It was late evening, dark, when he awoke, arms and ankles and face lumpy with itching bites. There were others in the hut, all with the same air of cowed misery as the owner. Their Spanish was a local patois, but just intelligible.

"Three years we have been here," one was saying to Machado. "We came here after the burning. We felled the trees, planted crops, thought that nobody would find us, that we might be left in peace."

"There were other groups like us," another said. "Over there, in the next valley," he waved vaguely, "and two in that beyond. But the Colonel ..."

"Colonel Almunia, the devil," the first interjected.

"I know of Almunia." Machado's tone was infinitely cold.

"Almunia, he fell on them with his horsemen. They hanged some and beat the others and drove them back to the plantation."

"Esclavos," Machado murmured to Dawlish in an undertone.

The word was explanation enough. Fugitive slaves who had fled to the hills when their sugar plantation had been burned during the insurrection. The rebels' tactics had been to wreck the economic

196

foundation of Spain's presence and they had turned much of the Eastern provinces' sugar plantations into a charred desert. "We fought with a machete in one hand and a torch in another," Machado had told Dawlish when they first met.

"They'll take us too. Our turn will come." The hut's owner spoke with miserable certainty and half a dozen heads nodded in despondent agreement. "With these we cannot outrun the horsemen." His sweeping gesture took in the women, the rickety children, the still-coughing baby. "They say the plantations are thriving again, need much labour – our labour. How can we escape it any longer?"

Dawlish felt angry as he listened. He had seen slaves before – had liberated them from the foetid holds of dhows off Zanzibar – and yet, he had to admit, the barrier of language had somehow made them seem a different species. But now a shared tongue revealed the people in this hut as intelligent beings, as rational as himself, as resentful of subjugation, as capable of affection. No barbaric Arab slaver was responsible for this oppression but a Western European nation which aped the manners of civilisation. And he felt shame also, stung by the memory that a year before he had helped condemn people like these to similar servitude on Paraguay's Rio San Joaquin, people who had briefly tasted freedom of a sort and who had fought to the death to retain it.. It would have been little comfort to them that he had refused the shares and the honorarium...

"It's hard, my friends." Machado feigned even greater hopelessness than his hearers. "But we must eat and we must live. As for myself – and for poor Nicolás – we have no choice. We're free men both, but our case is no better than yours. We must seek work if our little ones are not to starve. They say there is work at Boquerón, that as the plantations thrive again they need men to load sugar on the ships that come there."

Dawlish nodded slowly and solemnly in support, hoping he looked sufficiently stupid.

"There's paid work enough at Boquerón," said one of the men, "but it may be harder than on any plantation. They say the stranger there makes Colonel Almunia seem like an angel."

197

And that was all they knew, not even a name, for their information was based on scraps picked up from passing fugitives, yet it was enough to make Dawlish's heart beat faster, an indication that Topcliffe's intelligence must be correct.

They travelled again by night, guided for the first four hours by one of the slaves. The rain had stopped and the thicket about them steamed. The track's mud underfoot sucked at their feet and made the going slow and exhausting. Dawlish, slower than his companion – and feeling humiliated by the fact – set the pace. His feet, cosseted by years of socks and boots, were already cut and bleeding and his half-restored ribs ached ever worse as the night wore on. But there was nothing for it but to press on doggedly, to rest five minutes in every thirty, to ignore the insects and to watch in the moonlight for the exposed roots that might spell a trip and a sprain.

Dawlish tried to ignore the concern for Florence that had tormented him since they had parted, telling himself repeatedly that she was capable of the task she had so willingly accepted. The *Tecumseh* would have reached the port of Santiago to the west by now, would perhaps be moored in the outer harbour, would have undergone port inspection. Florence and Raymond – man and wife as far as the authorities there were concerned – might already have made their first sight-seeing venture ashore, millionaire tourists who would certainly be so entranced by the city as to wish to extend their visit there. Tomorrow there would be courtesy calls on the mayor, the military governor, invitations to the commanders of any Spanish naval vessels in harbour to visit the yacht.

And the charade must continue until… until Machado made good on the promise he had made about Boquerón.

By midnight they had passed into more open country and their guide left them. They skirted badly tended patches of yucca, saw several isolated huts, found their way to a wider track, one Machado recognised, and plodded westwards under a full moon. Most of the terrain was clothed in low, tangled vegetation.

"There was cane when I was last here," Machado said as they rested. "Sugar cane as far as you could see, and when we set it alight it was like a torrent of flame cleansing the land. And over there," his

198

voice was dreamy with recollected pleasure as he pointed, "over there, near Yateritas, we surrounded an entire column – twenty four men. It was two days before they surrendered and by then there were just ten left."

"And then?" Dawlish dreaded the answer.

"The machete and the rope and the knife, Nicolás. The only arguments the Spanish understand."

"This Almunia they spoke of. You said you know him."

"I know him," Machado's tone conveyed that the conversation, and the break, was ended.

Soon afterwards they encountered softly-rustling cane, already higher than themselves in this wet growing season. It walled the track on either side. The sky ahead had a reddish, flickering glow.

"The *ingenio*, the mill at Tres Caminos." Machado sounded bitter. "They have rebuilt it."

Furnaces fed with waste cane-fibre were powering crushers and boilers, transforming the last of the previous crop into syrup and raw sugar and molasses. The work would be hot, dangerous and endless but the restoration of Spanish power had ensured there would be no shortage of labour.

"This sugar will go to Boquerón?" Dawlish asked.

Machado nodded. "From here, from Hatuey," he gestured to a fainter glow further east, "from Rincón and San Juancito, all will go to Boquerón."

They pressed on until the first shanties fringing the ingenio came into sight and the low rumble of its machinery was audible. Now the undertakings that Machado had so earnestly given in St. Augustine must be put to the test. He had been confident – vehement – that resistance still smouldered beneath the Spanish heel, that swarms of loyal supporters only awaited his return to rise in yet another revolt.

"If I don't return by daybreak, Nicolás ..." His words trailed off.

Dawlish understood. The outlook for himself – alone and stranded – would be bad. For Machado it would be infinitely worse. He watched the Cuban trudge down the track towards the hovels, then withdrew into the cane and crouched down to snatch three hours of insect-troubled sleep.

*

The eastern sky was reddening when Machado returned, smiling for the first time since Dawlish had met him.

"Polycarpio Diaz is still there – a good man – and his cousin Diego, and Tarquino Serrano, all still defiant, even if they must toil like mules for Almunia and his vultures! *Cuba Libre,* Free Cuba, still lives, Nicolás!" He opened a small sack, produced cold cooked-yucca, bananas, a bottle of water and another of white rum. "What little they have they are proud to share."

"And passes, Julio?" The stealthy visit to the ingenio had not been to seek food.

"Tarquino has not lost his talent." Machado pulled two already creased and sweat-stained scraps of paper from inside his shirt.

Dawlish examined them by the growing daylight. Teniente Rafael Tosta, commander of the garrison at Jauco – forty miles to the east – had authorised Julio Paz and Nicolás Quinones to travel from their place of birth to seek work at Boquerón, attested their status as free men, not slaves, and confirmed that each had taken an oath of allegiance to His Most Catholic Majesty Alfonso XII. The signature straggled across a medallion stamped in purple ink. The exterior surfaces were dust-grimed and the edges frayed. To Dawlish's untrained eye it looked like a competent forgery but he wondered if it would fool any official. Machado seemed to sense his doubt.

"He makes few, and only when they're essential," he said. "Too many and there might be suspicion."

They moved on to the track again, in daylight now. They plodded through the village, looking neither left nor right, like men dourly, wearily resigned to an unwelcome journey, every step an agony for Dawlish on his lacerated feet. They ignored the increasing signs of life and the sentries slouching before the three sand-bagged blockhouses that accommodated the local garrison. They joined another track, a larger one, that led directly westwards through the high cane and found themselves overtaking a ragged procession of carts laden with casks of rough brown sugar.

"How far to Boquerón, amigo?" The question was addressed to a driver. Machado knew the answer but the bewildered rustic far from home whom he impersonated would not.

"A half day and longer for you. Longer still for your friend." The teamster looked with pity towards Dawlish's bloody feet.

"Perhaps he can ride with you a little then? He is..." Again Machado tapped his head meaningfully.

Dawlish looked up with what he hoped was an air of benign idiocy. "Por Dios, Señor," he whined, "Por Dios y su Madre."

"Por Dios," said the driver and Dawlish scrambled up behind him, snivelling thanks.

The sun was unmerciful now, though thunderheads gathered to the south. A cloud of flies buzzed and hovered around the sweet-smelling, unsprung ox-cart. For all its jolting Dawlish still drifted into a doze. He woke fitfully several times to see Machado still trudging alongside, another half-dozen carts ahead and the endless cane still extending across the plain.

The sound of hoof beats shocked him into wakefulness. Half-dazzled, he blinked as a score of horsemen came trotting from behind, their leaders gesturing the carts to pull over. The riders were clad in light cotton uniforms – white with thin blue pin-stripes – with dusty leather boots, canvas bandoliers and broad-brimmed straw hats, lean, mahogany-brown men whose seats indicated that they lived in the saddle.

"Get down! Be ready for inspection!" A sergeant was pacing his mount back and forth along the convoy.

Dawlish slid down with the driver, meekly joining the line of teamsters and helpers who were uneasily removing their hats and casting their eyes down, each more abjectly humble than the next. Machado was three places from him, head bowed. Several riders had dismounted but the remainder held carbines at the ready, some passing down the other side of the carts to block off the rear. Full packs and saddlebags confirmed that they were engaged in some mission longer than a local patrol.

The silence was broken only by the abrupt demands of the troopers working down the line. Once there was shouting, the sound of a blow and a whimpered apology, as somebody failed to produce his papers quickly enough, but neither Dawlish nor the others dared glance sideways. Sweat ran down his face, fear knotted in his stomach and his heart pounded as a trooper approached, hastily scanning documents and thrusting them back to their owners. He was suddenly conscious of the chirping of the crickets in the cane and wondered if it would be the last thing he remembered. And then it was his turn and his hands were shaking as he extended his pass. He glanced briefly into a leathery, moustachioed face and dark pitiless eyes, then dropped his gaze again.

"Buascas trabajo?" It sounded like an accusation.

"Si Señor. Mi mujer esta enferma y mis hijos…" The story was carefully rehearsed but the quaver in his voice was involuntary.

The soldier did not seem to hear, was holding the tattered paper up towards the light, seemed uncertain. "Wait," he said, unnecessarily, and he left to seek the sergeant.

Dawlish was trembling now and feared his bladder would loosen. His bloody feet suddenly seemed swollen and incongruous enough to attract the attention of the whole column. He fingered his hat, sensed the unease of the men to either side, glanced up to see if there was any vain hope of escape into the surrounding cane. A wall of horseflesh confronted him, the riders alert. Beyond them he glimpsed two mules with bodies lashed across them, the feet of one stirring weakly. The sight terrified him and he dropped his eyes again. He realised that the others in the line were as frightened as he was.

The trooper was returning, alone. He thrust the pass back to Dawlish without comment, took that of the man to his left, was satisfied and passed on. Dawlish felt relief wash through him briefly before concern for his companion replaced it. Now it was Machado's turn, but his document seemed satisfactory. "Un otro de Jauco, buscando trabajo," the trooper commented. Machado made some rejoinder that made him laugh and he passed on.

And so the inspection finished, the column of riders reforming and disappearing down the track towards Boquerón and leaving the carts to plod on wearily in their wake.

The sun blazed down. Dawlish dozed once more on his jolting perch, shocked into horrified wakefulness at intervals by the memory of twitching feet hanging from the two bundles he had seen disappearing westward on muleback with the horsemen.

*

The countryside was changing, the cane dying abruptly, replaced by scrub which in turn yielded to arid flats mottled with cactus. In late afternoon the convoy reached a knot of huts clustered around a well. A single creaking windmill raised water to troughs where the oxen might drink. Here the exhausted beasts would be rested for the night.

"You see the bay now, Nicolás?" Machado was slaking his thirst while Dawlish bathed his feet. A vee of water shimmered in the distance, just visible in the fold between two gentle slopes.

"How far?"

"Eight, ten miles. We could be there tonight were it not for your feet."

"We'll be there tonight," Dawlish said.

There was a spare shirt in his roll. Cut in strips, it might offer his feet some comfort. If it did not, then he must endure anyway. The memory of those columns of smoke crawling relentlessly onwards at two knots drove him. It was imperative that he arrive at the bay before they did.

They left the carts behind, made faster progress westwards in the two hours before darkness than they might have hoped. The rags protected Dawlish's feet them better than he had expected. The sun was sinking as the falling terrain exposed the full expanse of the island-littered bay and all its sub-inlets for the first time.

"That's Bahia Granadillo straight ahead," Machado said, "and there, extending to the south, that's the outer bay."

"And Boquerón?"

"We should see it soon." Machado pointed north-eastwards. "On this side of those narrows. There's Caimanera on the other side and that's Joa Bay to the north."

Dawlish could just discern the untidy collection of buildings and wharves that was Caimanera, the small port through which the sugar from the rich lands west of the bay and north as far as the town of Guantanamo was exported. But there was no mistaking the great, open expanse of Joa Bay, a huge shallow expanse fringed with salt-pans on its southern shore. But it was further south that Dawlish's attention was drawn, towards the great sweep of deep water that led to the open sea. He had memorised the chart on board the *Tecumseh*, well enough to identify Punta Caracoles on the distant shore and San Nicolás further seawards, and the island identified as Hospital Cay since Admiral Vernon had landed his sick there in 1741. For a few brief months before fever had forced retreat, this magnificent natural harbour had been known as Cumberland Bay. It had been the base for a thrust by British troops that had taken Guantanamo and that had been stopped just short of Santiago. It was in this outer bay that the *Hiram Metcalfe's* tugs would replenish their bunkers and where – he was sure of it – the ram would be eased stealthily into the water under cover of darkness.

Night fell and the last miles were made miserable by rain, a deluge illuminated by almost continuous lightning. What had been parched semi-desert was now a boiling sheet of water that raced and gurgled seawards through millions of self-torn channels and gullies. There was no shelter, and the track was invisible. The two bedraggled figures could only stumble onwards towards the dim, winking lights that identified Boquerón. Their shoulders were raw from the torrent's pounding and the rags protecting Dawlish's feet were now an abrading torture, but somehow they plodded on, cold and shivering, intent only on the next step and then on the next again. So, somehow, the lights drew steadily closer.

They gained Boquerón around midnight. There was no challenge to their entry among the squalid clump of shanties on the outskirts, only the sound of water beating dully on thatch roofs, and drumming more loudly on corrugated metal ones further on, and flowing ankle-deep through what passed as the few streets that constituted the village. The continuing lighting eased their search for the hut that Machado's contacts in Dos Caminos had identified as housing a sympathiser. It looked like any of a hundred others, a shack smaller than Florence's drawing room in Southsea. Dawlish crouched in the shadows while Machado knocked at the single dark, wooden-shuttered window.

When they gained entrance the atmosphere was sour with the sweat of a perhaps a dozen sleepers, women, children, an old man, somehow crowded in hammocks or on benches. The owner, Ambrosio, hushed those who stirred into slumber again and then lit a single candle. His worn face creased into a smile as Machado's features were revealed.

"Can it indeed be you, Don Julio?" he said. "Are you with us again, as you promised?"

"I could never forget you. Or the others. Or Cuba." Machado said. At another time and place it might have sounded sententious, but here, from this ragged, exhausted man, Dawlish found himself moved by it.

"Is there hope for us this time, Jefe?" Ambrosio's form of address – Chief – conveyed affection as well as respect.

"For now I bring only hope." Machado embraced him. "But with this gentleman's help" – he motioned to Dawlish – "there will be weapons, rifles, enough to arm five hundred men and more."

"You too are welcome, Señor. My house is yours." Ambrosio took Dawlish's hand in his. It was hard and callused.

"We're hungry, Ambrosio, hungry and tired," Machado said.

The food was meagre, the lodging miserable, and he was by now all but a cripple, but Dawlish dropped off to sleep content, fears for the morrow deliberately ignored. For he had reached here ahead of the dredger. However small a victory, it was his first since that rain-swept morning off Veglia.

*

The downpour had ceased and steam rose from the sodden ground. Daylight showed Boquerón's existence to be centred on a half-dozen zinc warehouses, a shoreline consolidated for a hundred yards with wooden piling and a jetty prodding out into deeper water. Smoke drifting from a brick chimney and the slow panting of a small engine identified an open-sided shed as a forge where belts slapping on overhead pulleys drove a lathe and drill for simple machinery repairs. Dawlish had an impression of overall decay partly arrested by haphazard signs of maintenance and patching. The recovery of the sugar plantations to the east since the cessation of fighting two years before had obviously saved this small port from extinction.

A low thick-walled, whitewashed structure constituted the customs-house. A veranda-ringed two-storey wooden building stood near it on a raised foundation. Close to the waterfront several ramshackle structures combined the functions of taverns and shops. The huts that accommodated the bulk of the inhabitants straggled beyond. The Spanish troop encountered the day before seemed to have camped in an empty warehouse, the horses munching contentedly at one end and the men cooking and eating at the other. Sentries were posted but showed no air of uneasiness or fear. These were men who were confident that all those about them were too cowed to constitute a threat.

A single brig – American by her ensign – was loading at the jetty and a larger vessel was moored further out, a lighter alongside. Three other lighters, rotten and decrepit, lay by the waterfront, awaiting the sugar and rum casks stacked in the warehouses. A knot of men was gathered there, stevedores being allocated their tasks by a loud-voiced overseer standing on a barrel. This was the man whom Ambrosio was bringing Machado and Dawlish to see.

They hovered on the edge of the sullen, reluctant crowd until its members had dispersed to their allocated chores. The overseer, the *capataz*, a thickset man, as dark as Machado, dropped heavily from his perch and started for a hut nearby that seemed to be a makeshift office. They followed at a distance, humble supplicant figures, and entered to find him already seated at a rough table, riffling through papers.

He looked up and recognition was instant.

"So it will start again, Jefe," he said, rising, hand extended. He showed no surprise at Machado's appearance and he sounded weary, resigned. "I did not expect it so soon. But we will do what we can."

Full explanations must wait. The first essential was work, jobs that would provide justification for the presence here of two penniless labourers from further east, and give them reasons for moving about, for observing and planning surreptitiously.

"Nicolás is in a bad way," Machado said. "He cannot manage heavy labour."

Dawlish nodded and felt the less for the admission. The last night's travel had all but finished him. His feet were flayed and were it not for the home-made ointment that Ambrosio had smeared on them this morning he might not have endured the walk this far. He had made himself ignore the constant ache of his ribs.

"Can he manage animals?" Esteban, the capataz, ignored his presence, spoke directly to Machado.

"Sí Señor!" It gave Dawlish a surge of pride to cut in. He had first hunted when he was six. "Horses, mules, anything on four legs."

"There'll be work tending them, Nicolás. But for you, Jefe, the work must be humble, must not bring you face to face with authority. Too many remember you."

"Labour has no shame," Machado said. "Not if it is for Cuba Libre."

"Cuba Libre," repeated Esteban and Ambrosio reverently, as if in prayer.

"Ambrosio tells me there is an Englishman here," Machado said.

"It's his town now." Esteban's tone was bitter. "He's a friend of the Spanish colonel, of Almunia. They say they fought together in Spain, against the Carlistas."

"I know Almunia." Machado's voice was emotionless.

"Forgive me, Jefe. God knows that you know him." Esteban looked embarrassed, then continued. "And while Almunia conscripts the labour for the plantations – and the masters have returned, Don Julio, for all that they fled before your fury, and now are even more rapacious than before – this Englishman organises the port. He makes deals with foreign merchants. He was away for some weeks, and now he's back, even more exacting than before, and he ensures that the sugar and molasses and rum flows out to the United States, to Europe. He runs the customs-house to his benefit and he divides the profits with Almunia and his jackals."

Esteban stopped, looked away, out to the bustle on the wharf. "And I'm part of it too, Don Julio," he said. "I'm his man from day to day, running this loading, organising this labour. I tell myself I do it because we need them to trust us until the day of reckoning comes. I do it and I hate myself for it."

"The day is near, my friend," Machado laid his hand on his shoulder. "But first we need forty like you here, in Boquerón. You can find them for me?"

"For you, Jefe, I can find fifty." He pointed through the door towards the men manhandling casks into a lighter. "That they seem docile and humble does not mean they do not hate. And with you among us…"

It would not be that easy, Dawlish knew. But it was a start.

*

By midday Nicolás Quinones, freeborn but half-witted, had settled into his new work. He moved among the oxen and mules corralled close to the wharves while the burdens they had transported were shifted on to lighters. He led them to the water troughs, shovelled dung, forked fodder and tended sores less painful than those encased by the rags bound on his own feet. He shuttled back and forth between the corrals and the newly arrived carts, greeted as friend the carter who taken pity on him the previous day, helped span oxen for the return trip with empty wagons. He moved painfully, and with downcast eyes, a meek, submissive figure, one of the wretched. But already he had noted the half-dozen coal-heaped barges moored further out in the bay, in the lee of one of the many islands dotting it, and the small steam tug that shuttled cask-laden lighters from the wharf to the three-master close inshore. His words with the men he

208

laboured with were few, but enough to confirm that there was no permanent Spanish garrison here, and no need of one.

Fear rather than force ruled here. At noon he learned exactly how.

A drumbeat, insistent and blood-chilling, summoned the inhabitants to the semblance of a square before the customs-house. Troopers, riding in pairs, urged the reluctant towards it with whips they showed every willingness to use. Dawlish tethered the mules he was leading and joined the straggling procession. Its anger and terror were almost palpable.

"It is the brothers García," he heard a woman say bitterly. "They brought them here yesterday, tied like sacks on mules."

"Those who disappeared?" her companion asked. "Mauricio and, what was the other's name? Sí –Ricardo. The widow's sons?"

"The same. Those who ran away after the older one was flogged."

"They won't be leaving again."

Yellow and red, a Spanish flag drooped limply from a pole before the customs-house. The large wooden house comprised the second side of the square and a small group, one in a formal white uniform, another a large woman in a purple dress, stood on the first-floor veranda. A row of low buildings formed the third side and here the resentful spectators were crowded. Troopers paced their mounts back and forth to contain them. Dawlish found himself squeezed on all sides, three or four back from the front of the crowd, but his height gave him view enough. Above and behind him a party of foreign sailors was gathered on a flat tavern-roof, several obviously drunk, cheering ironically and alone seeming to find the unfolding spectacle entertaining.

Still the drumbeat rolled.

The square's fourth side was open, fronting the flotsam-littered foreshore, looking out over the bay, the waters beyond clear, the jetty and shipping away to the left. A single rank of dismounted troopers stood there, six men, their carbines bayonet-tipped.

So few men, Dawlish thought as the onlookers about him shifted uneasily and muttered resentment, *so few men for so much fear.*

209

A murmur of anger and dread rose from the crowd as a small procession emerged from behind the customs-house. Two limping men, arms bound, were being hustled forward by other troopers. Their faces were black with bruising and congealed blood and their soiled, tattered clothing flapped in strips about them. A priest in a grubby cassock overlain with a lace surplice was keeping pace, intoning prayers they had no ears for, and barefoot boy, a torn vestment thrown over his rags, hurried alongside, waving before their faces a crucifix at the end of a pole. Four troopers followed with bayonets. One of the men stumbled, fell, was kicked as he struggled to rise, hampered by his roped arms. His companion cried out in protest, was cuffed into silence as the other was dragged to his feet again.

They stopped before the steps of the wooden house, below the group on the veranda. The drumming cut off suddenly, and with it the murmuring of the spectators and even the catcalls of the seamen above the tavern. The silence was broken only by isolated sobbing and whimpering from women in the crowd. Dawlish sensed a thrill of terror about him and a cold, horrible fascination within himself. He wanted to look away but found his gaze riveted on the two figures now hearing their doom confirmed. The white uniform had advanced to the top of the steps, was reading briefly and inaudibly from a paper, was folding it and putting it away, was turning on his heel and re-joining the small assembly behind him. The woman in the purple dress, fleshy, with a mass of dark curling hair, was smiling approval and turning for confirmation to the thickset, red-faced man beside her. The prisoners turned away and one tried to shout something to the onlookers before a blow silenced him.

"Ricardo García," an old woman whispered close by Dawlish. "He was a beautiful boy, so handsome, so brave. How could they…" Her voice choked in a sob.

The troopers prodded them towards the foreshore. They were trying to stay close together, shoulders touching, bound hands fluttering helplessly, uselessly, towards each other, but their escorts pushed them apart and the priest has inserted himself between them, upbraiding first one, then the other, with imprecations they turned

210

their faces from. The square they must cross seemed vast, endless, yet the distance was scarcely fifty yards. The single rank of troopers had turned now to face the sea and the prisoners were driven before them and halted at ten paces distance.

A sergeant called orders, carbine breeches were flipped open, single rounds inserted.

The García brothers were forced to their knees, their backs to their executioners. As they turned Dawlish saw that a ragged patch of hair had been hacked from the back of each head to provide an aiming mark. The skin beneath was white, but blood-streaked from the razor's slash. The men were five, six feet apart, and were trying painfully to edge towards each other for some last physical contact. One appeared to be too dazed to understand what was happening but the other still cried out encouragement and comfort to him and ignored the priest's last harangue. The brothers' last sight could have been of the tranquil, island-studded bay but instead their faces were turned to each other.

Then the priest too was stepping aside, drawing his boy with him. A new wave of silence and dread swept across the crowd and Dawlish felt himself sick with horror and pity. He had seen death enough in the fury and terror of battle but it had none of the cold, studied cruelty of this moment.

"Apunten!" The troopers were raising their carbines.

An eternity passed.

"Fuego!"

The kneeling men thrashed forward, blood fountaining from heads and torsos. One still writhed. The sergeant stepped forward and fired a single shot from his revolver into each head. A groan rose from the onlookers, of despair, of misery rather than of anger, of recognition that they were powerless, were nothing, in the face of such might.

They dispersed quietly, Nicolás Quinones among them, no less cowed and submissive. But as he left the square he trudged past the wooden house and dared raise his eyes briefly towards the veranda. A woman's shrill laughter greeted some humorous sally of the uniformed officer. The teeth of the man beside her were bared in savage grin beneath his white, closely cropped moustache. He was heavy man, though the weight he carried seemed more like muscle than fat, the man whose appearance had so shocked Florence in Fiume.

Major Clement Fentiman was satisfied by the morning's work.

20

"Disculpe, Señor!" Dawlish whimpered in apology, cringing and dragging to one side the sack-laden mule he led.

"I'll give you disculpe, you damned Dago!" The sailor, red-faced, in a sweat-sodden grey woollen vest and a nautical cap, and with an accent that could only hail from Liverpool, lashed out with his fist as his companion laughed.

Dawlish avoided the blow easily and shrunk away as the two drunkards who had just reeled into his path turned and staggered back towards the jetty. A British schooner was loading molasses there, replacing the American vessel that had just departed. Dawlish crammed his hat against his face to shield the grin spreading across it, pleased that after two days his masquerade was convincing enough to take in two of his countrymen.

His work was satisfying and undemanding, with the advantage that he could move about easily without arousing curiosity. Leading animals back and forth between the wharves and the corrals, on feet that were healing steadily, had already familiarised him with the life of the small port as well as with its physical features. His workmates accepted him easily – few expected lengthy confidences from the feeble-witted – and with rough kindness had assigned him a comfortable, if menial, position in their hierarchy.

Through the day, timid and stooped, he listened and watched. Already he knew how frequently vessels arrived – weekly in this season – and how Fentiman had managed the port for upwards of two years, making coal bunkering into a profitable adjunct to the export traffic. The Major's name was always spoken in fear, always linked with that of the dreaded Colonel Almunia, whose oppressions ensured an ample labour supply both for the port and for the plantations to the east that fed it. Since the execution of the García brothers Dawlish understood why Almunia did not need to station troops here. Memories of the butchery in the square, and knowledge that a single message from Fentiman to his ally would be enough to prompt a repeat, were enough to ensure Boquerón's sullen acquiescence in its servitude.

They plotted by night.

Machado and Dawlish had found separate lodgings, squalid huts whose owners were glad to provide a hammock in a corner for a pittance. They met after darkness, with each other and with Esteban, the capataz, and with Ambrosio, their first contact here. And afterwards meetings with others, gatherings of twos and threes in shacks and cantinas, furtive contacts that did little more at first than test resentment, probe willingness to act.

Dawlish spoke little – he was the Señor from the Estados Unidos, the mysterious agent who would supply Springfield rifles and limitless ammunition at the price of cooperation with his own needs. But it was Machado who dominated. Several knew him, all had heard of him, of his battles and escapes, of his cruelty no less than of his valour, of his wounds and endurance, of his sacrifice. But the reality was still more impressive than the reputation as Machado's eyes glistened when he heard of some recent outrage, as he rationalised how close success, Cuba Libre, had been before, how one last effort would surely now secure it, how the new flame of emancipation would be ignited here in Boquerón. He needed forty men for now – no more, he said – and then the rifles would arrive. Insurrection would again blaze irresistibly across the island like the fires that would consume the plantations and engulf Almunia and Fentiman and all the hated machinery of Spanish tyranny.

At first Dawlish could sense hesitation – well founded, since ten years of bloody rebellion had so recently ended in abject failure – and yet against all reason Machado seemed to carry his hearers with him.

"They've done their worst, worse by far than they did with those García boys," he would say, and all knew he meant his personal tragedy, never openly referred to yet always remembered. "They've

213

donc their worst, and still we endure! Spain is weak, another campaign will bring her to her knees..." and so it went on, a medley of cold fact and wishful thinking and Messianic conviction that drew even the most sceptical to his side.

And when all other arguments failed there was Fentiman, hated and dreaded in equal measure. Dawlish had seen him twice, both times with the dark-haired, heavy woman, once on horseback, once upon the veranda of the house that was part office, part residence, part fortress.

"Who is she?" he had asked.

"Dona Marta Martinez," As capataz, Esteban had dealt with her when she had run the port during Fentiman's recent absence. "Some say she's the widow of a Spanish officer, or the wife of an official in Havana, or the sister of a general in Cienfuegos. But whatever she is, she understands business and she loves money. And she's cruel."

"How?" Dawlish found himself simultaneously fascinated and repelled. He remembered her joking with the Spanish officer while the corpses on the square were still warm.

"When the major was away. There was a girl in the house, a maid, Dolores, slim and handsome. They say the major favoured her. There was no other pretext. Dona Marta flogged her herself, for an hour, longer, until she herself was tired, and left her hanging, and then came back to do it again. Afterwards she locked Dolores in the cellar under the house and there she died."

"What happened when the major returned?" Dawlish remembered Florence pale at Fiume.

"Nothing. There are so many girls. She was nothing special to him. But Dona Marta is."

Almost a week passed.

The circle of intrigue was growing, the plans hardening. They knew now that the dredger had been hailed by a Spanish patrol vessel off Baracoa, would be here in four, five days. Two troopers had brought Fentiman the news from further east – the cook in his house was part of Machado's conspiracy and his wife, a maid, had eavesdropped on their report. Boquerón's single, decrepit, steam tug

214

was being overhauled in anticipation of the shuttling of coal-laden lighters and the major had ordered Esteban to select a crew of the most able-bodied stevedores for the back-breaking transfer of fuel. Machado had arranged to be among them.

There were no conspirators among Dawlish's workmates, simple men who fed and tended and watered the animals and got drunk on rum when they could afford it.

"Come, drink coffee with us, Nicolás," one called as he loosed two mules into the corral.

"Vengo, Miguel, vengo." Dawlish wiped his brow.

It was midmorning, the heat merciless. He had been in a near trance, he realised, as he had led the animals – and that was dangerous, for he was becoming too relaxed here, his vigilance was slipping. Florence had been dominating his thoughts, concern as to how the sham in Santiago was progressing. Raymond should have gained the confidence of the authorities by now, and Florence should have charmed them, and all the while she would be disguising her anxiety as no message arrived from Boquerón. And none could, not yet...

He joined the men lounging under a palm-thatch lean-to, accepted the coffee. The conversation was of the harvest to come, of the never-ending convoys of wagons that would trudge here from the plantations and ingenios. He sipped, content to listen.

Suddenly one of the men – Miguel, the oldest – was falling forward, trying to rise, falling again. Dawlish caught him, felt his body shivering violently, sensed his fever.

"Water!" The voice was a croak. "Water! I'm thirsty!"

The others were starting back, their faces pale with fright.

"Bring him water," Dawlish said. The man was shuddering in his arms but still they held back.

"Look at his eyes," one said. "His eyes!"

They were protruding, terrified, and the whites were white no longer, but a light mustard- yellow. A pallor no less obscene was suffusing the face.

"El vómito!" The word was taken up by the others in hushed, terrified tones as they shrunk back further. One broke from the group and ran.

The man's tongue was rattling in his mouth, his breath foul. "El vómito," he croaked, and his dreadful eyes told that he knew that it was a sentence of doom.

"Leave him, Nicolás, leave him if you wish to live," another called, one of the few remaining, for the others were now edging shamefacedly away.

But Miguel was clutching him, and knew he was going to die, and needed some human close to ease his agony and fear. Dawlish, himself terrified, knew what he embraced – El Vómito Negro, the Black Vomit, Fiebre Amarilla, Yellow Jack. The names varied but the scourge was the same and it returned with inexplicable frequency to decimate entire communities across the Caribbean. It had halted that British drive on Santiago over a century before, had wiped out an entire French army in Haiti, had doomed entire cities. And there was no known cure, no palliative, no understanding even of its origin.

"Nicolás! Por Dios, Nicolás!"

He could not resist the dreadful croak, could not prise off the weakening fingers fastened on his sleeve. The doomed man had been kind to him, had accepted him. For an instant he remembered how he had once found Florence – and Agatha too – caring for a group of sick refugees somehow coping, somehow steadfast, as hell incarnate flooded towards them. He knew how they would both react now. He could do no less.

"I won't leave you, Miguel," he said. "I won't desert you."

He lifted him on to the lean-to's low bench, covered him with sacking, sent the one man who dared remain for water. His own heart was racing, his hands shaking. He forced himself to be calm, checked his own skin, found no yellow, no fever.

Not yet, a small internal voice told him, but he ignored it.

Through parched lips Miguel was complaining of agony unimaginable – a furnace and hammer-blows in his head, savage pain in his back and legs – and all the time great shivers racked his frame. He half rose and grasped the bucket when it was brought, drinking greedily, then suddenly tossing it aside and thrashing as a stream of vomit, black and foetid, burst from him. Dawlish found himself besmirched, was unreasonably angry for a moment, and then gently pushed the wretch back down and covered him again.

The day was a long one, longest of all for the victim. A small crowd, constantly shifting, changing composition, came and watched from a distance, muttering fearfully, shaking heads. Esteban came, warned by the sick man's companions, and Machado was with him. Dawlish let them come no closer than ten yards, told them what he needed, food, drink, clean clothing.

"Nicolás doesn't fear the vómito because he is simple," he heard Machado explain to the onlookers, touching his head with that now-familiar gesture. The priest came, his face pale with fear, but kept his distance. He forced others to kneel around him, prayed hurriedly, shook water towards the lean-to, uttered blessings and then left.

Miguel was cold now, his pulse weak. He vomited twice more, relapsed into a near coma. In mid-afternoon he seemed to rally and managed to hold down the water Dawlish gave him. But his eyes were deeper yellow and seemed too lifeless even for fear. He was unaware of the presence of his wife, who hovered, weeping, nearby, supported by an adult son and daughter and restrained by neighbours from coming closer. One hand held Dawlish's in a grip weaker than an infant's and yet strong enough to show that Miguel still lived, still valued this last contact with the world he was slipping from.

The sun dropped, the heat eased, the shadows grew.

Dawlish's own initial terror had declined to an awareness that within hours he too might be in no better state, that his own life – and his ambition, and his love for Florence, and all his joy in life and horses and books and the sea – could end in similarly squalid agony. He ignored the thought as best he could, concentrated on reassuring the dying man, on cleaning away his waste, on keeping him warm. Beneath the sacks his body was cold as stone now, and the shivering had ended, as if he were too exhausted even for this effort. Somehow he still lasted, to midnight and beyond, dribbling his last weak vomit, ever more frail, ever more desperate when Dawlish moved even a foot from him. A single lamp shed light on him and attracted the insects that tortured Dawlish's hands and ankles, and beyond the circle of brightness the man's family still wept and Machado and Ambrosio and a few brave souls provided what encouragement and support they could.

At last it ended, the final passing perceptible only as the relaxation of the hand's last faint pressure. Dawlish sat holding it for ten, fifteen minutes longer, himself exhausted, numbed.

"He must be buried immediately," Machado called to him when at last he stirred.

They did it together. Machado and the dead man's son dug the grave in scrub just outside the village. Dawlish manhandled the body on to a mule and transported it there. He alone touched it and he laid it as carefully as he could into the shallow trench. The effort drew on his last reserves of strength and a sense of desolation surged through him. Only sheer necessity had brought him here and he had not wanted to abase himself to the level of a labourer, a peon, and yet now, in their misery, these people seemed very precious to him. The widow, restrained by friends, was screaming in anguish and in fear – for she knew that she too might be infected – and Dawlish found himself weeping when he covered the face with sacking and began to fill.

Afterwards, with dawn reddening the eastern sky, he trudged away to find water – he wanted desperately to wash – and afterwards, his mind a blank, he lay down and slept on that same bench on which a man had so recently died. Machado had been blunt about it – until it was obvious that Nicolás was not himself infected he could share no hut, must be regarded as a pariah.

*

Fear reigned in Boquerón.

There had been other cases, six, seven within the first two days, some as rapid in their lethality as the first, others more prolonged and offering some hope of recovery despite the agony. There was no pattern among the victims – a dock labourer, a young mother, a clerk at the customs-house, all apparently healthy one day,

218

yet no less mercilessly stricken the next than an old man or an already-sickly child. Men and women watched each other furtively but constantly for the first tell-tale signs of infection. Many shrank into their homes and avoided all contacts. There was no doctor here and each had their own recipe for protection, their own desperately trusted antidote. Those who could afford to leave had done so at the first alarm – Fentiman's woman had ridden for Dos Caminos – and before the authorities could take any action to quarantine the village. But the word spread quickly and the produce flowing in for export soon died to a trickle. Fear was stronger than greed and not even Almunia and the plantation owners further east would run the risk of some carter carrying the pestilence back.

And yet, as far as possible, men still, though frightened, went about their daily tasks in the dead, steaming heat. Dawlish was no longer a man apart, could return to his toil again, another of a growing band who had succoured the stricken and had somehow survived uninfected. He searched constantly for symptoms in himself. Half-surprised, he found none and wondered if the malaria that had plagued him intermittently since his Ashanti days might have given him immunity. His workmates regarded him with something like respect now, still slow-minded perhaps, but not easily scared. In the nightly meetings – Machado's circle of support had expanded – there was a new deference when he spoke. The plans were well advanced now, success marginally more likely since the plague which had isolated the port was a potent if unwished-for ally. From Fentiman's cook they knew the layout of the major's house, his daily routine, the disposition and rosters of his half-dozen guards.

A key supporter was Geraldo, the skipper of Boquerón's single tug, the tiny, open-decked vessel with a kettle-boiler that manoeuvred lighters between the wharves and vessels loading offshore.

"You're sure he's reliable?" Dawlish asked. The vessel belonged to the major personally and the man who ran it for him was automatically suspect.

"The García brothers were his wife's cousin's sons," Esteban said. "He hasn't forgiven."

Preparations for the dredger's arrival continued. Fentiman was more visible now, always with a Remington revolver on his belt, always trailed by two civilian guards carrying Winchesters, accepting as a right that all should shrink from his path and doff their hats and bob their heads. He gave no second glance when Nicolás Quinones, tangle-haired and ragged, bowed low as he strode by, inspecting progress on the tug's overhaul, examining coal manifests, even checking the fitness of the squad that Esteban had selected for the loading. Machado, now a regular stevedore, aroused no comment but another, less well built and insufficiently apologetic about it, received a cut across the face from the crop the major constantly carried. It was all too obvious that any fears Fentiman had of el vómito were being kept at bay by copious doses of rum.

Two days passed, eleven more cases, four quick fatalities among them. And then, on a listless, steaming afternoon when the heat had brought all activity on the wharves to a halt, a low, white-hulled vessel came thrashing through the lower bay, rounded the point and dropped anchor a mile offshore.

The USS *Kanawaha* had arrived. Her charges could not be far behind.

21

Nobody came ashore. El vómito saw to that.

The *Hiram Metcalfe* lay far out in the bay close to the islands, a near twin of the low-freeboard raft that had been sent off from New York with such pomp what now seemed a lifetime ago. Patches of rust attested to the long, dreary tow thus far. Men moved on her decks, painting, repairing, readying her for the next long leg. Somewhere among the jumble of equipment on her decks, nestled between the pumps and boilers and engines, in the shadow of the huge inclined bucket-ramp, the Fenian Ram was hidden, just another black iron drum among a dozen others.

The two large tugs that had brought the dredger here swung at anchor closer inshore, overhauls in progress, their bunkers empty until the *Kanawaha's* coaling had finished. Two coal lighters were moored against the warship and a billowing cloud of dust hung about her as wheelbarrows, baskets and sacks were used to shift the fuel across. It was a routine Dawlish knew and loathed and his sympathies were with the American officers whose holystoned decks would already be soiled, dimmed by a dark film.

A Spanish patrol craft lay close by, the *Spinola*, a two-masted wooden gunboat with an auxiliary engine. She had entered with the visitors and had escorted them to their moorings. Boats had passed to and fro between her and the American paddler, courtesy visits that would have an edge of carefully disguised mutual suspicion for all the formal civilities on deck and forced bonhomie in the wardroom. Since the *Virginius* affair the possibility of United States intervention in Cuba could never be wholly discounted nor the chance of covert support to rebel groups ignored. Dawlish had no doubt that the Spaniard would be keeping close company with the American vessels until they were safely out of Cuban waters.

Machado had little news that night, or the next either. He had slaved during the coaling, first of the American warship, then of the tugs. They were now replenished but he had learned that they would be here for several days more while repairs and overhauls continued.

Boquerón's agony continued – more cases, more deaths, with no apparent logic or pattern to either – and the crews out on the clean blue waters chipped, painted, spliced and tightened. In the afternoons the *Kanawaha's* boats were lowered, races held, picnics organised on small, uninhabited islands where el vómito's absence could safely be assumed. The United States Navy's routines, Dawlish noted, were not unlike those of its British counterpart.

One more day and then again a gathering in another smoky hut, rain beating on the thatch above, water gurgling in the darkness outside, five men clustered around a rickety table, the owner's wife and children banished for an hour to neighbours. Machado, Ambrosio, Esteban and the tug-skipper. Dawlish knew each's strengths and weaknesses now and sensed that they in turn had come to regard him as something more than a *Yanqui* outsider who was buying co-operation for his own ends.

"Why should the barges be moored there?" Dawlish asked. The tug had spent the afternoon shifting the emptied coal lighters to new moorings beyond an islet further out in the bay.

"It's a new location," Esteban said. "But no better than where they were."

"It necessitated much work." The skipper, Geraldo, sounded weary. "We had to lift anchors, move buoys."

The changes in routine must mean imminent action. The dredger was ready to depart now and the ram was still on board. At their new moorings the lighters would provide the perfect cover. It was known also that the Spanish captain would give a dinner for the visitors the following night. Fresh food, beef and fruit and rum, had been shipped out to the *Spinola* this afternoon, and more would follow tomorrow. There were few secrets here.

"It will happen tomorrow night then," Dawlish said. It had to. The dredger was due to depart the morning after.

"But I've heard nothing, Nicolás," Geraldo said. "I've only been told to keep steam raised."

"You'll hear it at the last moment," Dawlish said. "Believe me, it will be tomorrow night."

He had to believe it himself. It was unthinkable that the ram might be carried onwards towards Panama, that his deadly masquerade here might be for nothing.

There was no moon the next night and Dawlish guessed that the tugs' repairs had been dragged out with this in mind. It rained intermittently as well so that the bay was a black void in which the lights of the moored vessels were frequently obliterated. Despite the wet and the discomfort, despite the random death stalking their homes, many of Boquerón's inhabitants crowded the waterfront, cowering under whatever shelter they could find, lured by the novelty of the music drifting across the still water, a glimpse of a life impossibly different to their own. Dawlish and Machado moved among them, acknowledging an acquaintance here, refusing an offer of a swig of rum there, their eyes straining into the darkness.

The *Kanawaha's* shadowy form was just visible – white hull, a single buff funnel and the paddle box amidships. Deck clutter and high bulwarks hid her meagre weaponry but rows of lanterns illuminated her lines and festive bunting festooned her. Now cleaned after her coaling, she gave an impression, even at this range, of neatness and efficiency. Aft, sheltered by an awning, her band had just concluded *Rally Round the Flag* and was launching into *Hail Columbia* for the fifth time. Most of her officers had crossed to the *Spinola* earlier, eager, Dawlish guessed, to enjoy Spanish liquor. The watch left behind would feel hard-done-by, would be paying little attention to any movement beyond the curtain of rain between the *Kanawaha* and the darkened dredger.

"Es muy linda, la musica, Señor," a little girl said to Dawlish as he stopped for a moment beside her and her mother. Beneath her matted hair her eyes were large and bright with pleasure in her pinched, grimy face.

"Si, es muy linda," Dawlish agreed. He patted her head. The mother smiled. She was hugely pregnant and looked exhausted, but her pleasure in this unaccustomed spectacle was no less than her child's, the menace of el vómito briefly forgotten.

They have nothing, Dawlish thought, *and they'll still have nothing when I've gone from here.* The realisation hurt.

Somewhere out there the tug must be at work.

She had been busy at the distant lighter-moorings earlier in the day and had not returned to the wharf at sundown. Now another rain squall was rolling in, drowning out *When Johnnie comes marching home*, driving the sodden, wistful listeners on the foreshore further under cover. The *Spinola*, dark-hulled, shabbier, less festively lit than her American sister, rocked slightly as the breeze caught her. Aft in her captain's quarters, in a haze of cigar-smoke and alcohol, there would be toasts and tipsiness and assurances of mutual esteem and undying regard. There would be little concern for what might be happening out on the black waters beyond – but Dawlish had, as he stood shivering under a dripping eave, eyes straining into the darkness.

He could visualise it as if he were there.

On the *Metcalfe's* unlit deck a winch would be rattling, and sheave-guided cables tautening. The ram would shudder while she swayed slightly on the chocks that had supported and restrained her.

223

Then, as the winch panted and laboured she would be lifting free, high enough to clear the piping and machinery that had hidden her from view. The boom would be hauled over to swing her out over the water and the tension would ease and she would settle at last into her own element. There would already be a cable attached to that shackle on the foredeck to which Carter had secured the tow on that impossibly distant night on the Mill River and the tug would be hovering alongside. Fentiman would be by the skipper's side, his eyes bright with greed and triumph and then the ram, awash, would wallow towards her clandestine mooring by the lighters. And in eight hours' time the other, larger, tugs would be crawling seawards, and the *Metcalfe* would be lagging in their wake, and the *Kanawaha* would be exchanging last courtesies with her Spanish counterpart as the *Spinola* ushered her from Cuban waters.

The plan was audacious, the execution brilliant. It made the memory of Dawlish's own fiasco at New Haven harder to bear.

There was nothing more to be gained here tonight. He turned away, cold despite the sack he clutched over his shoulders, and headed for the scant comfort of his hammock. Women were wailing in a shack as he passed – el vómito had claimed another victim. He had come to accept it now as just one more hazard and his mind was focussed only on what must happen when the last plumes of smoke had dispersed over the southern horizon.

*

The fear was back.

Dawlish had thought that he had left it behind that morning on Long Island Sound when he had dozed on Florence's shoulder and when New Haven and the memory of darkness and suffocation dropped astern.

Not just the fear, but the knowledge of his own weakness.

He had ignored it, had deliberately forgotten it, in the weeks when the ram had been some distant, abstract object to be reclaimed. But now the ram was real again, all but within his grasp, nestling unobserved between two lighters he could see from Boquerón's foreshore. Her presence was confirmed by the testimony of Geraldo, the very man who had towed her there under cover of night and rain not six hours since.

A small voice, insinuating, coldly logical, told Dawlish that it would not be difficult to sink the ram out in the broad expanse of the bay, her grave unmarked. That was all that had been expected of him, and afterwards he could find his way to Santiago where Florence and Raymond were still carrying on their own pretence, and depart in comfort on *Tecumseh* to claim *Leonidas*. The promised cargo of arms would reach Machado in due course and honour would be satisfied.

But another voice, uncomfortable and persistent, reminded him that sinking alone would not be enough, not for his valuation of himself. The memory of failure had been bitter, of the kicking he had endured in the sack, of his incarceration in foetid darkness, of the ruffian who had spat in his pitcher of water. He wanted revenge on these people, wanted not only to destroy their submarine vessel but to put an end for ever to the ambition they had invested so much in. Not only must the ram be destroyed but the ship that was meant to carry her also, and with her Driscoll's whole vision. Only by such retribution could the memory of so much humiliation be erased. And yet... he felt cold with dread, and something inside him screamed protest, as he remembered the terror no less than the agony when he and Holland has smothered slowly inside the ram's iron maw.

Holland!

It could be none other than Holland who had been bundled ashore in the early hours, the figure that the tug skipper had so imperfectly seen and described. Two of Fentiman's men had taken him from the dredger, muffled and ineffectually resisting. Now he was lodged in the major's house, in that same cellar where a servant had been thrashed to death by a jealous mistress. His presence was the surest confirmation that the *Old Hickory* was en route here from Mobile, that Driscoll's campaign was about to commence.

The last meeting was the shortest.

Night had fallen. The actors were for the most part still at their homes, oblivious that their leaders were even now deciding action. Dawlish could sense the fear of those about him, fear greater even than his own, the fear of men with families who knew the enormity of what they were precipitating and the wrath of retribution that would follow failure.

"You're sure he's in the house?" Only Machado seemed elated, eyes gleaming at the prospect of five hundred Springfield rifles within his grasp, of Cuba Libre, of new fury of machete and torch.

"Sí, Señor." The single woman present, the cook's wife, was clearly terrified. But she had answered the summons, was here nonetheless. Dawlish could only guess why she hated the major with such palpable intensity. "Like all nights since Dona Marta left, he will be drinking rum and brandy and afterwards they will carry him to bed."

"How many guards?"

"Two, Señor. The stupid one who loves to eat so much and Ramiro who cannot keep his hands to himself."

Dawlish knew them as he now knew all Fentiman's thugs. He had never seen them without firearms, and neither he himself nor any with him possessed anything other than cold steel.

"Two more guards are drinking by the customs-house and the others are at the rooms they share in the town. We have men watching." Ambrosio's network functioned even with death and fever a daily reality around them.

"We need those alive. That's understood?"

"Understood, Jefe."

"Go back now," Machado said to the woman. "But be on the watch for us."

She slipped away into the night.

"The traffic, Esteban?" Machado turned to the capataz.

"Nothing from Dos Caminos, nothing from anywhere."

The stream of sugar and molasses had ebbed to nothing since the fever had struck. Boquerón was effectively isolated. The *Metcalfe* and her escort – gone since that morning – were likely to be the last shipping to visit for some time. The *Spinola* had left also and would be in no hurry to return to a fever-infested port where three more had died today.

"To work then! Cuba Libre!"

"Cuba Libre!" Dawlish joined in the low chorus.

226

They dispersed into the dark to trigger the chain of contacts that would assemble groups of six or eight at three separate locations.

El vómito kept the streets deserted. Dawlish and Machado flitted through shadows to the empty shack close to the customs-house from where Fentiman's house could just be seen through an alleyway. The ten minutes until others joined were endless. Dawlish fingered his knife, a vicious twelve-inch blade with a pointed tip and a razor edge. He hoped he would not have to use it – it was an assassin's tool, unworthy of a commissioned officer – but it and a hardwood baton were his only weapons. A man entered silently, a powerfully-built stevedore, Pablo, then two lithe young men more he recognised by sight only, dark and crinkly-haired like Machado and introduced as brothers, Porfirio and Gervacio.

A light glowed behind a drawn blind in the house beyond the alley – Fentiman's room, where he sat so often, drinking steadily, brooding on his lost majority, on the society that had rejected him and which he perhaps still longed for. A single guard circled the lower veranda at intervals, armed with a shotgun. The second would be somewhere inside, maybe outside Fentiman's door. One other light burned, in the kitchen towards the rear. Dawlish had never entered, yet knew the house as well as his own in Southsea. He had had quizzed the cook and his wife, had traced a diagram in the dust and memorised its details. Success, even his life, would depend on its accuracy.

Movement now – an opening door, a figure emerging on the kitchen, calling to the sentry, ascending to the veranda.

"Now!" Machado breathed.

Porfirio and his brother glided from the hut, down the alley, gained the shadows at its end and froze there.

The cook's wife was speaking to the guard, overcoming her distaste for the stupid one who loved his food or for the other who could not keep his hands to himself. The sound of a laugh – the guard should be accepting the offer of food and coffee now. The stevedore moved down the alley, joined the brothers in the shadows. The woman descended to the kitchen again and the sentry seated himself on the rail to await her return, his back to the watchers.

Dawlish and Machado slipped from cover, joined the others in the shadows. It was no more than thirty yards to the house, but they were open.

The woman emerged again. She was holding a tray and she moved awkwardly as she ascended the steps. The guard made to assist her, reaching out to take the tray from her.

Porfirio streaked from cover, light-footed, feline. It took him seconds only to cross the open space and freeze again in the shadowed angle where the front steps rose to meet the veranda. The woman was lifting items from the tray, the guard was reaching out, already cramming something to his mouth, and she was saying something that made him sputter in laughter. Almost invisible in the shadows, Porfirio was gliding along the side of the house in a crouch, the veranda directly above him. Its floor would have been level with his shoulders had he risen. The woman was at the guard's side – she had taken the tray back, was urging something else on him – but he was too intent on his eating to notice her eyes search the darkness for movement. She stiffened as she sensed Porfirio's presence, then collected herself and handed a cup to the sentry. She took the tray back, holding it horizontally before her.

The guard's head was thrown back as he drained the coffee. He was half-seated on the rail against which he had laid his shotgun, his face towards the house, towards the woman directly before him, wholly oblivious of the dark figure now directly below him.

And then he died.

The woman lunged forward with the tray, driving it into his chest. He gasped in surprise, flailed his arms as he toppled backwards and smashed to the ground below. Bewildered, half-paralysed by shock, he tried to rise but Porfirio was already top of him, dragging his head back by the hair, tautening his throat for the single slash that would finish him. The blade jerked and the body thrashed momentarily, then relaxed. On the veranda above the cook's wife was reeling back, overcome by the reality of what she had lent herself to. For an instant Dawlish feared that she might scream and nullify all she had achieved but she somehow restrained herself.

Porfirio dragged the body deep into the shadows and beckoned them forwards. When they reached him the woman had descended, white-faced and trembling. She guided them towards the kitchen's open door.

"Pablo! You're the sentry now!" Machado motioned to the veranda and the stevedore climbed up and commenced his circuit. Were Fentiman or the other guard to listen then his footsteps would counterfeit those of the dead man.

Into the kitchen. The cook was there and was as frightened as his wife now that he was as irrevocably committed. "Only Ramiro is with the major," he said as he opened the door that led into the passage beyond. The cellar – Holland's prison – was to the left, the stairs to the right. Holland could wait.

They inched up the stairs, Porfirio in the lead, his brother directly behind, knives sheathed, batons in hand. Dawlish had been particular about that for he needed living bodies to carry off the pretence he intended. He followed them, heart thumping, Machado on his heels.

Porfirio reached the head of the stairs and paused. The others froze below him. Another flight of stairs led to the sleeping quarters above but their business was on this floor where Fentiman's light burned. A corridor extended to either side of the stair-head, lit only to the left, a soft glow from around the corner at its end that revealed bare varnished boards, a closed door and several paintings on the walls. Enough to pass for a palace in Boquerón.

Porfirio shook his head – no sign of the guard, Ramiro.

They split, Gervacio and Porfirio to the left, towards that glow, Dawlish and Machado to the right, towards the room where Fentiman sat. They moved with infinite slowness, one foot at a time, shifting their weight ever so cautiously, dreading of the squeak of a loose floorboard. A fan of weak light radiated from beneath the major's door. There was an empty chair by the side, obviously for use by a guard.

Dawlish glanced back. The brothers were crouching at the corner at the far end of the corridor, silhouetted against the light leaking around it. One was looking back to see Dawlish's and

229

Machado's progress, the other was poised to hurl himself around the corner towards the source of light. Dawlish realised that they must have Ramiro in sight now, dozing on a chair perhaps or telling off the tedious minutes until he would change places with the guard outside.

They gained the door. Dawlish flattened himself to one side, Machado to the other. There was no sound from within. It was impossible to imagine Fentiman reading, easier to visualise him already slumped in half-drunken somnolence. Dawlish looked to Machado, caught his nod of agreement and raised his arm in signal to the brothers down the corridor. They disappeared around the corner, batons upraised, feet pounding. There was a brief cry of terror and surprise and then the dull sound of thumping, and another cry, this of pain, and then silence.

Movement inside Fentiman's room now, the sound of something falling over as if a sleeper, alarmed, was thrashing into wakefulness and upsetting something close by. Then heavy footsteps, and the light seeping beneath the door died suddenly.

Silence.

Fentiman, Dawlish realised with sickening certainty, was too old a fox to come blundering through the door to investigate a clamour outside. He would be armed – his Remington never left him – and he might even now be inching towards the window, intent on getting on to the veranda and outflanking his attackers. The stevedore, Pablo, should have stationed himself outside the window by now, but that could not be relied on. There was no option but to go in.

Dawlish gestured. Machado understood instantly and picked up the chair by the door. Still no sound from within. Dawlish, still flattened against the wall, moved his hand to the doorknob on his side and twisted. It turned. He pushed gently and the door shifted fractionally – not locked. He looked to Machado and nodded, then flung it fully open, stayed glued to the wall. He heard a sharp intake of breath within the room, sensed the slightest shifting of a body, the creaking of a floorboard.

Twenty, thirty seconds passed. Fentiman had not panicked, was standing his ground, would have manoeuvred himself behind cover.

"Now!" Dawlish yelled and Machado swung around, flinging the chair into the room's soft darkness. It crashed into something and there was a sound of falling objects, of tinkling glass. A revolver exploded in the gloom, its brief flame exposing a white moustache for a flashing instant as Dawlish hurled himself through the doorway.

Blackness returned, almost total, but he had seen enough to know that Fentiman was on his feet behind a heavy settee. The major had turned toward the centre of the room to fire and must now be swinging round, but Dawlish was leaping up and forward from his side, one foot now on the couch and vaulting forward to impact against Fentiman

"Damn you! Damn your soul!" a voice shouted and Dawlish felt a body thrashing under him.

He groped for the arm, found it with his left and brought his baton smashing down on it with his right. He heard a cry of pain, felt the arm relax and something heavy fall to the floor. Fentiman was writhing free but Dawlish lashed out again, towards where his head must be, felt his club connect, heard a gasp, then struck again. Machado was by him now, also striking unmercifully, and Fentiman, knowing he was outnumbered, was twisted on to his front, hands clasped over his head to protect it from further blows.

"Hold him!" Dawlish panted, then sought for the dropped revolver.

Machado was kneeling on the major's back, dragging the head back by the hair, a knife against the throat. Dawlish found the Remington. It clicked loudly as he cocked it.

"If you move, Major, I'll blow your brains out." He spoke in Spanish. "Now keep still while my friend trusses you."

Machado worked quickly, binding his hands behind with a short rope he had brought, knotting a rag tightly as a gag. Dawlish felt for the table, located a lamp, matches close by. He struck a light, removed the shade, ignited the wick. Light filled the room.

Fentiman's head was bleeding but his eyes blazed defiance. He was choking with fury behind his gag.

"Take him to the cellar," Dawlish said. Porfirio and Gervacio had appeared at the doorway, a battered and immobilised guard propped between them.

They manhandled the prisoners down. The house was quiet again and the sound of the single pistol-shot seemed to have evoked no response from outside. The squads sent to deal with the other guards must have been equally successful.

"The key! Where is it?" Dawlish demanded when they paused outside the cellar door. The major had recovered enough to look defiant. Dawlish placed the Remington against his temple. "We'll remove your gag. If I don't get the key I'll kill you."

Fentiman told them. Gervacio hurried to find the key. As the gag was being pulled tight again about Fentiman's mouth recognition dawned.

"I know you, damn your soul!" Fentiman gasped in English. "You're the Admiralty buyer, you're…" His words were cut off but his eyes bulged in fear as well as fury now, in recognition that he was facing more than a revolt of local peons.

Dawlish ignored him. The door was creaking open and a slight, pallid man with a receding hairline, high cheekbones and a heavy moustache was blinking in bewilderment behind thick, rimless lenses.

"Good evening, Mr. Holland," Dawlish said. "I trust I find you well."

22

"Nobody seems sorry about the news."

Dawlish stayed behind the lace curtain as he looked out into the sunlit square. Several small knots had gathered, staring towards the house with bitter satisfaction and then dispersing to spread the welcome tidings that Fentiman was thrashing in the clutches of el vómito.

"It's quiet in the town," Machado said. "And the guards are co-operative."

As I'd be, Dawlish thought, *if I were taking turns to pace back and forth on a veranda with a shotgun trained on my spine by a watcher at a window not five yards distant.* Knowledge that one of their comrades was already buried, ostensibly as a victim of rapid onset of the fever, while another lay in a half-coma in the cellar, was a powerful inducement to co-operate.

It had gone better than Dawlish had dared hope – the off-duty guards overpowered without struggle, the spreading of the news of el vómito's sudden arrival in Fentiman's citadel, the virtual quarantining of the house. The cook's wife shouted details to friends hovering at a safe distance and, *Sí*, it was true – had her husband not wrestled the pistol from his hand the major would indeed have put a bullet through his own head last night when he realised that he was stricken.

The small tug was halfway to the bay's western shore by now. It would land a trusted messenger south of Caimanera, with money enough to carry him to Santiago by the following night, perhaps earlier. His memorised message was of the briefest, but enough for Raymond to send to the United Sates the innocuous telegram that would start five-hundred Springfields on their way to Cuba and to turn the *Tecumseh's* bows eastwards. It would mean easing of Florence's concerns too. Dawlish could visualise her trembling with relief.

"You'll be garrotted for this, the whole damn lot of you," Fentiman snarled when they questioned him.

Machado struck him on the face with his own Remington pistol and drew blood.

"That's enough," Dawlish said. "I've no doubt the major will see sense."

"I'm damned if I'll see your sense." But beneath the bluster the watery blue eyes registered cold cunning.

"Driscoll has a ship coming here. We know her name, the *Old Hickory*, even the yard where she's been converted, in Mobile, Alabama."

"I know nothing of it." A bruise was rising on Fentiman's face.

"What's the ram doing anchored in the bay then, Major? And projectiles for her pneumatic gun in your warehouse?" Dawlish had seen them that morning, knew now what was in the four sealed crates landed from the dredger while the *Kanawaha's* band thumped out patriotic airs. "So when does the *Old Hickory* get here, Major?"

"I don't know what you're talking about."

Machado moved to strike again but Dawlish restrained him.

"You're dead already, Major. Most of Boquerón believes you have yellow fever and even your friend Colonel Almunia won't be surprised to hear you didn't survive it."

Fentiman looked up, his face half-contemptuous, half-pitying. "Men like you don't kill in cold blood, Dawlish. Your damn sense of honour won't…"

Machado's blow knocked him to the ground. Fentiman struggled to rise but his hands were tied and so he was unable to avoid the kick that caught him in the groin.

"But men like me do kill, Major," Machado said quietly, "and I can call in a dozen who'll delight in tearing you apart. So tell my friend what he wants to know." He kicked again.

"In five, six days." Fentiman was retching in pain, his words all but inaudible, but his eyes still gleaming with calculation. "The *Old Hickory* will be here in five or six days."

"How recent is your news?"

Fentiman was close to vomiting. "The day before yesterday. A telegram, brought by courier from Guantanamo." He saw Machado poised to strike again and said "It confirmed that she'd left Mobile."

It was bad.

A week was the longest, the very longest, they could hope to hold Boquerón by this charade. Poor quality coal, adverse seas, an overheated bearing… there were a dozen reasons why the *Old Hickory's* arrival might be delayed. A week – any longer and Machado and his supporters would be melting into the countryside, heading for that rendezvous point on the north-eastern coast where Raymond's associate would be landing the Springfields.

"Do the Spanish know?"

Hesitation. Fentiman closed his eyes, clearly weighing his options. "The *Spinola's* captain's been squared," he said at last. "He'll be turning a blind eye. He believes we'll be shipping out some valuables we appropriated during the revolt."

"Who's we?"

"Almunia, myself."

They left him, sensing that there would be little more to be had from him for now.

"I don't want him ill-treated, nor Ramiro either," Dawlish said. "Give them light and food." He remembered the squalor of his own confinement in New Haven and recoiled from inflicting the same, the more so since he despised the man at his mercy. "But put a vigilant watch on the door."

Holland seemed aged since Dawlish had last seen him. A near-prisoner on the dredger, he had suffered inordinately from sea-sickness while it had wallowed in the brief spell of stormy weather it encountered. But most of all Holland was disillusioned by his fellow-countrymen.

"I won't have them coerce me, Mr. Page," he said. "Not them, not any man. I was damned if I was going to teach them to use it, not here, not anywhere, not after they stole it from me."

For that was Driscoll's plan, to use these quiet waters as the training ground, as the base for the *Old Hickory*. From here she could come and go as an innocuous trader in sugar and molasses, the ram secreted in her vitals.

The Brayton had been repaired. "She's running like a sewing machine now, I'll give them that," Holland said. The necessary spare parts had been fashioned at the same Stamford workshop that had produced the pneumatic projectiles.

"We had a bargain, Mr. Holland," Dawlish said. "It still stands. You'll have the funds you need for further development and you'll have your tests – not a fortnight's, maybe not even half that, and you'll train me in the course of them – and then the ram's mine to dispose of."

"Where would we test her Mr. Page?"

"Here, Mr. Holland. Where Driscoll would have expected you to train his men."

He shook his head. "I won't do it. I just want to go home, Mr. Page."

Dawlish took him by the elbow and led him gently to the window.

"Look out there, Mr. Holland" he said. "That's Cuba. Half those you see walking the streets are slaves and the other half might just as well be. It's ruled by Spain like Cromwell ruled your country and a week ago I saw two men butchered like animals in that square before you. It's rotten with yellow fever and two dozen people died of it in the last week, one of them in my arms"

"But…" Holland began.

Dawlish cut him off. "The wrath of God will be descending on this place when Almunia comes and nobody is going to ask whether you're an Irish schoolteacher or a Cuban revolutionary before they garrotte or shoot or fillet you with the rest. You can stay here if you want, Mr. Holland, but there's only one way home for you and that's by doing exactly what I suggest."

Raymond would have managed it more elegantly but the result was the same in the end.

Holland agreed.

*

The fear had not left him – Dawlish knew now that it never would. As the ram slipped away from the lighters in the fading light a long arrowhead of ripples marked her progress across the mirror-smooth waters. He dreaded the moment when the hatch would again clang shut. He could only hope to keep at bay his horror of death in darkness by slow suffocation. His head and shoulders protruded as he relayed instructions to Holland to bring the craft to open water.

"Steady as she goes, Mr. Holland. I'm coming below."

One last glance across the now moonlit water towards winking lights of Boquerón and then he closed the hatch and the familiar warm, oily darkness enveloped him.

They dived but briefly, on a straight course towards the centre of the bay. They remained shallow enough for faint traces of the dying day to filter mistily through the glass ports, but sufficiently deep to confirm that the seals and plating had survived the wrenching from the mud off New Haven without serious harm. Holland had been meticulous in his checks and preparations for this dive – they had occupied the best part of the last thirty-six hours. He was another man now, his air of confusion and bewilderment gone as he confidently called the orders for valve manipulation and was once more one with his creation.

Dawlish forced himself not to count, not to calculate how long they had been submerged, not to long for the moment when they must rise again. And then, at last, soon but none too soon, they were on the surface again and cold, fresh air, sweeter than nectar, was sucking down the hatchway as the compressor recharged the reservoirs. They were far from the shoreline and the water here was deep enough for manoeuvring without fear of grounding.

"It's easier to learn when we're not being hunted!" Dawlish tried to force heartiness into his voice. "I'm getting the feel of the valves and levers now."

"It'll come, Mr. Page, it'll come," Holland shouted above the clatter. "It's a simple system when all's said and done."

Then the second dive, fear less now, controlled, not absent. A thin stream of air jetting from the forward tank, enough to feed the panting Brayton, and to satisfy their own breathing needs. The clatter of gears and shafting. The smell of oil almost strong enough to induce vomiting. Above all the darkness and sense of incarceration. Dawlish might have lived to a hundred and never have known his weakness, and he half-hated, half-respected the crude, deadly, ingenious craft that had revealed it to him.

"You'll want to try the horizontal rudder now, Mr. Page." Holland had to shout to make himself heard. For this was the object of the night's excursion, Dawlish's first exposure to controlling the ram himself. "Never mind about direction. I'll steer. You concentrate on holding depth."

Holland's grasp guided him up beside him on to the cramped saddle.

"I think we're fifteen, twenty feet under," Holland said. "You hear the exhaust? You hear it labouring? That'll tell you. Are you a musical man, Mr. Page? No? A pity. But with time you'll get to recognise the tone."

He reached for his hand and guided it towards the horizontal rudder lever, held it there. Dawlish felt it rock back and forward in a series of tiny corrective movements. "You feel it, Mr. Page? She's not too stable, even at this speed. You feel the nose digging in? Pull it back! No, not too much, that's too far! She's rising now, she'll come to the surface! Forward now, gently! That's it. Now back, slightly. Good! Hold it there."

Only now did Dawlish fully appreciate the skill and smoothness with which Holland had guided the craft in three dimensions as Driscoll's launch had searched so remorselessly for them. As he concentrated on holding the ram on an even keel, the forward motion was a series of slow pitchings, each minute over-correction sending bow or stern heaving up.

"Relax now, Mr. Page, hold it loosely, not tightly. You're doing better now." Holland's voice was calm, that of a born schoolmaster, authoritative but reassuring. He was steering on the vertical rudder himself but he had removed his touch from Dawlish's hand, even though it could still be sensed hovering near. "Small movements now, Mr. Page. That's it, that's good. Listen for the note of the engine, always listen for that. She'll labour if you sink, speed up as you rise."

Sweat saturated Dawlish, not just because of the heat radiating from the engine beneath him but from the effort needed to hold this iron cylinder level. His throat was parched and his head ached but his fear was all but dormant now, smothered by concentration. And now – after how long, eight, ten minutes? – the pitchings seemed less violent, the oscillations less sudden, and he fancied he could even distinguish the variations in the exhaust beat.

"I'm starting to get it," he croaked with absurd pride as he felt himself neutralise a rising bow without plunging it down violently. "I think getting it, Mr. Holland."

"Stay there, Mr. Page, and now take this too." Holland guided his hand to the steering lever, then slipped off the saddle. "I'll blow the tanks and bring her up. Just hold her as you're doing and she'll come up by herself. Don't worry now."

The ram lurched to the surface for the second time that night, the second of five. Each dive ten to fifteen minutes of suppressed dread, and yet with a growing sense of the ram's latent power, Dawlish cautiously hopeful that in two, three days more he might just master it. If he could but keep his fear hidden and in check...

They docked again between the lighters shortly before dawn. Dawlish was exhausted as he heaved himself from the hatchway but his heart leapt as he glanced seawards.

A pale-hulled vessel, ghostly in the moonlight, was threading her way slowly into the outer bay. The *Tecumseh* was unmistakable . And Florence would be on the bridge, her bony face beautiful with love and longing.

*

"The Spanish have three gunboats along the southern coast at any time," Raymond said, "and at least another two refitting in Santiago." Even in the hour before dawn his white suit was creaseless as he sat back in his leather chair and drew on his cheroot. His elegance made Dawlish feel like an intruder in the yacht's saloon.

"They're not nice people, Nicholas," Florence said.

She sat close to him, his hand clutched fiercely in hers, and he sensed a still greater strength in her than before, an indignation, an outrage. There was no time yet for greater confidences or intimacy. This was a business-like Florence, reporting on what she had undertaken to accomplish.

"Once we were spending money like water they were open, boastful even, about what they're doing," she said. "The garrisons have been reduced. They say the country's too exhausted to consider rising for another twenty years and that a few men like that dreadful Colonel Almunia you mentioned will be enough to keep it that way."

The pretence had been carried off faultlessly. The *Tecumseh* had been searched thoroughly on arrival at Santiago – Raymond had been the soul of co-operation with the authorities – and once satisfied that no arms were carried there was no reason to suspect the meat-packer millionaire and his splendid wife. Raymond had spent lavishly and Florence, majestic in white lace and linen, had been assiduous in her visits to churches and convents, guide-book in hand, head modestly covered. Invitations had come in return. While Raymond drank and smoked with bureaucrats and officers and the governor himself, and applauded their robust handling of those who resented honest wealth and lawful authority – there were such people in the United States too, but they were indulged too much – Florence heard their wives' litanies on the ingratitude of those that served them.

"So when you cleared for here there was no suspicion?" Dawlish asked.

"None. There isn't a Spanish officer in Santiago who wouldn't vouch for us," Raymond said. "They swallowed the story whole that I was interested in Caimanera as a possible location for a canning plant, with due prospects of incentives for any official from the governor down who might need to sign an approval."

And so there was good reason why the *Tecumseh* should loiter here in the outer bay, waiting until the fever epidemic should subside.

"It won't be for long," Dawlish said. "Three, four days at the most." In that time he must master not only the ram, but the projector as well. "I'll need Egdean," he said, "I'm glad he's here. Holland's made it plain that he won't risk taking life, anybody's life, himself."

Florence laughed. "But designing infernal machines is his life's work, Nick! How can he be such a hypocrite?"

"What men choose to do with the weapons placed in their hands is something between themselves and their creator but I'll have no man's blood on my own hands!" Dawlish could not quite mimic Holland's slow lilt and though the others smiled he knew the man he imitated was adamant. He would never fathom this naïve genius.

"You're filthy and you're worn out, Nick," Florence said when they were alone. "It's always the same when I leave you to look after yourself." She tried to smile, to make a joke of it, but her concern was too great.

"You were wonderful, Florence. You carried it off superbly."

"It stuck in my throat to entertain them on this ship," she said, "and to feel their greed and cruelty and to appear with Mr. Raymond at their receptions and operas and their parades, to smile at their men and to gossip with their women and to listen to their contempt for those they consider less. To see slaves in their street! People like you and me, Nick, ordinary men and women, except that somebody owns them body and soul."

"You're becoming a regular socialist, Florence! But if I stay here much longer I fear I'll turn something of one myself." He buried his face in her rich, golden hair. "I love you, Florence," he said. "I've missed you, missed you badly."

They had half an hour, no more, and then it must be business again. But for now it could wait.

"I love you too, Nicholas," she said.

That made all else bearable.

*

Two days and nights of practice followed, broken only by brief snatches of rest, of maintenance and adjustment of the Brayton. The *Tecumseh* was moored close to the barges, in the lee of the islet, and the ram could be secured alongside, secure from prying eyes ashore. Holland was given quarters on board. He was a liability anywhere except at the controls of his creation and Egdean had appointed himself as his guardian.

In Boquerón the fever's grip waxed, waned, waxed again and the town was at a standstill. Those who could had left, carrying tales of its misery and of the vengeance that had overtaken the English major who had so oppressed it, and who still sweated in delirium within his guarded mansion. What business was left to manage was handled by the capataz Esteban, who moved into the major's office and looked after his interests with every outward sign of conscientiousness.

Machado was briefly absent, creeping away by night with a half-dozen men and as many mules to recover a cache of rebel weapons buried thirty miles away when the fighting had ended before. Dawlish took his place at Fentiman's house, listening to the reports from the lookouts at the town's outskirts, hearing the assurances that none of the cowed, fear-stricken population that remained realised yet that they had undergone a change of masters. The major still fumed in the cellar below but Dawlish needed no further information from him, and so he left him to his gaolers.

Egdean's presence was reassuring, even if his bulk did make the ram's interior even more cramped. He seemed to have no fear of confinement. He adapted effortlessly to acting by feel in the warm darkness and he absorbed Holland's patient schooling without effort. By now Dawlish himself was taking the Irishman's place on the saddle above the panting engine and was growing ever more assured in the vessel's underwater handling. In daytime, with light seeping cloudily through the glass ports to guide him, he could now hold the vessel at eight to ten feet depth as she crawled forward. His ear had been trained sufficiently by Holland to enable him to hold ten to twenty feet at night by the tone of the exhaust alone.

And the projector worked.

It worked as well as it done from Whitehead's tug, with water admitted to the ram's small trim tank aft to raise the bows and the muzzle a fraction above the surface. With hull awash, only Dawlish's head emerged through the open hatch, with the control lever of the horizontal rudder locked, his right hand grasped on an extension of the steering lever. With it he manoeuvred to align the two rod-sights bolted on the foredeck on a distant target on the islet. He was becoming adept now and it was as if the weapon had been conceived especially for the ram. Even Scrivello would have been impressed at the ingenuity and efficiency with which his creation had been built into a vessel that has been virtually disassembled and reconstructed to receive it. One of the packing cases landed contained practice dummies identical in dimension and weight to the actual missiles –

Driscoll had thought of everything. Trial and error confirmed that from two cables distance, and with the air pressure available, it was possible to land a projectile within twenty yards of the target. Dawlish could only hope that the ram would cope with the violent water-borne shocks such as had shuddered through that tugboat's hull in that remote bay at Cherso. The proof would come in action. Secrecy demanded that live rounds not be fired and Holland had been unable to test them before he had fallen out with the Brotherhood.

But the fear was still there.

Dawlish had known fear before – bowel-loosening terror in the quiet moments before combat, unspoken dread in an open boat as the sky turned black and seas mounted and there was no haven to scud for, sheer fright as Cossack hooves had come drumming across a frozen hillside, clods flying, lance-points gleaming – but action had so often delivered him from its shaming grasp. But what he had discovered in the ram's darkness was worse, a core of abject dread well capable of paralysing him, an enemy slow and untiring and insidious, waiting patiently to rob him of dignity and resolution at the very moment when he would need his courage most. Holland's presence, calm, obsessive, fatalistic, had somehow helped him overcome it off New Haven but that crutch would be gone when he steered this vessel himself towards the now-imminent *Old Hickory*. Day by day his doubts, however ignored, however rationalised, grew within him like some foul tapeworm whose existence even Florence must not guess.

Hell, he realised, must have some element of this.

23

Machado's expedition had been successful, even if the results were meagre – eighteen Martini-Peabodys and two Spencer repeaters, five boxes of ammunition, a small assortment of pistols, all well-greased and preserved in oiled canvas.

"The countryside's quiet," Machado said. "Almunia's patrols are avoiding the area because of the vómito. But we still can't risk staying here more than another two days."

He had chosen the men who would leave with him, young, strong, resentful men who had been children when revolt had last scorched its path though the eastern provinces, older men who had been hunted mercilessly though forest and mountains, bitter men with scores to settle. And Fentiman would come too, a hostage for whose life other lives might perhaps be bartered in a grim future of inevitable outrage, reprisal and revenge.

"If not tonight, then tomorrow," Dawlish said. The *Old Hickory* must have encountered problems. The chain of lookouts Machado had posted down as far as the southern coast should have sighted her by now and should have been igniting the fires that would signal her arrival.

So time for one last practice run. Intermittent curtains of rain drifted across the bay in the steaming afternoon and the interior of the craft was like an oven, impossible to endure for longer than ten minutes at a time.

"Show me again, Egdean." Dawlish's shirt was plastered to him with sweat and the blindfolded seaman's body was glistening in the few stray sunrays that slanted down through the open hatch.

"Aye, aye, Sir."

Oriented by touch alone, Egdean's hands found the hand wheels between the tangle of piping below the projectors breech.

"Two turns anti-clockwise." He touched the first valve, the main connection to the forward air reservoir, though not implementing the action. "And here, a single turn," the second valve, the back-up.

In action the piston in the projector's accumulator, a bulky cast-iron cylinder below the projector's breech, would be heaving forward, driving a smaller piston in a narrower tube, multiplying ten-fold the pressure of the charge of air that would blast the projectile towards its target. Then only a single plug-valve would lie between the compressed air and the missile. Egdean grasped its lever, ready for final the right-angled twist.

"Prepared for firing, Sir," he called.

No need to order firing. "Close the bow cap."

Another rod, turning the worm and pinion that hinged back and sealed the domed cap that closed off the open muzzle in the bows.

"Bow cap closed, Sir!"

They had rehearsed it a dozen times this afternoon, and a dozen times yesterday, and in the days before, sighted at first, blindfolded later. Now the actions were instinctive. But the firing was the easy part.

"Now the reloading, Egdean. You need a breather first?"

"Thank you, Sir, but I'll manage it one time more. Then I'd relish a break."

He reached for the copper hammer hanging by a thong from a hand wheel – each tool had its uniquely assigned place, locatable by memory in the darkness. Three blows on its lugs loosened the threaded cap that closed the projector breech. It swung free, supported by a chain to a frame overhead. In reality the trapped water in the tube would now be spilling back – Holland's improvised installation of the purloined weapon had allowed no time for any more elegant solution – but Egdean was already crouching and groping to his right.

His searching hands found the nearest of the four vertically-stacked projectiles there, each identical in everything but length to those fired in the Whitehead tests. The shaft behind the explosive head was shorter now by a foot to allow storage and manhandling within the ram's confinement but testing had proved stability in flight to be unimpaired. Egdean's practised fingers found and released the metal clasp that secured the shaft and he lugged the missile across to the breech. Muscles straining under the seventy-pound load, knuckles skinning as they jarred against metallic edges, he heaved it up and lodged the domed head in the breech. His grip shifted back along the shaft. He raised it and pushed, sliding it into the tube, shoving against the resistance of the leather gaskets until only the ends of the sheet-metal fins were visible. Then he grasped the dangling cap again, engaged the thread and locked it with four blows of the hammer. His shoulders slumped and he panted.

"Forty-two seconds." Dawlish snapped his watch closed. It had taken over two minutes initially. "Well done. And now it's time for a breather."

Ten minutes break and then the sequence would be repeated, and repeated, and repeated again. For on it might depend success – and their lives.

*

They moored next to the yacht afterwards and spent two hours checking seals and lubrication, tightening packings and adjusting spacers. They drained the fuel tank and lines, flushed them through twice, then refilled with fresh oil strained through five layers of cloth. Then, last of all, the eight live projectiles were lowered one by one into the cramped interior, stood on end and secured with clips, four to either side. The caps were still screwed over the heads of the water-actuated fuses in the missiles' bases and would only be removed just before loading. Dawlish repressed a shudder as he remembered how water sloshed from the projector tube after each discharge. There was enough dynamite inside the ram to blast her to atoms.

Florence was waiting when he emerged at last. "Have you remembered the most important thing, Nick?" she asked.

He was tired, must have looked blank.

"The marker buoy, Nicholas. The little buoy they found you by."

He had checked it, even had length added to the line, but only to keep her happy. Her trust in it was enough to move him to tears. He knew that he could not hope for a second miracle.

But he could not bear to tell her that.

*

246

It was Nicolás Quinones, ragged, grimy and slow-witted, who landed from the tug and plodded through the rapidly fading dusk towards Fentiman's house. The heat was easing now but the sour, foetid smell of sewage and poverty was as strong as ever. Lights burned in the shacks about but their occupants stayed within, prisoners of fear. El vómito's grip had not relaxed.

He recognised the guard on the veranda – after nearly a week of turns pacing there under duress the man seemed to acquiesce in his fate and even nodded to him as he came and left – but now he sensed an agitation that had been absent before. The man was clearly terrified by more than the shotgun aimed at his back.

"Don't enter, Señor," he said. He raised the unloaded weapon he carried and gestured Dawlish away. "Go back!"

"What? Why not?"

"The fever is within. The cook…"

Dawlish pushed past him. From somewhere within he could hear a woman wailing. Esteban met him at the door.

"Is it true?"

The capataz nodded but the pallor on his face would have confirmed it anyway. "The cook," he said. "He'll be dead before morning. And El Jefe…" his voice trailed away.

Machado! Not now! Dawlish felt panic rising within him, fought it down. "Bring me to him," he said.

He was slumped on the settee in the room where they had overpowered Fentiman and already it was foul with the smell of the pestilence. Machado was trembling violently and there was no mistaking the yellow tinge to his skin, the mustard in his eyes. He recognised Dawlish but the words he attempted were lost in a dry rattle through cracked lips.

"I won't leave you." The phrase were unavoidable, just as when the first victim had collapsed into Dawlish's arms, but his brain screamed out against the injustice of it. Machado was trying to sit up, and failing. Dawlish cradled him and laid him down gently. "This will pass, Julio, this will pass," he said and then turned to the frightened capataz. "Bring a blanket, and water, and cloths to clean him."

Left alone with the sick man, his mind raced.

He knew nothing of the disease or of its origins – nobody did – but he had survived one close contact and so there must be a good chance he could survive a second. And Machado must live, not just because he had come to admire the man, but because he needed him. Even the capataz who had been so reliable until now seemed near breaking point. He was going to have to care for Machado himself. He had no medicines – though there was quinine on the *Tecumseh* and it had always helped his own malaria, but he suspected that it might be of little value here. El vómito was more savage, more rapid in its killing. He heard the steady wailing of the cook's wife somewhere below and he thought of Florence – she would not hesitate to join him here, would not shrink from infection – but he dismissed the idea at once. He had already exposed her too much.

The night's agony began. Once Machado was sponged, given water and had lapsed into an uneasy doze Dawlish left him in Esteban's care. He checked the watch on the sentries – the men assigned the task were frightened, though all assured him they would stay – and then descended to the kitchen. From the cellar beyond he could hear sounds of a door being kicked, of Fentiman's indistinct curses. That could wait. One look told him that the cook would not last until dawn and that the wife who tended him so ineffectually between her fits of weeping was close to insanity from fear and grief.

"It's not el vómito," she sobbed. "He's been walking in the night air – he never would listen to me – and he's weak from too much rum and he's…" But her eyes told she knew the truth.

Dawlish helped her settle her husband more comfortably, wiped away the rank blackness that befouled him, wet his lips and was deaf to his weak babbling. He set her to making coffee, to bringing it to the others in the house . The activity calmed her and then he left her with the dying man. "Bathe his forehead, Señora," he said. "Keep him cool and by morning it should be better." He saw that she knew he was lying.

The cellar door was as substantial as the one that had imprisoned him in New Haven but it was trembling nonetheless under a succession of blows from within. They stopped suddenly. Fentiman had heard his footsteps.

"I'd advise you to keep quiet, Major," Dawlish called in English. "I've men enough here who'll be only too glad to persuade you."

"So it's you, damn your soul!" Even the door's solidity could not mask Fentiman's anger. "I can guess what's happening out there, damn you, and the man in here with me doesn't look any too healthy either! You can't keep a man – a British officer, a fellow Englishman, God damn it! – to rot where there's yellow fever! Have you no honour, Man?"

Dawlish was suddenly back in that hotel dining room in Fiume and a name was springing into his mind. "Had Beatrice Hollins no honour then, Major?"

"Beatrice Hollins?" Fentiman sounded genuinely bemused and Dawlish realised that he had not even known her name.

"Ten years ago, Major, a chambermaid, at Lord Kegworth's." Dawlish was glad a door separated them for he knew he could not have restrained himself. "Think about Beatrice Hollins while you rot there, Major. And if you kick again I'll loose my men on you."

"Damn your soul then!" There was a new note in Fentiman's voice, of a fear deeper even than of the epidemic, and when Dawlish returned upstairs the racket had ceased.

Machado had vomited again, needed cleaning and water. He was still weaker, shivering violently and complaining with gestures of the agony exploding in his head. But his frame was massive, his body still powerful and his constitution must have been that of an ox to have survived privation, sickness and wounds as a guerrilla in the mountains. There was still hope.

"I'll sit with him to midnight," Dawlish told Esteban. The capataz was calmer now but looked exhausted. "If you sleep now I'll wake you later and you can relieve me." His own body was crying out for rest and tomorrow there must be one last check of every seal and bearing and valve. For the *Old Hickory* must be well past Punta Guarico by now. If not tomorrow then … but Machado was starting to choke again and a dark stream was dribbling from his mouth.

The sick man needed constant attention but Dawlish left him at intervals to ensure that the captive sentries were rotated and that the men who menaced them from the windows were alert. Machado kept four men in the house by night, two to watch the sentries, the others as reliefs and to check the cellar. Dawlish sensed their fear – no less intense for being unspoken – and hoped he was raising their spirits by a show of confident optimism he did not feel. He passed through the dark, airless house, the silence emphasised rather than broken by the woman's distant wailing, the muffled choking of the sick men, the steady, reluctant pacing of the guards on the veranda.

Dawlish looked out. On one side Boquerón was quiet and lifeless under its pall of fear and squalor. On the other lay the island-doted bay, calm and beautiful beneath the moonlight, *Tecumseh's* lights pinpoints in the distance. Out there, if all went well, he would soon be unleashing yet more death. He suddenly wanted it to be over, to be able to turn away from this vast fever-scourged prison, to forget conspiracies and subterfuge, to return to the comfortable certainties of disciplined routine, to stand once more on a spray-lashed bridge and feel a deck heave and surge beneath him. But first he had to clean Machado again, to bathe his forehead, to pray that his agony might be resolved swiftly.

By midnight he was fighting to stay awake, wishing for when he could rouse Esteban.

"He's asleep now," he told the capataz. Machado was moving fitfully and sweat still rose in great globules and glistened on his dark skin, but his breathing was more regular and he had not vomited for almost two hours. "Wake me if there's any change."

He stretched himself on a bed in an adjoining room, placed Machado's own Colt revolver under his pillow and was instantly asleep.

*

It must be a nightmare, Dawlish's brain told him as he jerked upright, momentarily confused, knowing only that gunfire was exploding close by…

The room was dark and suddenly he remembered he was in Cuba, in a house in Boquerón, and between the shots unseen feet were drumming on floorboards and a horse was whinnying and a woman was screaming and there were shouts…

He was on his feet instantly, pistol in hand. He moved to the window, plucked the curtain aside cautiously, saw four horses rearing and neighing in terror before the house. A man – a trooper, that strange striped cotton uniform was unmistakable – was struggling to hold them as he raised a revolver and fired clumsily towards the veranda. A body slumped face-up on the ground close by – one of the sentry-prisoners – and suddenly more shots echoed, from somewhere inside the house, from the floor below.

There were noises from the next room, where Machado lay, and as Dawlish moved to his own door, and cracked it open, he wanted to shout to Esteban to stay put. But it was too late. The capataz as already rushing down the corridor, armed with another of those revolvers recovered from the weapons cache. He reached the top of the stairs, yelled something, and then jerked back and fell as someone blasted from lower down. He struggled to his feet, moaning, but the second shot finished him and threw him down. Dawlish levelled his pistol on the space above the body, ready for the rush that would carry the attackers on to this floor, but none came, just more gunfire, acrid smoke rolling up the stairs, more shouting from below and a woman's screaming cut off by a single isolated shot.

Whoever they were, they were not coming up.

Dawlish edged from the room, flattened himself against the wall and moved down the corridor. He reached the stairhead and forced himself to look around the corner and down. One of his own men was crumpled on the steps below, his torso a dark, sodden mess. Somebody rushed past, visible for an instant, then lost in the deep shadows, but Dawlish thought he recognised one of the captive sentries who had been forced to pace the veranda. The shooting had ended now – the implications filled him with hollow dread – but he could hear the sound of shouting from the direction of the cellar and a woman's voice, strong and strident, shrieking in delight and triumph and a man's roar that could only be Fentiman's.

The major's mistress had not forsaken her lover.

251

Down the stairs, Dawlish skirting the body there, sheltering against the wall. He peered around the corner. The stairs led on to the main hallway and to his left he could see the open door leading to the square – the horses were still whinnying there and he caught a brief glimpse of one still plunging – and to the right another door gaped open, that leading down to the kitchen stairs. Two more bodies lay in the smoke-wreathed hall – one of the sentries, and the man who should have killed him before he could have left the veranda, alike now in death. A bloody crater on the wall above told of a shotgun blast taken straight in the face. Another body lay contorted in an open doorway, but Dawlish had eyes only for the door at the hallway's end, for he knew now with terrible certainty that Fentiman would emerge from it at any moment, liberated by his harridan mistress and the escort she had brought with her. Whether she had come with troopers on a mission of compassion for her stricken lover and had stumbled on the truth, or whether she had received information beforehand, even how she had gained entrance, by bluff or by storm, was immaterial now. Dawlish knew only that he must kill the major.

Footsteps now, sounds of dragging feet. Dawlish looked around the corner again. The sentry he had glimpsed before was half-carrying a body with him, the arm slung across his shoulder – Ramiro, the injured guard who had been confined with Fentiman. Another trooper was following, and his demeanour too told of relief after action, of exhilaration at survival, of too-early relaxation of vigilance. They were almost at Dawlish's corner now and he shrunk deeper into the shadow. Still there was no sign of Fentiman, only the sounds of a woman's shrill laughter.

They were almost past, halfway to the main door, when Ramiro's head lolled to the side. His eyes met Dawlish's. There was a brief instant of incomprehension before he gave a strangled shout. Then the man who half-carried him wheeled around and the trooper behind was pushing past and raising his carbine.

Dawlish fired first, saw the trooper's body jerk, the look of shock on the face, re-cocked and fired again. The trooper was hurled down and lay motionless and the two others were edging backward.

252

Ramiro sobbed "Disculpe, Señor! Por Dios, Señor!"

Dawlish emerged from the shadow, the revolver held before him, held towards their heads. "Go!" he said, "Go now, quickly!" and they went shambling towards the doorway, out into the square.

He drew back into the stairway's shadows. Silence now from the cellar, nothing but the thumping of his own heart.

Then suddenly a scream, a woman's scream, not of pain but of surprise and indignation, suddenly strangled.

"You hear me out there? Answer me, damn your soul?" From the dark above the kitchen stairs Fentiman's English words came in laboured bursts, as if he was struggling to restrain something, somebody, as he spoke.

Dawlish remained silent.

"I know you're waiting for me, damn you! You'd like to shoot me like a dog, wouldn't you?"

Again the sounds of a struggle, and then of a sharp blow, and a whimper.

"I told you to keep still, you bitch" Fentiman spoke in Spanish.

Dawlish suddenly knew what was coming but, even so, what followed disgusted him.

"I'll have a woman in front of me when I come out," the major called. "You won't shoot a woman, will you? Your precious sense of honour won't allow that, will it?"

Sounds of ineffectual struggle again, of another blow, then footsteps.

Fentiman appeared above the cellar stairway. His left arm was wrapped around the throat of a heavy, dark-haired woman – his mistress, Dona Marta. His right hand held a revolver to her temple. Eyes staring in terror, she was no longer struggling. He was moving backwards towards the kitchen to make his escape that way, keeping her body before him as his shield.

Dawlish did not follow. He left the shadows and crept towards the main door to the veranda. Through it he heard stamping hooves – the horses were protesting – and the major's yells of command as he emerged from the kitchen's entrance. The space before the house was empty but for the single body there – the horses had been led around the corner. Dawlish emerged on the veranda, hugging the shadows, and inched towards the corner.

He looked around – the four horses were still terrified, still circling and protesting as the trooper dragged them towards Fentiman. Behind them lurched Ramiro and the man who supported him. The major was moving slowly backwards towards the horses, his eyes on the house, searching for any sign of movement, his left arm still locked around Dona Marta's neck.

Ramiro and his companion had reached the horses, were taking reins from the trooper, who was facing the house, pistol in hand. To his left Fentiman was bellowing for the horses to be brought to him. But Ramiro and his helper were intent on their own escape. Ramiro managed to get one foot in the stirrup but the terrified animal circled and stamped and he was too weak to pull himself upwards. The other man was already in the saddle and moving his mount across to help him.

"Get down, damn you! Help me!" Fentiman yelled.

Dona Marta was writhing in his grip, furious and betrayed, but still he managed to hold her between him and the house.

The trooper was still twenty yards away, too far to risk a shot, even though Dawlish had rested the Colt's barrel along his forearm and had locked the sight on the man's abdomen. He had four rounds only, too few to gamble with.

Two horses broke loose, ripping their reins from the mounted man alongside who was attempting to lift Ramiro. They drummed across the square and disappeared down an alley.

This was Dawlish's chance. He saw the trooper before him hesitate, look back, saw Ramiro fall back as he lost his support, heard the major's cry of anger. Dawlish hurled himself forward, vaulted across the veranda rail, landed heavily enough to shoot agony through his still half-bruised ribs, stumbled to his feet and raced towards the trooper.

The man turned back too late, swinging his own weapon round to meet this onslaught, but Dawlish was already almost on top of him, and firing. The trooper caught the full impact in the chest and so died. The mounted man was shearing away, Ramiro abandoned, and was dragging a carbine from the bucket holster before the saddle. Dawlish rushed towards him, pistol outstretched. The rider's nerve failed. He kicked his beast and went clattering away across the square.

The bark of a pistol and something screaming past his head froze Dawlish in his tracks. Beyond the single remaining horse, on the stirrup of which Ramiro hung doggedly, too weak to lift himself, Fentiman was advancing, the weapon in his right hand jerking as Dona Marta twisted and kicked.

"Stand back!" he shouted. "Back!" His body was fully masked by the woman's but her struggling made it impossible for him to aim.

Dawlish paced back, raised his revolver, steeling himself to kill both man and woman together.

And at waist level it froze. He could not do it.

Fentiman reached the stamping horse and he slashed the revolver's barrel down on Ramiro's head. He fell, and the horse whinnied and stamped and circled, but Fentiman was hauling himself into its saddle and somehow dragging the woman with him. She was screaming, flailing with her arms and trying to reach his eyes, and it seemed impossible that he could maintain his balance. Dawlish dashed forward again, pistol upraised. The horse was rearing …

One instant Dawlish was on his feet, and there were but three paces to cover, and the next a solid mass was smashing him to the ground and a body was thrashing on top of him. He struggled free, found Dona Marta clutching him, lurching to her feet, swearing, and beyond them the major was wheeling his mount around and sweeping his revolver towards them.

Fentiman fired once, twice, three times before he spurred away. One slug screamed harmlessly overhead but it was his own mistress, slightly to Dawlish's front and left, who took the full impact of the other two.

She died in Dawlish's arms, blood burbling from her lips and soaking her dress. Her last words were of hatred for the man she had come to rescue.

But by then that man was well on the road to Dos Caminos. Where Colonel Almunia was. And Dawlish knew that his own hold on Boquerón had only hours left.

Failure stared him in the face.

24

"El Jefe cannot lead you," Dawlish forced himself to be patient. He had repeated it at least a dozen times before.

"Without him we will be slaughtered like chickens." Ambrosio, the man who had first offered him shelter here, spoke with a mixture of pleading and despair. He had already assumed the role of the dead capataz.

A dozen fellow would-be rebels nodded behind. "We cannot fight in the mountains without him, and we cannot stay here."

"El Jefe's too ill to travel." Yet Dawlish could think of no way of saving the comatose man from the vengeance about to fall on Boquerón. Death confronted all the others with no less certainty.

They were gathered before what was still a charnel house, for decisions were more important in these hours before daylight than clearing the bodies that littered it. The sounds of shooting had brought Cuba Libre's believers here, hesitant and fearful, too late to prevent Fentiman's escape. Others hovered on the edges of the square, bewildered villagers who had never suspected until now the masquerade that had been acted out in their midst. But all of them knew that, whatever had transpired last night, retribution would be both savage and indiscriminate.

"El Jefe still lives," Ambrosio said.

It was true, just. Machado's pulse was feeble but the massive chest still rose and fell weakly.

"Those whom el vómito does not kill in the first hours often live," Ambrosio said. "In two days, he can be carried with us."

Others murmured assent. They had seen enough of the pestilence in recent days to recognise a pattern in its caprices.

256

"I'll care for him," Dawlish said. "I brought him here, I can take him to safety again. But your own danger is greater. You should take your weapons, leave now, immediately."

"It's too late already." It was Geraldo, of the small tug. "Almunia's patrols will be watching every path away from here, however small."

Dawlish could imagine it already – battle-hardened troopers on well-fed mounts hunting, at most, forty frightened men on foot, unfamiliar with the weapons they had so recently acquired, their pitiful supplies carried on a half-dozen mules. It could only be a massacre, another futile, quickly-forgotten episode in the long sequence of failed Cuban revolts. He tried to tell himself that it was not his affair but the despairing faces before him – faces that had put blind trust in the man he had brought here – were a reproach he could not ignore.

"We could hold the town until El Jefe can travel," Ambrosio said.

"Impossible!" Dawlish was stunned no less by the suggestion's naivety than by the blind loyalty Machado inspired.

"Almunia won't attack immediately," Geraldo was aligning himself with Ambrosio. "Not today, maybe not even tomorrow or the next day. We know his methods, Señor, he's patient, he'll close off the town, gather reinforcements, maybe even cannon from Guantanamo or Caimanera, send for the *Spinola* to return..."

"And then you'll be slaughtered here like chickens."

"But before then, Señor, we have my tug, we have the lighters. Once El Jefe can be moved safely we can shift our men by night along the bay. We can land behind Almunia's patrols and disappear towards the mountains."

"It would be suicide," Dawlish said, but a small voice within told him it might answer his own needs. For the *Old Hickory* must be steaming westwards along the southern coast now...

"It's our country, Señor," Ambrosio said, "our liberty, our battle. You will leave here and forget us but we must fight as we know best."

They argued, but Dawlish knew the issue was already resolved. The talk was of details now, of disposition of men and weapons, of how to secure the approaches, of what to tell the townspeople, of the manner of evacuation. And bodies must be buried.

As the rising sun threw its first long shadows the flag that drooped above the customs house was, for the first time, not Spain's red and yellow but the five stripes and single star of Cuba Libre.

The fever-tortured man in the darkened room across the square did not yet know it but his revolt had been launched for him.

*

"Chinese or Indian, Mr. Holland?"

Beneath the awning stretched over the *Tecumseh's* upper deck Florence presided over the silver pots and snowy cloth as calmly as at East Egg, as if fear and pestilence did not reign in the squalid town not two miles distant, as if the ram did not nestle alongside, as if violent action, even death, was not perhaps just hours away. The heavy late-afternoon air lay over the bay's still waters like a smothering blanket. The anxiety around the table was palpable, yet nobody alluded to it.

Holland, awkward as ever in Florence's company, muttered his thanks. Then it was Raymond's turn, and Captain Swanson's, each taking his china cup and settling back his wicker chair, each masking unease in his own way. Dawlish, rested after six hours sleep and now bathed, shaved and comfortable again in clean white ducks, found himself calm now that the crisis was at hand.

Florence had woken him.

"There's news of the ship, Nick." He saw that she was forcing herself not to sound alarmed. "That little tug has just brought it. The skipper is waiting for you."

A signal fire lit by one of the lookouts on the southern coast had given the first indication but when Dawlish emerged on deck there was stronger evidence, a thin smudge of smoke drifting in the afternoon haze from an unseen vessel beyond the mouth of the outer bay. The *Old Hickory* had completed her passage from Mobile.

"It will be too late for her to guide her to Boquerón, Señor," Geraldo said. His small tug doubled as pilot boat for leading arrivals through the scattering of islands in Bahia Granadillo.

"But not too late for mooring between Punta Caracoles and Hospital Cay," Dawlish said. It was a common location for ships to pass the night before negotiating the intricate approaches to Boquerón or Caimanera. If the *Old Hickory* moored there it would be ideal for his purpose. If all went well the *Tecumseh* could be heading for the open sea soon after midnight.

"You're sure it is necessary to guide her there immediately, Señor?" Geraldo sounded troubled.

So well he might, Dawlish thought. Geraldo's life, Machado's, his associates', all depended on availability of his tug. Now he was being asked to venture it in a cause that did not serve them.

"After this I will ask nothing more of you," Dawlish said. "Lead the ship to Punta Caracoles, leave her, and the rest will be up to me."

Geraldo looked doubtful.

"The Springfields will be delivered," Dawlish added. "You will not see me again, but you can rely upon it that you and El Jefe will have the rifles."

"I'll guide her to Punta Caracoles," the skipper said at length. "And then I'll head back straight to Boquerón." He extended his hand uncertainly. "Adios, Nicolás."

"I wish you luck, Geraldo, you and El Jefe and the others."

As he took his hand and drew him towards him in an embrace, Dawlish felt that a gulf had opened already. This brave, simple man knew that Cuba Libre was already none of Dawlish's concern, that the ragged feeble-minded Nicolás Quinones had been laid to rest.

Dawlish watched the tug depart. In less than an hour it would be hailing the *Old Hickory*. Geraldo had his story ready for explaining Fentiman's absence – a minor indisposition only, with no allusion to Yellow Fever. If no suspicion was aroused the steamer's bows would soon be nudging northwards towards its anchorage.

The last details were settled across the tea table. Swanson confirmed that steam was up, the safety valves all but lifting. He was sweating profusely, conscious that he was committing himself to action which could put a noose around his neck – and his crew's – in any maritime court in the world.

Holland seemed consumed with misgiving, for all that he had helped Egdean inspect the ram and confirm that the air-reservoirs were holding pressure, every linkage and bearing free, every seal resilient.

"It's a terrible thing to endanger a man's life, much less kill him," he said. "It's not something to do without just cause. I hope to God you're in the right, Mr. Page. I hope that you're not risking your immortal soul."

"There's none of us would be here without you, Mr. Holland!" Raymond slapped him genially on the shoulder, "so we'll leave you to worry about your own soul, and ours when you've time left over, and the rest of us will get on with the business in hand. You agree, Captain Swanson?"

Raymond had already slipped into the role that would be his in the hours ahead, that of spotting the first signs of hesitation, of quelling doubts, of holding the captain and his crew of mercenaries to the bargain they had made.

Only Florence had no obvious task but as he glanced towards her and caught her eye, and saw the sad, resolute, loving gleam in it, Dawlish knew that he was dependent on her most of all.

*

The *Tecumseh* crept ahead at quarter revolutions, wholly dark but for the masked glow within the binnacle, warm blackness enveloping her. A blanket of cloud blocked out the full moon above.

At the masthead, on the bows, on the bridge, every eye strained ahead. They were passing from Granadillo into the outer bay. There was as yet no sign of the newcomer yet even though Geraldo's tug had flashed confirmation that the *Old Hickory* was safely moored. Dawlish, with Raymond by his side, swept his glass slowly, searching for any sights of shipping lights against the land mass of the western shore.

Nothing.

The silence around him was broken only by Swanson's curt and irregular instructions to the helmsman. Egdean too had a telescope and searched the blackness with the calm thoroughness of the experienced lookout. Florence stood in the port bridge-wing, mute as the others, darkly shawled, alone with her worries. She and Dawlish had said their good-byes already and silence and patience were what he needed of her until... until... He pushed away the thought.

The bows swung to port, away from the dark strip that was Hospital Cay. Dawlish could sense that the *Tecumseh* was burdened as much with fear and apprehension as by the ram that strained on the tow-line astern. A projectile was already loaded in her launching tube. He had visited the yacht's boiler and engine rooms, had spoken personally to every deckhand, had assured each man of his trust in him, had emphasised again that payment was assured, to their families if they themselves could not collect. He had encountered forced cheerfulness and sullen resignation – in one case outright insolence, though he let it pass – but none of the pride, defiant good-humour and stubborn resolution that he would have taken for granted from a Royal Navy crew. Only Carter, the marine veteran who had helped Dawlish snatch the ram from the New Haven yard, seemed unconcerned by the risks ahead. He was whetting his knife as if in a trance, as apparently unworried as Egdean, even if he had not prepared himself, as Egdean had, with a half-hour's Bible reading.

Then Dawlish saw her, mooring lights winking somewhat over a mile ahead, a long, irregular, indistinct profile.

"See there..." he passed the glasses to Raymond.

A pause, and then the American said: "I'll stake my reputation on it." He alone had seen her before and when he did she was in a graving dock.

"You're sure?"

"It's the *Old Hickory*." Raymond's tone left no doubt.

"Captain Swanson," Dawlish said. "Heave to, if you please."

Now it was time.

"Go aft, Egdean. Light the pilot."

261

"Aye, Aye, Sir." Simple words that had so often confirmed this plain man's unconditional loyalty from Zanzibar to Paraguay, yet never so welcome as now.

Dawlish turned to Swanson, his voice a whisper. "I'll be casting off now, Captain."

They had rehearsed this moment a dozen times on hand-sketched diagrams, chewing endlessly over every detail, desperately hoping for a moonless night when the unlit yacht would be invisible in the darkness. The reality of this overcast night was better than they could have hoped for.

"Afterwards, if you don't spot us, if you don't..." Dawlish found himself groping for words, as if specifying the danger might make it more probable.

"I won't hazard the ship, Mr. Page." They had agreed this long before.

"Even if Mrs. Page protests?" As she would, with savage unwillingness to accept Fate's verdict.

"Even if Mrs. Page protests." Swanson's tone left no doubt. "But we won't talk of that, Sir. I'll be seeing you back. I'll be seeing you back, Sir, sure thing, no doubt of it."

Dawlish nodded to Florence, as if to a slight acquaintance, and left the bridge. She turned away, gripped the rail before her tightly.

The ram had been drawn against the yacht aft, little more than the hatch casing showing above the water. A Jacob's ladder reached down to it from the bulwark. Carter stood atop the curved deck and helped Dawlish down. Egdean was already below. Dawlish lowered himself through the hatch.

"She's warm, Sir, the pilot light's steady."

"Start the engine if you please."

Five turns of the hand crank, the flywheel spinning up and then compression closed. The Brayton fired immediately and settled down to a low, gurgling chug.

"Well done, Egdean. She's never sounded better." Dawlish stuck out his head and shoulders. "Ready now, Mr. Carter. I'll be obliged if you push us off now."

Dawlish glimpsed Florence watching from the deck where she had so recently dispensed tea, but he noted her remotely, as already gone for him, for his mind was concentrated totally on the ram. In the compartment below, Egdean was adjusting the engine to a slow, reliable idle.

"You show them sons of bitches, Mr. Page," Carter called as he hoisted himself back on to the Jacob's ladder. "Come back now, mind, and Jerry too!"

Dawlish settled himself on the saddle, grasped the extended control levers.

"Engage the clutch, Egdean."

A lurch and a drop in revolutions as gears meshed. Dawlish opened the throttle slightly. Brayton purring smoothly, hatch open, the ram glided into the darkness.

25

Dawlish could just see over the hatch rim as the ram headed for the *Old Hickory's* lights. They still seemed impossibly distant. He twisted and saw the *Tecumseh's* hull, pale and ghostly, fading into the blackness astern.

The slightest of breezes rippled the surface. The bow-wave building before the casing was scarcely higher than on the calm reaches of the Mill River. Dawlish aligned the two aiming rods set vertically in the foredeck on *Old Hickory's* shadowy profile, and opened the throttle slightly further. The exhaust was burbling steadily through the check valves aft and he estimated the speed at just over two knots.

"Anything to report, Egdean?"

"All steady, Sir, all steady."

For eight, ten minutes the moored vessel seemed to grow no nearer. At last her shape began resolving itself, a long, slim hull, raised islands at bow, amidships and stern, a single raked funnel, twin masts with their auxiliary sailing rig. There was nothing to distinguish her from a thousand other merchantmen, humble tramps that plied the trade lanes – nothing but the concealed compartment that would shelter the ram until she could be unleashed for its assassin's work. A coat of paint, a slight change of rig, the erection of a second, dummy, funnel, or of a canvas deckhouse, could transform the *Old Hickory's* appearance within a day, give her a new identity, allow her to fade into anonymity until it was time to strike again.

"Less than a mile now, Egdean."

He marvelled silently, and gratefully, at stolid acceptance of the seaman who crouched, blind and disorientated, in the hot darkness by the engine, his hands moving occasionally to check levers and hand wheels, his lips most likely moving in the prayers that gave him so much comfort. And Dawlish realised that the fear that he himself had so much dreaded was absent, forgotten in the press of care and concentration of the last half-hour.

Five minutes passed and the steamer drew nearer still. He closed the throttle slightly, slowed, anxious lest the tiny bow-wave show white against the darkness. That darkness was less intense now, for the first breaks were showing in the clouds, and diffuse moonlight was filtering through. He corrected the course slightly to port to keep the *Old Hickory's* lights winking against the shoreline's darkness.

Closer now – more tense, though not with fear, but rather with the controlled exhilaration of a stalker creeping ever-nearer to a stag. His gaze was riveted on the steamer, no more than eight cables distant now. With luck one shot might do it...

Time now to bleed air from the trim tank aft, to admit water and raise the bow, to expose the projector muzzle...

"Egdean!" His voice was calm. "Stand by to..."

And at that moment a cry rang out from off to starboard, incoherent, but its message of alarm unmistakable. Above the Brayton's low chatter and the bubbling of her exhaust Dawlish heard a second call ring out in Spanish "Por allá!" – "Over there!" – and then more voices.

He turned, saw a dark shape perhaps two cables away to port, towards the open sea, a white vee of foam breaking before a sharp stem and what looked like a three-pounder above it and smoke spilling from a tiny brass funnel on which the moonlight gleamed. He recognised it immediately as a launch and, worse, beyond it, two, perhaps three miles seawards at the very mouth of the bay, he saw a larger shape, unmistakable beneath the thinning clouds as the *Spinola*. If her captain had been squared, as Fentiman had claimed, then he was determined to raise his price and was sending a boat to levy it from the *Old Hickory*. Dawlish cursed himself for the single-minded concentration that had focused him on his target at the expense of all else.

"Por allá!" The cry echoed again and the white vee edged over, heading straight for the ram. A shout issued from the *Old Hickory* too and a light appeared there, and another, and he glimpsed figures moving across them.

Only one decision was possible.

"Open the air bleed, Egdean," he called into the dark void beneath him, "I'm taking her down."

"Aye, Aye, Sir."

The ram's bows were set directly towards the *Old Hickory*, six, seven, cables distant now, and the steamer lay squarely beam-on. He could not risk collision when submerged, yet if he did not hold as straight a course as possible there was no knowing where he might surface. He swung the hatch cover over and lowered it as gently as he could, then hammered the dogs closed. The familiar close, oily, warm darkness he loathed wrapped him like a shroud.

"Ballast, Egdean!"

Dawlish's own hand was on the horizontal rudder lever, pushing it slightly forward, nudging the stern up, the bow down, even as Egdean opened the air valve on the vent line of the tank underfoot. Air rushed through it, driven by the water entering through the open ports in the bottom. The ram shuddered and seemed to drop. On the surface the top of the hatch would be disappearing now and white froth would be boiling eight feet ahead of it as the last of the air was expelled from the ballast tank. There was a chance – a good chance, a small internal voice told Dawlish – that the *Spinola's* launch's lookout might interpret it as barracuda falling on a shoal of fish.

"Close the air line!"

The bows were dropping further, the slowly rotating screw driving the ram further under. Dawlish eased back the horizontal rudder, felt the bow lift slightly, eased a little more, and then he was holding to as near to level as he could sense by a series of tiny adjustments. He was listening intently to the exhaust – the engine revolutions were so low that it was by far the loudest noise – and he satisfied himself that the hatch must be at least ten feet under, and certainly not more than fifteen. It was a comfortable depth if he could maintain it. Even if the bows rose there was little chance of breaking the surface before he could correct it and yet it was not deep enough to put the seals under undue pressure.

He had held the vertical rudder unmoved since they had submerged. With luck they were still heading straight towards *Old Hickory*. He was counting steadily, pacing out the seconds, five hundred and thirty one, five hundred and thirty two… almost nine minutes. Measured runs a few days since had indicated some fifty yards to sixty yards per minute at this throttle setting. Provided the ram had not strayed off course it was now five hundred yards closer to the steamer than when she had dived, almost half way.

Options sped through Dawlish's brain – to continue submerged, or to rise and attack immediately, or to rise and reconnoitre. It would be simple were he to know what was happening above. Had the alarm on the *Spinola's* launch been construed as false? If not, had it been passed by lamp to the Spanish gunboat? That was what he most feared. The *Old Hickory* was not getting underway – that he was sure of, for it was close enough for any thrash of her screw to sound through the ram's hull. And yet even if the alarm had been raised, who might have expected a threat rising from below? Surprise was on his side. It would remain so until he had discharged the projector. Surprise, as so often before, was his most powerful ally.

He made his decision. Attack.

"Flood the trim tank!"

Egdean released the lever above the tiny tank aft, counted to fifteen, as trial and error had proved sufficient, then closed it sharply. Dawlish sensed the hull settling by the stern by some three feet, the bow rising. He felt Egdean's hand brush his leg, reaching for the valve on the main ballast tank's air line, grasping it, waiting for the command he knew was coming.

"Blow the main ballast!"

The ram heaved upwards, then rolled slightly and Dawlish knew she was on the surface, wallowing gently.

"Close the air bleed," he called, "Stand by the projector," then pounded the hatch's locking dogs free and hung his weight on it to stop the escaping over-pressure from within swinging it back like a bell-clapper.

For an instant he saw the sky above – the clouds were ragged and there was more moonlight now. He pushed his head and shoulders into the deliciously clean air and hinged the hatch down silently.

The submerged course had wandered slightly to port. The *Old Hickory* was just off the starboard bow, five hundred yards distant – and four-hundred was the ideal launching range. He glanced over his right shoulder to find the Spanish launch but it seemed to have turned away. The lookout had most likely been chided for seeing danger where there was none and would be hesitant to risk reproof a second time.

Dawlish reached down, felt for the throttle lever, edged it back. The rotations dropped to an idle, and the speed dropped even further. The projector's domed bow cap was just level with the surface ahead and water climbed over it and streamed away in the slightest of ripples. He pushed the rudder lever over slightly, let the ram curve over until the aiming rods were aligned on a point in open water some twenty yards to starboard of the steamer's stern. His heart was thumping, blood racing in his brain, his hands trembling, and nothing existed but the lamp-lit *Old Hickory* as the ram crept stealthily forward.

"Open the bow cap!" He dropped his face towards the hot darkness within to speak the command, detected Egdean's bulk crouched by the projector breech, the white blur of his raised face.

"Aye, Aye, Sir!"

The cap flipped up and Dawlish fought the awareness that the projectile might now be as dangerous to the ram as to the steamer. Water was surging aft into the projector tube, washing towards the rounded nose of the projectile within – fifty pounds of dynamite – and only the triple leather seals around the cylinder flanks blocked its access to the four fuses at the rear. Seawater would activate them, dissolving in ten seconds the plugs of salt that covered the exposed terminals of a small Daniel electric cell, shorting the minute gap between them, sending a tiny current coursing through the detonator, exploding the main charge. And that would be enough to obliterate the ram and both men she carried.

The range was closing. Almost perfect now. Another ten yards...

"Fire!"

Spray erupted before the bow like a huge half-moon fan and the champagne-cork report that attended it was loud enough to waken the most drowsy lookout on any vessel within a mile. The projectile was lost in the darkness but already Dawlish was shouting "Close the bow cap" and his eyes were riveted on the waters astern of the steamer.

"Bow cap clo..."

But Dawlish had no ears for the rest. He saw figures, two, three, dashing from the steamer's midships accommodation. They froze as they saw the splash climbing, thirty yards from the vessel's stern, standing still for an instant, then collapsing, leaving only a spreading circle of ripples. The aim had been perfect, and now the projectile would be sinking, and the water eating greedily into the salt plugs.

He started counting, one, and two, and three ... He reached for the hatch cover, drew it vertical, ready to slam closed ...and six and seven ... only the thinnest layer would cover the fuse terminals now ...

A hillock rose from the surface, ten, fifteen feet, and suddenly it was ruptured by a white geyser blasting up through its summit. Foaming concentric waves lashed out from this tortured centre.

"Brace yourself!" Dawlish yelled, but already a dull blow was slamming into the ram and he was flung violently against the hatch rim.

He steadied himself, transfixed by the sight of the *Old Hickory* rearing furiously upwards as a wall of water hit her, then plunging no less violently as it passed, funnel and ventilators and masts lashing in metallic agony as stays snapped. Yet it was not the damage above the waterline that mattered – that could be repaired – but how the hull's framing, and the plating that clad it, resisted the gigantic hammer blow. But now the racing wall of water was speeding towards the ram, high and fast enough to roll over her, and her own survival was Dawlish's first priority. He slammed the hatch down, drove the dogs home and clung tightly to the ladder rungs.

The wave hit and the convulsive rolling, plunging, pitching, jerking that followed was all the worse for the darkness and roaring that enveloped them. Dawlish was remotely aware of crying out as his forehead smashed against bare metal. He heard Egdean shout out involuntarily but one fear overrode all else, of rivets popping, of seams parting and the ram's structure rupturing under the very forces she herself had unleashed. But the Delamater Iron Works had produced a hull which would have been worthy of the Portsmouth Naval Dockyard itself and though it thrashed and leaped no sheets of water came spraying through rending flanks. At last the motion subsided and Dawlish sensed the craft wallowing as if on a turbulent surface.

"Are you hurt, Egdean?"

"I'll live, Sir."

He was suddenly aware of the Brayton's silence – and that could be more deadly than the maelstrom they had just survived.

"I'm opening the hatch. Start the engine as soon as I do."

He flung it open, thrust his head into the night, saw only blackness ahead, creaming foam surrounding the ram, diminishing waves racing off into the darkness. He could see no vessels, no lights and realised that the ram's convulsions had rotated her through some sixteen points. He twisted, looked astern.

The *Old Hickory*, battered, wounded, tortured, lit only by three lanterns now, was still afloat on an even keel. The attack had failed.

There was worse – the Spanish launch was cutting directly towards the ram, hastening to the stricken steamer's aid, oblivious of the obstacle in her path.

Safety lay in one direction only. Down.

Dawlish slammed the hatch shut and through the oily darkness heard Egdean heaving on the starting crank. But louder still was the approaching beat of the launch's propeller reverberating through the hull plating.

"She'll fire, Sir," Egdean gasped, "she surely will." He slammed the compression closed and the engine coughed, made three spluttering revolutions, then died.

"You've declutched her?" Dawlish felt mounting despair.

"I have, Sir, and..." He had the flywheel turning again, and this time Brayton responded, breaking into an irregular, choking idle.

"Now the ballast!" The pilot boat's screw was echoing louder now ...

Air blasted from the vent line and water rushed into the tank. The ram lurched, settled – she was sinking more quickly this time, for the trim-tank aft was full – and her plating was panting and booming to the churn of the nearing screw outside.

"Open the air bleed, Egdean! Open it fully!"

Dawlish pushed the throttle lever over slowly, engaged the clutch, heard the Brayton stutter, then smoothen, as her revolutions increased. The ram's own screw was biting now – he felt her surge forward, and he pushed the vertical rudder lever forward. The bow dipped, steeper than ever before, and he sensed the vessel burrowing deeper, impelled by the screw's thrust.

"God have mercy on us!"

Egdean's cry was involuntary as the noise above reached a crescendo, a rushing, thumping drumbeat superimposed on a roaring swish of waters surging past the launch's hull. The ram heaved, as if dragged by the suction of the keel racing scant feet above her, and then the pitch of sound was changing and it was diminishing and the danger was past. For now.

Dawlish had no idea of the depth. He knew only that the bows were still down, the ram plunging towards a level where external pressure might collapse it or the seabed trap it. The engine had slowed, was coughing, the exhaust hardly capable of opening the check valve against the weight of the water column. He eased the horizontal rudder past neutral, held it, felt the bows rising and the Brayton revolutions picking up again. His hands were shaking – the fear was back, worse even than at New Haven – and he guided the ram towards the surface, no matter what might lie there.

"They've never seen us," Egdean said, invisible in the darkness. Dawlish guessed he had his ear against the plating. "They're slowing, Sir, perhaps they're going alongside the steamer."

"Reduce the air-bleed," Dawlish said.

He closed the throttle, held the vessel on an even keel and used the vertical rudder to bring it into a slow, steady circular pattern, hoping he could hold it there, clear of the moored ship, for another three or four minutes. He hoped even more that he could control his rising terror.

"The bow cap's closed, Egdean? You're sure?" The tremor in his voice shamed him.

"It's closed, Sir."

And if it was not, if the violent manoeuvres had unseated it, a solid eight-inch water jet would come streaming in when Egdean opened the projector's breech. Against that influx, no deballasting could get them to the surface.

Dawlish hesitated. The ram was still apparently undetected, could still creep back to rendezvous with the *Tecumseh*. Then pride – or madness – reasserted itself.

"Load the projector, Egdean."

The copper hammer pounded on the closure's lugs. Then there was the sound of the last thread releasing, the cap swinging free, and water cascading back into the compartment to slosh underfoot. And then no further flow. The bow-cap had held.

"I'm unscrewing the protectors, Sir," Egdean called through the darkness. There was a tremor in his voice too, for once the covers were removed from the fuses the salt plugs would be exposed.

271

There was no shortage of water underfoot to dissolve them should the projectile slip from his grasp.

Dawlish heard Egdean release the clip that held the projectile against the side, and the scrape of the metal fins on the deck as he manhandled it towards the open breech. The huge seaman gasped with effort as he raised the head and lodged it in the tube. Leather seals squealed as he shoved it deep inside.

"It's home, Sir! Nearly done!" Slower than in the calm waters off Boquerón, but a credible effort for frightened toil in total darkness.

"Well done, Egdean!"

It was not only the steady blows tightening the closure that reassured Dawlish, but the very proximity of the simple, gentle man who had come through so much with him. Egdean must never suspect that without his presence he would have been sobbing in panic by now.

"Prepared for firing, Sir." An edge of pride in the tone, the pride that had carried tens of thousands like him through hell at Quiberon Bay, the Nile, Trafalgar.

"Blow the main ballast!"

As air rushed into the tank Dawlish told himself, unwillingly, that there would be no choice but to run the compressor if they were to have sufficient air for another dive. It would be noisy, but if all went well there would be sufficient confusion for nobody to notice...

The ram was wallowing slightly and through the glass ports Dawlish could detect the slightest pallor of moonlight. He swung his full weight on the hatch as he released the dogs but the overpressure was enough to jerk him with it as it escaped. He restrained the hatch with difficulty, laid it back, pushed his head out. The *Old Hickory* lay three cables to starboard and the ram was moving parallel to her.

Chaos reigned there. Lights danced over the steamer's superstructure – men with lanterns – and the Spanish launch had drawn alongside amid confused shouting that echoed clearly across the intervening water.

"Open the bow cap!"

The ram was undetected, the circumstances ideal for a stealthy approach ...

Dawlish nudged the rudder over, swung the bows until they were pointing just ahead of the steamer's bows, opened the throttle slightly and crept steadily forward. The range was closing ...

There were sounds of panic on the *Old Hickory*, men shouting, the flash of a single revolver shot aimed high as if to restore order and abrupt silence for an instant thereafter, then shouting growing again.

Five hundred yards, and figures were dropping down to the launch ... another thirty seconds, and another single pistol report... The closer the projectile landed to the hull the better, for the frames must be already strained, perhaps even seams ruptured, by the shock of the first explosion. Dawlish edged the bows over further, steadied, and the aiming rods were shaving just past the steamer's bow...

"Fire!"

Again the fan of droplets and the loud report and the call of "Close the bow cap!" as the projectile blasted on its low trajectory. The fan collapsed and beyond it a white column climbed up not five yards from the steamer's side, close enough for its spray to shower it as it collapsed.

Dawlish pounded the coaming in delight and shouted involuntarily "Bull's eye!" Then he checked himself, throttled back, and began to count, telling off the seconds to the fuses' detonation. Jerking lanterns on *Old Hickory's* deck revealed men rushing to investigate this new mystery and ...

The sea rose.

It rose like a smooth mound and the steamer was on the slope, the bow pitching up on the incline, the stern plunging under, and then from the very summit a frothing volcano belched forth, throwing a column of seething white, thirty, forty feet skywards. A hammer-blow hit the ram, jarring, brutal, though weaker by far at this distance than the impact that must have pounded the *Old Hickory*, but Dawlish was braced for it. His eyes remained locked in awe on the collapse of the boiling storm of spray. The steamer was thrashing down with it, only her superstructure visible as churning lather surged across her canting decks. The foremast whipped like a sapling in a gale, then tumbled sideways and the funnel toppled over in a swirling cloud of smoke and sparks, crushing the lifeboat on davits beside it.

A solid white-capped rampart of water was racing towards the ram.

"Hold on!" Dawlish yelled and slammed the hatch closed. The ram had endured this once before, and he was certain now that she would survive it again, but that made the tormented wrenching and rolling and buffeting no less easy to bear. And this time the Brayton did not die, so that when at last Dawlish dared to throw the hatch open again it was still somehow ticking over.

"Did we do it, Sir?" Egdean's tone was plaintive, that of a man who did not want to go through this again.

"We did."

And he was appalled by it.

The *Old Hickory* was heeling over into a cauldron of raging foam, her silhouette against the torn clouds different now, shorn of mast and funnel, her bow submerged and great bubbles gurgling from the shattered hull beneath. Amidships, where tongues of flame were starting to lick on the splintered decking around the collapsed funnel, men were leaping across the gap opening between the ship and the Spanish launch. The small craft was drawing away, her whistle shrilling, figures clustering her sides, some tossing lines toward others struggling in the angry waters.

Dawlish forced the image of suffering from his mind. He had seen ships die before, and men too, and he knew that to dwell on it was the road to madness. He pushed the rudder over and opened the throttle slightly, swinging the ram's bows away from the stricken vessel. The sky had cleared considerably and now only shreds of cloud obscured the moon. He searched the horizon, fancied he saw the faint blur that represented salvation, the *Tecumseh* holding station. Florence would be watching the growing flames in silent horror, and Holland would be torn between pride and anguish as he saw his vision realised and his countrymen frustrated, and Swanson and his lookouts would be straining for any sight of the tiny vee of white thrown up by the ram's low superstructure. Dawlish aimed the bows towards the yacht, opened the throttle further and called down to Egdean to engage the compressor. The noise level was high, but he gambled on nobody having ears for it.

Only now did Dawlish search for the *Spinola* and the full implications of her presence hit him. The gunboat was moving slowly up the bay, her yards bare, smoke billowing from her stack. The captain, surprised and horrified by the explosions that has erupted from nowhere, would be exercising extreme caution as he approached the sinking vessel, drawn onwards by the screams of his own launch's whistle. Every eye would be straining, every weapon would be manned – and the *Spinola* carried four six-inch Parrot rifled muzzle loaders, well capable of reducing the *Tecumseh* to a hulk with a half-dozen shots.

It could only be minutes before the *Spinola* spotted the white-hulled yacht hovering so suspiciously in the shadowy waters beyond the stricken steamer. Driscoll's dream might be foundering with the *Old Hickory* but retribution was already imminent.

Dawlish glanced towards the *Tecumseh* and he could all but feel Florence's presence. He had but one option.

"Load the projector, Egdean," he shouted, pushing the rudder bar over.

The ram's work was not yet finished.

26

The *Spinola's* hull was foreshortened, the red and green dots of her navigation lights showing that she was heading towards the burning *Old Hickory*. The range was over a mile, far beyond the projector's throw, yet even had it been closer Dawlish knew that the chances of hitting a moving target were negligible. Deterrence, not sinking, was the best he could hope for. Below him, despite the Brayton's clatter, he could hear Egdean manhandling the projectile into the breech, the thump of his copper hammer on the closure lugs.

Dawlish moved the rudder fractionally to align the sights on the ever-closer *Spinola*. The trim tank aft was flooded and the bows raised so that the domed cap there was just skimming the surface ahead.

"Prepared for firing, Sir!"

"Open the bow cap!"

An orange flash lit up the gunboat's bows, smoke billowed, and an instant later a Parrot's boom rolled over the ram, just before its shell screamed overhead. Dawlish twisted to look towards *Tecumseh*. Her white hull shimmered ghostly through the semi-darkness – the Spanish lookouts would have been blind not to have spotted her. Her proximity to the burning steamer could be no coincidence, but they had not seen, could not imagine, the nearer threat, the ram, awash, crawling towards them. The shell dropped in a frothing column off the yacht's port quarter – wide, but not bad for a ranging shot.

Dawlish turned again to face the oncoming gunboat. The ram's bows had wandered slightly and he nudged them over until the sighting rods were one with the *Spinola's* masts. The range must be fifteen hundred yards now ...

"Fire!"

He fancied he glimpsed the projectile's fall, a tiny dot against the now moonlit sky, and then the pale splash as it plunged down three cables ahead of the gunboat's bows.

"Close the bow cap!" he shouted, simultaneously counting in his head, telling off the seconds as the water ate into the salt covering the detonator terminals. Below, Egdean was struggling with the next projectile and ...

The eruption clawed upwards, a white maelstrom of spray and foam that blocked the gunboat from view. Still it climbed and Dawlish was calling "Brace yourself!" and pulling the hatch closed above him and throttling the Brayton back to an idle.

The hammer-blow smashed into the ram. As she thrashed and wallowed Dawlish felt his terror rise and forced himself to hold Florence's image in his mind. Terrified by the fall of the gunboat's shot, she would have seen his projectile's detonation, would know that he placed himself between her and danger, that he would...

But the buffeting was subsiding and he realised that he and the ram had once more somehow survived.

"Egdean?"

"I'm all right, Sir!"

"Reload!"

Dawlish threw the hatch open, thrust out his head. The ram had been hurled from her previous course and the *Old Hickory* was dead ahead, her stern lifting, her superstructure awash with flames. To port, beyond the creaming pool radiating from the projectile's explosion, the *Spinola* lay beam on and was turning away. The Spanish captain would have realised that no gunfire had preceded the fury that had risen before his bows, that its magnitude exceeded any conventional shell's. There could be only one explanation imaginable – a remotely-actuated mine. Confronted by this sudden apparent escalation in Cuban rebel capability the captain must be reasoning that where there was one mine there would be more. It was essential to reinforce that reasoning.

Dawlish opened the throttle – the engine had purred without interruption while the ram bucked and plunged – and again swung the bow towards the gunboat.

"Prepared for firing, Sir!" Egdean's voice was a croak in the suffocating atmosphere below.

The routine was familiar now, the loud "pop", the fan of spray, the finned projectile disappearing against the gunboat's silhouette, the brief splash and the long seconds as it sank. The *Spinola* was eight hundred yards and more beyond the point of fall. She had turned away and was already headed seawards, the *Tecumseh* ignored for now.

Some variation in dynamite quality, some difference perhaps in the depth at which the water devoured the last skin of salt, made this detonation the most spectacular of all, a boiling mountain of tortured water that climbed well over fifty feet before it froze and hung suspended before crashing down again.

The bow cap was already closed, the main hatch's dogs hammered tight, the engine throttled back, when the shock smashed into the ram, rolling and pitching her as before. But now, as he clung to the ladder and endured, Dawlish knew that he had saved the

Tecumseh for now. Only a lunatic or a hero would venture his ship closer inshore against a menace that could break his vessel's back – and the Spanish captain's caution so far had shown him to be neither.

Once more the heaving stilled and when Dawlish opened the hatch the *Spinola* was stern on, white cream beneath her transom as she thrashed away from the projectile's now-subsiding pool of seething froth. But she was retreating, not fleeing, and he did not doubt she would hover at the bay's entrance, far enough for safety from any mines the captain might imagine, near enough to observe any movement. The *Tecumseh* was still going to have to run past her for the open sea...

He glanced astern, searching for the yacht. He found her, a mile distant, her hull dyed crimson by the *Old Hickory's* flames and she was crawling on a course that would carry her between him and the blazing steamer. On her bridge every eye, Florence's most of all, would be searching for the tiny dot that was the ram's superstructure. He eased the throttle fully open and turned the bows for interception. Beyond the burning ship he spotted the Spanish launch straining for the western shore, too weighted down with survivors to represent a threat.

"Egdean!" He shouted into the suffocating darkness beneath. "Stand easy!"

"Shall I reload, Sir?" The seaman sounded surprised.

"No need. Rest yourself!"

The ram had served her purpose and soon he would be rid of her – the thought brought a brief surge of joy. He allowed himself to slump on the hatch rim, grateful for the clean air, and noticed that his hands were trembling. For the ordeal was not over. The *Spinola* still barred escape.

The *Tecumseh* was swinging over and accelerating. She had spotted the ram.

He closed the throttle, heard the Brayton splutter and die. Soon it would be time to flood the main ballast, to leave the hatch open as he stepped across to the yacht, and consign the ram to the oblivion he had undertaken to bring it to.

The *Tecumseh* was a cable distant now. Somebody in her bows was shouting incomprehensible instructions through a hailing-trumpet. Dawlish lowered himself into the warm gloom.

"Go on deck, Egdean!" He would handle the scuttling himself. He shoved the seaman up the ladder, and felt for the ballast lever, ready to pull it fully open to sink the ram permanently.

A metallic crash reverberated through the hull and he looked up to see the white of the *Tecumseh's* port side through the hatchway's disk. Then shouts, and scraping as hull ground against hull. The yacht's forward momentum died as her screw reversed briefly.

Dawlish's hands were on the ballast lever – and then he paused. Slow the ram might be, and incapable of hitting a moving target, but she was the only weapon he had, The *Spinola* and her Parrots still lay seawards. Suddenly he saw how he might still use this weapon and he released the lever as if it were hot, appalled at how close he had come to throwing away this best hope.

He felt hands grab his shoulders, Egdean pulling him through the hatch. Carter had descended to the curved decking.

"Rig a line to the towing shackle!" Dawlish gasped, swinging the hatch closed behind him. "Run it aft! We're taking her in tow again!"

As they set to it he moved to the Jacob's ladder. Hands reached down and lugged him over the bulwark. He glanced to the bridge. Florence was there, her hand raised, and he recognised and loved the discipline that kept her from running to him. He pushed through the knot of seamen and hurried to the bridge.

Swanson stood by the helmsman, his face ashen and expectant for orders but Holland and Raymond hardly noticed Dawlish's arrival. Both had glasses trained on the doomed steamer.

"What now?" Swanson said. He pointed seawards. The *Spinola* was all but stationary at the mouth of the bay. "We'll never outrun her." He did not mention the *Virginius* but fear of her crew's fate was plain on his features.

"We'll slip past her, Captain, never fear!" Dawlish knew he must radiate confidence. "We can give her three knots, maybe four. And we're taking the ram in tow and ..."

Florence was close, hesitant, reluctant to intrude at this moment of decision. Dawlish felt his hand reach for hers, but his mind was racing and he had no words for her. She drew closer and her hair brushed his cheek.

"It's horrible, Nick!" Her voice was hushed. "There are men on that ship still. They'll burn, Nick! They'll burn!"

"We can't leave those men, Mr. Page." It was Holland, no less shocked. "We can't let our fellow men burn alive, God help them! Look for yourself."

"He's right, Nick," Florence's voice was hushed. "I told you it was horrible. Just look, Nicholas!"

"We've got ourselves to save," Dawlish said. "Captain Swanson, I'll thank you for full revolutions once the ram's secure!"

"God and His Holy Mother would never forgive us!" Holland's voice was anguished, "It would be a mortal sin, I tell you, and God knows we've done murder enough tonight!"

"They're right." Raymond sounded wearily reasonable. He laid an arm on Dawlish's shoulder and dropped his voice. "They're right. It could give us something to bargain with. Here, look through here." He offered his glasses and Dawlish found himself accepting and putting them to his eyes.

The *Old Hickory's* bows had disappeared – were perhaps resting on the seabed – and water lapped against the front of the blazing midships superstructure. The inferno extended to the canted well-deck aft. Only the stern, risen high enough for the screw and rudder to be part-exposed, was still free of fire, though a dreadful glow illuminated it. Three men were there, one lying motionless. Another, obviously injured, slumped against the rail. Only the third, long and lean, was on his feet and attempting to keep the others from slipping down the incline into the ravenous flames.

"You recognise him?" Raymond shouted.

Dawlish nodded slowly. There was no mistaking the long and lean body and the closely cropped beard. Brigadier Stephen Driscoll

"You can't let them burn, Nick!" Florence was calm but insistent.

Dawlish found himself answering "No, Florence, I can't let them burn!" His reason was not Raymond's. He had wanted retribution, but not this. The *Old Hickory* had been enough. He could not turn from the man who would not abandon the injured wretches on that doomed ship. The man who had twice spared him from death when he himself had been at his mercy.

He turned to Swanson. "The ram's secure, Captain?"

"She's secure."

"Then take us under the counter of that vessel. Quickly now!"

"God bless you, Mr. Page!" Holland said. "And God help those poor souls!"

The *Old Hickory* lurched as the *Tecumseh* churned towards her on full revolutions. Blazing timbers collapsed into the pit where the funnel and ventilators had once stood and steam rose from the debris-strewn waters around as the hull settled deeper. A new geyser of flame erupted through an opening aft. Driscoll had one arm thrown up to shield his face as he used the other to hold the prostrate man, even as he used his body to jam the other survivor against the rail.

"Get a fire hose forward to the bows," Dawlish snapped, "and half a dozen good men!" He turned to Florence. "Get below, prepare to help with injuries."

"Gladly, Nicholas." Her face told him that she was steeling herself for horrors. Then she was gone and his heart went with her.

Driscoll's dream of revenge and liberation was dying hard. Even at a cable's distance, where Swanson signalled for quarter-speed, the heat was palpable and it grew as the yacht edged closer. The canvas hose snaking from a pump aft stiffened and the first gush spluttered from its brass nozzle, then stabilised to a solid jet. Carter was commanding the men holding it and now it was spraying a feathery plume ahead of the bows, reaching for, but not yet touching the steamer's canted stern.

Swanson pushed the helmsman aside and took the wheel himself, one hand on it, the other on the telegraph, signalling for yet lower revolutions, nudging the bows over, creeping ever closer to the inclined poop. Driscoll had seen them and was shouting encouragement to the two men he still sustained, just as he must have done when he had led his company to the very muzzles of Confederate rifles above Fredericksburg. He must be enduring agony, Dawlish realised, for even on *Tecumseh's* bridge all but Swanson and himself had retreated as far as possible from the scorching heat.

Tecumseh inched forward. Carter cheered and blasphemed as his men raised the hose to rain spray on the stern now towering above them. Holland had slipped from the bridge to join them, a small, scrawny figure helping to resist the hose's writhings, his collarless shirt plastered to his back and reflected flames flashing from his spectacles. The *Old Hickory's* screw was exposed, and ten feet of her keel, and the hull lurched and jerked as the poop rose ever higher. The last plunge must be imminent. A new volcano of flame erupted as the afterdeck's blazing planking fell into the hold beneath. Flames were licking over the last intact structure on which the three survivors cowered, held at bay only by the deluge the hose showered down.

Metal screamed as the yacht's bows ground against the curved strakes above the dying vessel's sternpost and Swanson rang for increased revolutions to hold his craft there. High above the forecastle, drenched and bedraggled, Driscoll was trying to heave an inert body across the rail. A grapnel-ended rope snaked up, skidded over the deck until it found a purchase, then tautened. A figure was raising himself, hand over hand – Carter, his feet seeking the plating and urging him up the overhang. He gained the rail, flame-dyed as he emerged from the shadow, and dragged himself over to join Driscoll. He shouted down, caught the rope thrown up to him and was instantly fashioning a bowline beneath the armpits of the prostrate man.

The vessels remained locked for little over three minutes and yet to all involved it seemed like as many aeons, an eternity of heat and smoke, of scraping metal and roaring flame, of drenching spray boiled instantly to steam, of shouting, terrified men and of bodies twisting and dangling as they were lowered jerkily to deliverance.

Driscoll was last off. Despite the heat he paused for an instant to look forward across the pit of fire that was all that remained of his dream. Then he turned, his face a mask of sadness, and swung himself across the rail, groped for the rope and lowered himself towards the *Tecumseh*. A dozen hands reached for him but it was Holland who wrapped his arms about him and supported him as he slumped exhausted against the bulwark.

The yacht surged astern, breaking the contact, and then ahead on quarter revolutions, curving away to starboard as the blazing wreck settled further.

"Neatly done, Captain." Dawlish's tongue rattled in an arid mouth.

"What now?" Swanson's hands were trembling. "What now, Mr. Page? We can't fight the Spanish Navy."

The gunboat was stationary, and beam-on, but she seemed closer now, little over two thousand yards. She had probed forward cautiously while the *Tecumseh* was focussed on rescue but her captain's resolution had baulked at any further penetration. And it was not necessary. She effectively blocked the bay.

"We can beat her by three knots, Captain." Dawlish hoped he did not sound as desperate as he felt. Better to go down fighting than to a Spanish firing squad or garrotter, better for Florence too, infinitely better. "We can make that four when we cast off the ram. And we can..."

The *Spinola* settled the issue. A flash again illuminated her and the crash reached the yacht a second before a white fountain blasted up a hundred yards short and to port. Another flash announced a second weapon coming into action – the gunboat carried two Parrots on each beam – and its shell fell closer still.

There's a competent gunner there, a small voice told Dawlish, *a very competent gunner indeed. And the sea is calm and the moon uncovered, and they can see us as well as we them, better perhaps, because of our white hull...*

"Full speed, Captain," he said.

Swanson needed no urging. He ground the telegraph handle forward even as he spun the wheel, responding to Dawlish's rapid commands that would take *Tecumseh* creaming across the bay. Then it would be time to swing southwards, to weave deliberately towards the gunboat and the open sea, to ready the ram for her last duty, to...

"Mr. Page." A hand touched his arm and he half turned to see Holland, red and sweat-drenched, yet smiling. "This gentleman wants to thank you."

He turned to see Driscoll, Carter's hand on his arm. And from his stance, his expression, his calm, Dawlish saw that this man was not defeated, for all his loss and exhaustion, that he had known failure before and was not cowed by it, that he might lose battles but never lose faith in his cause.

"I'm obliged to you for my life, Commander," Driscoll extended his hand, "though for damn little besides. You're even more persistent than I reckoned on."

Dawlish ignored the hand and turned to Swanson. "I'd be obliged to you, Captain, if you'd have this man put in the paint locker." His own eyes were locked on the *Spinola*. She had not moved. Tackles would be hauling her cannon across to track the *Tecumseh*...

"There are two injured men," Driscoll said. "They'll be seen to, I trust?"

"They'll be seen to." Dawlish snapped.

"The rest of the boys got away, the crew too. I'm glad of that. They're maybe a little scorched but your government won't have heard the last of them, Commander."

Dawlish did not answer.

"I guess I'll wish you Good Night then, Commander – and you too, Sir," Driscoll had noticed Raymond and half bowed to him. "It's Mr. Worth, isn't it, or whatever name you're calling yourself these days? I might have guessed you'd be involved."

"Worth?" Raymond smiled. "I can't recollect knowing a Mr. Worth."

"I wish you every success evading the gentlemen over there." Driscoll nodded towards the Spanish gunboat, then allowed Carter to lead him below. "I won't be giving you any problems," he said. "I can do with a little sleep."

The *Spinola* spoke again, one shell screaming high and wide and harmless but the other dropping fifty yards ahead of *Tecumseh's* bows. Dawlish called the instructions, Swanson swung the helm, and the yacht cleaved onwards in a series of zig-zags to throw off the gunners' aims.

"That ram's slowing us like a sea anchor," Swanson shouted. "Can't we cast off the damn thing?"

"Not yet, Captain, not yet." But Dawlish was frightened now, and even more so as the next salvo threw up fountains on either beam. One shell would be enough, and he dared not yet head for the open sea. It would be minutes yet before the gap widened enough to allow a turn and even then...

Tecumseh beat onwards, boiler straining, deck plates trembling as her screw thrashed and her pistons flailed, her crew cowering behind any cover they could find, the ram lurching and plunging in her wake. The sky was clear now, the bay flooded in moonlight and the yacht's white hull must be standing out against the dark of the land beyond. And the worst was yet to come, Dawlish knew, the moment when the yacht must slow, when the ram must be hauled alongside, when he must enter that dark maw once more, and only the knowledge that Florence would otherwise most surely die kept him from screaming at the prospect. He hated that oily darkness and...

The Parrotts fired together – the *Spinola's* black masts and yards illuminated in an orange flash before the rolling smoke obscured them, and then the crash expanding across the water, and the shells screaming in its wake. *Tecumseh's* helm was being flung over and one fountain was surging up ahead – and then an incandescent ball exploded against the after end of the deckhouse. A man fell howling, a splinter lodged in his back. There was no fire, but a jagged gap was torn in what had been the side of the saloon and steam screamed from a ruptured pipe somewhere below and enveloped the stern in a scalding cloud that drove all still on deck forward.

"My God! Oh My God!" Swanson was looking aft, horror-stricken, trembling.

"Take control aft!" Dawlish pushed him from the helm, took it himself. "Get that leak stopped!" Steam was power and every ounce was needed if the yacht was not to be a stationary target for the *Spinola's* fury. Already he could hear cries of panic and, worse still, sense the engine's throb lessening, the response to the wheel more sluggish. "Mr. Raymond!" he called, "Help him!" His white suit streaked with ash, Raymond followed the captain, as calm as if he were yachting on the Solent with the Prince of Wales.

Dawlish swung the bows northwards, deeper into the bay. Hospital Cay was a dark mass ahead. Billowing steam obscured the gunboat but his last glimpse told him she was not following – her captain was taking no chance of mines. Dawlish could only hope that whatever line had been fractured could be isolated before all power was lost. He heard voices raised aft, the captain's and Raymond's among them and then the hubbub of panic seemed to lessen and he sensed ordered teams moving into action. Egdean was up in the bows, dragging the now-deflated hose aft with two other men and Carter was yelling for the pump to be reactivated. A curtain of water would soon sizzle down on hot metal to protect some hero's search for an isolating valve.

The speed was down now, six, seven knots, and the engine was panting at half-revolutions and still slowing further. A double boom aft announced the gunboat firing again. Her shells landed wide, harmless feathery plumes rising off the starboard beam. The range was opening, even at this pace, and the shot that had landed had been a lucky one. If only *Tecumseh* could maintain speed...

Raymond was at Dawlish's side again, self-possession lost for once. "It's the siren line," he panted. He looked badly frightened.

"That's better than I feared." It was a non-critical line, small bore.

"Egdean's trying to reach the valve. He's wrapped in sacks and Carter's got the hose turned on him but the header's damaged also..."

"Which header?"

"The main steam header above the boiler. It's cracked and distorted below the valve, it's leaking badly."

Even as he spoke the shrill of escaping steam sharpened to a last high scream, then died. Egdean had closed the valve. Looking aft Dawlish could glimpse the jagged remnant of the pipe draped across the deck abaft the funnel and the crater torn in the superstructure – *Florence! Florence!* his mind howled and yet he could not leave this bridge – and from it steam still billowed and rolled, less violently, but enough to bleed the vessel's power within minutes more.

"It will need a patch, canvas, strapping..."

Raymond nodded. "The captain said as much. And the engineer is..."

Again the Spanish Parrotts blasted.

The shells fell short, a hundred yards and more astern, but it was the cracked header – the line that carried steam to the engine – that worried Dawlish more. A canvas patch might buy just enough time to carry the yacht to safety but it would be a temporary expedient only. If the *Tecumseh* was to have power enough to race past the waiting gunboat towards the open seat then more permanent repair was essential. That would need a forge, rudimentary machine tools – and twenty-four hours at least. That made only one decision possible.

Dawlish swung the helm, away from Hospital Cay's dark outline, and the vessel nudged sluggishly towards the moonlit expanse of island-dotted water off the starboard bow.

Towards the town he had hoped never to see again. Towards Boquerón.

27

The *Spinola* was blocked from view now and Swanson had the helm again, bringing *Tecumseh* crawling towards the town. Dawlish had gone aft to inspect the damage. Wisps of steam still jetted from beneath the patch that a sodden, parboiled, sacking-wrapped Egdean had somehow strapped about the header. It was however holding sufficient pressure to urge the pistons to a sluggish but sustained rhythm. The deckhands had been organised into a makeshift damage-control party but there was little more they could do for now. Most were peering nervously aft for any sign of the gunboat.

"Bear up, Lads!" Dawlish injected confidence into his tone. "We'll show those blackguards what the old *Tecumseh* can manage!"

He would have raised a smile, even a cheer, from a Royal Navy crew but here he earned only glum silence. One man spat ostentatiously.

"Where's Mr. Egdean? And my wife?"

"There. With Charlie Flanders." In the half-wrecked saloon, with the wounded man.

Glass crunched underfoot on the carpet and a yard-square gap of sundered panelling showed where the blast had torn through. Dawlish braced himself for what he must see – he had never become inured to the sight of wounds and agony. A body he had last seen lowered from the *Old Hickory's* poop lay quietly in one corner and another stirred weakly and moaned close by. Choking, piteous sound came from the sofa in the shadows where Florence was cradling the injured man to her. The front of her dress was saturated with his blood. He jerked weakly as Egdean, himself pale and trembling, wound something white and ragged around the exposed torso. An incongruous stretch of lace told that Florence had torn it from her petticoat. Carter held the weakly kicking legs. He looked up.

"The splinter. We got it out," he said. His hands and shirt were bloody.

"There, old fellow," Egdean was saying, ignoring the burbling scream, unearthly, dreadful, that came as he eased the wounded man towards him to pass the strip of cloth one more time around. "There, there, old fellow, we're nearly there."

Florence's eyes met Dawlish's. She said nothing, just shook her head slowly. She had seen death in Thrace often enough to recognise it now. This unconsidered, anonymous seaman who had just acquired a name had minutes to live.

"There's nothing to fear," Dawlish lied. "We're heading back briefly to Boquerón. I'll be on the bridge, with Captain Swanson. You might join me when…" The words trailed off.

He turned away, sick with apprehension for her.

Boquerón was still two miles distant when the first tongue of flame flashed against the dark mass of the hinterland rising beyond the town.

"What..." Raymond began.

Even before a small flash and a dull boom announced the arrival of its shell somewhere among the shacks beyond the warehouses, the sharp crack told what was out there in the scrub and cactus.

"It's a mountain gun," Dawlish felt cold.

No larger than the wheeled seven-pounder muzzle loaders Royal Navy ships carried for shore-landings, insufficient to cause major damage but enough to trigger panic. Colonel Almunia was announcing his arrival.

"We can't face artillery," Swanson said, and Raymond, silent, was nodding behind him.

"They're firing blind," Dawlish said. "If we can't repair the header we're done for anyway."

The yacht was crawling now and Boquerón and its forge and workshop still seemed impossibly distant. Sounds of shouting, and a brief rattle of rifle-fire, stilled by further yelling, echoed across the still waters. Then another flash, another report – it seemed to be from the same position as before – and an impact to the north of the first, closer to the customs-house. This time flames flickered and grew as a thatch roof caught fire.

"Twelve hours," Dawlish said. "That's all we need."

"But..."

"Hold her steady as she goes, Captain Swanson."

Men on deck were pointing to the town, others, frightened, were emerging from below and looking expectantly to the bridge. Any sign of irresolution, and control might be lost.

"And Captain Swanson? I'd like to see the engineer, and Mr. Carter and Mr. Egdean and Mr. Holland. We'll have need of their services. Can you send a man to bring them here, if you please? And Mr. Raymond? Could I trouble you for one of your Havanas?"

"Can your friends hold for twelve hours?" Raymond spoke in an undertone as he cupped his hands around a lucifer while Dawlish drew on the cigar.

"Not they, Mr. Raymond. We. We'll do our damnest." Dawlish paused as another report sounded and the shell's fall was lost somewhere in the dark warren of shacks. The rate of fire was slow, irregular. "You hear that?" he said. "I think it's a single weapon, that the gunners are out of practice and that our friend Almunia is taking his time. I think we'll manage twelve hours."

He strolled to the bridge wing, leaned on it with an air of nonchalance he did not feel and appeared to savour the tobacco. He ignored the men he sensed glancing up towards him but all the time his mind was racing, and every option seemed more hopeless than the last considered. The burning roof in town had been extinguished but smoke still drifted seawards and the clamour carrying over the still water was louder. Its tinge of panic was more ominous than any damage the next small shell might wreak on some wretched hut. He turned away as the men he had sent for joined him. None argued with what he asked of them. That at least was a start.

Figures clustered and lights danced on the jetty and foreshore as the *Tecumseh* neared. Dawlish was being rowed ashore even as the yacht's anchor splashed down. On the landing stage he discerned Ambrosio and Geraldo but they made no movement towards him when he ascended the ladder. They seemed smaller, more frightened, than when he had parted from them. Without Machado they were helpless, and they knew it.

"We thought we would not see you again, Nicolás." Ambrosio's tone conveyed no warmth.

"The gunboat, the *Spinola*," Dawlish said. "It's out in the bay."

"It will come here?"

"Not yet. Her captain fears to come closer." He did not voice his concern that the gunboat might probe cautiously around the edges of the imagined belt of mines, penetrate this far and blast the *Tecumseh* to flotsam even as she lay at anchor. A British captain would not hesitate to do so but he could not answer for a Spaniard.

"Almunia's guns will destroy us, Nicolás." An edge of despair in Ambrosio's voice. "We can do nothing against them."

"There's one gun, two at the most and they're small, they sound worse than any real damage they can do if they're lucky." Dawlish tried not to sound dismissive. "They're firing to break your courage before any real assault. I heard rifle-fire that died away. Did Almunia's men attack on foot?"

Geraldo shook his head and seemed the calmer of the two. "Our men are in position. Some shot wildly when the first gun fired, but we think it was at shadows. No, Nicolás, I don't think we're under real attack yet."

"They won't attack before daylight. There's time yet to prepare," Dawlish said. "And I can help you hold them when they come."

"Why, Nicolás? A few hours ago you told us it was impossible. So what do you want of us?"

Dawlish gestured towards the shed that sheltered the forge. Its furnace had been cool since the fever had struck. "We need repairs," he said. "We need to heat and bend metal, maybe even use the drill and lathe."

"We have trouble enough of our own," Ambrosio was trembling. Somewhere close a woman was screaming, not in pain but in terror. Figures were stumbling blindly through the half-darkness, away from the last point of shell impact. A bell was tolling dismally from the church north of the square.

"And El Jefe?" Dawlish asked, desperate to keep the negotiation going.

"The worst is past," Geraldo said. "But he's still bad. We'll kill him if we move him."

"You need time," Dawlish was grasping at straws. "I can hold the town for you," he said. "Against Almunia, against the Spanish Army if needs be! But only if you help us repair this ship, let us use the forge."

"You'll hold Boquerón for us, Nicolás?" Fear lent bitterness to Ambrosio's sarcasm. "How will you do that? Will God and his angels be assisting you?"

"You'd be assisting me, Ambrosio, and you, Geraldo, and all our friends." Another shell fell, harmlessly, perhaps in waste ground, for its crump was muffled, but the others flinched nonetheless. "I've half a dozen men on the yacht who've seen war service and who'll use a rifle because they know they'll be dead if they don't. And we can use what's stored over there." He pointed to the nearest warehouse, saw a gleam of understanding in Geraldo's eyes. "Work with me and I swear that I won't leave until Señor Machado is fit to travel with you, not even if this *Tecumseh* must leave without me."

He paused as he saw them turn away, heads together, murmuring and weighing his words. Two minutes passed. Then Ambrosio turned to him.

"Help us then, Nicolás," he said. "Help us, for God's sake, and the forge is yours."

Before the sun rose the first kindling was crackling in the furnace and in engine room the engineer and Holland and the stokers were scorching their hands and skinning their knuckles as they fought to unbolt the ungainly, still-hot, steam header and prepared to manhandle it ashore.

But by then Dawlish had another battle on his hands.

28

"We need more time."

Dawlish spoke half to himself as he pushed through another alley thronged with terrified families. Some were heading for the illusory sanctuary announced by the church's tolling bell. Others were creeping out into the dark scrub to the east.

"How much time?" Raymond hurried beside him.

"Two hours, three maybe."

Dawn, the most likely time for attack, was two hours away. Egdean and a handful of *Tecumseh* crewmen were already reinforcing the screen of three dozen zealots who had dedicated themselves to Cuba Libre. They crouched in huts at the outer fringes of the town but they were not soldiers, not yet even *guerrillas*, and ammunition was so short that most had never fired the weapons they had been so hastily trained to use. The urge to throw those weapons down and scurry towards the jetty, where Geraldo's tugboat offered the only means of escape, might well be irresistible if an attack were pressed with any resolution. Dawlish had seen enough to know that their disposition could be, must be, bettered – and that needed time, longer than two hours. Fentiman knew this warren well, would know by what best route, what lanes, Almunia's hard professionals could tear through like foxes through a pheasant hatchery.

"Two, thee hours," Dawlish repeated.

"That long?"

"Not less, Mr. Raymond. The defences can't be readied in less."

Boquerón's landward flank consisted of four-hundred yards of scattered hutments petering out into the scrub along a convex trace anchored in swampy ground to north and south. It was obviously too long to be held with the untrained, frightened force available. The track from Dos Caminos, which led almost directly to the customs-house and main square, divided the frontage into two sectors, the southerly twice the length of that to the north. Defending everything would mean defending nothing. Only a few, critical points could be held – and in selecting them Dawlish had never felt more like a sailor ashore, a seaman facing soldiers bred to such choices since childhood. Those key locations must be strengthened – barricades improvised, pitfalls dug, huts loop-holed. And Carter, who would be handy if you'd mislaid the key of a safe and was now ripping crates open in a warehouse, needed time to work. Five, six hours. And the men sweating with the header at the workshop might need longer still.

"We're going to have to talk to this Colonel Almunia," Raymond said.

"How?" Dawlish drew him into a doorway. A shell burst somewhere close, a brief glow and a dull boom, followed by the sounds of screaming and of running feet. "Just how are we going to talk to them?"

"Send out somebody with a white flag, someone who can get more than a hundred yards up the road without being shot."

"The priest," Dawlish remembered him haranguing the brothers kneeling before the firing squad. There had been no doubt on whose side he had been on that day. "The priest, he'll be glad to go because I doubt he'll want to come back. Somebody else needs to go with him. Somebody who can offer something they want."

"Driscoll," Raymond said.

"Driscoll?" Dawlish was taken aback. The idea would never have occurred to him.

"The major's old comrade, isn't he? And Driscoll can offer them twenty, maybe thirty thousand dollars' worth of sugar, rum and molasses in the warehouses that could go up in smoke if we're so inclined. They'll be interested in that."

"Why would Driscoll negotiate for us?"

Raymond shrugged. "Because we'll be letting him free to join his friends."

"I didn't come through all this just to..." Dawlish felt anger rising.

"You can't carry Driscoll back to hang off a yardarm. The man's a hero to half America – you'd provoke a war. And you won't murder him here in cold blood. You've killed his dream, Mr. Page, he's harmless to you, for now at least. But send him up that track under a white flag and he can buy you some time. Maybe not five hours, but time."

And time was what this argument was wasting. Ambrosio would be have assembled the labouring party in the square by now, men not cowed by the intermittent explosions but who knew that vengeance when it came would be indiscriminate, that they might as well support resistance as submission. They would need direction, to be routed where the need for barriers and defences was most urgent, to be set to work with pick and mattock. The decision could not be delayed.

"Get Driscoll," Dawlish found that the words all but choked him. "Have him at the square in ten minutes."

*

294

Dawlish left the priest under guard on the veranda and climbed the stairs to Machado's room. The sick man recognised him and lifted a weak hand. The yellow in his eyes had faded to a faint lemon.

"He's coming along well, Nick." Florence pushed Machado back gently on his pillow. She had changed, was once more immaculate. "Once he has some beef-tea inside him he'll be rearing to join you, won't you, Señor Machado?"

She had insisted on coming here once she was satisfied that the two *Old Hickory* survivors on the yacht were comfortable. Dawlish had been unable to dissuade her.

"You might catch the fever," he had told her. "You haven't seen it, Florence, you don't know how fast..."

She had held a finger to his lips. "I may be dead anyway within a day," she said, "and I'll go mad if I'm not busy."

Within an hour of coming ashore she had sponged Machado clean and had changed him into a fresh nightshirt of Fentiman's. She might have been a thousand miles from the shells dropping close by.

"Don't worry, Nick," she said. "I'll get him down to the pier by midday. He'll be..."

"I must go, Florence," he cut in. This moment was a luxury he could not afford. Raymond must be back soon. He paused, unmanned by the knowledge that he should never have yielded to her demand to accompany him, that this parting might be final. "I may not get back," he said. "You must promise me that if I don't..."

"... that I won't marry that gallant Brigadier Driscoll you've locked in a dungeon – I'm sure he'd accept me in a flash – or go to mass with Mr. Holland, or let Mr. Raymond buy me diamonds and racehorses, or run off with Captain Swanson." Her face was set in a frown of mock severity and she was telling off on her fingers. "I'll promise to live like a respectable old widow and wear black bombazine for the rest of my days and drape your picture with crepe and weep over it daily. That's what you want to hear, isn't it?" She kissed him lightly. "Go now, Nick." She turned away quickly.

On the veranda outside he caught the aroma of cigar smoke, saw two glowing tips in the shadows.

"Good Morning, Commander." Driscoll's voice.

"Good Morning, Brigadier." Dawlish had resolved on cold formality.

"We have a deal," Raymond was emerging from the shadow. "Brigadier Driscoll will be pleased to speak for us."

"Pleased is a bit strong, Sir," Driscoll said, "but I'll let it pass. You're offering the contents of the warehouses for a twenty-four hour truce. That's the offer?"

"And for evacuation without hindrance within that time."

"And myself?"

"You'll return under the same flag of truce and confirm it," Dawlish paused. The next words were difficult. "Then you're free to go. You'll be free to find your *Old Hickory* crew."

"And if there's no deal?"

"You're free to go anyway."

"You're generous, Commander. First my life, now my freedom."

"If you can call it freedom here," Dawlish said. "For a devotee of liberty you've found yourself some damn strange confederates."

Driscoll shrugged. "I don't suppose either of us have much choice when there's business to be done, but then again I guess we both want to live to fight another day. You're not offering much of a deal, Commander, not as far as those people over there are concerned." He nodded towards the priest who stood waiting. "That's the gentleman who's to carry the white flag?"

"Not a banner you're accustomed to carrying yourself, I think," Dawlish said. "I won't ask you to start now."

When the small procession assembled among the last huts at the edge of the village it was the barefoot lad who had waved the crucifix at the execution who now affixed a white cloth to a staff.

"He's devoted to me, a good boy," the priest said, "He won't leave me." His hands shook as he glanced towards the lightening sky eastwards and the still dark mass of scrub beneath it. He fumbled beneath his surplice and produced a creased and garishly coloured picture. He kissed it, extended it to the boy, and then to Driscoll. "San Benito," he said, "a sure protector. San Benito who..."

Driscoll shook his head. "You're not too concerned about leaving your flock, are you, Father?" he said in rapid Spanish. He ignored the priest's stammered excuses.

Over to the right there was a flash, a crack, and seconds later another small explosion somewhere among the crowded hutments. The mountain gun was still firing, though less frequently, and obviously blindly.

"I guess we'll need to be moving then, Commander?" Driscoll said.

"It's time."

The eastern sky was lightening, the merest pink glow, but growing, enough to disclose the track lying open before them and running straight and broad between the darker outlines of the low scrub on either side.

"Let's go then! Vamos!" Driscoll passed an arm around the boy's shoulder. "Raise that banner, Son! There's nothing to be afraid of." He clapped the priest on the back. "And we'll need a chant from you, Father, something solemn that'll carry!" He lunged forward, drawing them with him. "Quick march now! Left! Right! Left! That's it, Boys!"

They moved up the track, the priest's voice rising in a quaver, his fear all too apparent, the white rag flapping above them like a tormented ghost.

Dawlish turned to the hut behind him, the defence's foremost position. He entered. Gervacio and Porfirio, who had helped take Fentiman, were peering nervously through the loop-holed wall, armed with Martini-Peabodys.

"Help me up on the roof." Dawlish sensed their unwillingness to leave the protection of the hut, their bewilderment at what the intermittent shelling must convey. Only combat would decide whether they would stand or turn and run.

He scrambled up, digging his toes into the thatch to hold himself against the ridge. He raised the glasses he had brought from the yacht. They, and his revolver, were his only equipment. The eastern sky was red-streaked and at any moment sun would burst from the horizon like a molten ball. The features of the open plain, baked and seamed and scrub-scattered, were ever clearer. The three figures on the track were a hundred yards distant and the priest's singing was louder, more confident. Fifty yards beyond them was a low ribbon of continuous brush. Dawlish swept his glasses slowly along it, and then back, and then paused, heart thumping, eyes straining, for there, as the first sunbeams cast long shadows over the scarlet ground, was the briefest glint of metal. There was movement there, foliage shaking, and then a head and shoulders briefly visible and then another, as quickly withdrawn.

The party on the track had not seen it – the boy was too intent on his flag, the priest on his chant – and Dawlish felt an urge to call out to them even before a shot crashed out. They froze. The priest's voice was cut off in mid-note and the flag dropped and the boy made to scurry back, but Driscoll caught him and thrust the staff into his hands again. Dawlish sensed the group wavering, saw Driscoll's arms about his companions, heard his voice bellowing something into the long shadows ahead.

A minute passed, the silence all the deeper for the memory of that single shot.

The three figures remained motionless on the track but there was further movement in the brush beyond them, figures flitting briefly into view and disappearing again. Then a voice rang out, the distance too far for words to be distinguishable. Driscoll called back something equally incomprehensible while the boy waved the flag with renewed vigour. A man emerged cautiously from the scrub, his pyjama-like uniform crossed with bandoliers. Another shouted exchange and the trooper faded into the brush again. A moment later a head and torso rose above the foliage and then disappeared quickly rearwards, a horseman spurring away with news of the attempted parley.

Raymond had climbed up. Dawlish passed him the glasses. "I don't envy them," he said.

The group on the track stood stock still but Driscoll continued to call out, to elicit short shouted replies from the unseen men before him, to encourage the two wretches cowering by his side, their shadows shortening as the sun was soared. This was the moment which Dawlish had most feared, when the defences still needed hours to complete and when growing daylight favoured the attackers. Every minute of delay was golden.

Five minutes. The day's warmth grew.

Ten minutes now. The mountain gun had been silent since Driscoll had first been spotted – a good sign perhaps.

At last a horseman appeared, a single rider drumming down the track, slowing, circling and stamping around the group on the track, voice raised. The priest and his boy broke away, scurrying towards the scrub and stumbling over their cassocks, the horseman in a slow canter at their heels, leaving Driscoll standing alone. And while he stood there, while his lone presence demanded response, the forge within the open-sided workshop was glowing bright and hammers were reverberating on the damaged steam header and elsewhere in the village Carter was going about his deadly work and Ambrosio's labourers were digging and heaping and barricading.

Dawlish sensed a movement to his right, at the limit of his peripheral vision. He swung his glasses to catch five horsemen cantering over open ground parallel to the scrub, the leader riding his chestnut as elegantly as at a review. Dawlish glimpsed a long, dark, clean-shaven face and knew this must be Colonel Almunia, just as the heavy rider ploughing in his wake was all too clearly Fentiman. They wheeled on to the track and headed towards Driscoll. He stood unflinching as Almunia rode straight for him, drawing rein only feet away. The other horsemen seemed to flow around him, obscuring him from Dawlish's sight, as they too came to a standstill.

Minutes passed.

Fentiman had manoeuvred his mount next to Almunia's. He waved an arm as if angrily – Almunia appeared to be quietening him – and Dawlish could just discern his raised voice, the words indiscernible. The other riders looked nervously towards Boquerón, carbines crooked in their arms, their horses stamping impatiently and exposing Driscoll momentarily to view. He was talking earnestly, shaking his head, and Fentiman, seemingly furious, wheeled away as if to leave until summoned back by Almunia. Then, abruptly,

Almunia himself gesticulated towards one of the other riders and the man went cantering up the track until lost in the scrub.

The parley seemed stalled. The riders had backed away from Driscoll and waited ten, fifteen yards from him, their mounts snorting and swishing their tails in boredom. Almunia and Fentiman had lit cheroots, were obviously in no hurry. Driscoll stood motionless, hatless in the now-burning sun, deliberately ignored, a scarecrow in clothing that was torn and filthy since he had almost burned on the *Old Hickory's* poop. He looked neither towards the men before him nor to the village behind. Dawlish watched with growing apprehension, foreboding even. He had not known what to expect, but it was not this.

He turned to Raymond. "Go down. Quietly. Fetch Egdean and his people." The seaman had been posted with a half-dozen men in a cluster of shacks fifty yards to the rear. "Don't let them show themselves."

"What do you think..." for once Raymond sounded mystified.

"I don't. And pass me a rifle. Now, immediately."

Raymond slid down the thatch, lowered himself to the ground. Dawlish refocused on the group on the track. The riders continued to ignore Driscoll but Fentiman has wheeled around, was looking expectantly eastwards.

"Here, Señor." Gervacio pushed a Martini-Peabody towards him, and cartridges in a canvas bag. A few days since Dawlish had been Nicolás to these men, but now, in desperation, they deferred to him.

The rifle was loaded. He removed ten more rounds from the bag and pushed them nose-down into the thatch to his right, then settled himself more comfortably, laid the barrel along the roof-ridge and aligned on Almunia. The range was over two hundred yards, maybe two-twenty. He had not used the weapon, could not judge the accuracy of its sighting but he adjusted the backsight to two hundred yards and knew he would be lucky to hit anything.

The rider who had left Almunia's group was returning at a canter. A line of men, eight, ten, was emerging on foot from the scrub behind in faded striped uniforms, bandoliers and canvas leggings. But it was on the four figures they hunted before them, hands bound behind, faces bloodied, that Dawlish's gaze was involuntarily riveted. The priest who had so lately accompanied Driscoll up the track was keeping pace with them and flourishing his lithograph of San Benito for want of anything more sacred.

"I'm here, Sir," Egdean called softly from below and behind.

"You can depend on your men, Jerry?" The question was unfair, impossible.

"They'll do, Sir, if they get the example."

Dawlish had not shifted his gaze. The prisoners had been driven close to Almunia now and could only be fugitives who had slipped from the village as it had endured the night's random bombardment. They were innocents, neutrals who had wanted nothing of Cuba Libre, but were no less doomed, if only for example's sake, than if they had shared Machado's vision.

"Go to the corner of the hut, Jerry," Dawlish spoke very quietly. "Keep out of sight, your men too, but watch Driscoll. Be ready on my word to advance and to take the men out there under fire, and to fall back just as quickly."

"And Mr. Driscoll, Sir?" There was note of hesitation, a hint of respect for the enemy who had not deserted his injured men on that blazing deck.

"I don't know," Dawlish said. "I'll tell you."

The prisoners must know now what was inevitable, for they might indeed have stood anonymously by Dawlish when the García brothers had been butchered. One was thrashing his head and screaming in despair as he was forced to his knees, face towards Boquerón. The others, dumb with fear, bowed passively as the troopers lined up behind. The priest scurried from man to man, gabbling absolution. Dawlish heard Driscoll's voice bellowing out, saw his arms wave, and though the distance distorted the words knew he was protesting. Almunia ignored him and nudged his horse into a walk. He halted before the nearest of the kneeling men, then drew his revolver, cocked it and fired into the air. The report echoed over the scrub and a wail rose from the man cowering below him.

"Hold fast!" Dawlish hissed to Egdean. "He knows we're watching. He wants us to see. He wants all Boquerón to see."

Almunia's message was all too clear – no compromise, no mercy.

The Martini-Peabody's sights held Almunia and Dawlish had taken up the first pressure on the trigger. Another squeeze might not kill but it would distract. And yet a hard logical voice within Dawlish's brain told him that Almunia's calculated terror might be double edged, might evoke fury as much as fear in men who would see they had nothing to hope for from capitulation. He eased his pressure on the trigger.

"God pity them!" One of Egdean's men gasped.

Almunia wheeled towards the village, reared the horse and again fired skywards, defiant, proud in his power to draw every eye towards him. As the fore-hooves met the ground he spurred away from the prisoner cowering beneath him, leaving him briefly to his terror, and forward to the furthest of the kneeling men. He reached down and fired into his head. Even as the body smashed down, blood spouting, Almunia was wheeling towards the next man, whose face was lifted to him in silent imprecation. He fired straight into it and passed on and killed the third. The fourth, the last, had struggled to his feet and was stumbling towards Driscoll, who started towards him with arms outstretched. Almunia dropped his pistol to swing on its lanyard and unsheathed his sabre as he brought his horse pounding after him.

Dawlish swung his sights to follow, dropping slightly to the larger target of the horse's straining body. Almunia raised the sabre as Dawlish fired. Even as the butt kicked knew he had missed, yet it had been close enough to cause the rider to swerve momentarily, for the horse to plunge.

"Now, Jerry," Dawlish yelled as he ejected, plucking the next round for the thatch and pushing it into the smoking breech. "Save Driscoll!"

For the scarecrow had reached the running prisoner, was pushing him down behind him. He was holding his arm up and shouting in an impossible attempt to stay the doom bearing down on him as Almunia regained control of his mount and urged it towards him.

The chestnut's flank aligned on the sights for an instant and Dawlish tore off a shot, ejected, snatched for another cartridge. He saw the horse stagger sideways and Almunia jerking in the saddle as he fought to calm it. Shots crashed from the hut beneath him – Gervacio and Porfirio blazing through the loopholes. Egdean was racing forward, three, four men following him – the others' nerve had failed them – and Dawlish fired again towards the confusion of men and horses that was rushing to Almunia's aid.

Driscoll had grabbed the pinioned man, was hauling him towards the village, stopping and pulling him to his feet again when he tripped. He did not look back, must know that death was instants away. Another horse was down now, legs thrashing as it careered into Almunia's terrified brute, and its rider was struggling free, and Almunia himself was slipping from his saddle. Twenty yards behind, the dismounted troopers were hurrying forward on foot, some shooting wildly towards Egdean's oncoming group, and Fentiman wheeled towards them, shouting commands. Dawlish saw that if the troopers' fire was concentrated then neither Egdean nor Driscoll nor any man on that open ground would survive.

Dawlish fired again, and again, and never knew if it was his round or one from the hut's loopholes that plucked a rider from his saddle at the instant he was bearing down on Driscoll, sabre raised. Egdean had paused now, fired twice in rapid succession – he had commandeered one of the two Spencer repeaters – and one of the troopers fell close to Fentiman, who had now driven them into the semblance of a line. Two of Egdean's men were firing also while the others raced forward towards Driscoll, who was still dragging the terrified prisoner with him. Another horseman was sweeping in towards them from the left and Egdean spun towards him, blasting two fast shots, one of which took the animal straight in the chest. The rider flew over its head as it collapsed forward. He tried to rise, then fell writhing as Egdean's next shot caught him in the stomach.

Almunia's dismounted troopers were the danger now and Dawlish shifted his aim to them, yelling to Porfirio and Gervacio to do the same. His breech was hot, and smoke drifting up from the loopholes below him half-obscured his view, but another of the men by Fentiman had fallen. Egdean was driving forward again and scarcely ten yards separated him from Driscoll. Dawlish's own ready-use rounds were finished and he pulled more from the bag. Egdean had only a single man with him now – one had been hit and his companion had hoisted him on his shoulder to carry him rearwards while another had taken to his heels.

As Driscoll retreated past him Egdean dropped to his knee to fire deliberate, aimed shots towards the riflemen. The one man still with him, brave, but a novice to his weapon, might not even be aiming but he was blazing as fast as he could reload. Dawlish kept firing towards the line of riflemen and suddenly one was turning away and rushing back in panic, and though Fentiman spurred after him, flailing with the flat of his sabre, another joined him in flight and then another still. Then Fentiman must have realised that he could not rally them and he turned his horse, and urged it at a gallop towards Egdean.

"Fall back, Jerry! Fall back!" Dawlish bellowed, uncertain if he could be heard between the gunshots.

The order might already be too late. The man firing beside Egdean had gone down, a crumpled heap, and the seaman's repeater was empty. There was no time for him to push seven rounds into its tubular magazine. Dawlish tracked Fentiman's canter, past the fallen bodies, past the tumble of injured horses from where Almunia was retreating on foot, dragging his wounded mount behind him. The major was weaving, the view foreshortened, the aim difficult.

Twice Dawlish fired, and once saw the dust spurt a yard short of the drumming hooves, but he knew that his hopes of hitting the burly figure with the raised sabre were vain. Egdean must know that flight offered no salvation for he had risen to his feet and had taken the Spencer's barrel in his hands, drawing it back to swing like a club. Fentiman was urging his horse in a canter, had drawn his blade across his left shoulder to slice down, had eyes only for the huge seaman standing fast before him. Only at the last instant did he spot the other figure dashing up behind Egdean – Driscoll, who had left

304

his charge to find cover at the hut with the seaman's retreating men, and who now returned, shouting as he came.

Fentiman's attention was deflected for a moment only but his horse took advantage and sheared away from Egdean's flailing rifle. The major's downward-scything blade met only air and he fought to rein in the animal and drag its head around to attack again. Five yards away Driscoll had dropped, was rolling over the body of Egdean's dead companion and was dragging the Martini-Peabody from under it.

Wrenching his mount around, Fentiman lunged at Egdean. The seaman held his rifle with both hands, at muzzle and butt, and he swung it up to block the sabre's arcing slice. The blade glanced off but the impact knocked Egdean off balance and he staggered and fell. Fentiman reined in and circled, sabre raised for the kill but beyond the fallen seaman Driscoll was now on his feet, and raising the rifle. The distance separating them was too much for even the fleetest horse to cover before a trigger could be squeezed. Beneath the white moustache the major's teeth were bared in a howl of anger and despair as he dragged his horse's head over, set spurs to its flanks.

The movement saved him, for Driscoll's bullet tore along the side of Fentiman's face, and the horse, terrified, took its head. Egdean rolled free of its beating hooves as it stampeded rearwards, a stunned and bleeding Fentiman crouched across its neck. He somehow regained control as the track disappeared into the scrub. The firing had died and there was no sign now of the riflemen or of Almunia. Only scattered bodies marked the action.

Driscoll pulled Egdean to his feet. They jog-trotted wearily back towards the hut. As Dawlish met them in its lee the man whom Driscoll had saved, his bounds now cut free, pushed past and dropped to his knees. "Gracias, Señor, Gracias," he sobbed, drawing Driscoll's hand to his lips.

"De nada, amigo." Driscoll passed an arm around his shoulder and raised him. "Go with this man," he said in fluent Spanish, propelling him towards Egdean. "He'll show you how to fight." He turned to Dawlish. "They're butchers, Commander," he said, then paused, looked Dawlish in the eye. "They want blood, pure and simple. We've got a battle on our hands."

"We?" Dawlish could not resist sarcasm. "There's been a parting of friends, has there? The major wasn't overjoyed to see you?"

"We were never friends, Commander. We dealt strictly on a cash basis and now Fentiman finds me a distinct liability. As I guess you do also."

"They heard the offer?"

"I told you I didn't think it was much of a deal, Commander. They didn't either."

"And the contents of the warehouses?"

"Almunia says he couldn't give a damn – they're not his. It's more important to show Boquerón who's master, he says, and he wants somebody called Machado. And Fentiman wants you, Commander. They said they wouldn't hesitate to massacre the entire village to get the pair of you. They staged that exhibition of savagery to prove it." His tone held controlled anger and contempt.

"I gather then you've changed sides," Dawlish said.

"Not quite." Driscoll shook his head. "But I suspect I've joined you on their list."

"We'll be waiting for them." Dawlish glanced back towards the scrub, could imagine Almunia marshalling his forces beyond its cover.

"I don't mind waiting with you," Driscoll said. "If you'll let me hang on to this, that is." He held up the rifle he still carried. "You might even welcome a word or two of advice from an old soldier."

A small cold voice reminded Dawlish that this man had thrived, had even advanced himself, through four years of organised slaughter. He needed him.

"I fear that once again I haven't much of a deal to offer," he said, "even were I keen to make one with a Fenian."

"We all make temporary alliances we don't like, Commander," Driscoll said, "but I guess I've more in common with your Cuban friends than with yourself, brave man that you are." He extended his hand. "President Lincoln once did me the honour of shaking this," he said. "I guess you might bring yourself to do as much. Is it a bargain?"

Dawlish hesitated for an instant. Topcliffe could never have foreseen this.

And from somewhere beyond the scrub the mountain gun barked. An instant later an orange-streaked plume of earth exploded twenty yards to the right of the hut, too distant to harm them, but close enough to confirm that vengeance was imminent. Neither man flinched.

"It's a bargain," Dawlish said, and he reached for Driscoll's hand.

29

The outline of the village had been traced in the dust with a stick. Crouched over it, Dawlish realised how inept, how amateurish, his plans had been. Driscoll had quickly identified weaknesses and strengths that might have remain hidden for an eternity to a sailor's eye.

"We're safe enough on the flanks, Commander." He gestured towards the scribbles representing the marshy ground bounding the village to south and north, "but here's the problem." He swung the stick down Boquerón's eastern side. "We'll never hold it with the men we've got." He had already seen what they were, untrained, frightened, desperate.

"But we can delay them?" Dawlish had no word from the workshop, no idea of how far the header's repair had progressed.

"Hardly even that." Driscoll's deep-set eyes were half-closed, his long face a mask of concentration. "But the perimeter isn't important," he said at last. "Though they've got to think that we believe that it is, that it's all we've put our trust in." He prodded the main square. "You were right about this area, that's where we need to get them." Almunia's execution of those villagers and the skirmish that followed had bought time for Ambrosio's labourers to toil there. "You said an ex-marine was there? You can rely on him?"

"Carter. He didn't hesitate to save you last night."

"That was Carter? He'll do then. And I'll be with him. I'll put the bulk of our people there – eighteen, twenty men."

"And myself?"

"Here, Commander." The fringe of huts south of the track. "I can't spare you more than half-a-dozen men." There was no hint of arrogance about his assumption of compliance. "Hang on as long as you can. You'll have to decide yourself when to fall back."

Dawlish nodded. "And Egdean?"

"North of the track, with what's left." That would be five armed men, Dawlish calculated. Egdean could have Gervacio and Porfirio. They had kept their heads well earlier.

"The track?" It lay like an open gash between the clusters of shanties, a broad highway thrusting towards the customs-house and the square.

"They'll be welcome to come down it any time they like." The faintest smile hovered on Driscoll's lips as he looked up. "I haven't heard that gun of theirs for a while now."

"Is that important?"

"It must be. They're either shifting it or they're conserving shells. Probably both. They'll attack soon."

Time now, too little, to order the redeployments, a quick informal conference. Ambrosio had been fetched with two of his lieutenants, Carter also, pleased so far with his murderous preparations, and a grim Egdean, and Raymond, glum with news of frustrations the forge. The repair of the *Tecumseh's* header was progressing, but slowly. It was past eight now but it would be noon at the soonest before the work was completed. But the repair of the ungainly section of flanged piping was only the first step. Manhandling it into the yacht's cramped boiler-room and reinstalling it there would demand hours more. And then steam would have to be raised...

They listened quietly – it might have been the calm of despair as much as of resolution. They accepted Driscoll's changed status without query, for the story of his parley and its aftermath had spread like wildfire. They seemed to sense his hard professionalism and determination, and to draw strength from it. Dawlish felt his own

308

resolution stiffened. However short the alliance might last, he had in Driscoll an equal on whom he could rely implicitly. Together they assigned stations, men and weapons, repeated instructions, urged patience and coolness. Heads nodded, assuring understanding and commitment.

But when they hurried away there was no elation, only a shared unspoken awareness that the hours ahead might most probably be their last.

*

Air shimmered above the parched cactus-dotted waste as Dawlish swept his glasses across it for the twentieth time. Two hundred yards away in the line of ragged brush unseen eyes must be subjecting this cluster of huts where he now crouched to similar scrutiny. Until Driscoll had convinced him to thin the outer defences there had been a larger force here. Perhaps the Spanish still thought there was, for the withdrawal had been stealthy. Where fencing did not intervene, anything moveable had been dragged between the shacks to make rudimentary barricades. But Dawlish knew that the huts to be defended here with four rifles, a single carbine and his own revolver, and another four machete-armed men, would be overwhelmed in minutes if an attack were pressed with any vigour.

He glanced back. The corrugated roof of Fentiman's house was just visible over the ridges of intervening thatch. Raymond should be there now, convincing Florence that regardless of Machado's condition it was time to shift him – and herself – to the *Tecumseh*. He tried not to think of her, or to reproach himself that he had ever yielded to her demands to accompany him. Experience had taught him to fear the degradation of pain, but death itself, the ending of being, was terrible only because it meant leaving her – and here that meant leaving her to some end that could be atrocious. He suddenly wanted her back at a Southsea breakfast table in her silk dressing robe, laughing across the toast and marmalade, frowning in mock-horror as he read out some item in the morning's *Times*.

309

Rifle-fire crackled from the north – Egdeans's sector – individual shots, then brief ripples followed by silence, then isolated reports again. No general assault then, but cautious probing, testing of the extent of the defence.

Dawlish entered the nearer hut. An American, Aaron Powell – upwards of forty, but tough-looking and one of three volunteers from the *Tecumseh's* crew who claimed experience in the Union forces – pointed nervously through a loop-holed wall. Raymond had said that he would go to Hell and back for money, but for now Aaron knew he was in Hell. "They're close, Mister," he said, obviously worried. "I don't like it." Enrique, a labourer recognised from the earliest conspiratorial meetings, crouched by him with a carbine and looked terrified. The two other men in the hut had machetes.

"What have you seen, Aaron?"

"Nothing, Mister. Only the sound of shooting." They would see nothing so far distant through these slits, for brush and cactus obscured the line of sight towards Egdean's position.

Dawlish went outside to the rough barrier of casks and thorn-scrub thrown up between this hut and the next. He forced himself to stand – his head and shoulders were exposed and he knew a competent marksman could take him down – but giving example was crucial. He focussed his glasses. Wisps of gunsmoke were dispersing in the trembling air over the jumble of huts held by Egdean but the weapons there had fallen silent. Either Egdean was exerting an iron firing-discipline to conserve his scarce ammunition, or his men had lost their nerve and fled.

Closer to the ribbon of scrub, a hundred yards beyond the huts, a tumbled horse lay still. There was no sign of its rider but among the foliage Dawlish saw a single figure expose itself for an instant. He searched slowly, and saw another flit between bushes, and then a head and shoulders emerge, and a rifle, unhurriedly aiming towards the buildings and dropping out of sight again even as the weapon's bark reached him. It brought no response from the huts – Egdean must know that his strength was being probed and Driscoll had warned him that it was best they know he was there, but not in what strength. The enemy was taking few chances either – the single

310

dead horse indicated a mounted probe but the other riders had fallen back and dismounted.

Dawlish swept the glasses southwards. No sign of movement to either side of the track or directly ahead, only the quivering heat over seamed earth and baking scrub. A ripple of shots from the left drew his attention there again. It was impossible to guess how many men harassed Egdean at ineffectual range. A single shot, probably the seaman himself responding, was the only reply.

Then, suddenly, from the right, the mountain gun's report, and its smoke rising above the scrub, and the scream of its shell directly overhead and its explosion in dust and flame and flying thatch thirty yards to the rear.

A shriek from a hut to the right – fright, not agony, for the structure was untouched. "Look to your front," Dawlish bellowed and heard Aaron relaying the order. He glanced back – a mud wall partly collapsed, a roof smouldering, the shell's physical effect puny. But among the screening brush Spanish gunners would be sponging and ramming and re-aiming their miniature weapon. Is noise and flash alone could panic untrained men. He strode to the hut. The men within were looking fearfully towards the dispersing plume above the scrub.

"Their aim's bad!" Dawlish called, "You're safe where you are!"

"It'll take more than that to shift us, Mister!" Aaron shouted as Dawlish hurried on but his voice held a quaver.

The second defended shack was thicker walled. The American seaman within – Sam Eames, his name came back to Dawlish, another man Raymond had praised – had a Martini. So had two of the four villagers with him. Dawlish knelt beside them, looked though a loophole across the ground beyond. Almost immediately there was a flash in the scrub, a sharp crack, and then an explosion to the right and just ahead, showering pebbles on the thatch above.

Then heads were rising a hundred yards ahead, ten, fifteen, on foot in an open line. There was dead ground there, a dip too far from the edge of the village to be dominated from it, and the enemy approach through it had been unseen. Arms and shoulders appeared, rifles thrown across the hollow's lip, a single shot, then a ripple. Rounds slammed into the hut's outer wall and puffs of dust erupted from the surface within.

"Stay back!" Dawlish pulled a man back from a loophole. "Sam!" he shouted to Eames, "You and I! Only you and I watch them!" He crouched by the slit, peering out for short glimpses only, enough to tell him that the attackers had not left their cover.

The fusillade continued, irregular, staccato. A lucky shot screamed into the hut and buried itself harmlessly in the opposite wall. One of the machete men was cowering in the corner, babbling, but the others were looking at him with a mixture of pity and contempt and Dawlish sensed that they would hold. The urge to fire back, however blindly and wildly, was almost irresistible. Then the mountain gun was speaking again and this time its shell fell close, exploding in the yard behind, close enough to bring straw and dust cascading from the thatch above.

"There's more of them!" Eames yelled, jerking back from his slit.

The rifle-fire seemed no more intense – or effective – but when Dawlish looked again another half-dozen dismounted troopers were emerging from the scrub. Emboldened by the lack of return fire they were hurrying across the open ground to join their comrades in the dip. They were massing there and in minutes they would hurl themselves this way.

Dawlish's mind raced. This position could not be held if this was not an exploratory probe but rather the main attack, yet immediate withdrawal would be disastrous. Driscoll and Ambrosio and Carter still needed more time. And *Tecumseh's* engineer sweating at the forge needed it most of all.

"They'll come. Hold fire until they're within fifty yards," Dawlish told Sam Eames. He had seen enough to trust him. "I'm joining Aaron."

He reached the other door as the gun fired again and was over the threshold as the shell buried itself in the barricade of casks and thorn outside. The doorpost saved him from the hurricane of scorching air and screaming fragments blasting from the gap torn in

312

the barrier but he staggered to his knees, stunned by the detonation. The hut's interior was dim with rolling dust and dislodged thatch. Through the murk he saw faces pale with terror and Aaron crouching at a loophole, then turning back, his mouth open in a yell that was silent to him.

But even before his ears cleared Dawlish knew what that yell conveyed. Those grim men in striped uniforms were launching themselves from the hollow.

30

"Hold your fire!"

Dawlish plunged through the dust-choked hut towards the loopholes but his words were drowned in the first crash of the defenders' response as Aaron, the American seaman, and Enrique, the carbine-armed villager, blasted probably un-aimed rounds.

"Hold your fire!" he yelled again, throwing himself to his knees beside a jagged loophole.

The attackers were still eighty yards distant, perhaps thirty men in a broken line, rushing forward at a crouch with bayonets fixed.

"Select your targets. Aim low!"

Dawlish itched to snatch the carbine, knowing that his own revolver was useless until the onslaught would be practically on top of him. A single shot rang from the hut to the right, then Sam Eames' voice calling from there for fire to be held.

"Dios nos salva!" One of the machete-armed villagers, a willing volunteer an hour since but now unmanned by sunlight glinting on those bobbing tips of steel.

Seventy yards now, close enough to see bronzed faces grim beneath their straw-brimmed hats, to hear the exhortations of the sergeant on the right pounding forward, pistol upraised.

"I can take him!" Aaron's voice, more fearful than confident.

"Hold your fire!" Dawlish wondered how many trembling, untrained hands would still feed their breeches after the first two or three shots, would still seek a target, how long before blind panic took hold.

"Enrique!" he called, "I'm relying on you! You've chosen your man?"

"Si, Señor." This labourer, whom some vague vision of Cuba Libre had inspired to risk his all, had had three hours' instruction with his rifle, had fired only two scarce and precious rounds in practice and had most likely missed the target with both.

Then again the sharp crack of the mountain gun, and the scream of its shell directly over the advancing men, low enough to cause several to flinch, and the thump of its harmless detonation somewhere to the rear. But it seemed to hearten the attackers, for they were yelling now, something between a cheer and a howl, and the sergeant was pointing towards the gap torn in the barrier between the huts by the earlier shell. The line was closing, the troopers bunching and the range was fifty yards – still too great for accuracy but close enough if the ill-trained defenders were to have time to reload.

"Wait for it! Aim low!"

Dawlish steadied his revolver barrel on his forearm, tracked his foresight on the crossed bandoliers of large man in the centre of the line, dropped it lower still. Forty yards.

"Fire!"

Aaron and Enrique fired. Dawlish saw a trooper tumble next to his own target and then other shots echoed from the hut to the right also, and another man was down, two out of perhaps thirty. The line surged on with momentum unimpaired.

"Reload! Keep firing!" Dawlish yelled but he knew that all discipline was at an end and that each man was now fighting – or perhaps deciding to run – for his own skin alone.

He cocked his pistol, aimed, fired while the others blasted also. Smoke half-obscured the slits but another attacker fell, and then another, and they were a line no longer but an ever-denser mass clustering towards the gap in the barricade. Shots from the huts to either side tore into their flanks – an attacker tumbled, screaming, dragging at a comrade – and Dawlish fired again and heard Enrique yell with triumph and Aaron swear as he fought to clear a jammed cartridge. Even the two machete-men, helpless onlookers for now,

314

were shouting wildly. Most of the attackers were now concentrated between the two huts, the range point blank, close enough to see scarlet exploding through faded cotton, to sense fury and fear and blood-lust through the acrid smoke.

Dawlish jerked back from his slit to push rounds into his pistol's empty chambers. Dust exploded from the wall above him and a scab of dried mud fell away – the attackers were firing back. He glanced out to see some eight men breaking from the main assault on the breached barricade and heading directly towards the hut. Dawlish brought one down with blood fountaining from his leg and Aaron's rifle was cleared in time to take another but Enrique was fumbling to reload.

Then the figures were passing from Dawlish's view and thumping against the wall's exterior. Rifle muzzles were thrust through the loopholes and tongues of flame stabbed into the hut's choking murk. Hands reached inside and Enrique's weapon was dragged from his grasp. As he struggled to retain it a bayonet speared into his chest and he fell, his scream overtaken by a burbling moan. Dawlish jerked back from his own slit just as another bayonet plunged through and its rifle barked. Half-deafened, face seared, he pushed his revolver towards the gap and fired. He glimpsed a face frozen in horror outside, a body collapsing.

"They're through, Mister!" Aaron was silhouetted at the glow that was the back-doorway and then was gone.

Dawlish realised that only he himself was alive in the hut. More shots flashed into the pungent gloom that was now a death-trap. He launched himself towards the door. He stumbled over a corpse slumped there – the machete-man who had been so terrified – and was blinded for an instant by the glare as he emerged into the sunlight. He ducked instinctively as a Spanish trooper burst though the dazzle and lunged towards him, carbine raised to stab downwards. He swung up his revolver, fired, and sidestepped as the body fell past him, but beyond it a dozen men or more were pouring though the gap in the barricade. He had been spotted and three troopers were rushing towards him and another behind was raising his rifle.

He swung his pistol, fired at the nearest man – he might just have hit but he had already turned away and was sprinting towards an alleyway between two shacks to the rear. One had been tumbled by the mountain gun and he glimpsed a head and shoulders, and a raised rifle – Aaron, crouched among the rubble and aiming past him.

Shouts and shots echoed behind, and Dawlish heard pounding feet and wanted to scream for awareness of those terrible bayonets closing on his back. He raced onwards, seeing almost too late the crumpled form of another of the machete-men and leaping across it. Smoke spat from Aaron's rifle, and the shot must have shaved past Dawlish for he heard a gasp behind and then the clatter of a crashing body and a dropped weapon. Then he was gaining the wrecked hut's shelter and throwing himself down behind the low, jagged remains of its outer wall. He looked back. His pursuers were falling back, dragging a limp figure. The attackers were clustered around the second hut and three were on the roof, tearing away the thatch.

"It's time to go, Mister!" Aaron was feeding another round into his breech with steady hands. His boasts of service with Porter's Mississippi Flotilla must have had substance after all. "We can't do nothin' for Sam 'n his boys!"

Sam Eames and his men were dying hard in the second hut.

Troopers crouched to either side of the door were angling their rifles round to fire blindly inside – it must be like hell itself in there – and the men on the roof were blazing down through gaps they had torn. Others were dragging away the timbers barricading the single window and thrusting in weapons. Twice they must have believed resistance to have ended, for twice small groups flung themselves through the doorway with outstretched bayonets. Twice they staggered back, bloodied and hacked, for the cornered machete-men were selling their lives as dearly as any of their living comrades whose ammunition still lasted.

"Not yet!" Dawlish shouted and fired towards rear of the palpitating knot that was now too frenzied to notice the threat of Aaron and himself to their rear.

Eames and hi men are finished, a small cold voice told him, *only the dying remains*, and yet pride and pity made it impossible to abandon

316

them yet. A yelling trooper went down – whether to Dawlish's shot or Aaron's was immaterial – but then a savage howl rose from the troopers and they were pushing through the door again, and the rifles were falling silent.

"Come, Aaron!" Dawlish felt shame and fear as he scrambled through the rubble towards the lane beyond. Simple, untrained men who had placed their trust in him had died – were dying still, for a long, piercing shriek rose above the cries of triumph behind – and his defence had lasted less than five minutes.

He pounded on through the winding, beaten-earth alleys, always seeking the rusty corrugated roofs of the warehouses, the only point of reference rising above the huts, while Aaron panted beside him. At last they paused, chests heaving, breaths rasping. The emptiness about was oppressive, for the huts' occupants had fled for shelter to the church.

"They're not following." Aaron's voice registered surprise at survival as he looked back along the winding alley.

"They won't, not yet," Dawlish said.

For the attack had clearly been a probe, with too few men allocated to expect breakthrough. Stronger opposition would have driven them away to try elsewhere, would have bought more time. They were still too few to advance through this labyrinth unsupported but they had gained a position that would guarantee their fellows unopposed advance across the open ground between village and scrub. Already a messenger would be returning to confirm to Almunia that his point of entry had been secured. Within an hour his forces would be concentrating there to thrust into the heart of the village. And noon was still an hour away, and it would be hours yet before the *Tecumseh* was fit to sail...

A hundred blundering yards through the alleyways, and then a barricade, and loop-holed shacks, the last obstacle on this flank before the town square. A voice only too obviously terrified by the gunfire stammered a challenge and was instantly reproved by Ambrosio as his head emerged above the barrier.

"What happened, Señor?" He too sounded shocked by the sight of two smoke-grimed men only when he knew there should be more.

"They've taken the huts," Dawlish said.

He reached out and was pulled up and across the barrier. Aaron followed. Ambrosio held this petty fortress with six villagers, their faces familiar from those impossibly distant days when el vómito negro had seemed the greatest threat.

"And the men? Jésus and Paco and Enrico and the Americano and ..."

"Dead."

"God help us then, Señor."

"We must delay them, Ambrosio," Dawlish said. "They'll be attacking this way, not immediately, but when they do it'll be in force."

He felt despair as he surveyed the warren of shacks and alleys and yards around him, adobe walls and ramshackle wooden fences and ragged cactus hedges, all the clutter and confusion of a tropical slum. A company of marines would hardly suffice to save this position from outflanking. He forced himself to sound calm – one hint of irresolution and these men would scurry.

"One volley, that's all I ask, and then we fall back to the square," he said. "You can do that?"

A pause. "We'll do it, Señor." No conviction in the voice. Even one volley might be too much to expect.

Dawlish turned to Aaron. "Find Driscoll, tell him what happened, tell him I'm sure it's from this direction Almunia will attack. And tell him he must get my wife back to *Tecumseh* immediately."

Aaron turned, was gone and Dawlish had hardly time to acquaint himself with the position – three airless huts, linked by barricades, men crouched beneath loopholes hacked in the mud walls, sweat-soaked and terrified, weapons loaded. He passed from room to room, hoping his encouragement did not sound hollow.

318

They came, faster than he could have ever feared, their onset announced by the mountain gun's report – louder, sharper, closer, than ever before.

Dawlish twisted towards the doorway to the adjoining room – there were three men there – just as orange flame burst within it, and the blast rent his ears, and then smoke and dust rolled towards him as the intervening wall collapsed. Choking, throwing his hands involuntarily above his head, he heard shouts of agony and terror. He stumbled back as part of the roof cascaded down, thatch and rafters falling in a billowing heap and blasting a cloud through the breached wall. He called for the men within and got no reply. The barricaded window somewhere to his left – he could just see its lighter outline through the churning dust – was the only exit now and the rifleman who shared this room with him was tearing at the barrier.

One part of Dawlish's brain, cold and rational, told him that his position had been outflanked, that the mountain gun had been manoeuvred through the alleys to the left. The other, instinctive and animal, urged that only that barricaded window and the alley beyond offered any chance of survival.

The last obstacle was torn from the window. The villager threw a leg across the sill.

"Here! Your rifle!"

Dawlish thrust it towards him but the man had no thought beyond survival as he levered himself through. He raced across the alley, towards the hut occupied by Ambrosio. Dawlish picked up the rifle and threw himself through the window, then sprinted across. Heads and shoulders rose above the barricade to the side of the hut ahead, half-familiar faces. A rifle blasted, then another, their rounds howling past to either side of Dawlish as he ran and telling him that the first of the attackers were close behind. Hands reached out as he gained the barricade, and cactus thorns lacerated him as he was dragged across, but he had the rifle – worth gold this instant – and his revolver swung like a pendulum about his neck.

"Fall back!" he shouted to Ambrosio, who was firing from the barricade, "Fall back!" For at this minute the attackers would be manoeuvring the mountain gun forward over the rubble and grouping for the next rush. "I'll cover you!"

Ambrosio shouted to the hut's defenders to leave. Dawlish turned to the barricade – the men there were already taking flight – and saw splinters fly from it as shots sounded from beyond. Hands appeared, arms clad in striped cotton, and then a head and torso as an attacker was heaved over. Dawlish raised the rifle he had just acquired and too late realised that he had no ammunition for it, but the Spanish trooper was half-across and bringing up his carbine, and another was appearing to his right. Dawlish changed his grip to catch the muzzle with both hands, then swung his rifle like a club. The trooper cried out, twisted, but the butt was already smashing into his temple. Even as he collapsed Dawlish swung back to catch the second man with no less force. He slipped back from sight, but other hands and arms were appearing to either side. Dawlish turned, saw that he was alone, dropped the useless rifle and ran.

"Here, Nicolás!" Ambrosio's head appeared around a corner twenty yards beyond.

Dawlish pounded towards him, saw Aaron suddenly emerge by Ambrosio's side and drop to one knee, steadying his rifle. And behind him Stephen Driscoll followed, hustling a half-dozen riflemen before him.

Voices shouted from behind – the attackers were across the barricade – and Aaron was aiming, then holding fire. Driscoll was calmly drawing his men into a jagged line, and somehow they were responding to his shouted orders and raising their weapons. Dawlish's feet skidded as he gained the corner and Ambrosio dragged him round. Driscoll's voice was steady.

"Apunten!"

The villagers were squinting down their sights and they seemed somehow larger, more confident, than hours before. Eight, ten, striped uniforms were over the barrier already, and more were appearing, bayonets glinting evilly in the sun. Driscoll raised his own rifle and Dawlish hurried to his side, pistol raised.

"Fuego!"

The volley ripped into the attackers. Through swirling smoke Dawlish saw bodies crumple and bloody gouts erupt, and figures poised above the barricade drop back in panic.

"Fall back!" Driscoll urged his men into the cover of the corner, gesturing back down the short lane towards the open square beyond. They hesitated – Dawlish hesitated himself – for their success had surprised and heartened them. One was opening his mouth in protest as Driscoll shouted again.

"Fall back and reload!"

And then Dawlish understood. Carter had been busy here last night.

The men fumbled through the unfamiliar process of reloading as they hurried down the alley. Dawlish found himself alongside Driscoll.

"Keep 'em moving, Commander," he said. "Get them into the open."

"Into the square?"

"As far as the house. Where your wife is!"

Dawlish felt despair well within him. She was still here and he was drawing the attack towards her.

Now the wall to the left was of the tavern from where the drunken sailors had viewed the slaughter of the brothers García. The sunlit beaten earth at the end of the alley was the square itself.

"Over there, boys!" Driscoll pointed to Fentiman's house and Aaron urged them towards it in a shambling run. The customs-house was to the right and from beyond it – where Egdean's tiny garrison must still be keeping its lonely vigil, came the sudden crash of rifle-fire.

"That might be the main attack!" Driscoll yelled, still pounding onwards and pulling the panting Ambrosio with him.

Dawlish kept pace, conscious that once more striped uniforms must be surging across the barricade and into the alley, confident that the defence had broken. Hope rising, they would be rolling towards the square – where it was essential they must see the backs of the retreating defenders – and expecting to link with the attackers now smashing in through Egdean's screen.

A slim white figure emerged on the veranda a hundred yards ahead – the swirling linen skirt and the pyramid of golden hair were unmistakable – and Dawlish shouted for her to take cover even as the first shots rippled from behind. One of Driscoll's riflemen stumbled and clutched his leg, his face contorted in pain, and another fell, his arms thrown out in an attitude of crucifixion.

"Halt, Boys! Form up!"

Driscoll dragged the nearest man towards him and swung him about. Another paused in his flight and joined him.

"Form line, Boys!"

Aaron fell in beside him and Dawlish found himself, against all reason, wheeling around to join him.

Troopers were boiling from the alley beside the tavern, around the casks stacked against it – twenty, twenty-five, and still coming. Several were dropping to their knees and raising their weapons and Dawlish felt that every rifle was aimed at himself. Others were fanning out to either side and forming under the barked commands of their sergeants. A denser knot was emerging now, manhandling the tiny mountain gun forward. And from the left, beyond the customs-house, the rattle of rifle-fire was growing. Egdean's assailants must be cautious, were probing, had not yet broken through.

"Apunten!" Driscoll was as calm as on that distant night in the garden at Fiume.

Dawlish felt something whip past his cheek, heard the first reports crash out from across the square. Then he too was part of the volley Driscoll called for and his pistol was bucking in his hand and he never knew if his round had reached the kneeling trooper he had aimed for.

"Lie down! Get down!" Driscoll threw himself prone, pulling the man by his side with him.

Dawlish, understanding, did likewise and but for one man who turned and sprinted rearwards in panic the others followed suit. He pressed himself ever flatter into the ground as dust spurted before him – the troopers were lowering their aim – and braced himself for the hell that could be his only salvation. His bowels were liquid with

322

fear, the desire to burrow into the earth irresistible, and though Driscoll was yelling for them to cover their faces he could not resist glancing up to see an open line of Spanish lurching towards him.

"Carter!" Dawlish's inner voice was screaming, "Now, Carter! Now!"

Like a demon responding to an invocation a gale of flame and screaming debris exploded outwards from the tavern's wall. Fifty pounds of dynamite – an entire projectile intended for the ram – lodged within a sugar cask packed with stones, scythed a fan of searing death across the square. Its scorching breath tore past the buildings along the perimeter, carrying shredded bodies with it, and it lashed across the open ground, blistering the men who lay in terror there, killing the man next to Dawlish and roaring on to shower the house beyond with a rain of driven pebbles.

Driscoll, now more than ever a blackened, livid scarecrow, was struggling to his feet, shouting and gesticulating, though Dawlish was too dazed to hear him. He lurched up to see wreckage and limp bodies strewn and figures dragging themselves across the charred ground. The tavern's front was a smoking crater but the thick-walled adobe hut to its side, where Carter had crouched to manipulate his improvised detonation system, still stood. The ex-marine had lived up to Raymond's recommendation.

Now other figures were emerging, from the customs-house, from shacks near it, a handful of rifle-armed villagers and many more with machetes only. Driscoll's bellowed commands sent them cheering towards the stupefied survivors who were now shambling back into the alley they had emerged from only minutes since. Dawlish went with them, past the shattered mountain gun, slithering on dreadful fragments, ignoring the few wild shots the troopers loosed as they scurried for safety. Then the mob was upon them, hacking, stabbing, blasting, in an orgy of vengeance. Dawlish – or Nicolás Quinones perhaps, despised labourer – had a bayonet-spiked carbine in his hands. He could not recall picking it up from its lacerated owner and his empty pistol swung loose on its lanyard as he thrust and slashed with the others.

323

And suddenly it was over, the last striped uniforms – filthy, bloodied, now – slumped where they had died so hard, penned in the tavern's rubble. Bewildered villagers, astounded and frightened by what they had done, stood aimlessly, began to feel their wounds or sat, drained and empty, amid the carnage. One was weeping uncontrollably. Dawlish, weary, felt an urge to trudge across the square – the house seemed so close – and collapse into Florence's arms and sleep.

"Commander." Driscoll's hand on his arm, the voice insistent. "We need them back in their positions. Hurry Commander!"

For the sound of shooting from beyond the customs-house was dying away. Unbidden, the image rose in Dawlish's mind of Egdean and what survived of his tiny garrison falling back towards the square as he himself had done.

He nodded, found Ambrosio, whose cheek was bleeding but who seemed not to have noticed yet, and together they set to rousing the dazed villagers, setting them to collect fallen weapons, to scurry back to the loop-holed shacks and the customs-house from which they had so recently sallied. He steeled himself to disentangle an ammunition-laden bandolier from a headless, smouldering torso.

"You liked that, Mister?"

Dawlish turned to see a savagely triumphant Carter gesturing towards the blast-scoured square. "A twenty-four carat job, Mister," he said, "and we'll show those sons of bitches again, damned if we don't."

"You..." Dawlish froze.

Carter was pitching over, blood fountaining from his temple, his face a rictus of surprise. A volley was crashing out behind and Dawlish spun about to see troopers – two, three dozen men, spilling around the bend of the track that ran past the customs-house. Those at the front had halted, had dropped to one knee and were already reloading, and a burly figure in brown with upraised sabre was urging another rank, standing, to fall in behind them.

There was no mistaking Fentiman.

31

Three, four more men were down besides Carter. Others stood petrified in horror.

"Take cover!" Dawlish started towards the nearest shack.

He saw Ambrosio at the doorway and across the corner of the square, beyond the open track, Driscoll was being pulled through a half-obstructed window of the customs-house. And with Carter gone, a cold inner voice told him as he pounded forward, that was where he should be himself – but he would never make it in time. The shack was nearer.

Ambrosio was waving him on – no more than twenty yards to go, but his feet were skidding on rubble – and he was aware of five or six villagers pounding beside and behind him. Rifles crackled from the fortified customs-house, a handful against the troopers' massed carbines, but their reports were lost in the crash of Fentiman's disciplined volley.

Dawlish felt something pluck his left sleeve and sear his forearm. He heard the cry of the man to his side as he pitched over and the dull thudding of bodies falling behind him, but then he was at the door and Ambrosio was dragging him inside. A rifleman was firing from the window and two terrified villagers were fumbling to load weapons they had picked up in the square.

"Show them how, Ambrosio!" Dawlish fed a round into his own weapon.

He pushed his way to the window, jerked back as the frame splintered and a round thudded into the opposite wall, then looked out cautiously. Two of Fentiman's men were down and his first rank were firing again, individually now, but their targets had gained cover and were returning fire, however ineffectually, and the major was urging his second rank forward.

They were still forty yards from the sidewall of customs-house – and from the innocuous cluster of casks stacked against the chandler's store opposite. Dawlish remembered Driscoll's earlier words. They were welcome to come down this track any time they liked.

He raised his carbine, aligned his sights for an instant on the white, closely cropped moustache and then dropped it towards the chest. The major's sabre was raised again and he was calling a command – he was cool, he must be granted that – and Dawlish's finger was tightening on the trigger at the instant that one of the villagers blundered past him, weapon at last reloaded. Dawlish's muzzle jerked up and he realise he had missed his chance, for Fentiman was shielded by the resolute line now moving past him down the track.

Dawlish looked around. There was a doorway in the shack's rear wall. Even now other troopers might be working their way through the alleyways behind, probing and outflanking. He turned to Ambrosio and gestured across the square. Fear for Florence gnawed within him.

"Take these men," he said. "Get El Jefe to the ship, and my wife with him."

Then Ambrosio and his men were gone, and Dawlish was alone in the hut.

He raised his carbine – his view was diagonal up the track – and saw that Fentiman's men were hesitant now, and under his urging they had flattened themselves against the walls to either side. Still they inched forward – sometimes moving in short spurts from cover to imagined cover – and the stacked casks were still twenty yards ahead. The fire from the customs-house was less intense now, for the advancing troopers were coming into the windows' blind arc. Dawlish selected his target, a sergeant perhaps, judging by his gestures, but his shot was wide. He groped inside the unfamiliar bandolier and pushed another round into the breech.

The troopers were level with the casks now. Another twenty yards would carry them into the square itself and the fire that opposed them had died away. A half-dozen troopers rushed forwards, throwing themselves at the nearest window on the custom-house sidewall, thrusting carbines inside and firing. The building's main door, that opening on the square, burst open suddenly and six or seven men came rushing out. Dawlish felt a thrill of delight as he recognised Egdean among them, and Porfirio also – they must have

326

reached the custom-house's far side as they retreated. They raced across the square, heading for Fentiman's house, and the door swung gaping behind them.

But Driscoll did not follow them.

Dawlish could almost visualise him crouched inside a corner of the thick whitewashed walls. While shots smashed through the barricaded window he would be jerking the cord that Carter had so carefully strung through a concealed hole and along a small channel carefully dug across the track, then roofed over with boards and disguised with earth. The salt-covered detonator terminals would be plunging into a pail of water...

Fentiman was striding past the casks, twenty, thirty of his men ahead of him, as many behind, the sudden ending of fire from the customs-house encouraging them to greater haste. The first of them were flowing around the corner into the square and had spotted the fleeing defenders. Several were pausing to take aim. The major had raised his sabre again, and his brick-red face was contorted in a yell of anticipated triumph as he lurched into a run.

The casks erupted.

Confined between the solid frontage of the chandler's store and the massive wall of the customs-house across from it, the explosion's fury sent fire and stones screaming down the track in both directions. Fentiman and his men went with the hurricane, ruptured corpses carried on its blazing surge, all wrapped in the same deadly shroud. Even the handful who had gained the square could not escape the funnel of scything pebbles, more lethal than any shrapnel, that spewed from the track and lashed them down.

Dawlish threw himself below the window, arm flung across his face, as the hot gale swept past. When he rose it was to see a scene more dreadful than had followed the first detonation, bodies and parts of bodies strewn along the track and far out across the square, and plastered, even more dreadfully, against the once-white wall of the customs-house.

Isolated shots broke the sudden silence, villagers still concealed venting old resentment on any sign of life. Already the first figures were emerging from cover, machete in hand, rolling bodies over, hacking viciously whether there was life or not. Two wretches, dazed but uninjured, were being pinned in a corner and Dawlish looked away, unwilling to see their brutal end, yet knowing he had no right to deny the oppressed their vengeance.

He left the hut and emerged on to the square, disgust and weariness and relief washing through him in equal measure. He looked up the track. Beyond the point of explosion, whatever had remained of the attackers had taken to its heels. But the Spanish would be back, he knew, not today, but a week, a fortnight, a month from now, their retribution absolute, and even those innocents who had no part of this, who even now cowered in the church, would bear its brunt.

Driscoll was hurrying towards him.

"Let's gather the boys up, Commander," he said. "It's time to move out." There was a hard gleam in his eyes, cold satisfaction in his tone, the quiet pride of a professional in an unpleasant task competently executed. Topcliffe had been right to fear this man.

They imposed order of a sort, set a screen to watch for any further Spanish movements, put others to gathering weapons and ammunition – enough to equip an entire company and more – and to carrying them down to the jetty. Familiar faces were absent, villagers who had trained so desperately and who were already slipping from memory, the Juans and Pablos and Agustíns, and Sam Eames and Aaron Powell. Women had appeared and searching among the chaos, intermittent shrieks announcing that they had found what they had most feared. Wounded were being rolled into blankets and borne off to inadequate care.

"A good man," Driscoll was looking at Carter's body. "We'd have been finished without him."

"You know he helped me that night in New Haven?" Dawlish said. "I'd never have taken the ram without him."

"He was a good man anyway."

"And Fentiman?" They had found what remained of him and had turned quickly away.

"Better dead, Commander." Driscoll's voice held no trace of compassion.

Dawlish could at last head across the square, heart thumping, fear increasing as he saw how stone fragments had torn gashes in the house's frontage, had shattered windows. The entrance yawned open and he entered to see Egdean and Ambrosio among a knot of men clumsily descending the stairs, holding a door above them. It carried Machado, half-sitting, struggling to keep his balance. Florence was on the landing above, issuing instructions in poor Spanish. Her face broke into a smile as she spotted Dawlish and he saw she wanted to cry out in joy no less than he did himself, but then she stopped herself, and no word passed between them. She looked away and urged Machado to lie still.

They brought him out, rested the door on the veranda. He raised himself weakly on one elbow, brushing aside Dawlish's efforts to lift him. The fever had passed, though his skin still had a grey pallor and the eyes were still misted with yellow. He looked out across the misery-strewn square, and above the battered customs-house saw the tattered five stripes and single star flapping weakly.

"We prevailed then." Machado's voice was little more than a whisper. "Cuba Libre still lives."

"Cuba Libre!"

The words were taken up by the men about him, Ambrosio and Porfirio and the other exhausted, sweat-soaked men, not a cry of triumph or of hope, but a growl of savage determination, recognition that for them, no less than for Machado himself, there could be amnesty, no accommodation, ever again.

The small procession trudged along the foreshore, the improvised stretcher borne at shoulder height. The workshop was just visible through the cluster of huts by the jetty. Smoke drifted only lazily from its chimney now and the forge no longer glowed. The repaired steam header might even now be back on the *Tecumseh* and Holland and her engineer straining in her boiler-room to flange it in position. Yet the knowledge brought no elation, for Dawlish was looking beyond the jetty where gathered weapons were being stacked on a lighter and where Geraldo's tug waited for Machado with steam already up, and past the white yacht's shell-wounded profile, and out over the tranquil waters to the south.

329

And there, on the horizon, a black dot, crawling slowly back and forth across the outer bay, was the *Spinola* and her ship-smashing Parrotts, the last and most dangerous enemy of all.

Florence was walking by the door, telling Machado to lie back, be quiet. The face Dawlish loved so much was haggard with exhaustion. He moved closer, fell in with her pace and their hands brushed together briefly. What they felt could not be expressed here and so, business-like, she nodded towards Machado.

"I couldn't move him sooner, Nick," she said. "Even now he's very weak..."

But it was for himself she had waited, Dawlish knew, and had he not returned, had Fentiman prevailed, she would have been with those women searching for their men in the aftermath of carnage, no matter what the cost to herself.

"He'll live, Florence," he said, "and we'll live too. Just a few more hours and we'll ..."

And suddenly there were cries and shots – wild ones – but above all the terrible drumming of hooves. A knot of horsemen was bursting from an alley at the square's furthermost corner, half a dozen, no more, several blasting with pistols at the few defenders scattering from their path. The leading rider was crouched along his chestnut's neck, sabre extended, and with the slightest touch of the reins was urging it down on a fleeing rifleman. Screaming, the man threw down his weapon and half-turned, arms raised, too late to avoid the blade skewering into his throat and expertly plucked free as the animal thundered past. The rider rose in his saddle – he had spotted the group carrying Machado – and as he called to his men to wheel towards it the long, dark, clean-shaven face was that of Almunia.

"Put it down!" Dawlish yelled. "Florence, get down! Don't move!"

The bearers were setting the door down hastily and one of them, his courage at an end, broke away and ran back towards the house.

"I'm with you, Sir," Egdean was at Dawlish's side, bayonet fixed.

"Stand firm!" Dawlish yelled. "Form a line!"

It should be a square, for the horsemen could flow around, take them in the flank and rear, but he had too few for that. Ambrosio was struggling with his rifle, yet standing shoulder to shoulder with Egdean, his bloodied face registering a mix of terror and determination. Another man was joining him, and then another.

"Pick a target! Aim for the horses!"

Dawlish knew the orders might well be meaningless for these terrified men and when the riders crashed into them even this slight discipline might dissolve. Florence was crouched somewhere behind him...

The horsemen were halfway across the square now, Almunia's sabre upraised, his course straight towards Dawlish, the riders to either side drawing level, and curving round to engulf the knot before them.

"Hold fire!"

Dawlish had raised his rifle, was lining fore and back sight on Almunia's hatred-contorted face, could sense that this was a man who had lost everything and would sooner sell his life in one insane act of retribution than report his humiliation to his superiors.

"Cuba Libre!"

Machado was trying to raise himself, and he could only croak, but his words were echoed incoherently by the other men like some despairing invocation. They formed a ragged line before the door on the ground. One fired wildly, and Ambrosio was calling him a fool and he was struggling to reload. Suddenly the man next to Dawlish doubled up and fell backwards across Machado's legs, a bloody crater exploding from his back as a trooper's slug tore into him.

"Hold fire!"

The order was lost in an ineffectual ripple of despairing shots as discipline collapsed. A horse screamed, its rider fighting to regain control. Egdean's round tore another from his saddle but the line was dissolving and Dawlish found himself jostled, his sights flung away from Almunia. Men who had fired stumbled backwards, turning to find riders surging in behind. Porfirio fell across Machado, blood gushing from his chest, and Florence was trying to pull him away. A horseman who had swept in from behind was chopping at another, his blade slicing mercilessly through the hands raised so ineffectually to protect the head.

Almunia pulled his chestnut's head over. Foreleg and stirrup-toe came shaving past Dawlish and the sabre arced down. Dawlish threw up his carbine to meet it, and the shock of impact tore it from his grasp. Terrified now, he dropped, reaching for the fallen weapon, the stamping hooves crashing about him, Almunia's sabre probing and slashing.

A horse had fallen just beyond, legs flailing, its rider squirming beneath. From beyond it Egdean appeared. "I'll cover you, Sir" he called, and drove upwards with his bayonet towards Almunia. The Spaniard, hearing, twisted in his saddle, missed the spike, and gave spurs to his mount, urging it from the melee, then wheeling away to see where he could best strike again.

Dawlish had his rifle again – still with a round in the chamber – but almost too late heard Egdean cry "Behind you, Sir!" He spun to see a horseman drawing rein not ten feet distant and swinging a pistol towards him. Dawlish was first to fire – no time to aim, a lucky shot that took the horse in the chest . It tumbled and its rider spilled over its neck. Egdean was on him before he could recover, bayonet plunging.

"Nicholas! Nicholas!" Florence's cry went to Dawlish's heart.

A coachman's daughter, fearless of horses since birth, she had taken hold of Almunia's reins – he had cut in on the far side - and she was dragging the chestnut's head aside. She was somehow avoiding the snapping teeth, though her sleeve was blood-soaked where the sabre had already raked a glancing gash, but Almunia had eyes only for the figure that had rolled off the door beneath him.

"Machado!" he cried, his surprise as palpable as his hatred, "Machado!"

The sick man was wriggling to avoid the plummeting hooves and dragging himself free from Porfirio's body lying across his legs, hands scrabbling for the dead man's rifle. Almunia was leaning over, sweeping viciously with his sabre, oblivious of anything but the hated enemy beneath him. Unseen behind, Dawlish launched himself forward, his now-empty carbine grasped by the muzzle like a club, but yards still separated him from Almunia. The horse, enraged by the blows Florence was now raining with her free hand, was starting to plunge. Dawlish swung – the butt should have taken Almunia squarely across the back but the whinnying chestnut had reared up and the blow fell on the knee.

Almunia jerked upwards in pain as the horse pounded down again and, too late, twisted to confront Dawlish. The swinging carbine caught him square across the chest and he tumbled down on the beast's other side.

"Now, Nick! Now!" Florence screamed as she dragged the horse with her, and he ducked around the thrashing hooves to finish the fallen Spaniard.

There was no need.

Almunia was jerking weakly as blood spurted from his throat, soaking the sick man who had found enough strength to wrench a bayonet free from Porfirio's rifle and who still stabbed and hacked with merciless intensity.

At last the body stilled. Machado looked up, saw their horror.

"For my wife," he said. "For my wife whom he burned. For my three children."

And then he began to weep.

32

Dawlish struggled into wakefulness, shaken by Florence, and felt the last hammer blows that secured the header above the main steam valve reverberate through the yacht. He had needed the sleep, needed it if he must do what he must do tonight, and yet he had felt guilty for retiring while others slaved.

"It's time, Nicholas." Her voice trembled slightly. "Only three hours, but you told me to call you when Captain Swanson said the work was finished."

"What time?"

"Just after eight."

In the darkened cabin he could just make out that she was scented slightly of violets, her clothes changed, again immaculate.

He embraced her for a moment, buried his face in her hair, felt her wince.

"Your arm, Florence..." He remembered the gash now. He had cleaned and bandaged it himself. Now it was in a sling.

"It's nothing, Nick. Look – I can move the fingers." She tried to smile as she did so. She poured water from a ewer with her good hand and he dashed it in his face.

He was all but sure that he was going to die, for what he intended was suicidal, and yet the foreboding brought no fear, only a dull sorrow that he must leave this glorious woman. But there was no other way, and he owed it to her, a small voice told, him, to her and the others who would not have been here but for his blunders – and his ambition. *Leonidas* was a small prize to have hostaged so much for.

She had laid out clean clothes for him – the touch of a cotton shirt was a small joy – and he scalded his mouth in throwing back the coffee she had brought. She sensed his mood and confined herself to hurrying him out and to the boiler room.

Egdean, Holland and the engineer were slumped exhausted against the bulkhead, skins scarlet and glistening, sweat-saturated clothes clinging to them. The stoker was shovelling coal into an already glowing furnace. Protected only by a single blisteringly hot valve, the three men had balanced on a plank scaffold over the boiler and somehow flanged the mended header in place.

"The safety-valve will lift soon," Swanson said. "We're ready for sea." Dawlish saw fear on his face, knew the *Spinola* was uppermost in his mind also.

"A half-hour, Captain, a half-hour, not more."

For not only *Tecumseh* would be departing. Geraldo's tug, with a single lighter in tow, would also be creeping out into the darkness, carrying Machado and two score others to a landing further inland, on the northern shore of Joa Bay, to continue the reignited struggle for Cuba Libre.

Florence accompanied Dawlish when he crossed to the lighter. They pushed their way through a cluster of men transferring captured weapons from the jetty. Women were weeping and pleading among them, children wailing. They found Machado under an improvised awning aft. He thanked them both. Propped up, still too weak to stand, he reassured them that he was better now, infinitely better.

Raymond was present, and all business. "I've been telling Señor Machado that the bargain stands. Five hundred Springfields, ten thousand rounds of ammunition. The vessel carrying them will be off Punta Guarico within a fortnight. I sent the telegram myself before I left Santiago to confirm the shipment."

"Punta Guarico is a long way." Machado sounded wearily resolute. Forced marches, unrelenting pursuit, a litter carried on the bleeding shoulders of exhausted men, wounded despatched with a single shot to avoid capture – he knew what lay ahead. "But we'll be there, Señor," he said, "we'll be there."

"I have contacts if you should need further deliveries," Raymond said. "Quality guaranteed, straight from the arsenal, and at a price that can't be beaten."

"I guess you'll always be able to offer a deal that can't be beaten, Mr. Raymond." Driscoll emerged from the shadows, laden with three carbines and an armful of bandoliers. "It is Mr. Raymond – or is it Mr. Worth? I never did quite figure out the name correctly."

"Raymond will do, Brigadier." He smiled.

"You'll be leaving tonight also, Commander, Ma'am?" Driscoll laid down his load.

"Shortly."

"And the ram, Commander?" Driscoll looked wistfully towards the rounded hull lying awash at the *Tecumseh's* stern.

"You know I must take her." Dawlish had crossed an ocean to frustrate this man, and now he found himself speaking almost apologetically.

Driscoll shrugged. "You've got the advantage, Commander. And she's no good to me here now. I won't dispute it. Not this time." The same tone of weary resolution as Machado's.

335

"If..." Dawlish found himself reluctant to spell out the odds, even to himself, "...when the yacht makes open sea, Captain Swanson could drop you in Haiti, Brigadier." He tried to smile. "It's probably the furthest the patched header will last anyway." Topcliffe would never have authorised this, he knew, but he owed Driscoll something. It hardly mattered now. He might not anyway be there himself to face the admiral's wrath.

"You're going to take your chance with those fellows out there?" Driscoll nodded seawards, towards the *Spinola* waiting patiently there in the darkness. "You might be safer taking your chances with Señor Machado, Commander. But it's a handsome offer. You've two of my men still, injured both of them. I'd appreciate if you extended the courtesy to them, but you'll not take offence if I don't accept."

Driscoll looked around, taking in Machado, and the exhausted villagers stacking weapons and supplies, and the despair of the women on the dockside. "I guess these people might benefit from a little military advice, at least until – where was it? Punta Guarico? Maybe even beyond." He smiled. "Maybe I was a little too stale, Commander, maybe that's why you got the drop on me. Perhaps I can do with a spell in the field again and I'll need to find those boys who escaped from the *Old Hickory*. Cuba Libre, or Ireland Free, it's the same battle in the end."

"The offer stands, Brigadier." Dawlish felt a surge of respect and liking. "I wish the circumstances could have been different. Not this, not Boquerón, not Cuba, but your politics, your country."

"And you're leaving too, Ma'am?" Driscoll turned to Florence. She nodded.

"You're a damn fine woman, Ma'am. I'm glad to have known you." He reached out and took her hand and, in an unexpected gesture, kissed it. "You've been lucky in life, Commander," he said and reached out his hand to him.

Dawlish took it. The grip was firm.

"I look forward to the day we can meet as friends, Commander, but until then..."

"We're still enemies," Dawlish could not keep regret from his voice.

"I guess that's so, Commander, I guess that's the way it is." Driscoll turned away.

So too did Dawlish and Florence. In silence. Back towards the *Tecumseh*.

*

The yacht was still lay alongside the jetty and they were looking down from the bridge.

Wails rose from the wharf as Geraldo nudged the tug out into the still waters, the barge straining aft. Somebody shouted "Cuba Libre!", but it sounded half-hearted, and was not picked up, as if the full enormity of what they were undertaking had at last dawned. Machado had struggled to his feet, and Ambrosio was supporting him. They waved solemnly to Dawlish, and others waved also, faces familiar to him from hushed plotting in smoky huts, or as workmates of the half-witted Nicolás, or as terrified participants in this day's slaughter. At last the soft darkness enveloped them.

"What will become of them, Nick?" Florence said.

"What will become of us?" he wanted to rejoin, but instead he kissed her, said he loved her. "Go to the saloon now," he told her. "Don't come on deck again." He saw her tears glisten as she turned away.

He felt alone, wholly alone, knowing he might never see her again. Memories flooded back – a morning off Troy, a transcribed poem of Keats arriving unexpectedly at a bleak Black Sea anchorage, terror as Bashi-Bazooks stormed a Thracian caravanserai; hands touching in a boat gliding across the still waters of a Byzantine cistern; laughter exchanged across a breakfast table. He wanted never to leave her, to hold him to her forever. He felt a hollowness, and infinite regret, yet no fear.

Not yet, he thought, *that fear will come in the confined darkness*, and he was glad that Florence would not witness it.

33

Almost ready to cast off.

A last word with Swanson on the bridge, another with Egdean at the *Tecumseh's* stern. Two cables' length of narrow manila rope was flaked there, ready to run out free and fast, the most that could be found in the chandler's store ashore. One end was made fast to the same bollard as the ram's towing bridle, the other extended out into the darkness aft.

"A word, Sir, if you'll pardon the liberty," Egdean looked uncomfortable.

"Say it, old friend."

"You're a married man, Sir. I don't have nobody myself. There's no call for you to do this, Sir, and I know the drill as well as you – you know that, Sir. I can do what's needed just as well as you can."

"No argument, Egdean." Dawlish forced a harshness into his voice he did not feel. "Just keep your eye on me. Watch nothing, nobody else, no matter what those blackguards out there throw at this ship. Just watch me and wait for my signal. You understand?"

"Aye, Aye, Sir."

"You're my only hope, Jerry." Dawlish's voice softened. "I'd rely on nobody else for what I'm asking of you."

He thought briefly about speaking to Holland. He had been invaluable in assisting repair of the header but now he was slumped in exhaustion in the cabin assigned to him. It was better not to awaken him. The inventor would want no part in what must now happen to his beloved child.

Dawlish lowered himself down on to the ram's curved decking. He checked the lashings fastening *Tecumseh's* dinghy to the tiny superstructure abaft the hatch. The dark paint with which it had been daubed to reduce visibility was still wet. He reassured himself that the knife Egdean had whetted to razor-sharpness for him was still at his belt, then swung his legs into the space below and lowered himself. The familiar warm oily stench surrounded him and he fought back the first stab of terror at his dark confinement. He reached out – the levers and hand wheels were familiar now – and touched the projectiles stacked in their racks. Another four had been jammed alongside the Brayton engine that would never run again. He positioned himself on the saddle, head protruding through the hatch.

"Ready!"

Egdean, above him on the *Tecumseh's* stern, relayed the message. Crew scurried to cast off and the yacht's screw thrashed slowly. She drew slowly away from the jetty, leaving the ram wallowing gently astern until the towing bridle tautened and dragged her into the wake.

At first, his eyes eighteen inches above the surface, Dawlish's vision was filled by the white hull that towered ahead and by the slime-fouled pilings of the wharf. Then, as *Tecumseh* moved further from shore, Boquerón revealed itself in all its squalor and he remembered his first arrival here, and his labours, and the vómito, and all the cruelty and heroism and sacrifice his presence had triggered. The few onlookers who had remained where straggling home and somewhere in the great island's interior merciless men would soon be planning the retribution to fall on them. He craned to glance aft, past the bulk of the dinghy secured there so clumsily, but already the tug and her lighter were lost in the darkness, carrying Machado and Driscoll and the rest who no longer had a home towards some petty epic of revolt and desperation.

The sky was overcast directly above, but southwards, seen beyond *Tecumseh's* flank, the cloud was ragged over the mouth of the bay, letting moonlight filter through. Dawlish searched for any sign of the Spanish gunboat. Finding none brought no relief, for she must be there, her lookouts' eyes straining for any sight of movement. Swanson was hugging the coastline as close inshore as he dared as he moved seawards, merging the yacht's profile with that of the higher ground to port.

Dawlish heard Egdean's shouted query, and yelled back that he was ready for increased speed. He swung the hatch cover closed and tightened a single dog. The ram twisted and plunged and reared gently in a slow, steady, sickening rhythm as *Tecumseh's* screw beat faster. A regular bumping on the casing above told that the dinghy was still in place. Only the slightest paleness filtered through the thick-glassed ports, enough to confirm water breaking and seething outside, washing over the hatch.

He could only wait now, knowing from the steady reverberation through the plating that the yacht's screw was churning at close to maximum revolutions, guessing that the heading remained unchanged. The humid darkness was worse now that there was nobody to share it with, nor any activity nor drill to occupy him – not yet at least. Slightly nauseous from the closeness and the unfamiliar screwing, pitching motion, he wedged himself on the saddle above the engine, and tried to empty his mind of any thought of Florence, of his father, or his long-dead mother, of happiness past or of opportunities missed. He could imagine Swanson and the others on the bridge, eyes riveted on *Spinola's* lights, fearing the moment when they might swing away from their steady course, dreading the explosion of flame-dyed smoke that would herald a Parrot hurling its shell towards them.

Tecumseh steamed on, slight changes in heading signalled by lurches of the ram. Dawlish peered through the thick glass but through the foam surging without discerned nothing but dark to port, a slight lightness to starboard. The yacht must have covered half the distance to the mouth of the bay by now and still her luck was holding. The urge to lift the hatch ever so slightly and to check position – and *Spinola's* presence – was almost irresistible but he fought it down. If Swanson could have profited from running the Union blockade then he must be trusted now.

Time now to start the preparations.

He groped and found the head of the nearest of the four projectiles clipped in the starboard rack. At its base his fingers located the protective covers over the water-activated fuses. He twisted one loose, left it on a single thread, but did not remove it. Three more followed – there were four fuses on each head. One cover was jammed on the next projectile and he left it, passed on to the others. His hands were trembling slightly but the work stilled them, but not the thumping of his heart, the racing blood, the craving to fling the hatch open and breathe the night air, whatever the consequences.

340

The ram rolled viciously, almost throwing him from the saddle, and the bows plunged, then reared. The hull rang with the blows of the tethered dinghy fighting to break loose. *Tecumseh* was changing course – and violently. The ram's plating seemed to pant in resonance with her screw's beat, and the revolutions were increasing. *Spinola* must have spotted the yacht, must be swinging toward her, and Swanson must be telegraphing for maximum revolutions – and more. *Tecumseh's* furnace must be glowing white by now, the safety-valve perhaps screwed down a turn, the pistons flailing. The hastily-repaired header must somehow be holding.

Then a hammer blow, dull, yet all-enveloping, ringing through the ram, drowning the noise of *Tecumseh's* screw for an instant, doing no damage, but enough to announce that one of those fearsome Parrots had fired – and missed. But the Spanish gunners would be noting the splash, would be sponging and hauling the weapon over, and the gunboat's captain also would be calling for maximum speed.

Water sprayed over the hatch's lip as Dawlish flung it open and thrust out his head. He glimpsed the yacht thrashing ahead – and the land was falling away to port and the open sea was straight before her bows – but it was the *Spinola* he sought as he twisted clumsily. The calm waters were moonlit to starboard, towards Punta San Nicolás, and there the gunboat was, foreshortened, bows on, a mile and a half distant, not more, her yards bare and foam seething at her stem. She was still turning, curving into a course for a stern chase and, as she did, fire and smoke belched from her bows.

The shell's flight was seconds only, yet in that eternity Dawlish saw Florence exposed to its scorching, scything fury, her beauty and her goodness powerless before it. Any sacrifice of his seemed too insignificant to weigh against her peril. The trajectory was low and the round fell short, and a hundred yards before the yacht, in a skidding, tumbling plume that ended in a sudden climbing geyser. *Tecumseh* has survived. For now. The ram shuddered as the explosion's shock rippled through her, but her seams were holding even if she thrashed and rolled with it.

"Ready, Sir?" Egdean's voice booming across the yacht's wake.

"Not yet, Jerry! Not yet!" Dawlish bellowed back.

341

For though *Spinola's* gunners could afford salvo after salvo, methodically correcting their aim and range, bringing perhaps a second weapon into play, he could make but a single response. And the time was not yet, and until then *Tecumseh* must takes her chances. He glanced from ship to ship – the distance separating them was closing and despite all her repairs the yacht was conceding two, perhaps three knots to her pursuer. But that was perhaps to the good ... provided the Parrots did not get the range.

He lowered himself again to the saddle. Water was spilling over the hatch's brim and cascading into the ram's interior. His hands were wet – there was nothing to dry them with, and he hesitated before he spun the first of the fuse-covers free. The touch of the dry salt beneath sent a pang of terror through him but he dropped the cover – no going back now – and freed the second, and the third. Water fell on his back and he arched it to shield the projectile heads as he continued. Another head's detonators were exposed now – two to go – and then another shock came beating through the plating, *Spinola's* shot falling, closer than before, he judged by its intensity, but still somehow sparing the yacht.

All the covers were stripped away now – fifteen, one still jammed – and only the thinnest layer of salt shielded the detonator terminals. Four projectiles, each encasing fifty pounds of dynamite, were now naked to the ravenous seawater that would trigger their detonation, and with them the four other missiles stored on the opposite rack and another four jammed above the engine. Five feet of height separated them from the water sloshing on the deck below, but the there was little to shield them from splashes from the rain cascading through the hatch. Instant annihilation was perhaps seconds away.

He thrust his head through the hatch, heard Egdean's shouted query from the *Tecumseh's* poop.

"Not yet!" Dawlish yelled back, "Wait for my signal!"

The gunboat astern had closed the range to perhaps a mile, and was still gaining. Against the black pyramid of her rigging and masts and yards, and the yet darker hull, Dawlish could discern white-clad figures. The bow chasers were silent – they should have fired again by now – and then he saw that the Spanish captain must have realised that he could easily overhaul the yacht without sinking her. A boarding party would be standing ready and every man would be seeing prize money, and the satisfaction of an entire crew of gunrunners and rebels taken captive. Dawlish remembered that shooting alone had not sufficed for the crew of the *Virginius*. Their heads had been displayed on spikes. The thought of Florence exposed to such vengeance gave him the courage to drop back into the ram's darkness.

Water lapped around his ankles, fell on his head and shoulders in intermittent downpours. His hand groped for the main ballast lever, found it. Ninety degrees would open it fully, take the ram down in less than half a minute. He cracked it open, less than ten degrees but enough for a slow bleed of the air that restrained the inflow of water. And with that small action accomplished the ram was settling, slowly, ever deeper, and all the while waves would continue to wash in across the hatch's rim.

Now, furiously, he wanted to live, to escape the doom enveloping him, to breathe clean air no matter what the cost. He sprung up the ladder and threw himself through the hatch on to the foam-wreathed decking. He ignored Egdean's call, had no eyes for the oncoming gunboat, heaved himself inside the dinghy that still bucked and thumped on the ram's after decking. He felt for his knife and reached for the ropes that still tethered the tiny craft. He sawed frantically. The first parted, and the second, and the third snapped of its own accord. Suddenly the dinghy was leaping free, dropping to the side of the ram, leaping and plunging in its waves, all but throwing him out, still tethered to *Tecumseh's* stern by her manila tow rope and dragged, like the ram on her own thicker hawser, in the foaming wake.

He struggled to his knees. Egdean seemed impossibly distant but even in the dim moonlight the agony of expectation on his face was manifest

Dawlish cupped his hands. "Now, Jerry!" he yelled. "Cast off!"

He saw the arc of Egdean's sledgehammer as it swung down to drive the pin from the shackle securing the ram's tow. He saw the

343

end of the hawser come leaping over *Tecumseh's* stern and splash into the wake beneath. He felt the ram shudder, then wallow, alongside the dinghy and then drop astern as he was pulled forward after the yacht. He could hear Egdean bellow as he directed many hands to heave in the manila rope, to draw the dinghy forward, and under *Tecumseh's* curving counter, but he saw none of it, for he had turned to watch what he had set afoot.

The ram had lost all headway and was rolling gently, almost awash, nothing but the tiny superstructure visible, so tiny that any eye less accustomed than his own might miss her altogether. Beyond her the gunboat ploughed onwards, little more than a half-mile distant now, confident of her prey.

The dinghy leaped as it was dragged into the screw's churn. Dawlish turned, saw faces lining the poop close above – Florence was there, tight-lipped – and Egdean was flinging a heaving line. The weighted head plopped in the dinghy but slithered overboard before he could grab it, and then it was snaking back again, and this time he caught it. He dragged it toward him, and with it the bowline in the heavier rope that followed.

"Hurry, Sir, Hurry!"

A faint cry reached him as he thrust his shoulders through the loop – a voice from *Spinola's* bows booming through a speaking trumpet the order to heave to.

"Ready, Jerry! Now!"

He felt the rope about him draw taut, tugging him with it and he launched himself from the dinghy into the seething foam. Terror of the screw's slicing blades gripped him as he went under. He choked and came back up again, spluttering and retching, and then went under once more. His foot smashed into something hard – the rudder, a cold remote voice told him, and he was that close to the beating screw – and then his head was in the air and he felt himself rising. Shaking water from his eyes, breath heaving, he twisted as he dangled – and there still was the gunboat, ever closer, all the more menacing for the silence of her weapons.

Hands grabbed for his shoulders and he reached out himself and caught the bulwark. An instant later he was being lugged over and slumping on the deck.

"Nicholas!" Florence was reaching for him but even her he thrust aside as he dragged himself up to look astern.

Four cables astern, eight hundred yards, the *Spinola* cleaved onward remorselessly, and again her command to heave to echoed over the narrowing gap. A small black object lay directly before the gunboat and her bows were edging over to shave past. Some keen eye on the forecastle must have seen it – might have taken it for a barrel, maybe even for a floating mine, for anything but the hatchway of a nine-tenths submerged submarine boat – and the helmsman, alerted, was altering course ever so slightly.

And then the object disappeared in a brief flurry of bubbling froth. There was no sign that any on the gunboat were alarmed by it, for their quarry was too close now, their blood up. But Dawlish was counting, half-sickened, half-elated by the deliverance he knew was at hand as the seawater surging through the plunging ram's interior ate ravenously through the salt plugs.

The sea rose.

It heaved up and burst, vastly more violent, more furious, more sustained than when the *Old Hickory* had been mortally wounded. Foam and spray clawed upwards a hundred feet and more, blotting out all view of the gunboat half a cable beyond. A raging wave, circular, raced outwards and another followed as the towering white column collapsed back into the seething pool beneath. A wall of tortured water rolled towards the *Spinola* – her helm was over, the bows turning away, though too late – and smashed over the forecastle. The ship rolled and thrashed as the torrent surged across her deck, dragging men and equipment with it.

"The foremast's going, Sir!" Egdean's voice was awed, but others were cheering as the standing rigging snapped, the cordage lashing like whips, and the mast toppled to starboard. Still connected by a hundred tendons, it crashed into the white water and lay there, pulling the gunboat's bows over.

The boiling waters were subsiding now and the gunboat was righting herself, and wallowing, but the millstone she dragged alongside impeded all progress. The circular wave was rolling on, white-crowned, energy dying and height decreasing with distance from its origin, and it lifted the *Tecumseh* only gently as it passed, heaving her up to provide a better view of the Spanish vessel's agony.

"It's like a death, Nick," Florence gripped his arm, "like she's dying..."

But he could feel no pity, no regret. For Florence would live.

The *Spinola* would not die, he guessed, though her seams would have sprung, and machinery would have been dislodged – a plume of steam screaming from near the funnel confirmed a boiler being blown down – and that mast must be hacked free if she was to make port. A career, perhaps of an officer as ambitious as himself, would be in ruins. The memory of the humiliation inflicted by a Yanqui gunrunner and his Cuban associates would be erased by hundreds of merciless reprisals across the ill-starred island.

And then Dawlish heard a sob.

Holland was gripping the bulwark with a terrible intensity, tears coursing down from behind his thick, rimless lenses, his chest heaving.

Florence moved towards him. "Mr. Holland," she said, "Mr. Holland, there's no need..."

Dawlish drew her back. "Leave him," he said. "He still has his dream."

And some vague understanding of what that dream might be chilled him, of warfare more cold, more efficient, more absolute than he ever experienced himself, less passionate, less personal, more dreadful than Boquerón's agony. This insignificant, obsessive schoolteacher might weep now but others in unguessed times to come would weep yet more because of his dream.

The land was falling rapidly astern, a dark mass concealing vast hatreds and heroisms and miseries yet to come. The crippled gunboat was but a smudge against the moonlit waters and the *Tecumseh's* bows were lifting and plunging gently as they met the swell of the Caribbean. Soon they would be turning eastwards towards Haiti – a day's run – to find there all the shelter that a neutral port and corrupt officials could furnish and Raymond's dollars purchase.

Dawlish turned away.

"Come, Florence," he said, "it's time to rest now." She flinched as he touched her wounded arm but she took his hand with the other and held it too her cheek.

His feet were dragging with exhaustion, his body aching, but still his spirit soared.

For she was his – and so too would be *Leonidas*.

The End

A personal message from Antoine Vanner

 I hope you've enjoyed *Britannia's Shark* and that you've also enjoyed the previous books in the series, *Britannia's Wolf* and *Britannia's Reach*.

You probably know how important good reviews are to the success of a book on Amazon or Kindle, especially for a writer starting publishing a series. If you've enjoyed this book then I'd be very grateful if you would post a review on **www.amazon.com** or **www.amazon.co.uk.**

Your support does really matter and I read all reviews since readers' feedback encourages me to keep researching and writing about the life of Nicholas Dawlish.

If you'd like to leave a review then all you have to do is go to the review section on the *"Britannia's Shark"* Amazon page. Scroll down from the top and under the heading of "Customer Reviews" you'll see a big button that says "Write a customer review" – click that and you're ready to get into action. You don't need to write much – a sentence or two is enough, essentially what you'd tell a friend or family member about the book.

Thanks again for your support and don't forget that you can learn more about Nicholas Dawlish and his world on my website **www.dawlishchronicles.com**.

You might also "like" the Facebook Page "Dawlish Chronicles" or want to follow my weekly blog on **dawlishchronicles.blogspot.co.uk** in which I write short articles based on research which is not necessarily used in the novels but is too good to let go to waste.

And finally – I can assure you that further Dawlish adventures are on the way. I hope you'll enjoy them, even though Dawlish himself might not!

Yours Faithfully: *Antoine Vanner*

Historical Notes

John Phillip Holland (1840 – 1914) was to continue his development of submarines through the 1880s and 1890s. After breaking with the Irish Republican Brotherhood, and despite considerable setbacks and difficulties in securing funding, he persisted with systematic investigation of design and operational problems. The combination of a gasoline engine for surface running and battery charging with an electric motor for submerged operation, finally brought him success in 1897. A refined version of this design was purchased by the United States Navy in 1900 and named the USS *Holland*. Similar craft were purchased by the Royal Navy in 1901 and by the Japanese Navy in 1904, and the basis for all subsequent development. It is one of the supreme ironies of naval history that the Royal Navy vessel, HMS *Holland*, should have been named in honour of a man whose early work had been financed by a revolutionary group, the Fenians, which was dedicated to the overthrow of British rule in Ireland. Holland himself was to die without seeing either the vast suffering his invention would unleash or the independence of his native country.

Adam Worth, alias Raymond (1844 – 1902) was to continue his successful criminal career – and double life as a socialite – until 1892, when he was convicted in Belgium for an uncharacteristically bungled robbery of a major cash transfer. He served four years and on release promptly stole £4000 worth of diamonds in London to finance his new operations. He returned to the United States and negotiated a deal with the Pinkerton Detective Agency. This involved return of the Gainsborough portrait of *The Duchess of Devonshire*, which Worth had stolen in 1876, against a payment to him of $25000. He returned to London, where he died. He was buried, under the name of Raymond, in Highgate Cemetery, not far from Karl Marx. In his own lifetime he was referred to by senior Scotland Yard officers as *"The Napoleon of Crime"* and is believed to have been the inspiration for Sir Arthur Conan Doyle's Professor Moriarty, whom Sherlock Holmes described by the same title.

About Old Salt Press

Old Salt Press is an independent press catering to those who love books about ships and the sea. We are an association of writers working together to produce the very best of nautical and maritime fiction and non-fiction. We invite you to join us as we go down to the sea in books. The following pages show some of our more recent offerings.

More Great Reading from the Old Salt Press

The real-life adventures of a young women at sea in 1799, brought to life in her own journal, edited by Joan Druett

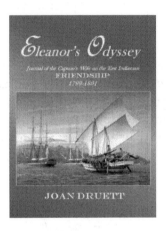

It was 1799, and French privateers lurked in the Atlantic and the Bay of Bengal. Yet Eleanor Reid, newly married and just twenty-one years old, made up her mind to sail with her husband, Captain Hugh Reid, to the Indian Ocean, the Pacific, and India. Danger threatened not just from the barely charted seas they would be sailing, but from the orlop deck of Captain Reid's ship *Friendship*, too—from the cages of Irish rebels he was carrying to the penal colony of New South Wales. Yet, confident in her love and her husband's seamanship, Eleanor insisted on going along.

Joan Druett, writer of many books about the sea, including the bestseller Island of the Lost, embellishes Eleanor's journal with a commentary that illuminates the strange story of a remarkable young woman.

A thrilling yarn
from the last days of the square-riggers

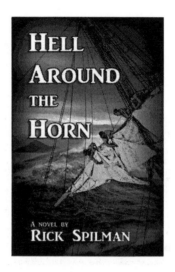

In 1905, a young ship's captain and his family set sail on the windjammer, Lady Rebecca, from Cardiff, Wales with a cargo of coal bound for Chile, by way of Cape Horn. Before they reach the Southern Ocean, the cargo catches fire, the mate threatens mutiny and one of the crew may be going mad. The greatest challenge, however, will prove to be surviving the vicious westerly winds and mountainous seas of the worst Cape Horn winter in memory. Told from the perspective of the Captain, his wife, a first year apprentice and an American sailor before the mast, *Hell Around the Horn* is a story of survival and the human spirit in the last days of the great age of sail.

ISBN 978-0-9882360-1-1

Another gripping saga from the author of the Fighting Sail series

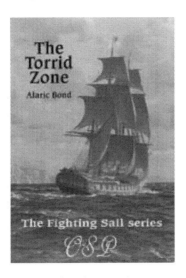

A tired ship with a worn out crew, but HMS *Scylla* has one more trip to make before her much postponed re-fit. Bound for St Helena, she is to deliver the island's next governor; a simple enough mission and, as peace looks likely to be declared, no one is expecting difficulties. Except, perhaps, the commander of a powerful French battle squadron, who has other ideas.

With conflict and intrigue at sea and ashore, The Torrid Zone is filled to the gunnels with action, excitement and fascinating historical detail; a truly engaging read.
ISBN: 0988236095

"Not for the faint hearted – Captain Blackwell pulls no punches! " - Alaric Bond

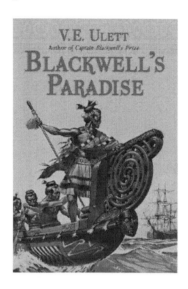

The repercussions of a court martial and the ill-will of powerful men at the Admiralty pursue Royal Navy captain James Blackwell into the Pacific, where danger lurks around every coral reef. Even if Captain Blackwell and Mercedes survive the venture into the world of early nineteenth century exploration, can they emerge unchanged with their love intact. The mission to the Great South Sea will test their loyalties and strength, and define the characters of Captain Blackwell and his lady in Blackwell's Paradise.

ISBN 978-0-9882360-5-9

Printed in Germany
by Amazon Distribution
GmbH, Leipzig